Henry W. Clarke

The Bústán by Shaikh Muslihu-d-dín Sa'dí Shírází

Henry W. Clarke

The Bústán by Shaikh Muslihu-d-dín Sa'dí Shírází

ISBN/EAN: 9783337085162

Printed in Europe, USA, Canada, Australia, Japan

Cover: Foto ©Andreas Hilbeck / pixelio.de

More available books at **www.hansebooks.com**

THE BÚSTÁN

BY

SHAIKH MUSLIḤU-D-DÍN SA'DÍ SHÍRÁZÍ,

TRANSLATED FOR THE FIRST TIME INTO PROSE,

WITH

EXPLANATORY NOTES AND INDEX,

BY

CAPTAIN H. WILBERFORCE CLARKE, R.E.

LONDON:
WM. H. ALLEN AND CO., 13 WATERLOO PLACE.
PUBLISHERS TO THE INDIA OFFICE.

1879.

LONDON :
PRINTED BY W. H. ALLEN & CO., 13 WATERLOO PLACE.

TO

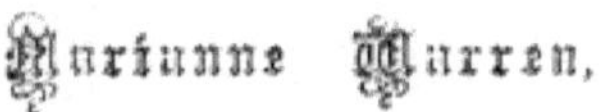

THIS WORK IS INSCRIBED

AS A TOKEN OF HEARTY AFFECTION,

AND AS A TRIBUTE TO HER UNVARYING KINDNESS DURING

HIS CHILDHOOD, BOYHOOD, AND MANHOOD,

BY HER NEPHEW,

THE TRANSLATOR.

PREFACE BY THE TRANSLATOR.

THE Reader's attention is invited to the following points in this translation of the Bústán of Shaikh Muslihu-d-dín Sa'dí of Shíráz:

a. The couplets are numbered, rendering reference easy.

b. Each line of the translation agrees with the corresponding line in the original Persian text; the two lines, forming a couplet, are *not* run into each other.

c. A full index to the discourses is given.

d. Foot-notes give information as to the couplets of the Bustán which are omitted in the 'Iḳd-i-manẓúm, while the index shows the stories of the 'Iḳd-i-manẓúm, which are omitted in the examination for " High Proficiency " in Persian.*

The Persian texts of the Bústán differ greatly. The Persian text of this translation is that which was brought out, under the auspices of the Oriental Society of Germany, by Charles M. Graf, at Vienna, in 1858.

The student, as he reads, should number the couplets of his Persian text, so as to make them accord with those of this translation. Much trouble in making references will thus be saved.

The Bústán, as a whole, or in part, is required for the—

<table>
<tr><td>High Proficiency
Higher Standard
Degree of Honour</td><td>Examinations in Persian,
in India.</td></tr>
</table>

---

* The 'Iḳd-i-manẓúm consists of Selections from the Bústán only.

The original is in Persian verse. This translation is in prose. In this I have but pursued the course which Mr. Wollaston has followed in rendering the verses of the Anvár-i-Suhailí. To render the Bústán in verse, one should be a poet, at least equal in power to the author. Even then it would be well-nigh impossible to clothe the Bústán in such an English dress as would truly convey its beauties. Moreover, if such a translation could be prepared,—no matter how beautiful it might be in execution,—it would be of little advantage to the student. That which is now offered is so literal and so annotated as to encourage the hope that it may in a great measure relieve the student from the labour of consulting a dictionary.

The following table shows the work done in this translation:

Number of	In Introduction.	In Chapter										Grand Total.
		1	2	3	4	5	6	7	8	9	10	
Couplets .	190	971	518	364	527	202	174	438	273	330	112	4099
Discourses	4	33	27	28	30	17	15	33	16	24	6	233

" When one couplet out of a thousand is pleasing to thee,
  In the name of manliness! restrain thy hand from criticism."
                    " Bústán," Introduction, couplet 124.

                    H. WILBERFORCE CLARKE,
                                        Captain, R.E.

CONTENTS.

NOTE ON THE FRONTISPIECE.

The Frontispiece is a portrait of Shaikh Muslihu-d-dín Sa'dí Shírází, by a Persian artist, from a picture in the Haftán, built by Vakíl Karím Khán in 1775–79.

The Haftán, near Shíráz, is an enclosure 33 by 110 yards, containing the graves of seven darveshes whose names are unknown; and an 'imárat, or edifice, in which are two oil-portraits—one of Sa'dí, half life-size, over the door on the west side; and the other of Háfiz, in a niche, over the door on the east side.

The bowl in Sa'dí's hand is called " Kashkúl," or alms-bowl.

For a full description of this picture see Vol. I. of Binney's " Travels in Persia."

Through the kindness of Mr. J. J. Fahie, of the Persian Telegraph Department, this copy of the picture was obtained for this work.

ERRATUM.

Page 325, line 9, *for* From which the wife's clamour issues loudly, *read* From which, loud issues the wife's clamour.

THE BUSTAN

OF

OUR LORD SA'DI.

INTRODUCTION.

In the name of the Lord life-creating!
The Wise One speech-creating within the tongue!

The Lord, the giver, hand-seizing!
Merciful, sin-forgiving, excuse-accepting!

A King such that whosoever turned away his head from
    His door
Found not any respect at the doors to which he went,

The heads of kings, neck-exalting,
(Are), at His court, on the ground of supplication.

He does not instantly seize the froward;
He does not drive away, with violence, those excuse-
    bringing.

" Sar az dar táftan " signifies to be disobedient.
" Azíze " signifies a king; it is applied to God.

And, though He becomes angry at bad conduct,
When thou didst return, He cancelled the past circumstance
  (in the book of sins).

The two worlds (this and the next) are (like) a drop in
  the sea of His knowledge ;
He sees a crime, but in mercy covers it with a screen.

If a person seeks a quarrel with his father,
Doubtless, the father becomes very angry.

And, if a relation be not satisfied with a relation (on
  account of bad conduct),
He drives him from before him, like strangers.

10 And if the clever slave is not of use,
The master holds him not dear,

And, if thou art not kind to friends,
The friend will fly from thee to the distance of a league.

And if a soldier abandons service,
The king army-leading becomes quit of him.

But, the Lord of high and low (God),
Shuts not the door of food on anyone, on account of his
  sin.

The embroidered leather surface of the earth is His common
  table ;
At this open table, whether enemy (infidel), or friend
  (the faithful)—what matter ?

---

14 "Adhím" is a sweet-smelling grained and coloured skin, which is
sometimes called "sakhtiyán." Kings and Amírs spread this skin, and
eat food from off it. God most High having made the "adhím" of the
earth the treasure-chest of his creatures, all the people eat off it.

"Khwán-i-yaghmá" is the tray of food which liberal people spread,
and to which they invite the poor.

15 And if He had hastened against one tyranny-practising,
   Who would have obtained safety from the hand of His
       violence ?

   His nature (is) free from suspicion of opposition and simi-
       litude ;
   His kingdom independent of the devotion of jinn and
       mankind.

   The servant of His order every thing and person :
   The son of Ádam, and fowl, and ant, and fly.

   He spreads so wide a tray of liberality,
   That the Símurgh (in the mountains of) Káf (the Caucasus)
       enjoys a portion.

   Grace and liberality diffusing, and work executing ;
   Because He is the Possessor of Creation, and Knower
       of secrets.

20 Grandeur and egotism are proper for Him,
   Whose kingdom is ancient, and nature independent.

   He places the crown of fortune on the head of one ;
   He brings another from a throne to the dust.

   This one (has) the cap of Good-Fortune on his head ;
   That one the blanket of Mis-fortune on his body.

---

15   The first line may also be rendered :—
            And, if he had hastened in the way of tyranny.
16   The nature of God is free from the evil imputation of similitude, and
   of being of the same nature, made by those opposed to His commands.
18   " Símurgh " is a rare fabulous bird, sometimes called " 'anká."
22   " Gilíme " is a " postín," which is a cloth made of the hair of the goat
   and sheep.

He makes a fire, a rose-garden, for Ibráhím;
He takes a crowd, from the waters of the Níl, to the fire
  (of Hell).

If *that* (making the fire a rose-garden)—it is the written
  order of His beneficence;
And, if *this* (the destruction of Far'ún in the Níl)—it is
  the sign manual of His order.

26 Behind the screen He sees bad acts:
By His own favour, He covers them with a veil.

If, with threatening, He draws forth the sharp sword of
  Command,
The Cherubim will remain deaf and dumb.

And if, from the tray of Liberality, He gives victuals to be
  carried home,
'Azázíl (*i.e.* Satan) will say, "I may carry away a good
  portion."

At the Court of His grace and greatness,
The Great Ones have put greatness out of their heads.

In mercy, near to those who are distressed:
A hearer of the prayer of those supplication-making.

30 Concerning circumstances not yet come to pass, His knowledge penetrating;
As to secrets unspoken, His grace informed.

By power, the Guardian of high (sky) and low (earth),
The Lord of the Court of the day of reckoning (Judgment-
  day).

23　" Khalíl," meaning "the friend of God," is one of the titles of Ibráhím.
Nimrúd threw Ibráhím into the fire; but **God** made the fire a rose-
garden for Ibráhím's sake, so **that** his auspicious body received no hurt.
　" Guroho" refers to Far'ún and his host, who were drowned in the
waters of the *Nile.* God sent them to Hell.

31　" Hasíb" is written for " hisáb" for poetry sake.

The back of a person is not free from obedience to Him
    (it must bend);
On His word, there is not room for the finger of a person
    (in slander).

The ancient doer of good, good-approving;
With the reed of Destiny, in the womb, picture-painting.

From the east to the west, the moon and sun,
He put into motion; and spread the firmament on the
    water.

The earth, from distress of earthquake, became stupefied;
On its skirt, He drove down a mountain as a nail.

He gives to the seed of man, a form like a parí;
Who has made a painting on the water?

He places the ruby and turquoise, in the back-bone (middle)
    of the rock;
The red rose, on the branch of green colour.

From the cloud, He casts a drop towards the ocean;
From the back-bone (of the father) He brings the seed
    into the womb.

From *that* drop, He makes an incomparable pearl;
And from *this*, He makes a form (of man) like the lofty
    cypress.

The knowledge of a single atom is not hidden from Him,
To whom the evident and the hidden are one.

He prepares the daily food of the snake and the ant;
Although, they are without hands, and feet, and strength.

God said:—(*Arabic.*) " He who paints you in the womb."
  For " tab," " zubmat," or " hamíy," as sometimes read.
  The earth is supposed to be stretched out flat, like a carpet, with the
hills planted on it, to keep it steady.

By His order, He pourtrayed existence from non-
    existence;
Who, except Him, knows how to make the existing from
    the non-existing?

Another time, He takes away (creation) to the concealment
    of non-existence;
And, thence conveys (it) to the plain of the place of assem-
    bling (the Resurrection).

(The people of the) world are agreed to His divine origin;
Overpowered in respect to the substance of His essence.

45 The people discovered not what was beyond His majesty;
The vision discovered not the extent of His power.

The bird of Fancy flies not to the summit of His nature;
The power of the intellect arrives not at the skirt of His
    description.

In this whirlpool, a thousand ships (of reason) foundered,
In such a way that not a plank was found on the marge.

Many nights, I sate lost in this journey (of thought
    of God),
When (suddenly) terror seized my sleeve, saying, "Get
    up!"

The knowledge of the King (God) is the encircler of the
    wide plain (of creation);
Thy conjecture becomes not the encircler of Him.

---

48   Terror overpowered me, so that I lagged behind; because the condition
of knowledge is the comprehending by a learned man of the thing found
out, or being equal with it. But this condition, on our side, is not.
    In some copies the first line reads :—
        Many nights, I sate silent in this world (of thought of God).
49   "Kiyás." God has no similitude, and His knowledge is without
equal; then conjecture regarding Him cannot be encircling or comprehending.

Genius reaches not to the substance of His nature,
Thought reaches not to the profundity of His qualities.

One can attain to (the 'Arab poet), Suhbán, in eloquence ;
(But) one cannot reach to the substance of God without
    equal.

Because the immature ones have on this road urged the
    steed (of thought),
At (the words) "lá ahsá," they have wearied of the
    pace.

One cannot gallop a steed in every place,
Places there are where it is proper to cast the shield (yield).

And, if a traveller (a pious one) becomes acquainted with
    the secret of God,
They (the angels) will shut on him the door of returning
    (to the world).

Suhbán Wail was an 'Arab orator, who was so eloquent that he would not repeat a word, but express his meaning in different language. .

I cannot reckon Thy praises of Thyself; but Thou art such an One that Thou hast made Thy own praise of Thyself. "Lá ahsa" signifies "I cannot count Thy praises." The meaning is—A person cannot attain to the substance of the God without equal so that he may describe His perfection; because the best of persons in respect to this truth have made conjectures, but at at this phrase, "lá ahsa," they were confounded.

According to the holy tradition :—(*Arabic.*) "I cannot reckon Thy praises, Oh God, as Thou dost know Thyself."

In this religious idea they have made this comparison :—If a person looks at the signs of the sun, his eyes become dark and obscure. Even so if a person looks at the signs of God most High, he knows that He is the Creator of the strange, and the One who causes wonderful things to happen. But, if he wishes to understand the substance of His nature, his reason becomes dark and obscure.

As in the traditions :—(*Arabic.*) "In this case think only that there is *one* God ; do not think of the substance of God."

"Sipar andákhtan" signifies—to fly, to make submission, to be feeble ; or, in respect to God most High, one cannot make reflection.

As in the traditions :—(*Arabic.*) "Who knows God, his tongue is dumb."

In the " 'Ikd-i-manzúm," couplets 54 to 67 are omitted.

55 In this banquet (of the mystery of God), they give a cup
(of the wine of the love of God) to that one,
To whom they give a draft of senselessness (that he may
not utter the mystery of God).

The wise man fears this sea of blood (the mystery of God),
Out of which no one has taken the bark (of his life).

Of this hawk (the Rationalist), the eye is sewn up (blind
to the knowledge of God);
Of the other (the holy man), the eyes are open (to the
knowledge of God); and feathers (of flight to the
world) burned.

No one went to the (buried) treasure of Kárún (mystery of
God);
And if he found a way, he found not (a way) out of it.

If thou art a seeker, who over this ground (of the knowledge of God) dost travel,
First thou shouldst pluck up the foot of the steed of
returning.

60 Shouldst reflect, in the mirror of the mind;
Shouldst acquire purity by degrees.

Possibly the perfume of the love (of God) makes thee
intoxicated;
Makes thee a seeker of the Covenant—" Am I your
God ? "

---

58   Kárún was born of the uncle, or sister, of Moses. He was famous for
his riches. The wealth of Kárun is here emblematic of the knowledge
of God.

59   " Zamín " here signifies—baznu-i-Maḥrumiyat, which the author calls
" the sea of blood," and " the treasure of Kárán ;" but, more properly,
it means the path of the desert of the knowledge of God, which is
dangerous.

   " Asp " here means—that which draws one to the world, *e.g.* avarice,
sensual pleasures, etc.

61   " Búe " has yá,e waḥdat.
   In the áyat of the Súra of I'rák, God says:—(*Arabic.*) " Oh,

With the foot of search thou dost travel to that place (the
    mystery of God);
And thence, thou dost fly with the wing of the love of
    God.

Truth tears the curtains of fancy;
There remains not a lofty curtain, save the glory of God.

Again for the steed of reason there is no running;
Astonishment will seize its rein, saying, " Stand ! "

In this sea (of God) only the man-guardian (Muhammad)
    went :
That one became lost, who went not behind the inviter
    (Muhammad).

Those persons, who have turned back from this road (of
    following Muhammad)
Travelled much, and are distressed.

Muhammad ! thy God took this confession from the descendants, the
offspring and race of A'dam ; and, I possess evidence on their bodies as
to—" Am I your God ? "

God most High, before the creation of A'dam (on him be peace), having
created the souls of men, said :—

    " Am I your God ? "

The souls answered " Yes." Those who said " Yes " in this world became
of the faith of Islám. Those who gave no reply remained as infidels.
Some of the Muslims, by reason of the affections of this world, forgot
that Covenant ; but, in the case of the souls of those who are lovers of
God, and solitary save as regards Him,—its sound still remains.

When the perfume makes thee intoxicated and a seeker of the Covenant—" Am I your God ? " then, with the foot of search, thou dost find
the path to that stage (am I your God ?)

God most High says to thee—" O Adorer ! " and thou dost reply—
" O Lord ! "

Thence, with the wing of love, thou dost fly and arrive at the side of
the Court of God, which is the end of the world. Certainty as to the
Unity of God is then acquired, and no veil remains between the Adored
(God) and the adorer (man) save the veil of splendour, beyond which
there is no passing for the steed of thought.

After that, thou dost reach the stage of astonishment at witnessing
the essence of the splendour of God.

That person, who chooses the way opposite to the Prophet,
Will never arrive at the stage (of his journey).

Oh Sa'dí! think not that the path of purity,
One can travel, except behind the Chosen One (Mu-
        hammad).

———

Generous of dispositions, beautiful of natures!
The Prophet of creatures, the Intercessor of nations!

70 The Imám of the prophets, the Leader of the road!
The faithful of God, the place of descent of the Angel
        Jibrá,il!

The Intercessor of mortals, the Lord of raising and dis-
        persing (the Judgment-day)!
The Imám of the guides, the Chief of the Court of
        Assembling (the Resurrection)!

The Speaker, whose Mount Sinai is the celestial sphere;
All lights are the rays of his light.

The orphan (Muhammad) who, the Kurán un-completed,
Washed the library of (effaced) so many religions,

When anger drew forth his sword of terror,
Struck, by a miracle, the waist of the moon in two halves.

———

69   "Karíma-l-sajáyá" is one possessed of great qualities and good habits;
who gives information about God to the people, and is an intercessor
with God for them; and who asks pardon from God for the Muslims of
the earth. From couplet 69 to 80 is in praise of Muhammad.
70   "Imám" is one who precedes, or leads, the prophets.
    Faithful, because Muhammad concealed not any part of the revelation
of God. The angel Jibrá,il descended on Muhammad with the Kurán.
72   Kalíme has yá,e wahdat. The ladder of Moses, "the Speaker of God,"
was Túr, or Mount Sinai. The author, having alluded to it, says, "Our
Prophet, Muhammad, is like Moses, whose Túr, that is to say his
ladder, is the sphere. They have said:—Although Musa spoke to God on
Mount Túr, the highest sphere is the base of the Túr of Muhammad.
    In the 'Ikd-i-manzúm, couplets 72 to 97 are omitted.
74   This miracle is said to have occurred at Makka.

When his fame fell in the mouths of the people of the
world,
An earthquake occurred in the court of Kisrí (King Nau-
shiraván).

By the words—lá iláha illa-lláh—he broke into small pieces
(the idol) Lát;
For the honour of religion, he took away the reputation of
(the idol) 'Uzzá.

He brought 'not forth the dust of (the idols) Lát and
'Uzzá (only);
But made the Old Testament and Gospel obsolete.

One night he sate (on the beast Burák); he passed beyond
the Heavens:
In majesty and grandeur, he exceeded the angels.

So impetuous, he urged (his steed) into the plain of propinquity (to God),
While Jibrá,il remained behind him, at the tree of paradise.

80 The Chief of the sacred house (of the Ka'ba) spoke to him,
Saying:—" Oh, bearer of the Divine Revelation! move
proudly higher.

" When thou didst find me sincere in friendship,
" Why didst thou twist the reins from my love?"

Jibrá,il said:—" The power to move higher was not to me:
" I remained here, because the power of wing remained
not to me.

---

75   Kisrí was the name of King Naushirawán the Just; it became a title
of the kings of Persia.

76   There is no god but God!

77   The revelation of the Old Testament descended on Moses; that of the
New Testament, or Anjíl, on 'Ísa, or Jesus.   See note 70.

78   From couplet 78 to 98 is on Muḥammad's ascent to the ninth heaven.
For a full account, see the Sikandar-Náma.

79   The Sudra is a tree in the seventh heaven; it is called the tree of
paradise, or "sudra u-l-muntahạ."   The angels cannot go beyond it.
The seventh heaven is the mansion of the angel Jibrá,il.

" If I fly one hair's breadth higher,
" The effulgence of splendour will burn my feathers."

On account of sins, a person remains not in restraint,
Who has such a Lord (Muhammad) as guide.

85 What acceptable praise may I say to thee?
Oh, Prophet of Mortals! peace be on thee!

May the benedictions of angels be on thy soul!
May they be on thy companions and followers!

First Abú-Bakr, the old disciple;
'Umar, grasp on the convolution of the contumacious demon
        (Satan);

The wise 'Usmán, night, alive-keeping;
The fourth 'Alí-Shán, Duldul, riding.

Oh God! by the right of the sons of Fátima,
May I, on the word of faith, conclude (my life)!

90 If thou dost reject my claim, or if thou dost accept,
    I, and the hand, and the skirt of the offspring of the
        Prophet (are together).

Oh chief happy footed! what loss occurs
Of thy exalted dignity, at the court of the Living One,

That there are a few beggars of the tribe,
Humble companions, guests, at the House of Safety
        (paradise)?

---

86   " Darúd " is a salutation, which means:—from God—mercy; from
angels—asking pardon; from men—praise and prayer; from animals—
praise.

88   " Duldul" was the name of 'Alí's mule.

89   In the traditions:—(Arabic.) "He whose last words are lá iláha illa-
l-láh! will indeed enter paradise."

92   Tufail was the name of a person of the tribe of Umayya, who, in a
state of distress and poverty, used to go without invitation to the
rejoicings of men and to their bridal feasts. The Persians call such an

God praised and honoured thee (oh Muhammad!)
Jabrá,il performed the ground-kiss of thy worth.

The lofty sky, before thy worth, (is) ashamed,
Thou created, and man yet water and clay.

95 Thou from the first, the essence of the existence of man;
Whatever else became existent is an offshoot from thee.

I know not what words I may say to thee,
Who art higher than what I say of thee.

To thee, the honour of—" but for thee "—is sufficient
    grandeur;
Thy praise in the verse of the Kurán—táhá wa yasín—is
    sufficient.

What praise may the imperfect Sa'dí make?
Oh Prophet! on thee be benedictions, and safety!

In the extremes of the world, I wondered much;
With every one, I passed my time.

100 From every corner, I found pleasure;
From every harvest, I obtained an ear of corn.

---

one "the uninvited guest," or "the uninvited companion of a person
going to a feast." The meaning of the sentence is—Thy great dignity,
Oh Muhammad! at the court of God most High, becomes not less, if,
at the feast of paradise, a handful of beggars, like the man Tufail, are
thy guests.

94   In the traditions:—(*Arabic.*) "Whatever God created,—my soul first."
And again:—(*Arabic.*) "I was Prophet, and Ádam between water and
clay."

97   According to the holy saying of God:—(*Arabic.*) "Oh, Muhammad!
hadst thou not been, I would not have created the sky."

99   "Ba sar burdan" signifies—to bring to an end, or finish. From
couplet 99 to 128 is on the cause of the versification of this Book.

Like the pure ones of Shíráz of dust-like (submissive) dis-
    position,
I saw not (one).—May mercy be on this pure soil (of
    Shíráz)!

The cultivating of friendship of the men of this pure soil,
Drew away my heart from Syria and Turkey.

I said to my heart :—" From Egypt, they bring sugar ;
They take it as a present to friends."

From all that garden (of the world), I was loath
To go empty-handed to my friends.

105 If my hand be empty of that sugar,
There are words sweeter than sugar—

Not that sugar that men apparently enjoy ;
But that, which the lords of truth take away on paper
    (with respect).

When I completed this palace of wealth,
I prepared in it ten doors (chapters) of instruction.

One chapter is on Justice, and Deliberation, and Judgment ;
The guarding of the people, and the fear of God.

(In) the second chapter, I laid the foundation of Benefi-
    cence,
That the benefactor may praise (by liberality) the excel-
    lence of God.

---

104   In the 'Ikd-i-manzúm, this couplet is omitted.
106   " Kande " has yá,e wahdat.
107   In the 'Ikd-i-manzúm, couplets 107 to 190 are omitted.
108   Before the words which constitute the subject of each chapter, the
word " dar " should be understood, as " dar 'adl."

10 The third chapter is on Love (of God), and Phrenzy, and
     Perturbation,—
Not the worldly love that men fasten, with force, on them-
     selves.

The fourth chapter is on Humility; the fifth,—Content-
     ment;
The sixth,—the description of the man Contentment-
     choosing.

The seventh chapter on the description of the Science of
     Education;
The eighth chapter,—on thanks for safety.

The ninth chapter is on Repentance and the way of
     Rectitude;
The tenth,—on Prayers and the Conclusion of the book.

On the august day, and happy year;
On the auspicious date, between the two 'ídds,—

15 It was fifty-five years more than six hundred,
Since that this renowned treasury (the Bústán) became full
     of pearls (of eloquence).

---

10   "Mastí" signifies—kharábí (intoxication), a state in which a person
makes himself (kharáb) enraptured in the knowledge of God.

    "Mai" signifies—bekhudí (senselessness), ecstacy, or the state in
which a person considers himself non-existent.

    "Kharábí wa bekhudí," signifying—the true state of the lovers of God.

    And it may may be mentioned that, similarly, sákí (a cup-bearer)
signifies :—

    The Divine promise; a spiritual guide; or, a source of Divine
bounties.

12   For "az" read "dar baiyán."

14   One 'ídd is the breaking of the fast of Ramazán; the other 'ídd is the
day on which sacrifices are offered ahmakkah, or the sacrifice of the
solemn festival of Bairám.

My jewel of speech has remained in a woman's veil;
Yet from shame, I carry my head on my bosom.

Because, in the sea there is the pearl and also the oyster
    (pearl-less);
In the garden there is the lofty tree and the small.

Ho! oh wise man of happy disposition!
I have not heard the skilful one, a defect-seeker.

If the coat be of silk, or if painted and embroidered,
Of necessity, its quilting (of cotton) is in the interior.

120 If thou dost not obtain the painted and embroidered silk,
    fret not,
Do the work of Liberality, and cover my redundant words.

I boast not of the capital of my own excellence;
I have brought my hands in front, in beggary.

I (have) heard that in the day of hope and fear (the resur-
    rection),
The Merciful One will pardon the bad for the sake of the
    good.

If thou also dost see evil in my words,
Act, in imitation of the world-Creator.

---

116   "Dámani" is a fine linen, or painted silk veil, worn by ladies; it is
sometimes called mikna', which signifies a coif of fine linen two cubits
(3 feet) long, worn by Arabian women at home and abroad. The word
is here used to show that the jewels of speech were so abundant that a
woman's veil was required to hold them.

    "Sar andar burdan *or* zadan" signifies—to plunge the head in the
collar of reflection, *or to* be thoughtful and amazed.

    I raise not my head, because in my words goodness (eloquence) and
evil (defect) are mingled.

123   God, on the day of resurrection, will pardon the bad for the sake of
the good. So, for the sake of my good words, do not thou sneer at the
ill words which may fall under thy notice.

When one couplet, out of a thousand, is pleasing to thee,
In the name of manliness! restrain thy hand from
    criticism.

Assuredly, in Persia, my creation (the Bústán),
Is priceless, like musk in Khutn.

Like the noise of the drum, the fear of me was afar.
In my absence, my defect was veiled.

Sa'dí brings the rose to the garden
With sauciness; and pepper to Hindústán.

Like the date, skin with sweetness encrusted;
When thou dost open it, a bone (a stone or difficulty) is
    inside.

My disposition had no desire for this kind (of composition);
It had no wish for the praising of kings.

But, I threaded the pearls (of poetry) in the name of a
    certain one;
Perhaps, the holy men may unfold,

That Sa'dí, who snatched the ball of eloquence,
Was (lived) in the days of Abú-Bakr, the son of Sa'd.

If in his time, I boast—it is fit;
Even as, the Lord (Muhammad) in the time of (King)
    Naushírawán.

Khutn is a musk-producing country of Turkistán. Sa'dí remarks
that, in Persia, there are many compositions like the "Bústán"; hence,
only out of Persia will the "Bústán" be valued.

Those afar off knew not my defects.

"Shankhí" signifies—without fear, bashfulness, or shame.

From couplet 129 to 175 is in praise of :—

Muhammad Atábak Abú Bakr-i-Sa'd-i-Zangí, to whom this work is
dedicated.   He died in $\frac{658 \text{ A.H.}}{1260 \text{ A.D.}}$

Muhammad was born in the time of King Naushírawán the Just.
Muhammad says:—(Arabic.) "I was born in the time of the just king."

A world-guardian, and Faith-cherisher, and justice-distri-
    buter—
Came not after (Khalífa) 'Umar, like (King) Abú-Bakr.

---

133   Abú-Bakr was the first, 'Umar the second, and 'Usmán the third
Khalífa. They reigned respectively 2, 12, and 12 years. Abú-Bakr was
the father of 'A,isha, Muhammad's favourite wife. King Abú-Bakr is
not to be confounded with the Khalífa of the same name.

These Khulafá were succeeded by 'Alí, the cousin of Muhammad, who
had married Fátima, the daughter of the Prophet. The Sunnís acknow-
ledge Abú-Bakr, 'Umar, 'Usmán and 'Alí. The Shíahs reject these, and
consider that 'Alí was the rightful heir to Muhammad. 'Alí was assas-
sinated in A.D. 660 in the Masjid, at Kúfa; he was succeeded by his
eldest son Hasan, who gave place to Mu'awiyya, the enemy of his father.
It is believed that Hasan was afterwards poisoned.

'Alí's younger son Husain, on the death of Mu'awiyya and accession
of his son Yazíd, escaped to Makkah. Misled by the representations of
the people of Kúfa, he set out for that city with 100 men.

On the plains of Kerbela, 5,000 men were opposed to him; his party
were massacred. The corpse of Husain was subjected to many indig-
nities. This took place in A.D. 680.

The Persians (Shí'ah) venerate the three imáms 'Alí, Hasan, and
Husain; they execrate the memory of the three successors of the Prophet;
to wit, Abú-Bakr, 'Umar, and 'Usmán.

The masjid of Muhammad is at Makka; of 'Alí, at Najuf, near
Kúfa; of Husain, at Kerbela, near the ruins of Babylon.

The orthodox Mussulmán was ordered to make a pilgrimage to
Makka at least once in his life. Hárunu-r-rashíd visited Makkah nine
times, and spent (£700,000) on the way. Ibráhím Adham, who had
abandoned the throne of Khurásán, spent twelve years on the pilgrimage,
in consequence of the number of genu-flections which he had vowed to
perform.

The Ka'ba, at Makka, is a square building protecting a black stone,
which is said to be one of the precious stones of paradise, which fell to
the earth with Ádam. The angel Jibrá,il brought it to Ibráhím when
he was re-building the Ka'ba. The stone is set in silver in the S.E. corner,
seven spans above the ground; it was originally white as snow, but has
become superficially black—either by the touch of a menstruous woman
or by the kisses of numberless pilgrims; it is said to be lighter than
water.

The pilgrims, free from sin and impurity, have to circulate seven times
around the Ka'ba. The first three circuits should be at a quick pace,
and the last four slowly. As they pass the stone it is incumbent to
kiss it, or to touch it with the hand, which should immediately be applied
to the lips.

Chief of the head-exalting ones, and crown of the great
  ones !—
The world will boast, in the time of his justice.

35 If a person comes from tumult into shelter,
He has no shelter-place, save this country (Shíráz).

Happiness for the door (of Abú-Bakr), like the old house
  (Ka'ba) !
From every broad road around it, men come.

I saw not such a country, and treasure, and throne
Which is a bequest to the child, and to the young man, and
  to the old.

The style and title of the ceremony is—
        tawáf-i-baytu-lláhí-l-harám.
With the Persians the pilgrimage to the shrine of Husain is more
popular than that to Makka, which is in the hands of their opponents,
the *Sunnís* (Turks).

From all parts of Persia, bodies (often in an advanced state of decom-
position) are brought to Kerbela.

It is allowable, for those who cannot make the pilgrimage, to get a
substitute. There are men whose sole occupation is to make the journey
for others.

The deaths of Hasan and Husain are commemorated during the first
ten days of the Muharram.

The play is acted on a stage : when the audience has been worked up
into passionate grief, it is not unusual for men to rush through the
streets, cutting themselves with knives, and crying "Hasan ! Husain !"
The acting usually takes place in a tent called a takiyá.

The Shí'ahs only believe the interpretations of the Kurán given by
'Alí, Husain, and the next seven lineal descendants of the Prophet, who
form their nine imáms. They do not call the Sunnís infidels, but
refuse them the appellation of "al mumín," the faithful.

36   As the roads to the house of the Ka'ba are open, and men come from
every quarter for the sake of performing Hajj, even so the door of King
Abú-Bakr is open, and men, for the sake of justice and repelling of their
needs, are present in his presence.

37   The bequest of treasure to children, who are fond of gold and silver,
of country to youths desirous of renown, and of throne to wise old men
versed in state affairs, they have assigned.

2 *

The one sorrowful on account of a grief came not to him,
On whose heart he placed not a plaster.

He (Abú-Bakr) is a seeker of good, and hopeful (of good) :
Oh God ! fulfil the hope that he has.

140 A corner of his hat on the highest Heaven,—
Yet, from humility, his head on the ground.

If the beggar supplicates,—it is his nature ;
Humility from the neck-exalting ones is good.

If an inferior falls (in humility) it is proper ;
The superior prostrate (in humility) is a man of God.

The recollection of his grace is not concealed ;
Nay, the clamour of his liberality travels in the world.

A wise man of happy disposition like him,
The world, so long as it was a world, recollects not.

145 In his age, thou dost not see a sorrowing one,
Who complains of the injustice of the one of strong
  grasp.

No one has seen this custom, and order, and regulation :
King Firídún, with the majesty that he had, saw not this.

On that account, his dignity before God is great ;
Because by his might, the hand of the weak ones is
  strong.

Some say that "wakf" signifies—dastína, a wrist-ornament. The
couplet would then mean—that country, treasure, and throne, were the
adornment and boast of child, youth, and old men.

112 The superior is humble only from fear of God.

143 "Kí" here signifies—balki.

146 Firídún was a king, who reigned over Persia in 750 B.C. He placed in
bonds King Zahhák, who was notorious for cruelty.

He so spreads his shadow over a world,
That an old man fears not a Rustam.

In every age, men of the violence of time,
And of the revolution of the skies,—groan.

Oh great monarch ! in thy just age,
No one complains in respect to time.

In thy time, I behold the peace of the people ;
After thee, I know not (what will be) the end of the
      people.

It is also by reason of thy fortune of happy ending,
That the date of Sa'dí is in thy era.

So long as the moon and sun are in the sky,
In this book, remembrance of thee is eternal.

If kings have gathered a good name,
They have learned a good way of life from former kings.

Thou, in the administration of thy own kingdom,
Surpassed former kings.

Alexander, with a wall of brass and stone,
Confined the way of Ya,júj from the world.

Thy barrier against Ya,júj-kufr is of gold ;
It is not brass, like the wall of Alexander.

"Ya,júj" and "Ma,júj" signify—Gog and Magog; they represent the
descendants of Japhet, son of Noah ; they lived in cities to the north of
Kohistán, whence they were wont to issue and oppress the neighbouring
nations. Alexander the Great built a wall one hundred farsangs in
length between two mountains, and so confined them. See the Sikandar-
Náma, by Nizámí, **Discourse** 13, couplet 49.

"Ya,júj Kufr," or Changez Khán. King **Atábuk** made peace with
him, by paying money, so that the Muslims of Shíráz obtained safety
from his tyranny. The Author gives pre-excellence to his praised one,
Abú-Bakr.

That eloquent one—who, in security and justice,
Utters not thy praise,—let him not have a tongue!

Well done! The sea of gift and mine of liberality!
Because the implorer for aid is existent from thy existence.

160 I consider the qualities of the King beyond computation;
　　Within this narrow plain of the book, they are not
　　　　contained.

If Sa'dí writes all thy good qualities,
He will assuredly make another book.

I desist from thanks for such liberality;
It is indeed better, that I should spread forth the hand of
　　　prayer:—

May the world be to thy desire, and Heaven thy friend!
May the Creator of the World be thy guardian!

Thy lofty star has illumined a world;
The declination of thy star has burned the enemy.

165 Of the revolution of Time let there not be grief to thee!
　　And of reflection, let there not be dust (of grief) on thy
　　　　heart!

Because a single grief, on the heart of kings,
Disturbs the heart of a world.

May thy heart and territory be tranquil and prosperous!
May confusion be far from thy kingdom!

May thy body be always (sound) like thy true religion (of
　　　Islám)!
May the heart of thy enemy be sluggish, like deliberation!

May thy inward parts, by the strengthening of God, be
　　　joyful!
May thy heart, and religion, and territory be prosperous!

70 May the World-Creator have mercy on thee!
Whatever more I may say is empty talk and wind.

This indeed is enough from the Glorious Omnipotent One,
That the grace of thy welfare is on the increase.

(King) Sa'd, the son of Zangí, departed not with pain from
    the world;
When he begot a renowned successor, like thee (Muham-
    mad Sa'd).

This branch, from that pure stock (Sa'd, son of Zangí), is
    not wonderful;
Because his soul is on the summit (of paradise), and his
    body in the dust (of the grave).

Oh God! On that renowned tomb (of Sa'd, son of Zangí),
By Thy grace, let the rain of mercy fall!

175 If of Sa'd, son of Zangí, an example and recollection
    remain,—
May Heaven be the Protector of Sa'd, son of Abú-Bakr!

Atábak Muhammad, a king of good fortune,
Lord of crown, and Lord of throne.

A youth of fresh fortune, enlightened mind;
In fortune, young; in deliberation, old.

---

172   Zangí was the grandfather of Abú-Bakr; Sa'd, the son of Zangí,
was the father of Abú-Bakr, who was King of Persia, in the time of the
poet Sa'dí. There was another Sa'd, who was the son of Abú-Bakr.
Vide couplet 175.

175   "Atábak" signifies—an instructor. Sa'd, son of Zangí, was instructor
to Sultán Sanja, of Shíráz; one night the Sultán, in a state of intoxication, gave the sovereignty of the country of Shíráz to Sa'd, son of Zangí.
After the death of Sanjar, Sa'd and his heirs were called Atábak.

176   Muhammad was the son of that Abú-Bakr; they used to call him
Muhammad Sa'd. From couplet 176 to 190 is in praise of Muhammad
Sa'd, son of Bú-Bakr, son of Sa'd son of Zangí.

In wisdom, great; and in spirit, lofty;
In arm, strong; and in heart, sensible.

Oh happy fortune of the mother of Time!
Who cherishes such a son in her bosom.

180 With the hand of liberality, he took away the water (of
    reputation) of the river:
In exaltation, he took the place of the Pleiades.

Bravo! may the eye of Fortune be open (joyous) on thy
    face,
Oh chief of monarchs, neck exalting!

The oyster, that thou dost see full of pearl-grains,
Has not that value that one pearl-grain has.

Thou art that hidden (rare) pearl of one grain;
Because, thou art the ornament of the house of the
    kingdom.

Oh God! preserve him by Thy grace:
Keep him from injury and the evil eye.

185 Oh God! make him renowned in every horizon:
Make him precious, by the grace of devotion.

Keep him a dweller in justice and piety;
Fulfil his wish in this world and the next.

Let there not be grief to thee on account of the hateful
    enemy!
Let there not be injury to thee, from the revolution of the
    world!

---

180   He made the river ashamed by his liberality, and diminished the
splendour of the Pleiades by his grandeur.

182   "Yak dána" signifies — a jewel, incomparable, without equal, and
unrivalled.

187   In some places "tá" is replaced by "ash."

The tree of paradise like thee brings forth fruit :
The son fame-seeking ; the father fame-possessing.

Know that welfare is a stranger of that household
Who are evil speakers of this household.

190 Bravo ! Religion and knowledge. Bravo ! justice and
    equity.
Bravo ! country and government.— May it always be
    lasting !

CHAPTER I.

ON JUSTICE, EQUITY, AND ADMINISTRATION OF GOVERNMENT.

1 The beneficences of God are not contained in the imagination ;
What service does the tongue of praise offer ?

Oh God do thou—this king (Abú-Bakr son of Sa'd), the poor man's friend,
Since the case of the people is in his protection,—

Keep long established over the head of the people ;
By the grace of devotion, keep his heart alive (fresh).

Keep his tree of hope fruitful ;
His head green, and his face, with mercy, fair.

6 Oh Sa'dí ! go not in the way of dissimulation (in regard to the King's praise) ;
If thou hast honesty, bring and come.

---

1   In the 'Ikd-i-manzum couplets 1 to 21 are omitted.
5   According to the demands of truth, direct to goodness the Poet addresses himself.

Thou (Sa'dí) art a stage-recogniser, and the King a road-
    traveller :
Thou art a speaker of truth ; and the King, the bearer of
    truths.

What necessity that nine thrones of the sky,
Thou dost place below the foot of (the King) Kizil-Arsalán.

Say not :—place thy foot of honour on the Heavens.
Say :—place the face of sincerity in the dust.

Place, in devotion, the face on the threshold (of God) ;
Because this is the highway of the righteous.

10 If thou (Abú-Bakr) art a slave of God, place thy head on
    this door (of God) ;
Place, from off thy head, the cap of lordship.

At the Court of the Order-giver possessed of Majesty,
Bewail, like a darwesh, before a rich and powerful man.

When thou dost perform thy devotions, put not on the
    kingly raiment ;
Like the poor darwesh, bring forth a cry,

Saying :—"Oh Omnipotent One ! Thou art powerful ;
" Thou art strong ; Thou art the darwesh-cherisher.

---

6   " Manzil shinás" is a spiritual guide, or one who knows God.

7   The following couplet was composed by the poet Zahír-fariyábí, whose
patron was King Kizil Arsalán :—

    " Reflection places beneath its foot nine thrones of the sky,
      So that it may kiss the stirrup of Kizil Arslán."

The poet Sa'dí, in praising Abú-Bakr, says What need to say so much?
because in saying so, pride and arrogance are found, and pride is the
mark of misfortune.

12   Let Ritualists observe this passage.

" I (Abú-Bakr) am neither a monarch, nor an order-giver;
" I am one of the beggars of this Court.

15 " What springs forth from the power of my conduct,
" Unless the power of Thy grace is my friend ?

" Give to me the means of liberality and goodness ;
" And, if not,—what goodness can come from me to any-
          one ?

" Oh God ! keep me on the work of goodness ;
" Otherwise, no work can come from me."

At night, like the beggars, pray with ardour,
If, by day, thou dost exercise sovereignty.

The obstinate ones (courtiers) are at thy door, loin girt ;
Thou (shouldst be thus)—thy head on the threshold of
          devotion.

20 Oh, excellent !—for us slaves, the Lord-God ;
For the lord a slave, duty-performing.

They relate a story of the great men of the faith,
Recognisers of the truth of the essence of truth,

---

19   " Gardan-kashán " signifies — men possessed of power, and arrogant.
" Kamar-bastan " signifies — to choose, to be of stout heart in deeds, to
show solicitude in work.

21   " 'Ilmu-l-yakín " is—proof of the certainty of a thing is obtained to
such a degree that the doubter is incapable of entertaining doubt, though
the thing itself may not be viewed as—
          The conception of the form of fire from smoke.
" 'Ainu-l-yakín " is—the viewing of a thing is obtained so that a person
sees the form of fire with his eye. This yakín is superior to the first.
" Hakku-l-yakín " signifies—the effacing of one thing by another in
such a way that, apparently, it becomes that other thing itself, as—
          Iron in the fire of the smith's stove appears exactly like the fire
          itself.
The " Nineteenth Century " magazine, October 1878, " Faith and Veri-

As follows :—A pious man sate on a panther ;
Snake in hand, he urged his long, pleasant paced steed.

One said to him :—" Oh man of the way of God !
Guide me to this road by which thou didst go.

" What didst thou, that the rending animal became obe-
    dient to thee ?
" That the seal-ring of good fortune went to thy name ? "

25 He said :—" If the panther and snake be submissive to me,
" And if (also) the elephant and vulture,—be not asto-
    nished.

" Do thou also from the order of the Ruler (God) twist not
    thy neck,
" So that no one, from thy order, may twist his neck."

When the ruler is obedient to God,
God is his Protector and Friend.

It is impossible when He loves thee,
That He will leave thee in the power of an enemy.

---

fication," page 677 :—" A fact only is proved when the evidence can leave
us no room to doubt; when it cannot be denied without absurdity ;
when it becomes a necessity of the reason that we give our full assent
to it." Page 678 :—" This great scientific axiom is an utterly false
one." " It is in diametrical opposition to truth." " It is only the
meanest and most subordinate truths that are capable of being proved
at all."

24   That like Salaimán thou didst become master of ravening beasts.
25   In some places the following occurs :—
        I saw one, in the bed of a river (or, from the plain of the city of
            Rúd-bár),
        Who came towards me riding on a panther :
        Such terror, on account of that state, sate on (overpowered) me,
        That fearing bound the feet of my going.
        Smiling, he took his hand to his lip,
    but saying—Oh Sa'dí ! at whatever thou didst see be not astonished.

This is the road, and turn not thy face from the way ;
Place thy foot (on this road), and obtain the object which
    thou dost desire.

30 Advice of a person is profitable to a person,—to him,
To whom the saying of Sa'dí is agreeable.

I have heard that, at the time of the agony of the soul (the
    last breath),
(King) Naushíraván (the Just) thus spoke to Hurmuz (his
    son),

Saying :—" Be observant of the heart of the poor
" Be not in the desire of thy own ease.

" A person rests not within thy territory,
" When thou dost seek thy own ease, and no more.

" In the opinion of the wise, it is not approved—
" The shepherd asleep, and the wolf among the sheep.

36 " Go : protect the poor and needy one,
" Because, the king is the crown-holder for the sake of his
    subjects.

" The subject is like the root, and the king the tree ;
" Oh son ! the tree is strong by reason of the root.

" So long as thou canst, wound not the heart of the
    people ;
" But, if thou dost,—thou dost pluck up thy own roots.

---

29 " Sharí'at," the laws of Muhammad.   ⎫
    " Taríkat," the way (to God).   ⎬ By these four means, a
    " Hakíkat," the truth (of existence of God). ⎪ man may find God.
    " Ma'rifat," the knowledge (of God).   ⎭

33   In the 'Ikd-i-manzúm, this couplet is omitted.

35   In some places :—
    Thou hast slept cool, in the retired place, half a day ;   .he fire
    Say,—to the traveller, burn in the heat outside.
                                              . and Veri-

" If a straight road (of safety) is necessary for thee—
" The way of the pious is hope and fear.

" The disposition of man is towards wisdom,
" In the hope of goodness, and fear of wickedness."

---

40 If thou didst find these two doors (hope and fear) in the
        King,
Thou didst obtain shelter in the territory of his kingdom.

(The King) brings a gift to the hopeful one,
In hope of the gift (of pardon) of the Creator of the World.

" The injury of persons is not pleasing to him (the king),
" Who fears lest injury should come to his kingdom.

" And if there is not this disposition, in his nature,
" There is not the perfume of ease in that territory.

" If thou art foot-bound (by wife and family), accept con-
        tentment;
" But, if thou art a single horseman (solitary), take thy
        own desire.

45 " Seek not plenteousness in that land and region,
" Where thou dost see the subjects of the king sorrowful.

---

38   After the first line, understand:—have fear of wickedness and hope of
goodness.   See the second line of couplet 39.

39   The Ṣúfís have said:—(Arabic.) " Find out whatever desire there is
in hope and fear."

              (Arabic.) " Fear and hope are to man, as wings to a
bird."
        the 'Iḳd-i-manẓúm, couplets 39 to 41 are omitted.

43   "Bú,e " (lit. a smell) signifies—a portion, a share, wish.

44   That is:—
      In thy hand, there is nothing although thou art a king. More-
      over, affairs are in the hand of God. Hence thou also hast hope
        and fear.

۲

" Fear not the proud haughty ones ;
" Fear that one, who fears God.

" In a dream, he sees the territory of another populous,
" Who keeps the heart of the people of his country dis-
      tressed.

" From violence come ruin and ill-fame ;
" The prudent man reaches to the profundity of this
      speech.

" It is not proper with injustice to slay the peasants,
" Who are the shelter and support of the kingdom.

50 " For thy own sake preserve the villagers ;
" Because, the labourer of happy heart executes more
      work (for his master).

" It is not manliness to do ill to that one (the villager),
" From whom, thou mayst have experienced much benefit
      (in tribute)."

———————

I have heard that King Khusrau said to (his son) Shírwiya
At that time when his eyes slept (rested) from seeing (at
      the time of death),—

" In that state be, so that whatever resolution thou mayst
      make,
" Thou mayst consider the peace of the peasant.

———————

46   In the text, in the second line, a negative is wrong   See the
Sikandar Náma, Discourse 34, couplet 41—
            In business, I have fear of none,
            Save that one, who is God-fearing.
1   The splendid clothes and delicate food of kings, and other delights   of
3.   life, are purchased with the gold of the villagers.
35   Khusrau Parvez, son of Hurmuz, reigned 590–625 A.D. He
      lover of Shírín. Shírwiya, in order to increase his sensual appe
            Say,—to which proved to be poison : he reigned six months

" Be sure, so long as thou dost not turn thy head from
        equity and judgment,
" That men will not turn aside their feet, from thy power.

55 " The peasant flies from the tyrant ;
" He makes his bad repute, a stock story in the world.

" Much time passes not, that his own foundation,
" That one plucked up, who laid a bad foundation (of
        tyranny).

" The enemy, skilful with the sword, lays waste,
" Not so much as, the smoke (grief) of the heart of an old
        woman.

" The lamp (of grief) that the widow-woman lighted up,—
" Thou mayst often have seen that it burned a city.

" Who, in the world, is more favoured than that one,
" Who with justice, in sovereignty, lived ?

60 " When the time of his travelling from this world arrives,
" (The people of the world) send mercy to his tomb.

" Since bad and good men pass away (die),
" It is best indeed that they connect thy name with good-
        ness (and bless thee).

" Appoint the God-fearing one over the peasant ;
" Because, the abstinent one is the architect of the country.

" That liver-eater of the people is thy enemy,
" Who seeks thy profit, in the injury of the people.

" Government is a fault in the hand of those persons,
" From whose power, the hands (of the people) are (up-
        lifted in prayer) before God.

Khud should be pronounced with fatha for poetry sake.

65 " The cherisher of good sees not evil ;
" When thou dost cherish evil, thou art the enemy of thy
    own life.

" Exercise not retribution against the despoiler by (con-
    fiscation of) his property ;
" But, it is proper to bring forth (to destroy) his root from
    the foundation.

" Exercise not patience with the agent of the friend of
    tyranny ;
" Since, on account of his fatness (from extortion) it is
    proper to flay his skin.

" It is also proper, *at first*, to cut off the wolf's head,
" Not at the time when he tore in pieces the sheep of men."

How well said the captive merchant
When the robbers gathered around him with arrows !

70 " Inasmuch as courage comes from highwaymen,
" Whether the men of the army, or a troop of women, what
    matter ?"

---

66   In the second line, " ki " may have the force of—because ; *or*, nay.
    " Málish " signifies—punishment.
    " Málash " signifies—his property, as given in the text.

67   " Zulm dost " signifies—one who loves tyranny
    Exercise not patience ; nay, dismiss him, because I will plunder this
tyranny-practising one, after that he has become fat, and amassed by
oppression much wealth from the peasant, and will take his plunder from
him.
    Again :—
    Exercise not patience ; because it is necessary to flay this tyranny-
practising one. If not, having become bold, he will exercise on all still
greater tyranny.

68   In the 'Ikd-i-manzúm, couplets 69 to 264 are omitted.

70   The army should repel robbers ; when it does not exercise sufficient
bravery to do this, the author asks—what difference is there between it
and a troop of women ?
    The gist of this speech is :—That a king should protect merchants
and travellers.

The great king, who injured the merchants,
Shut the door of well being on the (people of the) **city and
the army.**

How may **wise men again go** there,
When they **hear the rumour of bad custom?**

Are a good name and favourable reception necessary **to**
thee?—
Hold in esteem merchants and envoys.

Merchants heartily cherish **travellers;**
Because, they carry their **good name to the world.**

75 That **kingdom soon becomes ruined,**
From **which, the** injured heart **becomes a traveller.**

Be the acquaintance **of** the foreigner, and **friend of the**
traveller;
Because **the traveller is one who hawks about a good**
name.

Hold dear the guest, **and** precious the traveller;
But also be on guard from injury from them.

To beware of the stranger is good;
Because, possibly, he may be an enemy **in** the guise of a
friend.

---

75   In some places:—
        When the king broke faith, in whom may he seek faith?
        When the villagers fled, from whom will he seek fame?
        What goodness, does that-one-without-purity expect,
        In whose rear are curses?
        Neither poverty, **nor helplessness;**
        Neither rebuke, nor oppression—at once.
        When memory of former kings comes to thee,
        Recite that same writing after thy own time.
        They possessed this very desire, and pride, and pleasure;
        In the end, they departed, and abandoned the world.

Advance the rank of thy own old friends;
Because, treachery never comes from the cherished one.

80 When thy servant becomes old,
Forget not the right of his years.

If old age has bound the hand of his service;
Yet, thou hast power, in respect to liberality.

———

I heard that Sháhpúr heaved a sigh,
When Khusrau drew the pen on (cancelled) his pension.

When, from want of food his state became distressed,
He wrote this tale to the king,

As follows :—" Oh king, clime-spreader, in justice !
" If I remain not (die still), thou dost remain in excellence.

85 " When I spent for thee my youth,
" Drive me not from before thee, in the time of old age."

The foreigner, whose head is intent on strife,
Injure not ; but, expel him from the country.

If thou dost not become angry with him, it is proper ;
Because, his own bad nature is the enemy, in pursuit of
    him.

And, if Persia be his native country,
Send him not to Sin'án, Slavonia, or Turkey.

Even there (in Persia) give him not respite, until the mid-
    day meal (slay him) ;
It is not proper to establish a calamity on any one.

---

82   " Sháhpúr" was the attendant, who used to be employed as
messenger between " Khusrau Parvez " and his mistress " Shírín."

88   Sin'án is a town in Yaman, in Arabia ; Sakláb is a country in the north.

89   " Chásht " is one watch out of the four watches into which the day
(not night) is divided.

Because they say :—May that country be overturned,
Since such men come out of it !

If thou dost give service (place and rank) recognise the
    beneficent man ;
Because, the poor man has no fear of the king.

When the poor man lowers his neck to the shoulder (in
    humility),
Only lamentation proceeds from him.

When the inspector has not two hands of rectitude,
It is necessary to appoint an examiner over him.

And if he (the examiner) agrees with his heart,
Pluck away service from the inspector and his examiner.

95 The God-fearing man, fidelity-displaying, is necessary ;
Hold him not faithful, who fears thee (and not God).

The faithful one is necessary, fearing the Ruler (God) ;
Not eminence of the minister, nor reproof, nor ruin.

Scatter (thy money), and reckon, and sit at leisure ;
Because, thou dost not see one faithful out of a hundred.

Two persons of the same nature, old, of the same pen
    education),
It is not proper to send together to one place.

How dost thou know that they may become mutual helper
    and friend ?
This one may be a thief, the other a confidant.

---

92   " Faro burdan gardan ba dosh " signifies—to practise humility ; to
reflect ; to obey.
95   See couplet 46.
    When a man is in doubt as to how much he possesses, he spreads out
his long purse (the scrip suspended at the girdle), and counts his money.
99   " Ham dast gardan " signifies — to become concordant.

100 When thieves have fear and terror of one another,
A Kárawán goes safe, in the midst of them.

One whom thou didst dismiss from dignity,—
Forgive his crime, when some time elapses.

To accomplish the desire of the hopeful
Is better than to break (the bonds) of a thousand fettered
    ones.

If the pillar of the office of the scribe
Falls, he cuts not the rope of hope.

The just monarch, with his subjects,
Becomes angry like a father with a son.

105 Sometimes, he strikes him so that he becomes sorrowful;
Sometimes, he makes water (flow) from his pure eyes.

When thou dost exercise gentleness, the enemy becomes
    bold;
But, if thou art an anvil, he becomes wearied of thee.

Severity and mildness together are best,
Like the vein-striker (bleeder), who is surgeon and plaster-
    placer.

Be generous, and pleasant tempered, and forgiving;
Even as God scatters (favour) over thee, do thou scatter
    over the people.

---

102   The second line may be rendered :—
            Is better than to subdue a thousand fortresses.
103   If the official be dismissed from office, he despairs not of being
reinstated.
108   As God ordered :—(*Arabic.*) " Do good as God has done good to thee."

No one came into the world, who remained,
Save that one, whose good name remained.

110 That one died not, after whom there remained—
Bridge, or masjid, or khán, or guest-house.

Every one, behind whom, a token remained not,—
The tree of his existence brought not forth fruit.

If he departed (from this world) and the marks of his well-
    doing remained not,
It is not fit to chaunt, after his death,—" Al hamd ! "

When thou dost wish that thy name may be eternal,
Conceal not the good name of the great ones.

After thy own time (death) call to mind that same descrip-
    tive picture,
That, after the age of former kings, thou didst behold.

115 One took away a good name from the world ;
The bad custom of the other remained behind him for
    ever.

---

109   In some places :—
         Whosoever came into the world will be one who passes away ;
         He who is permanent and lasting will be God.
110   " Khán " signifies — Kárawán-house.
       " Mihmán saráe " signifies — the place where they give food to the poor
    and necessitous.
112   " Al hamd ! " refers to the Súra fátiḥa of the Ḳurán. It here signifies
    —du'á,e khair.
114   In some places :—
         They possessed this very desire, and blandishment, and joy ;
         In the end, they departed (from the world) and passed away.
       The picture, regarding their lifelessness and namelessness, which after
    the death of former kings thou didst see on the tablet of possibility—
    behold that same picture (of non-existence) on the page of Time after
    thy own epoch. That is—like former ones, thou also wilt become name-
    less and traceless.

With the ear of approval, listen not to a person's injury ;
But, if the speech comes probe its depth.

Accept the excuse of forgetfulness of the sinner ;
When he asks for protection, give protection.

If a sinner comes to thy shelter ;
It is not proper to slay him, at the first fault.

When once they uttered advice, and the sinner heard not ;
Punish him, the second time, with imprisonment and
    bonds.

120 And, if advice and bonds are of no advantage to him ;
He is an impure tree ; pluck up his roots.

When anger comes to thee, on account of a person's crime,
Reflect much on his punishment ;

Because, it is easy to break the ruby of Badakhshán.
Broken,—it is not possible to fasten it together again.

A certain one came from the sea of 'Ummán,
Much sea and plain travelled ;

Arabia and Turkistan, and Majanderan, and Turkey seen ;
Sciences of every class of men, in his pure spirit ;

125 World travelled, and knowledge gathered ;
Travelled and society-versed ;

In form strong, like a large-bolled tree ;
But very weak without leaf.

Two hundred rags, one on the other stitched ;
He in the midst burnt from their heat.

---

122   Badakhshán is a country between Hindústán and Khurásán; in that
place is a mine of rubies and gold. Some say that there is no mine of
rubies, but that they bring rubies to Badakhshán and call them rubies
of Badakhshán.

By a river-bank, he entered a city ;
A great one (was) king in that locality.

Who had a disposition reflecting on good name ;
Who held the head of submission, at the foot of the dar-
    wesh.

130 The servants of the king washed,
In a bath, his head and body from the dust of the road.

When he placed his head on the threshold of the king,
Lauding, he placed his hand in his bosom.

He entered the hall of the great king,
Saying :—" May thy fortune be young, and power thy
    slave ! "

The great king said :—" Whence didst thou come ?
" What happened to thee that thou camest to me ?

" In this territory, what sawest thou of good and bad ?
" Oh one of good name and good disposition !   Say ! "

135 He replied :—" Oh lord of the face of the earth !
" May God be thy helper, and Fortune thy friend !

" In this country, I went not one stage,
" During which, I saw a single heart calamity-distressed.

" For the king, this very kingdom and ornament (of
    justice) is sufficient,
" That—he is not pleased with injury done to a single
    person.

" I saw not one, head heavy with wine ;
" Indeed I also saw the wine taverns desolate."

He spoke, and expanded his skirt of jewels of speech,
With such a grace, that the king extended his sleeve in
    rapture (was astonied).

140 The excellent speech of the man was pleasing to the king;
He called him near to himself and did him honour.

Gave to him gold and jewels and thanks for auspicious
    arrival;
Inquired of him his original birthplace.

Whatever the king asked of past events, he told;
In propinquity to the king, he surpassed other persons.

The king was in talk with his own heart,
Saying:—" I may commit to him the chief dignity of
    wazír-ship,

" But by degrees, so that the assembly of courtiers
" May not laugh at my judgment, on account of negligence.

145 " First it will be necessary to prove him in wisdom;
" To exalt his rank, according to his skill."

From the power of grief, there may be burdens on the
    heart of that one,
Who, untried, performs deeds.

When the Kází, with thought, writes the decree,
He becomes not ashamed of turban-wearers (nobles,
    learned and pious men).

---

130   " Astín bar afshándan " signifies—to be astonished.
147   " Sijjil " is the written degree, in which the judge writes the order of
decision with the reasons.

Glance (at the butt), when thou hast the arrow-notch in
    the bowstring-seizer,
Not, at that time, when thou didst shoot the arrow from
    the hand.

Like Joseph in rectitude and discretion, (for) a person—
Many years are necessary (in order) that he may become
    'azíz (king).

50 So long as much time passes not,
One cannot reach a person's profundity.

The king discovered his good qualities of every kind;
He was a man wise and of pure religion.

The king saw his good way of life, and illumined
    judgment;
His considerate speech, and capability of man-appraising.

Considered him in judgment better and greater than the
    great ones;
Placed him above the power of his own wazír.

He acquired such skill, and knowledge of work,
That he wounded not a heart by his order and prohibition.

155 He brought a kingdom beneath the (sway of his) pen;
Because, from him, sorrow came not to a single person.

He closed the tongue of all word-seizers;
Because an evil thing issued not from his hand.

---

148   "Shist" signifies—the bowstring-seizer; it is like a ring, made of
bone; they place it on the thumb at the time of shooting and pull the
bowstring with it.

149   "'Azíz" was the title of the wazír of Egypt.

The envious one, who beheld not (in this conduct) one grain
    of deceit,
Trembled, on account of his work, like wheat on the frying-
    pan.

From his illumined mind, the country acquired light;
Grief, on account of the new wazír, seized the old minister.

He, in respect to that wise one, saw not a single breach (of
    observance)
On account of which, he could express reproach.

160 The faithful one is a basin, and the evil one an ant;
The ant cannot, by force, make a breach in the basin (when
    within it).

Two sun-shaped slaves of the king
Used to be always loin-girt (in service).

Two pure forms like " húr " and " parí "
Like the sun and moon, free from a third likeness.

Two forms, of which thou wouldst have said—one is not
    greater (than the other),
Made themselves equal (in reflection) in the mirror.

The words of the wise one (the new wazír), sweet of
    discourse,
Took the heart of those two (youths) box trees (in stature).

165 When they saw that the qualities of his disposition were
    good,
They became, in inclination, his well-wishers and friends.

The inclination of humanity (love) also affected him;—
Not an inclination (lust) like that of short-sighted ones for
    evil.

---

160   Even so, the evil one cannot prevail over the upright one.

He used to possess news of (enjoy) ease at that time,
When he used to glance in their faces.

When thou dost wish that thy power may remain high,
Oh Sir! attach not thy heart to the smooth-faced ones.

And although desire (lust) itself be not present;
Exercise caution because there is fear of loss.

70 The old minister in respect to this obtained a little informa-
        tion;
    In villainy, he carried this story to the king,

Saying:—"I know not this new wazír, what they call
        him, nor who he is,
"In this country, he will not live in chastity.

"Those who have made journeys live without fear,
"Because they are not cherished by the country and
        government.

"I heard that he has an affection for the slaves;
"He is a treachery-approver and lust worshipper.

"It is not fit that such a dissipated, black-faced one
"Should bring bad repute to the halls of the king.

75 "Perhaps, I forget the king's favour,
"Because, I see ruin and am silent.

"On suspicion, one cannot quickly speak;
"So long as I was uncertain, I spoke not.

"One of my followers observed
"That he had one of them in his bosom.

---

71   "Sámán" signifies—ease, rest, repose, innocence, chastity.
74   "Khíra rúe" signifies—shameless, saucy-eyed.

“ I this have said ; now, oh king of ripe judgment !
“ As I tried, do thou also try.”

He explained the matter in the worst manner,
May there not be a happy day to the bad man !—

180 When the evil one obtained power over a small matter,
He burned the vitals of the great ones in the fire.

One can light a fire with fragments ;
After that, one can burn the large tree.

This speech made the king so wrath,
That his sigh came forth from the heart to the mouth.

Anger, in respect to the blood of the darwesh (new wazír),
  held sway ;
But, tranquillity held the hand in front (forbade)

Because to slay the cherished one is not manliness,
Tyranny after justice is coldness.

185 Injure not one cherished by thyself,
When he has thy arrow, strike him not with the arrow.

It was not proper to cherish him with wealth.
When, with injustice, thou dost desire to drink his blood.

So long as his skill was not certain to thee,
In the royal halls, he was not thy associate.

Now, so long as his crime is not certain to thee,
Seek not, at the suggestion of an enemy, his injury.

---

179 The second line is uttered by the Poet.
185 When kings go a-ravaging and desire to spare any of the inhabitants
of the country from rapine, they give to them an arrow, on seeing which
the soldiers refrain from plundering.

The king held concealed this secret in his heart;
Because, he preserved the saying of the sages.

90 " Oh wise man! the prison of the secret is the heart,
" When thou didst speak, it came not back to chains."

In respect to the work of the man, he secretly looked;
In the way of the sensible man, he saw defect.

When he (the new wazír) suddenly glanced at one of the
    slaves,
The fairy-cheeked one covertly laughed.

Of two persons, who are soul and sense together,
The silent lips are telling a tale.

When, by looking (at them), he used to make the eye bold,
Like the dropsical one of (drinking) the Euphrates, he used
    not to be satiated (of looking).

95 The king's suspicion of evil became confirmed.
From frenzy, he wished to be enraged with him;

But, from right deliberation and perfect judgment
He said to him, in a whisper:—" Oh, one of good name!

" I considered thee sensible;
" Held thee faithful to the secrets of the kingdom:

" Reckoned thee wise and intelligent;
" Regarded not thee shameless and unworthy.

" Such lofty station is not thy place.
" The sin is mine; it is not thy fault.

---

92   This couplet describes the nature of the defect mentioned in couplet
196.
94   "As the one stricken with dropsy becomes not satiated of drinking
water, so he became not wearied of looking at the youths.

200 " When I cherish one of bad stock, assuredly,
" I permit treachery in my house."

The man-much-knowing raised his head :
He thus spoke to King Khusrau, work-understanding :—

" When my skirt is free from crime,
" Fear of the villainy of the evil-intent one comes not.

" This thought never passed in my heart :
" I know not who said what never chanced to me."

The great king said :—" What I have said to thee,
" Enemies will say to thy face.

205 " Thus spoke the old wazír to me ;
" What thou dost know, also say ; and, do (what thou
   canst)."

He laughed, and placed his finger on the lip,
Saying :—" What he uttered,—is no wonder.

" The envious one, who sees me in his own place,
" Brings on (utters with) his tongue—what, but evil of me?

" I considered him my enemy, that hour,
" When Khusrau placed him lower than me.

" When the Sultán places my worth above him,
" Knows he not that an enemy is behind me ?

210 " Till the Judgment-day, he will not accept me as a friend,
" When he sees that, in my honour, is his degradation.

" On this point, I will thee a true tale,
" If first to (this) slave thou dost give an ear.

---

201 In the text, " dárad " is an error for " dáram."
206 " Angusht bar lab giriftan " signifies :—
   Angusht ba dandán gazídan ; ta'ajjub wa tahrír namúdan ; angusht-
i-hairat bar lab giriftan.

" I know not where in a book I have seen,
" That a person in a dream saw Iblís.

" With the stature of a fir-tree, with the countenance of a
      Húr,
" Light, sun-like, burned from his face.

" He went before him and said :—' Oh wonderful ! art thou
      this Iblís ?
" ' There is not an angel with this goodness (of appearance).

" ' Since thou hast this face with the beauty of the moon,
" ' Why art thou a stock-story as to ugliness in the world !

" ' They considered thee terrible of face ;
" ' In the bath-room, they painted thee hideous.

" ' Why, in the halls of the king, have they painted thee,
" ' Dejected of face, distorted of hand, ugly, ruined ? '

" Shaitán of overturned fortune heard this speech.
" In lament, he raised a shout and cry,

" Saying :—' Oh, one of good fortune ! that is not my form,
" ' But the pencil is in the hand of an enemy.

" ' I threw out their root (A'dam) from Paradise ;
" ' Now, by reason of malice, they depict me ugly.'

" Just so I (the new wazír) have a good name ; but,
" For reason, the evil-intent one speaks not good (of me).

" The wazír, whose reputation my rank spilled,—
" It is necessary to fly from his deceit to the distance of a
      league.

In some places :—
                A person, in a dream, saw Iblís :
                In stature, a cone-bearing tree ; in face, a sun.

" But, I think not of the anger of the king ;
" One without sin is brave in speech.

" If the inspector of measures seizes,—there is sorrow to
    that one,
" Whose weight of the standard balance-weight is deficient.

₂₅ " When a word comes happily from my pen,
" To me,—of word-seizers, what care ? "

The king remained confounded at his speech :
He spread the tip of the hand of Order-Giving,—

—Because the malefactor, by fraud and eloquence,
Becomes not free from a crime which he has (committed)—

Saying :—" Assuredly from an enemy, I have not heard
    this ;
—" Have I not seen thee, in short, with my own eyes ?—

" That, of this crowd of people in my court,
" Thou hast only a glance for these two slaves."

₂₃₀ The man of eloquence laughed, and said :—
" This speech is right ; it is not proper to conceal the truth.

" In this matter there is a subtle point, if thou wilt listen.
—" May thy Order be current, and government strong !—

" Dost thou not see that the darwesh, without resources,
" Looks with regret at the rich ?

---

224   " Sang-i-tarázú " is the weight used in weighing.
226   " Sar-i-dast afshándan " signifies — to be angry, to give up, to refuse.
    Thus :—A person utters a speech, and the person addressed agrees not.
    He turns the back of his hand towards the speaker, and shakes it in his
    direction, signifying that he disagrees with him and does not allow the
    speech to pass.

" The resources of my youth have passed ;
" Life in play and pastime passed.

" **Of the** appearance of **these (two slaves) I** have **no**
    patience ;
" Because, they are the possessors of the **capital of beauty**
    and grace.

5 " I had even such a rose-coloured face ;
" My limbs were crystal by reason of beauty.

" In this extremity, it is proper to spin my shroud ;
" Since my hair is like cotton, and my body like a spindle.

" I had even such night-coloured **ringlets** ;
" **My coat was tight on** the body from **delicacy (fatness).**

" **Two rows of pearls had a place in my mouth,**
" **Erect like a wall of silver bricks.**

" Now, at **the time of speech, glance—**
" **One by one, like an old city-wall, they have fallen.**

10 " Why **may I not look** with envy at these (two slaves),
" When **I bring to memory my ruined** (mis-spent) life ?

" Those precious days (of youth) departed from me ;
" Suddenly, this day (of old age) also arrives at an end."

When **the wise** man pierced this pearl of lustrous truth,
The king said :—" To speak better than this **is** impossible."

The king glanced at the nobles,
Saying :—" Desire **not** words and truth more beautiful
    than this.

---

35   **Like crystal,—white and** flashing bright ; but we should say, like *ivory*
rather **than** *crystal.*

" The glance towards a lovely one is lawful, to that one,
" Who knows how to utter excuse with such argument.

215 " If I had not in wisdom acted deliberately,
" I should have injured him by the speech of an enemy."

With severity, to carry a light hand to the sword
Is to carry the back of the hand of regret to the teeth.

Beware that thou hearest not the speech of the designing
    man ;
Because, if thou dost set to work (on his speech), thou
    wilt become regretful.

The dignity and honour, and property of the one of good
    name
The king increased, and to the evil speaker (the old wazír)
    he gave rebuke.

By the deliberation of his learned prime-minister,
His name, in the country, became renowned for goodness.

250 With justice and liberality, years he governed the country;
He departed (died), but his good name remained.

Such kings, who cherish religion,
With the arm of religion (of Islám), carry off the ball of
    empire.

In this age, I see not one of those kings ;
But if there be, it is Abú-Bakr, son of Sa'di, and no other !

Oh King ! Thou art the tree of paradise.
Because, thou hast flung thy shadow (of justice) to the dis-
    tance of a year's journey.

---

252   *Those* kings are the kings mentioned in couplet 251.

From fortune of happy star, there was to me greed;
That it might cast the shadow of the Humá's wing over my
    head.

5 Wisdom said :—" The Humá gives power."
(Nay !) if thou dost desire prosperity, come into this shadow
    (of Abú-Bakr).

Oh God ! in mercy Thou hast looked ;
Since Thou hast diffused this shadow (of Abú-Bakr) on the
    people.

Slave-like, I am a prayer-utterer for this kingdom :
Oh God ! keep perpetually this shadow (of Abú-Bakr).

It is proper to imprison before slaying ;
Because, one cannot join the head of the slain one.

The Lord of Command, and Judgment, and Dignity
Becomes not distressed, on account of the clamour of men.

10 Head full of pride, void of patience,—
To him, the kingly crown is forbidden.

I say not :—When thou dost fight, keep the foot (firm) ;
(But) when thou dost gather anger, keep reason in place.

Whosoever has reason endures ;
Not a wise man is he, whom anger makes subject.

Like an army, anger rushed from ambush :
Justice remained not, nor piety, nor religion.

I saw not such a demon (as anger) beneath the sky,
From whom so many angels fly.

---

54   The Humá is a fabulous bird, found in the Caucasus. He, on whom
its shadow falls, arrives at power.

56   Abu-Bakr was a just and liberal monarch.

64   The word " angel " refers to justice, piety, and religion.

265 Is it not a crime to drink water, without the order of the
   Law of Religion ?
But, if by decree of the judge, thou dost shed blood, it is
   lawful.

Whomsoever the decree of the Law of Islám gives to
   destruction,
Oh Sir ! beware, that thou mayst not have fear of slaying
   him.

And if thou hast (about thee) followers in his tribe,
Bestow gifts on them, and cause ease to arrive.

It was a crime on the part of the tyrannous man ;
What is the crime of his wife and helpless children ?

Thy body is powerful, and army great ;
But, into the country of the enemy (of the kings of Islám)
   urge it not.

270 When, the enemy flies to his lofty citadel,
Injury arrives to the innocent people of the country.

Look into the affairs of prisoners :
It is possible that a guiltless one may be among them.

When a (foreign) merchant died in thy country,
It is paltriness to carry thy hand to his property

Because, afterwards they will bitterly lament for that merchant ;
His relations and tribe will openly speak,

Saying :—" The wretched one died in a foreign country ;
" The tyrant took away his property that remained."

---

265 Water-drinking is allowable ; but it is a crime to drink it in the auspicious month Ramazan, when it is forbidden by the law of Islám.
  Blood-shedding is considered abominable in all religions ; but when
the law has decreed it, it is lawful.

Think of that poor child, without father;
And be cautious of the sigh of his sorrowful heart.

(There is) many a good fame of fifty years,—
Which one disreputable act treads under foot.

Those of approved acts of everlasting fame
Exercised not tyranny over the property of the people.

If he is king over the whole world,
When he takes property from the rich man, he is a beggar.

The noble liberal man dies of poverty;
He fills not his belly from the side of the distressed one.

I heard that a just order-giver
Used to have a coat, both surfaces of lining (cheap) material.

One said to him: " Oh Khusrau of happy days!
" Sew a coat of brocade of China."

He said :—" (Cloth of) this quality is covering and ease;
" And thou dost exceed this (rule), it is ornament and
        decoration.

" I take not the land tax for the sake,
" That I may put embellishments on my own body, and
        throne, and crown.

" If like women, I put ornaments on my body,
" How may with manliness I repulse the enemy?

" A hundred times, I have even greed and desire for it;
" But, the treasury is not only for me.

" The treasuries are full for the sake of the army;
" They are not for the sake of ornament and decoration."

The soldier, who, on account of his king, is not happy at
        heart,
Watches not the borders of the kingdom.

When the enemy carries off the villager's ass,
Why does the king enjoy tribute (levied from the people)
    and the tenth part ?

The enemy took away his ass, the king tribute ;
In respect to that throne and crown, what fortune
    remains ?

290 Violence to the fallen one is not manliness :
The mean bird carries off the grain from before the (weak)
    ant.

The peasant is a tree ; if thou dost cherish it, (Oh King-
    Gardener of the kingdom !)
Thou mayst enjoy the fruit to the desire of the heart of
    thy friends.

With mercilessness, pluck it not out with root and fruit ;
Because, the fool does injury to his own body.

Those persons enjoy the fruit of youth and fortune,
Who act not severely to their inferiors.

If an inferior becomes distressed
Beware of his complaining to God.

295 When it is possible to take the country with gentleness,
In contest, bring not forth blood from a single pore of the
    body.

In the name of manliness ! because, the country of the
    whole earth
Is not worth one drop of bood that trickles on the earth.

---

290   " Uftáda " signifies—weak and faulty.
    The weak ant, with great labour, collects his store of food.
294   " Az páe dar ámadan " signifies—" 'ájiz shudan ; sakat shudan ;
uftádan."
295   " Masámi "=" bíkh-i-múe."

I heard that King Jamshíd of happy nature
Wrote on a stone, at a fountain head.

" At this fountain, many like us took rest ;
" They departed (in death), just as the eyes twinkled.

" With manliness and force, they took the world ;
" But, they took it not with themselves to the tomb.

100 " They departed, and each one reaped what he sowed :
" There remained only good and bad fame."

When thou hast power over an enemy,
Injure him not ; because this (the power) is indeed sufficient
        sorrow to him.

A living enemy, head-revolving (raging), about thee (in
        desire of thy blood),
Is better than his (life-) blood revolving (circulating) about
        thy neck.

I heard that Darius of august family,
Became separated, on a hunting day, from his retinue ;

---

297   Jamshíd was a famous Persian king who practised sorcery, by which
jinns and devils became subject to him. It is said he reigned three
hundred years, during which time there was no sickness among the
people. At length he laid claim to godship, and was slain by Żuḥḥák.
    In the 'Iḳd-i-manzúm couplets 297 to 302 are omitted.

298   " Damkardan " signifies—to rest, or delay.
    In some places :—
    What use is there in boasting, or complaining, of prosperity and
        misfortune ?
    If thou dost twinkle the eye, thou dost see neither this, nor that.

303   Darius III. (336–330) B.C., was a Persian king.
    In the year 333 B.C., on the bank of the Issus, Darius with 600,000
men met the army of Alexander consisting of 30,000 foot and 5,000
horse. Darius fled from the field. Alexander gained a complete victory
over the Persian Army, of which 110,000 were slain.

A herdsman came running towards him :
Darius of happy sect said to his heart :—

305 " Perhaps, this is an enemy who has come to battle :
" From a distance, I will pierce him with a white poplar
        arrow."

He adjusted the royal bow to the bow-string :
He desired in a moment to make his existence, non-
        existence.

The herdsman said :—" Oh Lord of I'rán and Túrán !
—" May the evil eye be far from thy time !—

" I am he who cherishes the king's horses :
" In this meadow, I am in thy service."

The heart of the king, (which had) gone (in fear), returned
        to its place.
He laughed and said:—" Oh one of contemptible judg-
        ment !

310 " The auspicious angel (Jibrá,il) assisted thee ;
" Otherwise, I had brought the bow-string to the ear."

Alexander then conquered Egypt, and was prepared in 331 B.C. to
meet the forces which Darius had collected.

Darius wished for peace. He offered to Alexander the provinces
west of the Euphrates, and a vast sum for the release of his family.

Alexander, being determined to conquer Persia, refused.

In 331 B.C. the two armies met near Arbela. Darius had 40,000
horse and myriads of infantry. The horsemen came from the Khurd and
Turkoman tribes ; the footmen from Afghanistan and Bokhára.

Alexander mustered 7,000 horse and 40,000 foot.

As at the battle of the Issus, the courage of Darius gave way ; he
fled, and his flight decided the fate of the day. Darius escaped the
hand of Alexander, to fall by the hand of his own satrap Bessus.

This event is most graphically described by Shaikh Niẓámí in Discourse 30 of the " Sikandar Náma," translated by Clarke.

308   The student should note that "parwaram" is used in the text, not
" parwarad."

The guardian of the land-pastured laughed and said :—
"It is not proper to conceal advice from a benefactor;

" It is not laudable deliberation, nor good judgment,
" That the king knows not an enemy from a friend.

" The condition of living in greatness is such,
" That thou shouldst know each humble person—who he is.

"Thou hast many times seen me in the presence :
" Thou hast asked me concerning the herd of horses and
        the meadow.

315 " Now in love I returned before thee :
" Thou dost not again recognise me from an enemy.

" Oh renowned monarch !   I am powerful ;
" Because, I can bring a particular horse out of a hundred
        thousand.

" By reason of wisdom and judgment, I have the guardian-
        ship of the horses ;
" Thou also shouldst keep thy own herd permanent (free
        from loss)."

When Darius heard this counsel from the man,
He spoke fairly to him, and did him kindness.

Darius kept going and saying in his shame,—
It will be proper to write this advice on the heart.

320 On account of anarchy, there may be sorrow in that throne
        and country,
When the deliberation of the king may be less than that
        of the shepherd.

———

318   In the 'Ikd-i-manzúm, couplets 318 and 319 are omitted.

How mayst thou hear the lament of one crying for
    justice,—
The curtain of thy bed-place at Saturn?

So sleep, that the lamentation may come to thy ear,
If the crier for justice brings forth a shout.

Who complains of the tyrant, who is in thy time,
When every violence that he commits is thy violence?

The dog tore not the skirt of one of a Kárawán,
But the ignorant villager, who cherished the dog.

325 Oh Sa'dí! thou camest boldly into speech:
When the sharp sword of (true) speech is at thy hand,
    be victorious.

Say what thou dost know; because, truth spoken is well:
Thou art not a bribe-taker, nor a blandishment-giver
    (hypocrite).

Bind avarice (to thyself) but (then) wash the book of philo-
    sophy;—
Bid farewell to avarice, and say whatever thou dost desire.

A certain neck-exalting one (a king), in Media, came to
    know
That a wretched one beneath an arch kept saying:—

" Thou even art hopeful at the door (of God):
" Then accomplish the hope of those, door-sitting."

----

321   Kaiwán, or Zuḥal, is the planet Saturn in the seventh heaven.   Such
is its loftiness that the cry for justice cannot reach so far.

322   In the 'Iḳd-i-manzúm, couplets 322 to 358 are omitted.

327   When thou madest avarice thy garment, wash philosophy from the
book of thy wisdom; because, by reason of avarice, thou wilt not be able
to act according to philosophy.

130 Thou dost not wish, that thy heart may be sorrowful—
Bring forth from fetters the heart of the sorrowing ones.

The distress of the heart of the one justice-seeking
Casts a king from his kingdom.

Thou hast slept cool half a day in the retired place (haram);
Say to the foreigner, burn in the heat outside.

God is the taker of justice for that person,
Who cannot ask for justice from a king.

———

One of the great ones, possessed of discretion,
Tells a story of the son of King 'Abdu-l-'Azíz.

135 Saying :—He had a ring-stone set in a ring,
In respect to the value of which, the (Court) jeweller
    was confounded.

At night, thou wouldst say it is the orb, world-
    illuminating ;
A glittering star it was, in light like the day.

By chance, a drought-year occurred,
When the full-moon of the face of men became the new-
    moon.

When he saw not ease and strength in man,
He considered it not manliness to be himself at ease.

When a person sees poison in the jaws of men,
How will the sweet water pass to his throat?

———

334   The name of the son was 'Umar, a just and liberal prince.

340 He ordered : they sold the ring-stone for silver
Because pity came to him, on account of the poor and
    orphan.

He gave its value, in spoil, in one week :
He gave to the poor, and needy, and necessitous.

Those reproach-making fell on him,
Saying :—" Such a ring will not again come to thy hand."

I heard that he said, and the rain of tears
Ran down, like wax, on his cheeks—

As follows :—" Ugly is the ornament on a monarch,
" The heart of a citizen afflicted with powerlessness.

345 " A ring, without a stone, is fit for me :
" The heart of a sorrowful populace is not fit for me."

Happy is that one, who, the ease of man and woman,
Prefers to his own ease.

The cherishers of skill displayed not desire
For their own pleasure (acquired) from the grief of others,

If the king on the throne sleep pleasantly,
I think not the poor man sleeps at ease.

But if he keeps at night a long time awake,
Men will sleep in ease and repose.

350 Praise be to God ! this way of life and straight road,
Atábuk Abú-Bakr son of Sa'd has

In Persia, a trace of another calamity, a person
Sees not save the figures of the moon-like ones (lovely
    women).

These five couplets came pleasantly to my ear,
Which they sang in an assembly last night :—

" Last night, I had ease of life ;
" Because, that moon-faced one was in my embrace.

" When I,—head intoxicated with sleep—saw her,
" I said :—' Oh lovely one ! the cypress before thee is low
   (in stature).

355 " ' One moment, wash the narcissus (the eye) from sweet
   sleep ;
" ' Laugh like the rose-bush ; and sing like the nightingale.

" ' Oh calamity of the age ! why art thou asleep ?
" ' Come ; and bring the luscious red wine.'

" Confused with sleep, she glanced and said :—
" ' Thou dost call me a *calamity*, and sayst,—sleep not.' "

In the time of the Sultán (Abú Bakr) of enlightened spirit,
A person sees not another calamity awake.

———

In the annals of former kings, it is written,
That when Tukla sate on the throne of Zangí,

360 In his age, a person offended not another ;
If this were indeed so, he surpassed (former kings) and
   (for a king) enough.

————————————

358 This couplet is by the Author, in praise of the King; its meaning is:—
In the time of the Sultán of enlightened spirit, men experience only the
calamity of Lovely-Ones !
359 " Tukla " is the name of one of the Atábuks, who ruled in Shíráz ;
Zangí is the grandfather of Abú-Bakr, the son of Sa'd.
360 The qualities of justice of Tukla were high. In his time, no one
injured another. Sa'di says :—if this be so, he surpassed former kings,
and for a king this is enough.

He (Tukla) once thus spoke to a pious man,
Saying :—" My life in uselessness became accomplished.

" When country and rank, and throne pass away,
" Only the fakír carries away empire from the world.

" I wish to sit in the corner of devotion,
" That I may obtain this period of five days that is (left
    of my life)."

When that wise one of enlightened soul heard,
With anger, he arose, saying :—" Oh Tukla! this is
    enough.

365 " Religion is only in the service of the people ;
" It is not—in the rosary, and the prayer carpet, and
    darwesh-garment.

" Be a king on thy own throne ;
" Be a darwesh in pure morals.

" Keep loin-girt in truth and desire (of God) ;
" Keep tongue-bound from idle speech and pretension."

In religion, the foot (of action) is necessary, not the breath
    (of words) ;
Because, breath without action has no real essence.

The great ones, who possessed the ready money of purity,
Wore, beneath the outside coat, such a habit (of truth and
    desire of God).

---

361   Because I exercised not enough devotion to God.

362   Seven days were required for the creation of the world. Man is born
on one day; he dies on another. Thus five days are left which
metaphorically represent his life.

360   Belief is not to be reposed on *appearance*, but on the *way-of-life*.

70 I heard that the Sultán of Turkey wept,
   Before a good man, possessed of sciences,

   Saying :—" From the hand of the enemy, power remained
      not to me,
" Save this fort and city nothing remained to me.

" Much I tried that my son,
" After me, might be chief of the assembly (*i.e.* army).

" Now the enemy of bad descent prevailed ;
" He twisted the tip of my hand of manliness and exertion.

" What plan may I prepare, what remedy may I make ?
" Because, the soul in my body is consumed from grief."

75 The good man said :—" Oh brother ! suffer sorrow for
      thyself
" Since, the best and largest portion of thy life has gone.

" This extent (of country) is sufficient for thee, so long as
      thou dost remain (in the world) ;
" When thou dost go, the world is the place of another."

If he be wise ; if he be foolish ;—
Suffer not grief for him, because he will endure his own
      grief.

The world is not worth the trouble of having ;
Of seizing by the sword, and of abandoning.

Whom of the Kings of Persia knowest thou,
Of the age of Firídún, and Zahhák, and Jamshíd,

80 In respect to whose throne and country, did not declina-
      tion come ?
There only remained the country of God most High.

---

70   In the 'Iḳd-i-manẓúm, couplets 370 to 414 are omitted.
75   In some places :—
      The wise man was amazed, saying :—" Wherefore is this weeping ?
      It is proper to weep, on account of this reason and spirit."

To whom remains the hope of remaining for ever in this
    world,
When thou seest no one who remained for ever?

If silver and gold and treasure and property remains,
It becomes trodden under foot, after a few days.

But of whomsoever a good act remains current,
—May mercy perpetually arrive on his soul!—

A great one, whose good name remained,—
One can say with the pious, as follows :—*he remained.*

385 Ho ! take care that thou dost cherish the tree of liberality,
In order that thou mayst have hope that thou mayst enjoy
    its fruit.

Practise liberality that to-morrow (the Judgment Day)
    when they (the angels) place the account-book,
They may give thee dignities, according to the extent of
    thy beneficences.

One, whose foot-struggle is greater,
(Has) greater dignity, at the Court of God.

One, a backslider, deceiver, shameless,
Greedily desires the wages for work not done.

---

381   In some places :—
Make thy own deliberation ; because that one full of wisdom,
Who is after thee, endures his own grief.
Boast not of this five days' stay ;
Prepare for the thought of the plan of departing (from the world).

387   " Sa'í kadam " signifies — to run, to make an effort. It may be
translated by " 'amal " work. In some copies the first line runs :—
        One whose foot is foremost in endeavour.

388   The other—whose foot, in endeavour, falls backwards, and who practises deception—will remain in God's court, disappointed and un-
rewarded.

Quit him, so that he may carry the back of his hand (in
    regret) to the teeth :
An oven (of ability) so hot,—yet he baked not the bread
    (of good deeds) !

At the time of corn-gathering, thou wilt know,
That idleness is—not seed-sowing.

———

A wise man, in the boundaries of Syria,
Took a cave, for his dwelling away from the world.

By reason of his patience, in that dark corner of a place,
His foot descended to the treasure of contentment.

I heard that his name was—"Khudá-dost" (friend of
    God) ;
He was of an angelic nature, man-in-form.

The great ones placed their heads at his door ;
Because his head entered not at their doors (for petition-
    ing).

The holy man of pure practice desires
The abandonment of lust, by the beggary of the body.

When every hour, his lust says :—"give,"
It makes him wander, in contempt, from village to village.

In that land, where this wise man was,
There was a lord of the marches,—a tyrant.

Such that every feeble one, whom he used to find,
He used to twist his hand (torment), with his strength of
    grasp.

———

9   This is uttered by the poet.
1   " Páe fano raftan " signifies—ṣabát-i-ḳadam warzídan ; ístádagí
kardan.

World-burner (a tyrant), and merciless, and malevolent-
    slayer,
The face of a world became distressed by his bitterness.

400 A crowd of people went (from the country) on account of
        that tyranny and shame,
They took his bad name into the districts.

A crowd of people (women), wretched and miserable, re-
    mained :
Behind the spinning wheel, they uttered curses.

In the place, where the hand of tyranny becomes long,
Thou dost not see the lip of man, open from laughing.

The tyrant used now and then to come, to see the shaikh ;
" Khudá-dost " used not to look at him.

One time, the king (the tyrant) said to him :—" Oh one
    of good fortune !
" Gather not together thy face severely, in abhorrence
    of me.

405 " Thou dost know that I have the desire of friendship for
        thee,
" For what, dost thou bear enmity to me ?

" I grant that I am not the chief of the territory ;
" (But) in honour I am not less than the darwesh.

" I say not—place my excellence above any one,
" So be with me, as (thou art) with every one."

The wise 'ábid heard this speech :
He arose in perturbation, and said :—" Oh King ! hold thy
    ear (listen).

---

401   The student should note the use of " pesh giriftan."
408   " Bar ashuftan " signifies — to be grieved and angry.

" The distress of the people is on account of thy existence :
" I love not the affliction of the people.

" Thou art an enemy to him, with whom I am a friend ;
" I consider thee not a friend of mine.

" Why, in vain, should I hold thee my friend,
" When I know that God considers thee enemy ?

" Give not a kiss on my hand, like a friend :
" Go,—love my friends (the creatures of God).

" If they tear off the skin of ' Khudá-dost,'
" He will not become the friend of the enemy of the friend."

I wonder at the sleep of that stony-hearted one,
On account of whom, a whole nation sleeps straitened in
     heart.

Oh great one ! exercise not violence on the humble ;
Because, the world remains not in one way.

Twist not the grip of the hand of the powerless,
For, if he prevail, thou wilt rise to nothing.

I said to thee :—take not the feet of men from their
     place (distress them not) ;
Because, if thou dost fall into distress, thou wilt become
     weak.

---

1   In some places :—
        If friendship for me chances to thee,
        Perhaps then God holds thee an enemy.
5   That is—Wealth and power become changed.
6   " Panja pechídan " signifies—to vex, to cause distress.
7   That is :—
Drive not men from their place, and cause them not to slip from their
    station and rank.
    " Páe az jáe bendan " signifies—
        Az kadar kase rá afgandan wa ba árám sákhtan.
    " Páe " has here the force of " tákat."
    " Az pá, e dar ámadan " signifies—to fall into distress.

It is not proper to reckon the enemy at a low estimation ;
Since I have seen a great mountain from a small stone.

Dost thou not see that, when the (weak) ants assemble
together,
They bring trouble and torment to fighting lions ?

420 The (slender) hair is not less than a thread of silk :
When it becomes manifold, it is stronger than a chain (of
iron).

The heart of friends collected (tranquil) is better than
the treasure collected :
The empty treasury, better than men in grief.

Throw not the work of any one at his feet ;
Because it may often happen, that thou mayst fall at his
feet.

Oh feeble one ! endure (the tyranny) of the strong ;
Because, one day, thou mayst be stronger than he.

With resolution, bring forth a cry against the oppressor ;
Since, the arm of resolution is better than the hand of
force.

425 Say to the withered lip of the oppressed one,—laugh !
Because they will dig out the teeth of the tyrant.

By the noise of the drum, the rich man became awake ;
What knows he as to how the night of the watchman
passed ?

---

418   In the 'Ikd-i-manzúm, couplets 418 to 421 are omitted.
So, when the weak gather together they become strong.

422   " Dar páe andakhtan " signifies—
Tahkír wa ihmál wa ta'lîl kardan.

424   As they have said :—(Arabic.) The spirit of men is the cause of
the moving of mountains.

426   That is :—the rich one, all night, is in sleep and ease ; the poor one,
all night, is awake and in agitation.

The man of the Kárawán **suffers** grief on account of his
  own load (of merchandise);
His **heart** burns not at the wounded back of the ass.

I have **granted that thou art not** of (the number of) the
  fallen:
When thou dost **see** a fallen **one**, why dost thou stand (and
  not give help)?

On this point, **I will tell** thee a tale of past event;
Inasmuch **as** it would be slothfulness to pass by this **speech.**

———

° Such a famine **occurred in the city of Damascus,**
That lovers forgot love.

The sky over the earth became such a miser,
That the crops and the date-trees wetted not their lips.

The spring of the **ancient** fountains dried **up;**
Water remained **not, save the water of the eyes of**
  orphans.

Only the sigh of a widow-woman, **it used to be,**
If smoke went forth from a window.

I saw trees, leafless (poor), like a darwesh;
Those strong of arm, languid and greatly distressed (by
  the severity of the famine).

---

28   "Giriftan" is frequently used in this sense, as " farẓ yáḳabúl kardan,"
to **grant, to assume, to agree.**
30   Damascus was founded by Damsháḳ, son of Nimrúd.
    Friends **on meeting** said in former times—" 'Ishḳ," **love be to thee!**
Say **in these**—" Salám 'alayḳa," peace be to thee!
    In the drought year, for fear of being asked for something, friends
saluted not each other.
34   "Barg" signifies—the leaf of a tree; and also, provisions.

435 Not in the mountain, verdure; not, in the garden, a
      branch :
The locusts ate the garden ; and men, the locusts.

In that state of things, a friend came to me :
To that extent broken down,—merely a skin on his bones.

Although, in dignity, he was of strong state ;
Was lord of rank and gold and property.

I said to him :—" Oh friend of pure disposition !
" Say, what wretchedness has happened to thee ? "

He angrily shouted at me, saying :—" Where is thy
      reason ?
" When thou dost know, and dost ask,—the question is a
      fault.

440 " Dost thou not see that distress has reached to an exceed-
      ing great degree,—
" Trouble arrived to an extreme limit ?

" The rain from the sky descends not ;
" The sigh of the complaining ones ascends not."

At length, I said to him :—" For thee, there is not fear ;
" The poison (only) slays where the antidote is not.

" Though another person should perish from destitution,
" Thou hast wealth. To the duck, what fear of the
      storm ? "

The lawyer, vexed, glanced at me :
The glancing of a learned man at a foolish one.

445 Saying :—" Oh friend ! although a man is on the shore,
" He rests not,—his friends, drowning.

" I am not yellow of face, by reason of want of victuals ;
" Grief for those food-less has made yellow my face."

The wise man wishes not to see a wound
Neither on the limbs of a man, nor on his own limbs.

I am one of the first of those of sound body;
When I behold a wound, my body trembles.

The pleasure of that sound-bodied one becomes disturbed,
When he is at the side of the languid sick.

50 When I see that the wretched darwesh eats not,
The morsel of food within my palate is poison and grief.

Thou dost take one of (his) friends to prison :—
Where is his pleasure in the garden ?

One night, the sigh of the people lighted up a fire.
I heard that a half of the city of Baghdád was burned.

One, in that state, quickly uttered thanks,
Saying :—" Injury has not reached my shop."

A world-experienced one said to him :—" Oh father of
    lust !
" For thee the grief of thy self was sufficient.

155 " Thou dost approve that a whole city should burn by fire,
" If thy house is on one side, away from danger."

---

148   In some places :—
            Thank God, although I am free from wound.
152   In the 'Iḳd-manẓúm, couplets 452 to 479 are omitted.
154   The text gives " bú-l-hawás," which is said to be wrong; because
" hawas " is Persian.   The construction in—
            " bú-l-faẓúl " ⎫
            " bú-l-'ajab " ⎭ is correct, as the words are Arabic.
    For this word, " bul-hawas " should be read, in which " bul " signifies
—" bisiyár."

Except the stony-hearted one, how may he make his
    stomach tight (with food),
When he sees persons stone-bound on the belly ?

How does the rich man himself eat that morsel,
When he sees that the darwesh devours the blood (of his
    heart from grief) ?

Say not to the care-taker of the sick one :—"He is of
    sound body,"
Because he writhes from grief, like a sick one.

The one of tender-heart, when friends arrive at a stage,
Sleeps not, when the wearied loiterers are in rear.

⁴⁶⁰ The heart of kings is a load carrier,
When they see the ass of the fire-wood drawer in the clay.

If a (worthy) person is in the house of happiness,
One word of the saying of Sa'dí is enough.

This also is sufficient for thee, if thou wilt hear,
To wit :—if thou sowest thorns, thou reapest not jasmine.

———

Thou hast knowledge of the Kings of Persia,
Who exercised tyranny over their subjects.

---

456   The way of the most excellent of the pious was such that, when over-
taken with famine, they begged not of any. Rather, lest any should
become acquainted with their famished condition, they bound a stone on
the belly, by which they mitigated the pain of hunger and obtained an
appearance of fulness of belly, as from eating food.

458   The care-taker of the sick is, by sympathy, himself sick.

461   As they have said :—If a person is in the house, one word is enough.

462   As they have said :—
                The sage of Ghuznaví has said :—
                Oh Brother! whatever thou sowest, thou wilt reap.

That dignity and sovereignty remained not;
That tyranny over the peasant remained not.

465 Behold **the crime which issued from** the hand of the
    tyrant!
The world remained; **he, with his acts** of oppression,
    departed (died).

The body of the justice-giver is happy on the day of the
    place **of** assembling (resurrection);
Because, **he has an abiding place in the shadow of the**
    throne of God.

To a tribe, whose goodness **He approves, God**
Gives a king, just, of good judgment.

When He **wishes to** waste a **world,**
He places the country, in the grasp of a tyrant.

The pious ones think cautiously of the tyrant;
Because, the oppressor is (the personification of) the anger
    of God.

470 Recognise greatness **from Him, and** understand **the ob-**
    ligation;
Because, **the prosperity of the ungrateful one becomes**
    frail.

If thou dost express thanks (to **God)** in respect to this
    country and property,
Thou mayst reach to a property and country without
    decline (Paradise).

---

466   When, in the Day of Judgment, the Sun ascends to the height of one
spear only (and will be very near), there are three persons whom God
will place beneath the shadow of His throne.
    One of the three will be a just king.
    On the Judgment Day **there** will be no shadow save that of God's
throne.

471   **If thou dost exercise justice, equity, liberality, and generosity,—**
thou mayst obtain a property and country without decline, *i.e.* Paradise.
Because,—thanks for country is the exercising of justice; and thanks
for property is bestowing on the poor.

But, if in sovereignty thou doest violence,
After sovereignty, thou mayst practise beggary.

Sweet sleep is forbidden to a king,
When the weak one is the load-carrier of the strong.

To the extent of a mustard seed-grain, injure not a people ;
Because, the Sultán is the shepherd, and the people the
    flock.

475 When they experience strife and injustice from the king,
He is not a shepherd ; he is a wolf. Cry out against him.

He went to a bad end, and thought ill-advisedly,
Who exercised tyranny over his inferiors.

By negligence and severity towards these inferiors, he
    passes away ;
A bad name will for years remain attached to him.

Thou dost not wish that, from behind, they should curse
    thee ?
Be good : so that a person may not utter evil of thee.

———

I have heard that, in a territory of the west,
There were two brothers (prince-sons), of one father (a
    king),

480 Army-commanding, and neck-exalting (headstrong), and
    stout,
Good of visage, and wise, and expert with the sword.

The father considered them both to be terrible men ;
He found them seekers of warlike action and strife.

---

472   The beggary of this world is evident to all! The beggary of the next
world consists in being there contemptible and void of its ready money.
481   " Yáft " here signifies—" did."

He went (and) divided the country into two parts;
He gave a portion of it to each of the sons.

God forbid! that on account of one another, they should
 wrangle,—
Should draw forth, in contest, the sword of rancour.

After that, the father lived a short time;
(Then) he surrendered his precious soul to the Soul-
 Creator.

Death caused his rope of hope to break;
Death tied down his hands from work.

On two kings was established that kingdom,
In which were treasure and army, beyond limit and
 computation.

According to their own view, in respect to their own
 welfare,
Each one took a different way.

One (pursued the path of) justice, so that he might bear a
 good name;
The other, tyranny, so that he might amass wealth.

One made benevolence, the way of his life;
He gave money, and provided for the darwesh.

Laid foundations (of buildings), and gave bread, and
 cherished the army;
Made night-houses for the sake of the night of the darwesh.

In some places:—
  When Death broke the rope of his hope,
  The hand of Death tied down his tongue.
 " Bih uftád " signifies—" bihbúd," or " khairíyat," welfare.
 According to the guidance of their reason, to whatever they recognised
as best for them, they each took their way.

Made empty the treasuries, but made full (numerous, or
  satisfied) the army;
Even as people, the time of festivity.

The noise of gladness, like thunder, kept rising,
Like Shíráz, in the time of (King) Abú-Bakr, son of Sa'd.

A wise monarch of happy disposition,—
May the branch of his hope be fruitful!

Hear the tale of the youth, fame-seeking;
He was of approved conduct, and happy temperament;

495 Assiduous in the consolation of high and low;
A praise-utterer of God, morning and evening.

In that country, Kárún used to go boldly (fearless of the
  robber);
Because, the king was a giver-of-justice, and the darwesh,
  satisfied.

In his time, there came not to a single heart (the injury of)
—I say not—a thorn, nay, a rose-leaf!

By the assistance of fortune, he became chief of chiefs:
The chiefs placed their heads (in submission) on the line of
  his order.

The other (prince) desired to increase the power of his throne
  and crown,
He augmented the tribute from the men of the villages.

---

491 In the East, a great deal of money is spent at a festival.
493 *Or* auspicious descent.
498 " Sar bar <u>khatt</u> nihádan " signifies—to be obedient to order.
499 In some places :—
    Hear the end of the other brother!
    If thou art a good man, and manly run.

500 Greedily thirsted for the property of the merchants ;
     Poured calamity on the lives of helpless ones.

     Bestowed not and enjoyed not, in the hope of augmenting ;
     The wise man knows that he did not well.

     Because, while he collected that gold, by cheating,
     The army became distressed and dispersed by reason of
         weakness.

     The merchants heard the news,
     To the effect that,—in the land of that unskilled one, there
         is tyranny.

     They cut off (abandoned) buying and selling from (in) that
         place :
     Cultivation was not; the peasant burned in heart (on
         account of scarcity).

505 When Fortune turned away her head from his friendship,
     The enemy necessarily prevailed over him.

     The anger of the sky plucked out his root and fruit ;
     The hoof of the horse of the enemy dug his country.

     In whom may he seek faith, when he broke his promise ?
     From whom does he wish the land-tax, when the villagers
         fled ?

     What goodness does that unfaithful one hope for,
     When imprecation is in pursuit of him ?

---

501   "Peshí" is for "pesh-búdan"; it is called the "yá,e maṣdariya" or
     infinitive yá.
505   "Biná-kám" signifies—without desire, unasked, i.e. necessarily.

When, in the beginning of creation, his fortune was
    reversed,
Whatever the good men said to him—do; he did not.

510 What said the good men to that good (unjust) prince ?—
Enjoy the fruit (of power; do justice); because the unjust
    one enjoys not.

His imagination was a fault, and his policy languid;
Because, whatever he sought in oppression was (to be
    found) in justice.

Of this one, a bad repute remained; of that one, a good
    name :
The pinnacle of a good end is not for the bad.

A certain one (was sitting) at the end of a branch, and the
    butt end kept cutting :
The Lord of the garden glanced, and saw.

He said :—If this man does evil,
He does it not to me, but to his own body.

515 Advice is in place (proper), if thou wilt hear;
With the strong shoulder cast not down the weak ones.

---

509   "Káf Kun."

"Kun," the order of God in the beginning of the creation of the world.

Verse of the Kurán :—(*Arabic.*) "When God wished to create a
thing, His command was indeed as follows :—God said to it—'Be !'
Then it became."

"Káf" is the first letter of the word "Kun." Immediately on God's
order, all created things became.

512   "This" refers to the unjust prince ; "that" to the just prince.

512   In the 'Ikd-i-manzúm, couplets 512 to 547 are omitted.

Because, to-morrow (the Judgment Day) to God, the king
    brings
The beggar, who before thee is not worth a barley-grain.

Since thou dost wish that, to-morrow, thou mayst be a
    great one,
Make not an humble one thy enemy.

Because, when this kingdom passes from thee (in death),
That beggar will, in anger, seize thy skirt.

From the feeble, restrain thy hand; do not (such a deed);
Because, if they cast thee down, thou wilt become ashamed.

20 In the opinion of those free from worldly cares, there is
    shame,
In falling by the hand of the fallen.

The great ones of enlightened mind and good fortune
Won, by learning, a crown and throne.

In rear of the upright, swerve not:
And, if thou dost desire truth, listen to Sa'dí.

————

Say not—there is no dignity, higher than sovereignty;
Because there is no empire safer than the empire of the
    darwesh.

Men, the more lightly loaded, the more quickly go:
This is true; and the pious ones listen (and obey).

———————

16   The agent to " barad " is " gadá,e "; and its subject is " Khusrau,e."
In the endeavour to keep the two lines distinct, the couplet is obscure.
The meaning is:—
    On the Judgment Day, the oppressed beggar (who in thy opinion is
not worth a grain of barley) brings the king (his oppressor) before
God.

525 The empty-handed one suffers distress, on account of a loaf
   of bread :
The king suffers grief, to the extent of a world.

In the case of the beggar, when the bread of the evening
   is obtained,
He sleeps as pleasantly, as the Sultán of Syria.

Grief and joy proceed to an end ;
By death, these two quit the head.

Whether this one, on whose head they placed the crown :
Or that one, on whose neck the (paying of) tribute came,

If the exalted one be in Saturn ;
And, if the straitened one be in prison.

530 When the cavalcade of death hastes to the head of these two,
It is not possible to recognise one from the other.

The guardianship of country and empire is a calamity :
The beggar is king, but his name is beggar !

———

I once heard that, in a certain place,
A skull spoke to an 'ábid,

Saying :—" I possessed the pomp of order-giving ;
" I had on my head the cap of greatness (a crown) ;

" Heaven and concordant fortune gave me aid ;
" With the arm of empire, I seized Babylonia ;

535 " I had greatly desired that I might enjoy Kirmania,
" When, suddenly, the worms ate my head."

Pluck out the cotton of carelessness from the ear of sense,
That the advice of dead men may come to thy ear.

———

535 Tama' karda búdam may be rendered :—
    I was desire-making ; or, I was wishing.

The man of good work—evil is not to him :
No one practises evil, that good may come to himself.

The man mischief-stirring is also in the desire of wickedness,
Like the scorpion, that seldom goes as far as his own
    house.

If in thy disposition, there is not (the wish for) a person's
    advantage,
A jewel and the hard stone are even so identical.

40 Oh friend of happy disposition ! I uttered a mistake ;
Since there is profit in iron, and stone, and brass.

Even so, for the sake of reputation, the dead is best, the
    man
Over whom the stone has pre-excellence.

Not every man-born-one is better than a rapacious animal ;
Since the rapacious animal is better than the bad man-
    born-one.

Man, endowed with wisdom, is better than the beast of
    prey,—
Not the man, who, like a beast of prey, falls upon men.

When a man understands only eating and sleeping,
What excellence has he over the reptiles ?

45 The unfortunate horseman, going without a road,
The footman surpasses in travelling.

No one sowed the grain of generosity,
Who gathered not up the harvest of the desire of his
    heart.

------

38   When the scorpion, for man-injuring, issues from his house—men cause
him injury, so that it is seldom they let him return to his house alive.

In our lives, we have never heard,
That goodness befell the bad man.

————

A man of war had fallen into a well
Such an one that the male-tiger became female, from fear
    of him.

The evil-intent one ever experiences only evil :—
He fell; and saw no one weaker than himself.

550 All night, from complaint and lamentation, he slept not;
One struck his head with a stone, and said :—

Didst thou ever come to a person's call (for help),
That to-day thou dost desire a grievance-redresser?

Thou didst sow every seed of unmanliness;
See assuredly what thou hast taken up.

Who places a plaster on thy soul-wound,
When hearts keep complaining of the wounds inflicted by
    thee?

Thou usedst to dig a pit in our path,
In the end, without doubt, thou hast fallen into the pit.

555 Two persons, for the sake of high and low, dig a pit :
One of good walk of life; the other, of bad repute.

———————————

548   "Gazír" signifies—an officer, a hero.
549   "Khud" should be read with fatḥa for poetry sake.
550   *Lit.* "One stuck a stone on his head."
553   Whatever thou dost sow, thou dost take up its produce.
553   In some places :—
        Souls will bewail, on account of thy power.
    And again :—
        Thou hadst no grief, for the pain of hearts.

This one, that he may make the throat of the thirsty one
    fresh;
The other, that people may fall into it, up to the neck.

If thou doest bad, expect not goodness:
Because the tamarisk never brings forth the grape-fruit.

Oh thou barley sown in autumn! I think not
That thou wilt obtain wheat, at reaping-time.

If with soul, thou dost cherish the tree of hell,
Think not, that thou mayst ever eat its fruit.

The wood of the colocynth brings not the green date:
Whatever seed thou didst cast,—expect that very fruit.

They relate a story of a certain good man,
That he paid not respect to Hujjáj, the son of Joseph.

In frenzy, he cast on him such power (of argument)
That the power of altercation remained not to Hujjáj.

---

558   Another poet says :—
        Be attentive to this speech and listen well:
        Wheat springs from wheat; barley from barley.

559   "Zaḳúm" (properly written "zaḳḳúm") is a fruitless, thorny tree of
the desert; its white sap is of foul smell; it is called the tree of hell.
    In the 'Iḳd-i-manzúm, couplets 559 and 560 are omitted.

560   "Khar-zahra" is called in Arabic "sammu-l-ḥimár." Originally, in
Persian, it was written "khar-zahraj"; in medical works, it is called
"ḥinzal," that is, colycinth.

561   Hujjáj, the son of Joseph (not the Joseph of Bible history), was an
amír of Baghdád, notorious for tyranny. He lived in 685 A.D.
    The good man gave advice with severity; and, whatever Hujjáj said,
rejected.

562   "Saudá" signifies—frenzy, anger, passion.
    "Dast-i-hujjat fishánad." That is to say, Hujjáj became convinced.
The custom of Hujjáj was this:—He would slay a guiltless man. If it
were his pleasure, they would spread the decapitation carpet before him;
place the victim on it; cut off his head; and take away the slain one on
it. In this way, the spot, in front of Hujjáj, was unstained with blood.

Hujjáj looked sharply at the officer of the court,
Saying :—" Cast down the decapitation-carpet, and spill his
  blood."

When argument remained not to the violence-seeking one,
He draws, in contest, his face together.

565 The man of God laughed and wept:
The stony-hearted one of obscure judgment wondered.

When he saw that he laughed, and again wept,
He inquired, saying :—" Why is this laughing and
  weeping ? "

The Man of God said :—" I keep weeping, on account (of
  the violence) of time ;
" Because, I have four helpless children.

" I keep laughing on account of the grace of the pure God ;
" Because I, the *oppressed one*, go to the dust,—not the
  oppressor."

One said to Hujjáj :—" Oh good-hearted monarch !
" What dost thou desire of this old man ? touch him not.

570 " Because a people look towards, and lean upon him :
" It is not lawful, to slay a crowd at one time.

" Practise greatness and forgiveness, and liberality :
" Think of his little children.

" Perhaps thou art the enemy of thy own household,
" Because thou dost approve of evil to households ?

" Think not—hearts (being) torn by thy tyranny—
" That, on the last day, good may befall thee."

---

573 For " resh," read " resh-shuda."

I heard that Hujjáj listened not; but shed his blood.
Who knows how to fly from the decree of God?

75 That night, a great one slept in that thought:
In sleep, he saw him, and asked (his state); the
    slaughtered one said:

" Hujjáj urged not his punishment, in regard to me, more
    than one moment;
" Punishment remained to him, till the Judgment Day."

The oppressed one slept not; fear his sigh:
In the morning time, fear the sigh of his heart.

Dost thou not fear, that, at night, the one of pure heart
May bring forth, from the burning of his heart,—Oh
    Lord!

Iblís did evil, and experienced good?—No;
The pure fruit comes not from the filthy seed.

80 Shout not against rough lion-like men,
When with boys, in boxing, thou dost not prevail.

———

One gave advice to a son
—Preserve the counsel of the wise—

---

76   " Siyásat " signifies—order, regulation of government.   Here it means
punishment.
77   Muhammad ordered :—(*Arabic.*) Fear the claim of the oppressed one;
indeed God Most High has not hung a curtain between this and that
(*i.e.* between Himself and the oppressed one.)
79   As they have said :—
      Tree and fruit continually speak to thee,
      Saying :—Oh Sir! whatever thou wilt sow, the same grows for thee.
    In some places :—
      At the time of quarrelling, rend not the curtain of any one;
      Because, thou also mayst have shame in secret.
81   The second hemistich has no connection with the first, nor with couplet
582.   The author says to the reader as follows :—
      I am relating the advice given by a certain one; listen, and hold
        dear.
    In the 'Ikd-i-manzúm, couplets 581 to 588 are omitted.

" Oh son ! exercise not violence on small folk,
" Because one day, a great one may attack thy head."

Oh wolf of deficient understanding, dost thou not fear,
That, one day, a panther may rend thee in pieces ?

In youth, I had strength of grasp ;
The heart of inferiors was distressed on account of me.

585 I suffered one blow of the fist of the strong ;
I exercised not force, again, against the weak.

Take care thou sleepst not in carelessness ; because sleep
Is improper for the eyes of the leader of a tribe.

Beware ; sympathise with the grief of inferiors ;
Fear the violence of time.

The advice, that is free from design,
Is like bitter medicine,—the repelling of disease.

They relate a story of one of the kings,
Whom the disease of guinea-worm made like a spindle.

590 Weakness of body to such a degree overthrew him,
That he envied his subjects.

Although, the king on the chess-board is famous,
When weakness comes, he is less than a pawn.

A courtier kissed the ground before the king,
Saying :—" May the country of the Lord be eternal !

" In this city, is a man of happy spirit,
" Like whom, in abstinence, a man is rare.

" They brought not before him the important affairs of any
        one,—
" Whose object was not obtained, in a breath.

595 " An improper act has never issued in regard to him,
  " (He is) one of illumined heart, and one whose prayers are
        answered.

" Call (him), so that he may utter a prayer, on account of
      this disease
" That mercy from heaven may arrive on earth."

The king ordered, so that the chiefs of the servants
Summoned the old man of happy footstep.

They went and uttered the message.   The fakír came—
Body powerful in contemptible dress.

The king said :—" Oh wise man ! utter a prayer ;
" Because, in respect to the guinea-worm, I am foot-bound,
      like a needle."

600 The old man, bent as to his back, heard this speech :
With severity, he brought forth a harsh shout,

Saying :—" God is compassionate to the just ruler :
" Forgive ; and behold the gift of God.

" How may my prayer be profitable to thee—
" The oppressed captives, in pit and fetters ?

" Thou hast not made presents to the people,
" Whence mayst thou experience the empire of easiness ?

" It is necessary to ask pardon (from God) for thy fault,
" Then, beseech a blessing from the holy shaikh.

605 " How may his (the shaikh's) prayer aid thee,
" The prayers of oppressed ones behind thee ? "

---

595   The eye of the needle is considered the foot.   When it is threaded, it
is said to be foot-bound.

The monarch of Persia heard this speech ;
From anger and shame, he frowned.

He grieved and then said to his heart :—
" Why do I grieve ? this, that the darwesh said, is right."

He ordered : so that whoever was in fetters,
Him, by order, they quickly freed.

The world-experienced one (the shaikh), after two in-
    clinations of the head in prayer,
Lifted up the hand of supplication to God,

610 Saying :—" Oh uplifter of the sky !
    " In battle (against thee) thou didst seize him ; in peace
    invite him."

The saint thus held up his hands in prayer,
When the king raised his head (from the pillow) and
    leaped on his feet.

Thou wouldst say :—" From joy, he will fly,
" Like a peacock, when he saw no longer the thread (of
    captivity) on his foot."

The king ordered :—the treasury of his jewels,
They scattered on his (the shaikh's) feet, and gold on his
    head.

The shaikh shook his skirt from all that (treasure) and
    said :—
" For the sake of the false, it is not proper to conceal the
    truth.

---

610   " Jang wa ṣulḥ " signify—"mukẖálifat wa muwáfiḳat," *i.e.* in opposition
and concord.

611   " Dáman afshándan," *or* " dáman bar afshándan," signifies—to
journey, to abandon, to turn away the face from. That is :—for the
sake of *wealth*, it is not fit to conceal the truth.

615 " Go not again to the end of the tether (of injustice),
    " Lest that again the guinea-worm should raise its head."

When once thou hast fallen, take care of thy foot,
That once more it slips not from its place.

Listen to Sa'dí, for this speech is true,—
" Not every time, has the fallen one risen."

———

Oh Son ! the world is not an everlasting country ;
There is no hope of the sincerity from the world.

Morning and evening, on the wind, used not to go,
The throne of Sulaimán ?—on him be peace !

620 In the end, didst thou not see that it went to the wind
        (became non-existent),
    Happy is that king, who went (from the world) possessed
        of learning and justice !

That person seized from the midst (of the world) the ball
    of empire,
Who was in consideration of the ease of the people.

Those things which they took up (to the future world)
    came of use ;
Not those things which they amassed and abandoned
    (in this world).

I have heard that, in respect to the glorious chief of Egypt,
Death hastened an army on his life.

———

615   " Sar-i-rishta " signifies—desire, or object.
         Practise not again the tyrannies which thou didst once exercise.
617   The second hemistich is the true speech referred to.
618   In the 'Iḳd-i-manzúm, couplets 618 to 636 are omitted.
622   In some places :—
              This space of five days' prosperity is his,
              Whose pleasure is—the vexing of men.
623   " Ajall " is glorious ; " ajal " signifies—death.

The beauty went from his cheek, heart-exalting :
When the sun becomes yellow, much of the day remains
    not.

625 The wise men (in sorrow) bit the hand of annihilation ;
Because, in the medical books, they saw no remedy for
    death.

Every throne and country declines—
Save the country of the Eternal Order-Giver.

When the day of his life came near to the night (of non-
    existence),
They heard him say beneath his lip,

As follows :—" A king like me, in Egypt, there was not :
" When this is the fruit, sovereignty is worthless.

" I gathered the world ; I enjoyed not its fruit :
" Like the helpless ones, I passed from its desire."

630 The one of approved judgment who gave and enjoyed ;
Gathered the world, for the sake of his own body.

Strive in this work, so that wealth may be a dweller with
    thee ;
Because, whatever remains behind thee is regret and fear.

The rich man, on the couch, soul-fleeting, makes
One hand short ;—and the other, long.

At that moment, he shows thee by the hand,
—Because, fear has bound his tongue from speaking,—

---

625   The Sages chose the hand of annihilation ; or became captive to its
power and resigned themselves to his dying.
627   " Dar zer-i-lab guftan," signifies—to whisper.
629   " Az sar raftan," signifies—to abandon.
634   " Dast" has yá,e waḥdat.

To this effect :—extend one hand in generosity and
    liberality ;
Contract the other hand from tyranny and avarice.

635 Now, that thou hast the power, take action ;
How again (in the grave) mayst thou bring forth the hand
    from the shroud ?

Often the moon and pleiades and sun will shine ;
But thou wilt not raise thy head from the pillow of the
    grave.

King Kizil Arslán had a strong fort
That exalted its neck above the mountain Alwand.

There was not fear of any one ; nor need of anything :
Like the ringlets of brides, its road fold within fold.

It had fallen strangely in a garden, in such a way,
As a white egg on a green tray.

640 I heard that a man of favourable mien
Came, from a long journey, to King Kizil-Arslán.

A truths-recogniser ; world-experienced ;
A skilled one ; world-travelled ;

A great one ; an eloquent one, work-knowing ;
A wise one ; speech-weighing ; much-knowing.

Kizil said :—" So much as thou hast travelled,
" Hast thou seen another place, strong like this ? "

-----

635 " Dast zadan " signifies—to assist, or to show manliness.
637 Alwand is a lofty mountain in the territory of Hamdán.
638 Because the fort was strong, and all things were ready within it.
    " Zulf " is the ringlet that goes round about the ear.

He laughed, saying :—" This fort is joyous;
" But, I do not think it is strong.

645   " Did not the obstinate ones (kings) possess it before thee !
" A few moments, they were; and they abandoned it.

" May not other kings take it, after thee,
" (And) enjoy the fruit of thy tree of hope ?

" Remember the revolution of the country of thy father;
" Set free the heart from the knot of reflection.

" Fortune placed him, in a corner (of the grave) in such
        a way,
" That power remained not to him, over a particle.

" When hope remained not as to any thing, or person,
" Hope remained to him of the excellence of God only."

650   To the wise man, the world is straw;
For, every moment, it is the place of another.

———

A frantic one, in Persia, thus spoke,
To Naushíraván, saying :—" Oh heir of the country of
        Jamshíd !

" If country and fortune had remained to Jamshíd,
" When would crown and throne have become attainable
        by thee ? "

If thou bring the treasure of Kárún within thy grasp,
There only remains—what thou dost give (to the indigent)
        thou mayst take away.

———

---

644   If it were strong, the Angel of Death and Death would not enter it.
646   " It " refers to the fort.
647   This world, which was lent to them, remained not in their hands.
650   In the 'Iḳd-i-manzúm, couplets 651 to 655 are omitted.

When Alap-Arslán gave his soul to the Soul-giver,
The son placed the royal crown on his head.

655 From the crown-place, they consigned him to the tomb,
The target-place was not a spot for sitting.

Thus spoke a distraught wise one,
—When he saw his son, the next day, on horse-back,—

"Oh excellent government and country!   When head
    down-cast,
" The father departs (in death), the son's foot is in the
    stirrup."

Thus is the revolution of time
A gad-about, and bad-of-faith, and inconstant.

When the One of ancient days brings his life to an end,
One, whose fortune is young, raises his head from the
    cradle.

660 Place not the heart on the world, for it is a stranger,
Like the musician, who is, every day, in a different house.

Pleasure is not proper with such a heart-ravishing one,
Who has, every morning, a fresh mate.

This year, when the village (of the world) is thine, do
    good :
Because, next year, another will be village-chief.

A sage prayed for King Kaykubád,
Saying :—" In thy sovereignty, may there be no decline ! "

----

655   " Amáj-gah " is the place, where they fix the target ; it is also applied
to a king's throne.
656   Distraught as to the things of this world ; wise as to those of the
next.
657   The speaker jests at the transient nature of things.
658   " Sar dar nashíb " signifies—sar-nigún ; ma,yús ; be bahra.
663   In the 'Iḳd-i-manẓúm, couplets 663 to 677 are omitted.

A great one, upon this, reproached him,
Saying :—" The wise man utters not the impossible,—oh
  wonder !

665 " Of the kings of Persia, whom dost thou know,
" Of the time of Firídún and Zahhák and Jamshíd,

" In respect to whose throne and country, decline happened not ?
" (To utter) the impossible is not decorous, on the part of
  a wise man.

" To whom remains the hope of existing always,
" When thou seest no one, who remains for ever ? "

The learned sensible man thus replied,
Saying :—" The wise man utters not unsuitable speech.

" I sought not perpetual life for him ;
" I sought for aid, by the grace of his liberality.

670 " For, if he be devout, and pure in conduct,
" Religion-understanding, advice-hearing,—

" The day, on which he plucks up his heart from this
  country (of the world),
" He pitches his royal tent in the other country (of
  Paradise).

" Then, there is no decline to this empire ;
" There is translation from the (transient) world to the
  (everlasting) world.

" If he be devout, what harm in his death ?
" For he is a king even in the future world."

Whosoever has treasure, and command, and army ;
Government, and dignity, and desire, and pleasure,—

675 If his disposition be good,—
Ease, at all times, is prepared for him.

But, if he exercises violence against the poor,
This same command and dominion are his for five days.

When **Far'ún** abandoned not wickedness,
He exercised sway only up to the **brink of the grave.**

I have **heard** that of the monarchs of Ghúr,
A certain king used to seize asses by force.

The asses, beneath heavy loads, fodderless,
Wretched, perished in the space of two days.

When Time makes the mean one rich,
He places a load on the straitened heart of the darvesh.

When his roof is lofty, the self-worshipper
Pollutes, and casts rubbish on the humble roof (of his
 neighbour).

I heard that, one day, with the intention of hunting,
The **tyrannous** monarch went out.

He urged his steed in rear of the game,
Night overtook him; he remained far from his retinue.

Knew, in solitude, neither the turning nor the path;
Cast at length his head (himself) into a village.

A certain old man was residing in that village,
Old-of old men, men-recognising.

He kept saying to his son :—" Oh happy portion!
" Take not thy ass, in the morning, to the city.

Ghúr is a country near Kandahár.
" Rú,e " may mean—súe; jánib.

" For this one, ungenerous and of reversed fortune
" — Would that I might, instead of his throne, behold his
        bier ! —

" Has his loins girt in a demon's service,
" A cry, on account of the hand of his violence, goes to
        the sphere.

" In this territory, ease and cheerfulness
" The eye of man saw not and sees not.

690 " Perhaps this one whose book of sins is full, void of
            purity,
" Will go to hell,—curses in his rear."

The son said :—" Long is the way and difficult ;
" Oh one of good fortune ! I cannot go on foot.

" Consider a way, and express an opinion ;
" For thy judgment is more luminous than mine."

The father said :—" If thou wilt listen to my judgment,
" It is proper to take up a large stone ;

" To strike the ass, the load-carrier, several times with it ;
" To wound his head, and his leg, and his flank.

695 " Perhaps, that base one of ugly religion
" An ass,—lame, wounded—may be, for his work, useless.

" Like Khizr, the prophet, who shattered the ship,
" And, thus, stayed the hand of the powerful tyrant.

" In the year, in which the tyrant seized the ship at sea,
" He won many years of bad-repute."

---

696   " Khizr " was a celebrated prophet ; his history is written in the Súra
    Kahf of the Kurán ; he is said to have discovered the water of life.—See
    Sikandar Náma, Discourses 68, 69, and 70.

When the boy heard this tale from his father,
He took not his head beyond the writing of the order.

He struck down the helpless ass with a stone ;
The ass became feeble of leg, lame of foot.

The father said to him :—" Now, take thy own way ;
" Take that road even which is desirable to thee."

The son fell in with a káraván ;
As much abuse as he knew, he gave (to the tyrant).

And, on this side, the father—face towards the sky,
Saying :—" Oh Lord ! by the prayer-carpet of the true,

" Give me, from Time, as much tranquillity,
" As ruin springs from this oppressing tyrant.

" If I witness not his destruction,
" My eyes, in the night of the grave, will not sleep in the
        dust.

" A woman,—much better than an injurious man ;
" A dog,—better than the man, man-injuring.

" The hemaphrodite, who shows injustice towards himself.
" Better than that one, who shows evil towards man."

The tyrant-king heard this speech, but said nothing ;
He tethered his horse ; and, head on saddle-cloth, laid
        himself down to sleep.

All night, in wakefulness, he counted the stars ;
Through frenzy and reflection, sleep took him not.

When he heard the voice of the morning-bird,
He forgot the night's distress.

The (king's) horsemen, all night, galloped (in search) ;
Recognised, in the morning, the track of his horse :

Beheld, on horseback,—in that plain, the king,
On foot ; the whole of the troop went (towards him) :

Placed the head, in service, on the earth,
—From the wave of the multitude, the earth became like
    the sea.—

The great ones sate down, and asked for food ;
They ate, and set the assembly in array.

One of his old friends said :—
—Who was his chamberlain, at night ; and courtier, by
    day.—

715 " Last night, what victuals did the peasants place before
    thee ?
" As for us, neither eye nor ear reposed."

The monarch could not relate the adventure,
Which, from bad repute, occurred to him.

He brought his head, very slowly, before the courtier's
    head ;
(And) whispered, secretly, to his ear :—

" No one brought before me the leg of a bird,
" But the leg of an ass,—dislocated beyond measure."

When the tumult of joy came into the king's nature,
Memory of the villager of the previous night came to him.

720 He ordered :—they searched, and firmly bound him ;
Cast him, with ignominy, at the foot of the throne.

The black-hearted one drew forth the sharp sword ;
The helpless one knew not the way of flight :

---

714   The second line describes the friend.
      In the 'Ikd-i-manzúm, couplets 714 and 715 are omitted.
718   They brought him—not the leg of a bird to eat,—but the dislocated
    leg of an ass, as evidence of his tyranny.

Reckoned that moment the last of his life ;
Said whatever revolved in his heart.

Seest thou not that when the knife is at the head
Of the pen—its tongue (nib) is swifter ?

When the villager knew that flight from the enemy was
    impossible,
Fearless of him, he poured forth the arrows of his quiver
    (of speech).

He raised the head of despair, and spoke :—
" On the night of the grave, it is not possible to sleep in
    the house.

" Oh monarch ! not alone, said I to thee,
" That thou art of reversed fortune and unfortunate.

" I (alone) cursed not the power of thy oppression,
" But a people ; suppose—one slain, out of a people :
    (what then ?)

" From the mercilessness that exists in thy time,
" The whole world is the proclaimer of thy violence.

" Why getst thou angry with me only ?
" I spoke before thee ; but, all the World behind (thy
    back).

" It is strange that cursing on my part comes harshly to
    thee,
" Slay ; if thou canst slay the whole world.

" But if rebuke, on my part, appears severe
" Pluck up, in justice, the root of reproach (of injustice).

" When thou doest injustice, expect not,
" That thy name for goodness will go into the country.

" And, if—oh mean one !—it be that my speech is hard
    to thee,
" Do not to another,—what is hard to thee.

" For thee, the remedy is to turn away from tyranny ;
" It is not an innocent matter, to slay the helpless.

735 " Suppose—for thee, five days more are remaining ;—
" Suppose—two days more of enjoying pleasant ease.
    (What then ?)

" The tyrant of bad walk of life remains not (in the world),
" (But) everlasting curses will remain on him.

" I know not how thine eyes sleep,
" The oppressed, through thy hand of oppression, sleepless.

" For thee, there is good advice, if thou wilt listen ;
" But if thou wilt not hearken, thou thyself wilt become
    sorrowful.

" Know,—how praised becomes a king
" Whom the people praise in the Court.

740 " What profit—the applause, at the head of the assembly,
" The old woman,—cursing behind the spinning wheel."

The villager thus spoke,—the sword above his head ;
The soul surrendered to the arrow of Fate.

The king, from the intoxication of carelessness, came to
    reason ;
The auspicious angel Surosh (Gabriel) whispered to his ear,

Saying :—" Restrain the hand of torture from this old
    man ;
" Suppose,—one slain, out of thousands of thousands
    (what then ?) "

---

741   " Safr kardan " signifies—to surrender.

His head remained sometime in the collar (of reflection) ;
After that, he filled his sleeve with pardon.

Took off his fetters, with his own hands ;
Kissed his head, and took him into his bosom.

Gave him greatness and lordship ;
His welfare sprang forth from the branch of hope.

This story became related in the world ;
Good fortune goes behind the upright.

Thou wilt learn an adorned walk of life,—from wise men ;
(But) not to the same degree as from the ignorant (the
        enemy), fault-finding.

Hear thy own character from the enemy ; because,
In the friend's eye, whatever comes from thee is good.

Those singing praises are not thy friends ;
Those reproaching are thy friends.

It is a crime to give sugar to the sick one ;
When the bitter medicine is fit for him.

The one of sour face rebukes better,
Than friends of pleasant disposition, of sweet temperament.

No one utters to thee better advice than this :
If thou art wise, a hint is enough.

————

When the turn of the Khiláfat came to Mámún
He purchased a damsel with a face as the moon.

In the 'Iḳd-i-manẓúm, couplets 742–747 and 753–797 are omitted.
  Mámún, one of the Khulafá of 'Abásiya, was the son of Harúnu-r-
Rashíd, so often mentioned in the Arabian Nights.

755 In face, a sun ; in body, a rose ;
     In wisdom, wise,—a wanton one.

     In the blood of lovers, her hand deeply imbrued ;
     Her finger-tips, jujube-stained.

     Saffron—on the eye-brow, devotee-enchanting,—
     Was like the rainbow on the sun.

     On the night of the rites of Venus, that enchanting toy,
          Húr-born,
     Perhaps gave not her body to Mámún's embrace.

     The fire of anger fiercely seized him ;
     He wished to make her head two portions, like the Gemíni.

760 She said :—" Lo ! my head, with the sharp sword,
     " Cast down ; but, exercise not sleeping and rising with
          me."

     Mámún said :—" From whom, has injury reached thy heart ;
     " What feature of mine was disagreeable to thee ? "

     She replied :—" If thou slayst me, or if thou cleavest my
          head
     " (I must say)—from the smell of thy mouth, I am in
          distress.

     " The sword of contest, and the arrow of oppression slay,
     " At once ; the smell of thy mouth, gradually."

     Sarwar (Mámún) of happy fortune heard this speech ;
     He was greatly astonied, and sorely grieved.

---

757   " Ḳaus " signifies—a bow.
         " Ḳazaḥ " is the name of a devil.
         " Ḳaus-i-Ḳazaḥ " is Satan's bow ; and also the name of Rustam's bow.
         In Persia, rain is precious. When the rainbow appears, rain usually
     ceases. The people then say that " Shaiṭan " has stopped the rain with his
     bow.

765 Was, all night, in this thought, and slept not ;
Spoke, the next day, to the wise ones.

Those of every clime, constitution—understanding,—
With every one of them, he spoke on every matter.

Although, at that time, his heart was vexed with her,
He took medicine ; and, became fragrant of smell, rose-like.

He made the parí-faced one, companion and friend ;
Saying :—" This one uttered my defect ; she is my friend."

In my opinion, that one is thy well-wisher,
Who says :—" A thorn is in thy path."

770 To say to the road-lost—" Thou goest well,"
          t cruelty and atrocious crime.

At tha   e, when they utter not before thee thy defect,
Thou, from ignorance, considerst thy defect, skill.

Say not :—" The sweet honey is the superior sugar "
To that one, for whom scammony is necessary.

How well did the druggist, one day, say :—
" Is convalescence necessary to thee ? drink bitter
      medicine."

If sharbat is good for thee,
Take, from Sa'dí, the bitter medicine of advice.

775 With the sieve of knowledge, sifted ;
With the honey of devotion, mixed.

I have heard that, on account of a good man, a fakír,
The heart of a proud king became troubled.

---

772   " Sakmuniya " is Greek ; in Arabic, it is called " Mahmúdat."
      The Persians say it is a bitter juice, possessing the power of purging
the bile from the body.

Perhaps, on his tongue, a truth had passed;
He became, through pride, enraged with him.

He sent him from the Court to the prison;
For, the arm of a king is strong proved.

One of his friends said secretly to him (the fakír) ;—
" It was not well to utter this speech."   He replied :—

780 " To cause God's order to be accomplished is obedience to
      God;
" I fear not the prison, which is for a moment."

That very moment, when this secret, in private, went forth
      (from his tongue),
The tale also went to the ear of the king.

He laughed, saying :—" He entertains a foolish idea,
" He knows not that he will die in this confinement."

A slave brought that speech to the poor man;
He said :—" Oh slave ! say to Khusrau,

" I have not the load of grief on a wounded heart;
" For the world, this very moment, is no more.

785 " If thou helpst me not, I am joyful;
" If thou cutst off my head, grief comes not into my
      heart.

" If thou art prosperous in command and treasure,
" Another is dejected, in fear or grief.

" When we enter at the gate of death,
" We become, in one week, together equal.

---

784   In some copies :—
       Since, this very moment, the world is no more,
       Grief and joy are not present to the Darvesh.

" Place not the heart on this empire of five days,
" Consume not thyself, with the sighs of the people's heart.

" Did not the kings before thee collect together more than
        thou ?
" In exercising injustice, they consumed the world.

790 " Live even so, that they may commemorate thee with
        praise ;
" May not recite curses, over thy grave, when thou
        diest.

" In regard to a bad custom, it is unnecessary to lay laws ;
" For they say :—May a curse be on him, who laid this evil
        custom !

" But, if the Lord of Force raises his head,
" Does not the dust of the grave in the end make his head
        low ? "

The narrow-hearted one, by way of oppression, ordered—
That they should dig out his tongue, from the back (of the
        neck).

The man, truths-knowing thus spoke
Saying :—" I have no fear of this even that thou hast said.

795 " I have no grief of tonguelessness ;
" For, I know that God understands the unspoken word.

" And if, through tyranny, I suffer foodlessness,
—" If, in the end it be well with me, what grief ?

" The sound of mourning (for thy death) may be nuptial,
" If thy end be good."

A certain boxer had neither fortune nor victuals;
The means ready—neither for his evening nor for his
    morning repast.

On account of the cravings of his belly, he used to carry clay
    on his back;
For it is impossible to enjoy (gain) victuals, by means of
    the fist.

Through distress of fortune, always—
His heart, grief-stricken; his body, spindle-like.

For him, sometimes, battle with a malevolent world;
Sometimes, his face bitter, from distressed fortune.

Sometimes, from beholding the sweet pleasure of the (rich)
    people,
The bitter water (tears) used to descend to his neck.

Sometimes, he used to weep on account of perplexed work,
Saying:—" No one experienced a more bitter life than
    this ! "

The people eat honey, and bird, and lamb;
The surface of my bread sees not herbs.

If thou desirest justice,—this is not good,
I naked; but, to the cat, a coat (of fur).

How well would it have been, if my foot, in this clay-work,
Had descended to the treasure of my heart's desire.

Perhaps, for a time I would have urged the desire (of
    lust);
Would have scattered from myself the dust of affliction.

I heard that he was, one day, breaking up the earth;
He found a rotten chin-bone.

Within the dust, its joints dissevered;
The jewels of teeth scattered.

810 The tongueless mouth mysteriously uttered advice,
Saying :—" Oh sir ! be content with want of sustenance.

" Is not this the state of the mouth, beneath the clay ?
" Suppose—sugar eaten; or blood of the heart (grief)
  suffered (what then ?)

" Have not grief of time's revolution ;
" For much time will revolve without us."

That very moment, when this idea appeared to him,
Grief placed aside its burden from his heart.

Saying :—" Oh spirit ! void of judgment, deliberation and
  sense,
" Endure the load of grief, and slay not thyself."

815 If a slave carries a load on his head ;
Or if he rears his head to the summit of the sky,

At that moment, when his state becomes changed,
In death, both ideas leave his head.

Grief and joy remain not; but,
Requital for work and good name (work) remains.

Liberality, not diadem and throne, has permanence ;
Oh one of good fortune !—give that this may remain after
  thee (in the world).

Rely not on country, and rank and pomp :
For, they were before thee, and will be after thee.

820 Thou wishst not that thy country should come to confusion ?
It is necessary to suffer sorrow for both country and religion.

---

813 " Rú,e dádan " signifies—tawajjuh kardan ; mutawajjih shudan.
  In the first line, " khátir " signifies—ánchi ba dil khatúr kunád.

Scatter gold, since thou wishst not to leave the world,
As Sa'dí scattered pearls (of counsel), when he had not
    gold.

————

They relate a story of a certain violence—scatterer,
Who held sway over a country.

The day of man was, in his time, like the evening;
At night, the hands of the pure were, through fear of him,
    in prayer.

All day, the good, through him, in calamity;
At night, the hands of the pure, against him, in prayer.

Before the Shaikh of that time, a crowd of men
Wept bitterly, on account of the tyrant's power,

Saying:—" Oh wise man of happy disposition !
" Say to this young man,—Fear God ! "

The Shaikh replied :—" I am loath (to utter) the name of
    God ;
" For, every one is not worthy of His message."

Whomsoever thou seest apart from God,
Oh Sir ! reveal not to him the name of God.

It is sorrowful to speak of the knowledge (of God) with
    the mean ;
For, seed in salt soil is wasted.

When it affects him not, he considers thee an enemy ;
Grieves heartily, and vexes thee.

————

In the 'Ikd-i-manzúm, couplets 822 to 880 are omitted.

Oh King! thou hast the custom of a right walk of life;
The heart of the man, truth-speaking, is, on this account,
  firm.

Oh one of happy fortune! the seal-ring has a quality,—
Such that, it takes an impression in wax, not in the hard
  stone.

It is not wonderful, if this tyrant, of me, heartily
Grieves; for, he is a thief; and I, a watchman.

Thou art also guardian as to justice and equity;
May the protection of God be thy guardian!

835 In the way of reason, thanks (of the people) are not for
  thee;
Grace, and obligation, and praise—for God.

When God holds thee, in service, in the work of goodness,
He left thee, not abandoned, like others.

All are in the plain of struggle;
But, not every one wins the ball of empire.

Thou didst not, by endeavour, gain Paradise;
God created within thee, a disposition Paradise-like.

May thy heart be illumined, and time tranquil!
May thy foot be firm, and dignity exalted!

840 Thy life, pleasant; and, thy conduct, (bent) on rectitude!
Thy devotion, agreeable (to God); and, prayer, accepted!

———

So long as thy work prospers by deliberation,
Courtesy to an enemy (is) better than contest.

831
and   The king alluded to is Abú Bakr.
834

When one cannot, by force, defeat the enemy ;
With cajolery it is proper to close the door of strife.

If there be fear of the injury of the enemy,
Fasten his tongue with the charm of beneficence.

Scatter gold for the enemy, in place of crow's feet ;
For, kindness makes blunt the sharp teeth.

845 When it is impossible to bite the hand, kiss it ;
For, with superiors, the remedy is deceit and flattery,

Even as the friend, pay observance to the enemy,
Whose skin, at the time of opportunity, one can flay ;

By right judgment, there came to bonds Rustam,
From whose noose, Isfandiyár escaped not.

Exercise caution as to contest with the meanest person ;
For, I have seen many a torrent, from a drop.

Express not—so long as thou canst,—a knot (frown) on
     thy eyebrow ;
For, the enemy though weak (is) better a friend.

850 His enemy may be fresh ; and, friend, wounded,—
That one, whose enemies are (in number) more than
     friends.

Strive not with an army more powerful than thy own ;
For, one cannot strike the fist on a lancet.

And, if thou art stronger, in contest, than he,
It is not manly to exercise force against the feeble.

If thou art of elephant-strength, or of lion-claw,
Peace is, in my opinion, better than strife.

When the hand is broken as to every artifice,
It is lawful to carry the hand to the sharp sword.

855 If the enemy seeks peace, turn not aside the head;
And, if he seeks battle, turn not aside the rein.

For, if he shuts the door of conflict
Thou hast the power and awe of ten thousand.

And, if he bring the foot of battle into the stirrup,
The Ruler (God) will not desire from thee an account at
    the rising (Judgment Day).

Be thou his battle-opponent, when he seeks strife;
For with the malicious kindness is a mistake,

When thou speakst, with kindness and pleasantness, to
    the mean,
His pride and obstinacy become greater.

860 With Arab-steeds and manly men,
Bring forth the dust (of destruction) from the nature of
    the enemy.

But, if he returns, with gentleness and understanding,
Speak not to him, with severity and anger and harshness.

When the enemy enters at thy door, with submission,
Put out malice from thy heart; and, anger from thy head.

When safety demands, practice the trade of liberality;
Pardon; but, reflect on his (possible) deceit.

Turn not away from the deliberations of old men;
For, one years-endured is work-experienced.

865 They pluck up the brazen foundations from its root,—
Young men with the sword; and, old men with judgment.

Consider a place of retreat, in the heart of battle;
Of that, what knowst thou,—that he may be conqueror?

When thou beholdst the enemy in discord,
Give not, alone, thy sweet life to the wind.

And, if thou art on one side of the army, strive to go
    (from the slaughter) ;
But, if in the midst (of the enemy), put on the guise of
    the enemy.

And, if thou art a thousand, and the enemy (only) two
    hundred,
Stand not in the enemy's territory, when it becomes night.

870 In the dark night, fifty horsemen, from ambuscade,
Will, with terror, rend the earth like five hundred.

When thou wishst to travel the road at night,
Be cautious first of ambuscade.

When one day's march between two armies
Remains,—pitch thy tent in some place.

If he displays aggression, have no fear ;
And if he be Afrásiyáb, pluck forth his brains.

Knowst thou not, that when the enemy pursues one's day
    march,
His grasp of force remains not.

875 Thou tranquil,—strike at the wearied army ;
For, the ignorant one practised oppression against his own
    body.

When thou hast defeated the enemy, cast down the
    standard,
That his wound may not come together again (heal).

Urge not far, in rear of the routed army ;
It is not fit that thou shouldst go far from thy companions.

Thou mayst behold, the air cloud-like, from the dust of
    conflict ;
With javelin and sword they will gather around thee.

Let not the army urge in pursuit of plunder,
Lest that (the place) behind the king's back be void.

80 For the army, the guardianship of the monarch
    Is better than battle, in the circle of contest.

    The warrior, who has once showed ardour (in battle),
    It is proper to increase (his dignity), according to his
         worth.

    That, the next time, he may place his heart on destruction;
    May have no fear of contest with the (tribe of) Ya,júj.

    Keep the soldier happy, in peace;
    That he may be of use in the time of distress.

    Kiss the hand of fighting men, now,
    Not, at the time when the enemy beats the war-drum.

85 The soldier, whose duty is (lies) not in (getting) victuals,—
    Why should he, on the day of battle, place his heart on
         death?

    From the enemy's hand, the quarters of the country,
    Keep by the army; and, the army, by wealth.

    Of the king, the hand is bold against an enemy,
    When the army is tranquil of heart, and satisfied.

    They enjoy the price of their own heads;
    It is not right, that they should endure severity.

    When they keep pay from the soldier;
    He is loth to carry his hand to the sharp sword.

90 What manliness may he exhibit, in the battle-ranks,
    When his hand is empty, and work despised?

    Send warriors to the contest with the enemy;
    Send lions to the conflict with lions.

---

91   In the 'Iḳd-i-manzúm, couplets 891–971 are omitted.

Execute work, according to the judgment of those world-
    experienced ;
For, the old wolf is experienced in hunting.

Fear not the young men, sword-striking ;
Be cautious of the old men of much science.

The young men, elephant-overthrowing, lion-seizing,
Know not the artifices of the old fox.

895 The man, world-experienced, is wise ;
For, he has experienced much the hot and cold (vicissi-
    tudes) of life.

Young men, worthy of good fortune,
Turn not aside their heads from the saying of old men.

If further, a well ordered kingdom be necessary,
Give not a great work to an aspirant.

Make none leader of the army, save that one,
Who may have been, in many battles.

Entrust not a difficult matter to the young ;
For, one cannot break the anvil with the fist.

900 Peasant-cherishing and being chief of an army,
Are not work of sport and folly.

Thou wishst not that time should be lost ?
Entrust not work to one, work-unseen.

The hunting-dog turns not his face from the panther ;
The tiger, inexperienced in battle, fears the fox.

When the son is brought up to hunting,
He fears not, when contest meets him.

In wrestling, and hunting, and shooting at a mark, and
    ball-play,
A man becomes a warrior, and contest-seeker.

905 One reared in the hot bath, and pleasure, and luxury,
Will **fear, when he sees the door of conflict open.**

Two men place him in the saddle;
It may be a boy strikes him to the earth.

The one, whose back thou seest in the day of battle,
Slay,—if the enemy slay him not in the ranks.

An impotent one is better than the swordsman,
Who, in the battle-day, turns away his head, woman-like.

How well said the hero Gurgín to his own son,
When he (the son) shut up the bow-case, and quiver of
      battle :—

910 " If, women-like, thou wilt seek flight,
" Go not (to the battle-field); spill not the honour of
      fighting men."

The single horseman, who, in battle, showed his back,
Slew not himself, but those of renown.

Bravery comes not,—save from those two friends,
Who fell, in the circle of conquest.

Two of the same quality, of the same table, of the same
      speech,
Will strive mightily in the heart of conflict.

For shame comes to him of fleeing from before the
      arrow,—
The brother, a captive in the enemy's grasp.

915 When thou seest that friends are not friends (in contest),
Consider flight from the battle-field,—gain.

The first line means :—
    Though by reason of his size it requires two men to place him, &c.

Oh king, territory-conquering! cherish two persons—
One a man of arm (strong); the other, a man of judgment.

Those carry of the ball of empire from those renowned,
Who cherish the wise man and sword-man.

Whoever exercised not the pen and the sword,
If he dies,—say not over him :—" Alas ! "

Take care of the pen-striker (pen-man) and sword-striker
    (sword-man);
Not the musician; for manliness comes not from the striker.

920 This is not manliness,—the enemy in the affairs of war;
Thou,—confused with the wine-cup, and sound of the
    harp.

Possessed of sovereignty, sate down to play, many a one
Whose wealth went in play from the hand.

I say not—fear battle with the enemy;
Fear rather him, who is in the state of peace.

Many a one recited, in the day, the verse of peace;
(And) urged, when it became night, his army at the
    sleeper's head.

Warriors sleep mail-clad;
Since, the couch is the sleeping-place of women.

Within the tent, one, sword-striking,
925 Sleeps not naked (unarmed), like women in the house.

It is necessary to prepare secretly for war;
So that one can secretly assault the enemy.

Caution is the business of men acquainted with work;
The advanced guard is the brazen fence of the army-place.

---

919   In the second line, " zan " signifies—striker, possibly a harp-striker
or player; and also woman.

Between two ill-wishers of short hand (weak),
It is not wisdom, to sit secure.

Because, if both, together secretly, deliberate,—
Their short hand becomes long (powerful).

930 Keep one engaged with deceit ;
Bring forth the destruction of the other's existence.

If an enemy chooses war,
Spill his blood, with the sword of deliberation.

Go ; accept friendship with his enemy ;
That the shirt on his body may be a prison.

When discord occurs in the enemy's army,
Place thou thy own sword, in the scabbard.

When wolves approve of each other's injury,
The sheep repose in the midst.

935 When the enemy becomes engaged with enemy,
Sit down, in ease of heart, with thy friend.

When thou liftst up the sword of contest,
Look out, secretly, for the path of peace.

Because army-leaders, helmet-cleaving,
Seek secretly peace ; and, openly, the battle-ranks.

Seek secretly (in friendship) the heart of the man of the
    battle-field ;
For, it may be, that he may fall (in friendship) at thy
    feet.

When an officer of rank of the enemy falls to thy grasp,
It is proper to exercise delay in slaying him.

940 For, it may happen that a chief of this half (thy own army)
May remain a captive, in bonds.

If thou slayst this wounded captive,
Thou wilt not again behold thy own captive.

Fears he not that Heaven's revolution may make captive
    him,
Who exercises violence towards captives?

That one is hand-seizer (helper) of captives,
Who himself may have been a captive in bondage.

If a chief places his head on thy writing (of command),—
When thou keepst him well, another chief places his head.

945 If thou, secretly, bringst to thy hand ten hearts,
It is better than that thou shouldst execute a hundred
    assaults.

———

If a relation of the enemy be friendly to thee,
Beware; be not secure of craftiness.

Because, his heart becomes torn for vengeance against thee.
When, memory of the love of his own relation comes to
    him.

Consider not the sweet words of an enemy;
For, it is possible, there is poison in the honey.

That one took his life safe from the trouble of the enemy,
Who reckoned friends as enemies.

950 That knave preserves the pearl in his purse,
Who considers all people purse-cuts.

The soldier, who is an offender against the Amír,
So long as thou canst,—take not into service.

He knew not gratitude towards his own chief;
He knows not thee also: be afraid of his deceit.

Hold (consider) him not strong as to oath and covenant;
Appoint a secret watchman over him.

Make long the tether of the aspirant;
Break it not, lest thou shouldst not see him again.

955 When, in battle and siege, the enemy's country,
Thou seizst,—consign it to the prisoners.

Because, when a captive plunges his teeth in blood,
He drinks blood from the tyrant's throat.

When thou pluckst away a territory from the enemy's
    clutch,
Keep the peasantry in more order than he.

For, if he beats open the door of conflict,
The people will pluck out the essence of his brain.

But, if thou causest injury to the citizens,
Shut not (vainly) the city-gate in the enemy's face.

960 Say not :—" The enemy, sword-striking, is at the gate ! "
When the enemy's partner is within the city.

Essay with deliberation battle with the enemy ;
Reflect on counsel ; and, conceal thy resolution.

Reveal not the secret to every one ;
For, I have seen many a cup-sharer, a spy.

Sikandar, who waged war with the Easterns,
Kept, they say, his tent-door towards the west.

When Bahman wished to go to Záwulistán,
He cast a rumour of (his going to the) left, and went to
    the right.

---

954   If a mistake occurs, overlook it ; for, if thou becometh angry and
makest severance of his hope,—thou wilt not see him again.

965 If one, besides thee, knows what thy resolve is,—
It is fit to weep over that judgment, and knowledge, and
    resolution.

Exercise liberality;—neither conflict, nor rancour,—
That thou mayst bring a world beneath thy signet-ring.

When a work prospers through courtesy and pleasantness,
What need of severity and arrogance ?

Thou wishest not, that thy heart should be sorrowful?
Bring forth from bondage the hearts of those sorrowful.

The army is not powerful by the arm ;
Go ; ask a blessing from the feeble.

970 The prayer of the hopeful weak ones
Is of more avail than the manly arm.

Whosoever takes to the darwesh, his request for aid,
If he strikes at Firídún, he would overcome him.

---

971   In some copies, " o " occurs in place of, " az," which, otherwise, is redundant.

CHAPTER II.

On Beneficence.

1 If thou art wise, incline to truth;
For truth, not the semblance, remains in its place.

To whomsoever, there was neither knowledge, nor liberality,
    nor piety,—
In his form, there was no reality.

Beneath the clay, sleeps at ease that one,
By whom, men sleep tranquil at heart.

Suffer thy own grief in life; for the relation,
Through his own avarice, busies not himself with one dead.

5 Give now gold and silver, which is thine;
For, after thy (death), it is out of thy command.

Thou wishest not, that thou shouldst be distressed in
    heart?
Put not out of thy heart those distressed.

---

1   In the 'Iḳd-i-manẓúm, couplets 1 to 28 are omitted.

Scatter treasure in alms, to-day, without delay ;
For, to-morrow, the key is not in thy hand.

Take away with thy self, thy own road-provisions ;
For compassion (after death) comes from neither son, nor
    wife.

That one takes away the ball of empire from this world,
Who took, with himself, a portion to the future world.

10 With sympathy, like my finger-tip,
No one in the world scratches my back.

Place now, on the palm of the hand, whatever there is ;
Lest that, to-morrow (the Judgment Day) thou shouldst
    with the teeth bite the back of the hand.

Strive as to covering the shame of the darwesh,
That the veil of God may be thy secret (defect) -concealer.

Turn not the foreigner portionless from thy door,
Lest that thou shouldst become a wanderer (in beggary) at
    doors.

The great one causes alms to reach the indigent ;
For he fears that he may become necessitous (as to the
    need of others).

15 Look into the state of the heart of those wearied ;
For thy heart may, perhaps, one day be broken.

Make the hearts of those dejected happy ;
Remember the day of helplessness (the Judgment Day).

Thou art not a beggar at the doors of others ;
Drive not, in thanks to God, a beggar from thy door.

Cast protection over the head of the one father-dead ;
Scatter his dust (of affliction), and pluck out his thorn.

Knowst thou not, how very dejected his state was ?
May a rootless tree be ever green ?

20 When thou seest an orphan, head lowered in front (from
    grief),
Give not a kiss to the face of thy own son.

If the orphan weeps, who buys for his consolation ?
And, if he becomes angry, who leads him back (to
    quietude) ?

Beware ! that he weep not ; for, the great throne of God
Keeps trembling, when the orphan weeps.

Pluck out, with kindness, the tear from his pure eye ;
Scatter, with compassion, the dust (of affliction) from his
    face.

If his (the father's) protection departed from over his
    head,
Do thou cherish him, with thy own protection.

25 I esteemed my head crown-worthy, at that time,
When, I held my head in my father's bosom.

If a fly had sate on my body,
The heart of some would have become distressed.

If now, enemies should bear me away captive,
None of my friends is a helper.

For me, is acquaintance with the sorrows of orphans,
For, in childhood, my father departed (in death), from my
    head.

____

A certain one plucked out a thorn from an orphan's
    foot ;
The Khujand Chief, saw him, in a dream :—

19   The father is the root, the son the branches of the tree. A tree's
freshness is due to its root.

20   Khujand is a village in the country of Máwara,u-n-nahr, between
the Jíhún and Síhún rivers.

30 He was talking and sauntering in the gardens of Paradise,
    Saying :—" How many roses blossomed from that thorn ! "

So long as thou canst, be not free from mercy ;
For they bear pity to thee, when thou bearst pity.

When thou hast done a favour, be not self-worshipping,
Saying :—" I am a superior ; and, that other an inferior."

Say not :—" The sword of Time has cast him ! "
For, the sword of Time is yet drawn.

When thou seest a thousand persons, prayer-uttering for
    the empire,
Give thanks to God for favours.

35 For the reason that many men have expectation from thee,
    Thou hast expectation at the hand of none.

I have said that liberality is the character of chiefs ;
I uttered a mistake ;—it is the quality of prophets !

———

I have heard that, one week, a son of the road (a traveller)
Came not to the guest-house of (Ibráhím) the friend of
    God.

Through his happy disposition, he used not to eat in the
    morning,
Unless one, foodless, came from the path (of travel).

He went out, and looked in every direction ;
Glanced in the quarters of the valley ; and saw :—

40 One, willow-like, in solitude, in the desert ;
    His head and hair white with the snow of old age.

For consolation, he said to him :—" Marhabá ! "
Uttered, according to the custom of the liberal, the invi-
    tation,

Saying :—" Oh pupil of my eyes !
" Do me a favour, as to bread and salt."

He said, " Yes "; and sprang up and lifted his feet ;
For, he knew his temperament :— on him be peace !

The guards of the guest-house of Ibráhím
Placed the abject old man, with respect.

45 He ordered ; and, they arranged the table ;
All sate around.

When the company began :—" Bismi-llah ! "
A word from the old man reached not his ear.

He spoke to him, thus :—" Oh old man of ancient days !
" I behold not thy truth and heart-burning, like old men.

" When thou eatst food, is it not the custom
" That thou shouldst take the name of the Lord of
    Victuals ?"

He said :—" I accept not a religion,
" Which I have not heard from the old men, fire-wor-
    shipping."

50 The prophet of good omen knew
That the old man, of state-become ruined, was a Gabr.

He drove him away, with contempt, when he saw him a
    stranger (to Islám) ;
For to the pure, the filthy is forbidden.

The angel Surosh came from the glorious Omnipotent,
With majesty, reproaching, saying :—" Oh friend of God !

In Arabic, " Marhabá "; in Persian, " Khúsh Ámadí."

" I had for a hundred years given him victuals and life;
" Abhorrence of him comes to thee, in a moment.

" If he takes his adoration to the fire,
" Why withdrawst thou thy hand of magnanimity ? "

55 Make not a knot at the head of the ligature of beneficence,
Saying :—" This one is of fraud and deceit : and, that one
      of treachery and guile."

The man, Kurán-knowing, does injury,
When he sells, for bread, the Kurán and sound doctrine.

Where do wisdom and law give the decision,
That one of wisdom should give religion for the world?

But, do thou take ; because the wise man
Buys gladly from those cheap-selling.

———

One, tongue-knowing, came to a pious man,
Saying :—" I have stuck firmly in the mire.

60 " Ten dirams of a mean one are (weighing) on me,
" In such a way that a fourth part of them is ten mans on
      my heart.

" Through him, all night, my state distracted ;
" All day, (he is) shadow-like, behind me.

" From words, heart-confounding, he has made
" A wound, like a house-door, within my heart.

" Perhaps since he was born of his mother, God
" Gave not (to him) anything save these ten dirams.

" Of the book of Religion, Alif unknown ;
" Unread, save the chapter :—Spend not.

---

55   In the 'Ikd-i-manzúm, couplets 55 to 121 are omitted.
60   The diram = 0·03248 lbs.
          man = 13·0033 „
63   Alif is the first letter of the alphabet.

5 " The sun raised not its head a single day above the
  mountain
" That that scoundrel knocked not at my door.

" I am in reflection,—What liberal one
" May take my hand (help me) with silver, from that one
  of stone heart."

The old man of happy disposition heard this speech,
He placed two gold coins in his sleeve.

The gold fell into the hand of the tale-teller ;
He went out, thence,—a face fresh like gold.

One said :—" Oh Shaikh ! knowst thou not, who this is ?
" It is not proper to weep over him, if he dies

0 " A beggar, who (by deceit) places a saddle on the male
  lion ;
" Who places (on one side) the knight and queen of Abú-
  Zaid (the chess-player)."

The 'ábid was confounded, saying :—" Be silent !
" Thou art not a man of tongue ; listen !

" If what I thought (regarding him) was right
" I preserved his honour from the people.

" If he practised impudence and hypocrisy,
" Thou knowst not that he beguiled me.

" For, I preserved my own honour ;
" From the hand of such a deceiver, foolishness-uttering."

---

0 " Asp va farzín nihádan" signifies—asp va farzín ba tarh dádan va
bází rá burdan.

75 Spend silver and gold on the bad and the good;
For, this is the trade of liberality; and, that the repelling
of evil.

Happy he who, in the society of the wise,
Learns the qualities of the pious.

Wisdom, and judgment, and deliberation, and sense are
thine;
Listen, with reverence, to Sa'di's advice.

Because, Sa'di, for the most part, has words (of counsel)
in this fashion;
Not—as to eye, and ringlet, and lobe of the ear, and mole
(of lovely ones).

One departed (from the world), and a hundred thousand
dínars of his,
The heir, a sensible pious man, took.

80 He clutched not his hand on the gold, like the misers;
He took off the fastening from it, like the nobles.

The darvesh used not to be empty at his door;
Nor, the traveller, within his guest-house.

He made the heart of stranger and relation happy;
Tied not up the gold, like his father.

One, reproach-making, said to him :—"Oh one of wind-
hand !
" Make not altogether scattered what treasure there is.

" Gold, and consequential airs, and favour, remain not
long.
" Perhaps, no one has told thee this tale ?

---

75   Expenditure on the good is liberality; on the bad, the repelling of
evil.

85 " In these days, a certain Záhid, to his son,
" I heard—kept saying—' Oh soul of father !

" ' Go alone ; and be house-emptying ;
" ' Be liberal, and wealth-dispersing.'

" The son was fore-seeing and work-experienced,
" He praised his father, saying :—' Oh one of good judg-
      ment !

" ' In one year, one can gather together the harvest ;
" ' To burn it in a moment, is not manliness.'

" When thou hast no patience, as to straitened circum-
      stances,
" Consider the account, in the plenteous season.

90 " How well spoke the lady of the village to her daughter,
" Saying :—' Put aside, in the time of plenty, means for
      adversity.

" ' Keep full, at all times, the water-bag and pitcher ;
" ' For, the rivulet in the village is not always running.'

" By this world, one can obtain the next ;
" By gold, one can turn aside a lion-grasp.

" If thou art straitened, go not before a friend ;
" But, if thou hast silver, come and bring (that silver).

" If thou placest thy face, on the dust of his feet,
" He utters no reply to thee, with empty hands.

95 " The lord of gold plucks out the demon's eye ;
" He brings the jinn Sahar, by craft, to his net.

---

86   " Khána-pardáz " signifies—tamám kunanda, casbáb-i-khána.
     " Mujarrd " signifies—one who flings away all his goods that he may
devote himself to God.
95   Sahar is the jinn who obtained possession of Sulaiman's ring.

" Associate not, empty-handed, with lovely ones ;
" For without anything, a man is not worth anything.

" The hope of the empty-handed one prospers not ;
" With gold thou mayst pluck out the eye of the white
     demon.

" Scatter not gold, all-at once, on friends ;
" Be in contemplation of the trouble of the enemy.

" And if, on the palm of the hand, thou placest whatever
     thou hast,
" In the time of need, thou wilt remain empty (handed).

100 " By thy effort, the beggars—ever strong,
" Become not ; I fear, thou dost become lean."

When the forbidder of liberality uttered this tale,
The young man's vein, through anger, slept not.

He became perplexed in heart as to that censorious one ;
Was confounded, and said :—" Oh foolish talker !

" The power that is around me,
" My father said—was the heritage of my grandfather.

" Did they not first preserve it ?
" They died, in regret ; and, left it.

105 " To my hand, did not my father's property fall,
" That it might fall after me to my son's hand ?"

It is best indeed that men should to-day enjoy ;
For, to-morrow, after me, they will take it away in rapine.

---

97   Dev-Safaed is the name of a hero of Mázandaran, whom Rustam, son
of Zál, slew.

Eat, and clothe thyself, and bestow, and cause ease to
    arrive;
Why keepst thou (money) for the sake of the people?

The lords of judgment, (by alms) take away with them-
    selves from the world;
The base one remains, in regret, in his place.

With this world, thou canst buy the future world;
Oh my soul! purchase; and, if not, suffer regret.

Gold and wealth are of use to that one,
110 Who makes the wall of the future world, gold decorated.

He (the heir) enjoyed and gave away, so that those endowed
    with vision
Beheld the marks of that money-loss in him.

A person, out of nobleness, praised him,
Saying:—" In the path of God, thou enduredst much
    grief."

Head in the collar of shame, he kept saying :—
" What (good deed) did I, to which one can attach the
    heart ?

" The hope that I have is in the grace of God;
" For, to exercise reliance on my own effort is a crime."

Religion is this indeed,—that people of truth
115 Are good-doers, and (their own) fault-perceivers.

The Shaikhs have, all night, uttered prayers;
Have, in the morning, spread the prayer-carpet.

In the name of manliness! listen to the words of men;
Not Sa'dí; but, of Sahrwadí, hear.

---

117   Shaikh Shahábu-d-dín Abú Hifz 'Umar, son of Muhammadu-l-Bakríu-
s-Saharwadí, was of the offspring of Abú Bakr Sadík, the Khalífá.

For me the shaikh of knowledge, the spiritual guide, Shaháb,
Uttered two maxims of counsel,—boat on the water :—

" One,—be not in the assembly of those evil-viewing;
" The other,—be not in the lust of self-beholding."

120 One night, I know, that, from fear of hell, Shaháb slept not;
In the morning, it came to my ear,—that he said :—

" How well would it have been, if hell had been full of me;
" Perhaps, for others, there might have been escape ! "

———

Once upon a time, a wife lamented to her husband,
Saying :—" Purchase not again bread from the general vendor of the street.

" Go to the market of the wheat-sellers.
" For, this is a barley-seller, wheat-exhibiting.

" Not on account of purchasers, but from a swarm of flies,
" No one has seen his face for a week."

125 With heartiness, that indigent man,
To his wife, said :—" Oh light (of my eyes) ! be content.

" In hope of us, the vendor took here a shop ;
" It is not manliness, to take back from him profit."

Take the path of good, noble men ;
When thou art erect, seize the hand of the fallen.

Bestow ; for, those who are men of God
Are the purchasers (at) of the shop without splendour.

His connection with Sufí,ism was through his uncle Abú-n-Najíb Sahar-wadí. He attained to the society of Shaikh 'Abdu-l-Ḳádir of Gílan, and many others. His birth occurred in the month Rajab in the Muham-madan year 539; and death in 630.

Shaikh Sa'dí enjoyed his society ; and travelled, by water, with him.

If thou desirest truth,—the saint ('Alí) is the generous man ;
Liberality is the profession of 'Alí, king of men.

——

130 I have heard that an old man, on the road to Hijáz,
Used to make two prayer-motions, at every step.

So impetuous in the path of God,
That he used not to pluck the ghílán thorn from his foot.

At length from temptation, heart-disturbing,
His work seemed good in his sight.

By the craft of Iblís, he fell into the pit (of pride),
Saying :—" One cannot go on a road, better than this."

If the mercy of God had not found him,
Pride would have turned his head from the path (of religion).

135 An angelic messenger gave voice, from the invisible,
Saying :—" Oh one of happy fortune ! of good disposition !

" If thou hast performed devotion, think not,
" That thou hast brought a rarity to this court.

" By beneficence a heart tranquil making,
" Is better than a thousand sacred inclinations of the head
at every stage."

——

A wife thus spoke (to her husband) an officer of the Sultán,
Saying :—" Oh fortunate one ! arise ; knock at the door of
food.

" Go ; so that they may give thee a portion from the
(Sultán's) tray ;
" For, the children are looking to thee for food.

140 He said :—" To-day, the kitchen is cold ;
" For, the Sultán made the resolve of fast, at night."

The wife, through helplessness, cast down her head;
Heart torn with hunger, she kept saying to herself :—

" What did the Sultán wish from this fast-talking,
" The breaking of which is the festival of my children ? "

The devourer, from whose hand liberality issues,
Is better than one, who, world-worshipping, perpetually
    fasts.

Fast-keeping is reserved for him,
Who gives, to the wearied one, the bread of the morning
    meal.

145 Otherwise, what need that thou shouldst endure the trouble
        (of fasting);
Shouldst keep back from thyself (food in the day); and
        shouldst eat it (at night)?

The imaginings of the ignorant one, sitting in solitude!
He confounds, at length, infidelity and religion.

Purity is in water; and, also, in the mirror;
But, discretion is necessary for purity.

———

To a certain one, liberality was; but power was not;
Means of subsistence, to the extent of his generosity, were
        not.

Let not the mean one be lord of wealth!
Let not straitened means be to the generous man!

150 To him, to whom lofty spirit chances,
    The object of his desire seldom falls within the noose.

Like the pouring torrent, which, in a mountainous country,
Takes not ease in the midst of the heights.

He exercised not liberality, according to his means;
On this account, assuredly, he used to be of small worth.

One straitened wrote to him two words,
Saying:—"Oh one of happy end, of auspicious tempera-
　　ment!

" Take my hand (help me) once with some dirams;
" For, it is some time that I have been in prison."

155　The request was, in his eye, of no value;
But, in his hand, there was not the smallest coin.

He sent a man to the enemies of the captive,
Saying:—"Oh men of good name, and noble!

" Restrain, for a little, your hands from his skirt;
" And if he flies, security for him (is) on me."

And, thence, he came to the prison, saying:—"Arise!
" Flee from this city, so long as thou hast feet."

When the sparrow beheld the cage-door open,
Repose within it remained not to it, a moment.

160　Like the zephyr-wind, from that land he travelled;
Such travelling, that the wind would not have reached the
　　dust of his feet.

They, at once, seized the generous man,
Saying:—"Thou mayst obtain the silver, or the man."

152　　A poet has said:—
　　　　" Last night, in a dream, I beheld money.
　　　　I said: ' Why comest thou not to me?'
　　　　The money replied: ' Thou recognisest not my worth;
　　　　Thou givest, in liberality, to this and that.
　　　　Misers know my value;
　　　　I therefore go to the misers.'"

He took, in helplessness, the path to the prison ;
For, one cannot take the bird, gone from the cage.

I heard that he remained some time in prison ;
He neither wrote to any one a complaint ; nor, uttered a
    lament.

Times, he reposed not ; nights, slept not ;
A devotee passed by him, and said :—

165 " I think not thou devourest the property of man ;
     " What chanced to thee, that thou art in prison ? "

He said :—" Oh comrade of happy spirit !
" I enjoyed, by fraud, the property of no one.

" I beheld one, powerless, torn by captivity ;
" I beheld no release for him, save by my own confinement.

" It seemed, in my opinion, not proper,
" I, at ease ; another, in the noose (of torment)."

At length, he died ; and, took away a good name ;
How excellent, the life of him, whose name died not !

170 Beneath the clay,—a body dead, a heart alive ;
Is better than a world alive, heart dead.

The living heart never becomes destroyed ;
If, the body of the living heart dies,—what matter ?

———

A certain one found, in the desert, a thirsty dog ;
He found not beyond a spark of life in him.

He of approved religion made a cap-bucket ;
Bound to it his own turban, rope-like.

———

171   " Zinda-dil " signifies—roshan-dil wa neko kár.
       "Murda-dil " signifies—tárík-dil wa bad-kár.

Bound his loins in service; and stretched forth his arm;
Gave a little water to the powerless dog.

175 The Prophet gave intelligence of the man's state,
Saying:—"The Ruler (God) pardoned his sins."

Ho! if thou art a tyrant, reflect;
Choose fidelity; exercise liberality.

How does liberality become lost to the good man,
Since he lost not goodness done to a dog?

Pactise liberality so far as it may (suitably) come from thy
    hand,
The world-keeper closes the door of beneficence on none.

To bestow from the treasury, to the extent of an ox's skin
    of gold,
Is not like half a dang from the hand of toil.

180 Every one carries a load suitable to his strength;
The locust's foot is heavy to the ant.

Oh one of happy fortune! do good to the people,
That to-morrow, (the Judgment Day) God may not take
    hard (measures) with thee.

If he come from his feet (fall), he remains not captive,
Who was hand-seizer (helper) of the fallen.

Give not, with rebuke, an order to the slave;
For, it may be that he may fall (come) to order-giving.

When thy majesty and rank are lasting
Exercise not violence on the weakness of the common dar-
    wesh;

185 For, it may happen that he becomes possessed of rank and
    majesty;
Like the pawn, that suddenly becomes a queen (at chess).

Listen to the counsel of men, far-seeing ;
They scatter not the seed of rancour, in any heart.

The lord of the harvest suffers loss,
When he displays arrogance towards the corn-gleaners.

Fears he not that they (the angels) may give wealth to the
    wretched one ;
And from that one place the load of grief on the heart of
    this one ?

Many strong ones,—who fell suddenly ;
Many a fallen one,—Fortune assisted.

190 It is not proper to break the hearts of inferiors ;
Lest that, one day, thou shouldst become an inferior.

———

A certain darvesh complained of weakness of state,
To one of stern face, lord of wealth.

The one of black heart gave him neither dínárs, nor dángs ;
(And) shouted at him, moreover, in anger.

The beggar's heart, from his violence, bled.
He raised his head, with grief, and said :—" Oh wonder !

" Why, indeed is the rich man of severe visage ?
" Perhaps, he fears not the bitterness of begging."

195 The one of short sight ordered,—so that his slave
Drove him away, with contempt, and utter scorn.

By not offering thanks to the Omnipotent,
I heard that Fortune turned from him.

———

188   That refers to the wretched one ; this, to the arrogant one.
192   "Sar-bar" is a small load placed on a large load ; the word is here
metaphorically used.

His greatness placed its head towards ruin ;
Mercury put his pen in the ink (in record against him).

Wretchedness made him sit naked, like garlic ;
It left him neither chattels nor baggage-taker (the ass).

God's decree made him, through poverty, sit, dust on the
  head ;
Juggler-like, purse and hand empty.

200 His state, head to foot, became of another kind ;
Some time passed on (after) this occurrence.

His slave fell to the hand of a liberal one.
Generous of heart, and hand ; and luminous of temperament.

By the sight of the wretch of overturned state,
He used to be as much pleased, as the poor one with wealth.

A certain one sought, at night-time, a morsel at his door ;
From hardship-enduring, his steps were slow.

The lord of gift ordered the slave,
Saying :—" Make the dejected one happy."

205 When he carried to him a portion from the table ;
He involuntarily raised a cry.

He returned, heart-broken, to his master,
Tears on his face, mystery revealing.

The chief of happy temperament inquired,
Saying :—" From whose violence, came those tears on thy
  face ? "

He said :—" My heart sorely grieved,
" At the state of this old man of distracted fortune.

" For, in former times, I was his slave ;
" He,—the lord of goods and property, and silver.

210 " When his hand, from honour and luxury, became short,
" He makes long the hand of begging at doors."

He laughed and said :—" Oh son ! it is no violence ;
" For the revolution of Time, there is oppression against
    none.

" Is he not that merchant of stern countenance,
" Who used, from pride, to bear his head against the sky ?

" I am that one, whom he drove, that day, from his door ;
" The world's revolution has placed him in my day (state).

" The sky looked, again, towards me ;
" It scattered the dust of grief from my face."

215 If God closes one door, in wisdom,
He opens another, in grace and liberality.

Many a poor one, foodless, became satiated ;
Many a work of the rich one became overturned.

———

Hear a trait of good men,
If thou art a good man, and of manly gait.

When Shiblí, from the shop of the wheat-seller,
Carried a wallet of wheat, on his back, to the village,

He glanced ; he beheld, in that wheat, an ant,
That ran, head-revolving, in every corner.

———

213   See couplet 195.
219   Abú Bakru-sh-Shiblí was Ja'ffar, the Egyptian, son of Yúnis. He
came to Baghdád ; repented of his sins in the assembly Khair-Mizáj ;
was the disciple of Saint Juníd, a learned man, lawyer, and adviser ;
was of the sect of Málik ; was born in A.H. 247, and died in A.H. 334, at
the age of eighty-seven years.

220 He could not sleep, at night, for pity of that ant ;
He brought it back to its own dwelling, and said :—

" It is not manliness that this wounded ant,
" I should cause to be separated from its dwelling."

Keep tranquil the hearts of those distressed,
That tranquillity, from time, may be thine.

How well said Firdausí of pure birth,
—May mercy be on that pure tomb !—

" Wound not the ant, that is the grain-carrier ;
" For, it also has life ; and, life is pleasant."

225 He is of black vitals, and of stone-heart,
Who wishes that an ant may be of straitened-heart.

Strike not the hand of force on the head of the powerless,
Lest that thou shouldst, one day, fall ant-like beneath his
       foot.

The candle bestowed no pity on the moth's state ;
Behold how it (the candle) burned in the assembly !

I have assumed,—many are less powerful than thou ;
Also there is a certain one, in the end, more powerful than
       thou.

———

Oh son ! bestow ; for, the one man-born, a prey,
One can make by benefits ; and, the wild beast, by re-
       straint.

---

223   The second line is uttered by Sa'dí.
       Firdausí wrote the Sháh-Náma, containing one hundred and twenty
thousand lines, at the desire of Mahmúd of Ghazní ; he died A.D. 1021.
       The Sháh-Náma has, in part, been translated into English.
229   In the 'Iḳd-i-manẓúm, couplets 229–234 are omitted.

230 Bind the enemy, by showing kindness;
For, one cannot sever this noose, with the sword.

When the enemy experiences liberality, and courtesy, and
generosity,
Villainy from him comes not, again, into existence.

Do not evil, lest thou experience evil from the good friend;
The good fruit comes not from the seed-stone of wickedness.

When with a friend, thou art difficult and hard to please,
He desires not to see thy painting and colour (of face).

But, if a man desires good to his enemies,
Much time passes not, but they become friendly.

———

235 A young man came before me, on the road,
A sheep, running in bounds, behind him.

I said to him:—"This is a cord and ligature,
"Which draws the sheep behind thee."

He quickly undid the collar and chain from it;
Left and right, it began to bound.

Yet, from behind him, gambolling, it proceeded;
For, it had eaten barley and green-corn from the man's
hand.

When it returned to its place from pleasure and sport,
He regarded me, and said:—"Oh man of sense!

240 "This cord draws it not to me;
"But kindness is the noose about its neck."

From the kindness, which the raging elephant has expe-
    rienced,
He attacks not the elephant-keeper.

Oh good man ! cherish the bad ;
For, the dog keeps watch, when he devours thy bread.

The leopard's teeth are blunt against that man,
On whose cheek, he rubs, for two days, his tongue.

———

A certain one saw a fox, legless and footless,
He was astonied at the grace and creation of God,

245 Saying :—" How does he pass his life ?
  " With this leg and foot, how does he eat ?"

The darvesh of disturbed complexion was in this thought,
When a lion came forth, a jackal in his claws.

The lion devoured the jackal of reversed fortune ;
Whatever remained,—of it, the fox ate to satiety.

Again, the next day, the event happened,
That the Victual-sender (God) gave to him the day's food.

Truth made the man's eye capable of vision ;
He went ; and relied on the Creator,

250 Saying :—" I may, after this, sit, ant-like, in a corner ;
  " Since, elephants eat not their daily food by force."

He lowered, for some time, his chin to the collar (of reflec-
    tion),
Saying :—" The Giver of daily food sends from the un-
    seen."

———

241   Muslims regard a dog as being very unclean.
244   " Be dast wa be pá," signify—be tábí wa be ṭákatí.

Neither stranger nor friend suffered toil for him ;
Harp-like, his veins, and bones, and skin remained.

When, from weakness, his patience and sense remained not,
From the wall of the prayer-place, there came to his ear :—

" Oh impostor ! go ; be the rending lion ;
" Cast not thyself, like the crippled fox."

255 Strive so that, lion-like, there may remain (something)
   from thy (trade)
Why art thou, fox-like, depending upon the lion's leavings.

Whose neck is stout, like lions,
If he falls (into idleness) fox-like, a dog is better than he.

Bring to thy grasp ; and, drink with others ;
Pay no attention to others' leavings.

Eat, so long as thou canst,—by means of thy own arm ;
That thy strength may be in thy own balance.

Endure toil, like men ; and cause ease to arrive (to others) ;
The impotent enjoys the gain of others' toil.

260 Oh young man !   Take the hand of the old darvesh ;
Cast not thyself down, saying :—" Take my hand ! "

The gift of God is on that slave,
By whose existence, the people are at ease.

That head, in which is a brain, exercises liberality ;
For, those of mean spirit are skin,—brainless.

That one experiences good, in both habitations,
Who causes good to reach the people of God.

---

258 On the Judgment Day thy endeavours will be estimated.
263 In the 'Iḳd-i-manẓúm, couplets 263 to 265 are omitted.

Didst thou not see (hear), on the foot-binding (difficult)
    road to Kesh,
What that camel-driver said to his own son?

" Enjoy food, with good men ;
" For, they will not eat in solitude."

I have heard that there was a man of pure birth-place,
A recogniser, and road-traveller (in the way of God), in the
    confines of Rúm.

I and some other travellers, desert-wandering,
Went a-travelling for the sake of seeing the man.

He kissed the head, and eyes, and hands of each one ;
Caused us to sit, with reverence and respect; and sate
    down.

I beheld his gold, and sown fields, and attendants and
    goods ;
But, without generosity, like a fruitless tree.

As to manner and grace, he was attentive ;
But, his cooking-pot-place was very cold.

All night, there was neither rest, nor sleep,—for him,
As to praising God and reciting—" There is no God, but
    God " ; and, for us, from hunger.

In the morning, he bound his loins and opened the door ;
Began the very same courtesy and hand-kissing.

" Pá-band " signifies—foot-binding. It may be by clay, by stones, or
other impediment on the path.
   " Tasbíh " signifies—subhánu-lláh !
   " Tahlíl " signifies—lá iláha illa lláh !

There was one, who was of sweet and pleasant temper,
Who, was, in that inn, a traveller with us.

He said :—" Give me the kiss, by letter-translating,
" Because, for the darvesh, food (tosha) is better than
    a kiss (bosa).

275 " Place not the hand in service, on my shoes;
" Give me bread; and, strike then on my head."

Men have, by gifts, excelled;
Not those night-alive-keeping, heart dead.

This indeed I experienced from the Tatár watchman,
Heart dead, but night-alive-keeping.

Liberality is—generosity and bread-giving;
Foolish speech is the empty drum.

At the Resurrection, thou seest, in Paradise, that one,
Who sought truth, and let go pretension.

280 By truth, one can make a proper claim;
Breath, without action, is a slothful resting-place.

———

I have heard that, in the time of Hátim, there was,
Among his horses, one swift footed, like smoke.

A black steed of zephyr swiftness, thunder noise,
That used to surpass the lightning :

---

274   " Tashíf " signifies—the altering of the dots of letters; thus, بوسه
bosa, " a kiss," (using " tashíf ") means توشه tosha, " victuals."

277   The author signifies—by the watchman, a holy man; by the Tátár
watchman, one not holy.

280   " Ma'ní " signifies—good deeds and approved qualities.

281   Hátim, a celebrated liberal man, was the son of 'Abdu-lláh, the son
of Sa'du-t-Tai Shamsu-d-dín, the son of Khulfán. See the book in
Persian, " Hátim-Tai," which is easy to read

Used, in the gallop, to scatter hail over mountain and
　　　plain ;
Thou wouldst have said :—" Perhaps, an April-cloud has
　　　passed ? "

Such an one, torrent-moving, desert-travelling,
That the wind, from the front, used to lag, like dust.

285　Of Hátim's qualities, in every land and clime,
They mentioned a little to the Sultán of Rúm,

Saying :—" A man, there is not, like him in liberality ;
" A horse, there is not, like his in moving and journeying.

" Such a desert-traveller, like a boat on the water,
" That the crow flies not above his journeying ! "

The Sultán of Rúm spoke to his learned Vazír, thus,
Saying :—" The claim without evidence is shame.

" Of Hátim, that steed of Arab descent, I
" Will ask ; if he should exercise liberality, and give,

290　" I shall know that, in him is the pomp of greatness ;
" But, if he refuses, (his pretension) is the noise of the
　　　empty drum ! "

An envoy, skilful in the world, to (the tribe of) Tai,
He despatched ; and, ten men along with him.

The ground dead ; but, the cloud weeping over it,
The zephyr again placed life in it.

At the halting (dwelling) place of Hátim, the envoy
　　　alighted ;
(And) became tranquil, like the thirsty one, by the Zinda
　　　river.

293　" Zinda " is a stream near Iṣfahán ; its water is very sweet.

He (Hátim) spread a table, victual-covered; and, killed a
    horse;
Gave them sugar in his skirt; gold in his fist.

295 There, they passed the night; and, the next day,
The man of information (the envoy) uttered what he knew.

The envoy kept talking; and, Hátim distracted, like one
    intoxicated,
Kept gnawing his hand with the teeth of regret,

Saying :—" Oh partner, learned, of good name !
" Why didst thou not utter before this thy message?

" That wind-moving, fast, Duldul,—I
" Made roast-meat, last night, for your sake.

" For, through the dread of rain and torrents, I knew
" It was impossible to go into the pasture place of the herd
    (of cattle).

300 " For me, there was, in no other way, either turning or
    path ;
" There was only that horse at the door of my court.

" I considered it not generosity, in respect to my usage,
" That a guest should sleep, heart torn with hunger.

" For me,—a name conspicuous in the climes (of the world)
    is necessary ;
" Say :—let there not be (for me) another famous steed."

He gave to the individuals of the envoy's retinue dirams,
    dresses of honour, and horses.
—The good quality is natural, not an acquisition.—

---

295   The envoy asked for the horse, desired by the Sultán.
298   See Longfellow's poem, entitled " Sir Frederigo and his Falcon," one
of the tales of the Wayside Inn.

News of the young man of Tai went to Rúm ;
The Sultán uttered a thousand benedictions on his disposi-
    tion.

305 Be not content with this incident of Hátim ;
Listen to this more beautiful circumstance.

———

I know not, who told me this tale,
That there had been, in the country of Yaman, an order-
    giver.

He snatched the ball of empire from those renowned ;
For in treasure-bestowing, there was no equal to him.

One could call him—" the Cloud of Liberality,"
For, his hand used to scatter money like rain.

No one used to take to him the name of (mention) Hátim,
At which (mentioning), phrenzy used not to go to his head,

310 Saying :—" How much—of the words of that wind-weigher,
" Who has neither country, nor command, nor treasure ? "

I heard that he prepared a royal feast,
(And) harp-like entertained the people, in the midst of the
    banquet.

One opened the door of mention of Hátim ;
Another began to utter his praise.

Envy held the man to the desire of revenge ;
He appointed one for his blood-devouring,

Saying :—" So long as Hátim is in my time,
" My name will not go (into the world) for goodness."

315 The calamity-seeking one took the path to the tribe of Tai,
     He set out for the slaying of the young man.

     There came before him, on the road, a young man,
     From whom, the perfume of affection came up to him:

     Good of visage, and wise, and sweet of tongue;
     He brought him a guest, that night, to his own abode:

     Exercised liberality, and sympathised, and made excuses;
     Snatched the enemy's heart, by kindness:

     Placed the morning-kiss on his hands and feet,
     Saying :—" Stay at ease, a few days, with us."

320 He said :—" I cannot here become a resident;
     " For I have before me an important matter."

     He replied :—" If thou wilt reveal the matter to me,
     " I will with soul exert myself, like friends of one heart."

     He replied :—" Oh young man ! listen to me;
     " For, I know the generous one is a secret-concealer.

     " Thou knowest, perhaps, in this land, Hátim,
     " Who is of happy judgment, and good manners?

     " The King of Yaman has desired his head;
     " I know not, what hatred has arisen between them.

325 " Show me the short path to where he is;
     " Oh friend! this indeed, I look for from thy courtesy."

     The youth laughed, saying :—" I am Hátim:
     " Behold ! separate, with the sword, the head from my
         body.

---

315   " Pai giriftan " here signifies—ķaşd namúdan.

" When the morning becomes white, it is not proper that,
" Injury should reach thee ; or, that thou shouldst become
    disappointed."

When Hátim placed, with nobleness, his head (for
    slaughter),
A cry issued from the young man (the guest).

He fell upon the dust ; and, leaped to his feet ;
Kissed now the dust ; now, his feet and hands :

330 Threw down the sword ; and placed the quiver (on the
    ground) ;
Put, like the helpless, his hands on his breast,

Saying :—" If I strike a rose on thy body,
" I am, in men's sight, a woman, not a man."

He kissed both his eyes ; and, embraced him ;
And, took his way, thence, to Yaman.

Between the two eyebrows of the man, the king
Knew, immediately, that he had not performed the duty.

He said :—" Come ; what news hast thou ?
" Why didst thou not bind his head to thy saddle-strap ?

335 " Perhaps a renowned one made an assault against thee ;
" Thou, through weakness, sustainedst not the fury of
    the contest ? "

The clever youth gave the ground-kiss ;
Praised the king ; and, the majesty of his nature,

Saying :—" I discovered Hátim, fame-seeking,
" Skilful, and of pleasant appearance, and of good visage :

----

327   My relatives may do thee an injury for slaying me ; therefore slay me
at once, and get thee away.
330   " Bar pá,e jastan " here signifies—to leap on the feet, in joy.

" Considered him generous, and endowed with wisdom ;
" Regarded him, in manliness, my superior :

" The load of his favour made my back bent ;
" He slew me, with the sword of kindness and grace."

340 Whatever he experienced, from his liberality,—he uttered ;
The monarch recited praises on the offspring of Tai :

Gave the envoy gold-money,
Saying :—" Liberality is the seal on Hátim's name."

It (the evidence) reaches (touches) him, if they give evidence ;
Since, truth and fame are his fellow-travellers.

————

I have heard that, in the time of the Prophet, the tribe of
    Tai
Made not acceptance of the faith (of the Kurán).

The Messenger of good news and the Observer (Muhammad) sent an army ;
They took captive a multitude of them.

345 The Prophet ordered them to slay them with the sword of
    hate,
Saying :—" They are unclean, and of impure religion."

A woman said :—" I am Hátim's daughter,
" Ask (pardon for me) from this renowned Ruler (Muhammad) :

" Oh revered sir ! exercise generosity as to my state ;
" For my lord (Hátim) was endowed with liberality."

---

342   Report is not a liar ; his liberality is a settled matter.
343   In the 'Ikd-i-mangúm, couplets 343 to 367 are omitted.

By the command of the Prophet of pure judgment,
They loosed the fetters from her hands and feet :

Drew the sword upon the rest of that tribe,
So that they caused, mercilessly, a torrent of blood to flow.

350 With weeping, the woman said to the swordsman :—
" Strike my neck also with all the rest :

" I consider, not release from fetters, generosity ;
" I—alone ; and, my friends in the noose (of calamity)."

She kept uttering lamentations, over the brothers of Tai ;
Her voice came to the Prophet's ear.

The rest of that tribe, he gave to her,
Saying :—" One of true origin never erred ! "

———

From Hátim's store-house, an old man
Demanded ten diram's weight of sugar candy.

355 From the historian, I remember news such,
That he sent him a sack of sugar.

The wife said, from the tent :—" What is this ?
" The old man's need was exactly ten dirams."

The man-cherisher of Tai heard this speech ;
He laughed, and said :—" Oh heart's ease of Hai!

" If he demanded (what was) suitable to his own need,
        (and got it),
" Where is the liberality of the offspring of Hátim ? "

———

354   " Fáníz," in Arabic ; " páníz," in Persian, signifies—a confection
like shakar-barg ; shakar-ḳalam.

Another in generosity, like Hátim,
Comes not, perhaps, from the world's revolution,

360 That Abú Bakr, son of Sa'd,—the hand of munificence,
Whose magnanimity places on the mouths of beggars.

Oh peasant-refuge !   May thy heart be glad !
May Islám, by thy endeavour, flourish !

This dust of happy soil raises its head (ascends),
By thy justice over the climes of Greece and Rúm !

Like Hátim, if his name had not been,
No one, in the world, would have taken the name of (mentioned) Tai.

In books, the praise of that renowned one (Hátim) remains;
For thee, both praise and also reward remain.

365 Whereas, Hátim sought for that reputation and renown (in
the world) ;
Thy struggle and endeavour are for the sake of God !

There is no ceremony for the darvesh ;
Save this one word,—there is no other counsel :—

" As much as may be in thy power, do good ; "
Good remains, after thee (Oh Abú Bakr !); and, speech
after Sa'dí.

————

Of a certain one, an ass had fallen into the mire ;
The blood, through phrenzy, had gathered to his heart.

---

360   Abú Bakr, without being asked, gave to beggars ; and, thus closed their
mouths.

Read :—Whose magnanimity places the hand of munificence on the
mouths, &c.

Desert and rain, and cold, and torrent ;—
Darkness let down its skirt on the horizon.

370 He was in this grief, all night, till the morning ;
Spoke passionately ; and gave curse and abuse.

Neither enemy, nor friend, escaped his tongue (of reproach) ;
Nor the Sultán, whose land and produce it was.

By chance, the lord of that wide plain
Passed by him in that reprehensible state.

He heard these words,—far from rectitude ;—
Neither patience of hearing ; nor, way of answer.

He looked at him, with the eye of punishment,
Saying :—" For what is this person's anger against me ? "

375 He said :—" Oh king ! strike him with the sword ;
" Pluck up his life's root, from the earth's surface."

The Sultán of high rank glanced ;
He himself saw him, in calamity ; and, his ass in the mire :

Forgave the man, on account of his ruined state :
Swallowed the anger of his cold words :

Gave him gold, and a horse, and a coat of fur ;
—How good is love, at the time of hate !—

One said to him :—" Oh old man, void of reason and sense !
" Thou didst escape wonderfully from slaughter."   He
        said :—" Be silent :

380 " If I complained on account of my own grief,
" He gave me presents suitable to himself."

For evil, the return of evil is easy ;
If thou art a man, do good to him who did evil to thee.

I have heard that a proud man, from pride-intoxication,
Shut the door of his house in a beggar's face.

The man, helpless, sate down in a corner ;
His liver hot (with rage) ; and, sigh cold, from the heat (of
    despair) of his chest.

A certain one, covered as to the eyes (blind), entered ;
He asked him, the cause of his hate and rage.

385 He related—and wept, on the dust of the street—
The violence, that chanced to him, from that person.

He said :—"Oh certain one ! abandon grief,
" Break fast, only to-night, with me."

He drew his collar, with politeness and kindness ;
Brought him to his lodging ; and, spread the victual-table.

The darwesh of luminous disposition became comforted ;
He said :—"May God give thee luminosity (as to thy
    eyes) ! "

At night, from his eyes some drops trickled ;
In the morning, he opened his eyes ; and, beheld the world !

390 Within the city, the story went ; and tumult occurred—
For, last night, an eyeless one opened his eye.

He heard this report,—the rich man of stone heart,
From whom, the darwesh turned away straitened in heart.

He said :—" Oh fortunate one ! relate this tale,
" How this difficult deed became easy to thee.

" Who turned back to thee this candle, world-illumi-
    nating ? "
He replied :—" Oh tyrant of troubled days !

---

387   With kindness and compassion, having seized his collar, and placed
his hand on his neck, he drew him to his own house.

" Thou wast of short vision, and of sluggish judgment,
" For, instead of the humá (an auspicious bird), thou wast
　　engaged with the owl (a filthy bird).

15　" That one opened this door (of vision) on my face ;
" On whose face, thou didst shut the door.

" If thou dost express a kiss on the dust of men,
" In the name of manliness ! luminosity comes to thee.

" Those, who are covered as to the eye of the heart,
" Are, indeed, careless of this antimony."

When the one of overturned fortune heard this rebuke,
He bit the finger-tip of regret, with his teeth,

Saying :—" My falcon became the prey of thy net ;
" I had fortune ; to thy name, it went."

20　How may he bring the male falcon to his grasp,—that one,
Like a mouse, teeth plunged in avarice.

Verily, if thou art a seeker of the pious one,
Exercise not carelessness, a moment, as to his service.

Give food to the sparrow, and partridge and dove,
That the humá may, one day, fall to thy net.

When thou castst the arrow of supplication, in every corner,
There is hope that thou mayst, suddenly, make a prey.

From many oysters, a single pearl comes forth ;
Out of a hundred arrows, one comes to the butt.

16　　The first line means :—If thou dost ask for aid from man.
20　　The falcon here signifies—mardum-i-ma'ní wa kámil; ṣáḥib-i-dil, a
pious one.
　　" Dandán faro burdan " signifies—khám ṭam' namúdan.

405 The son of a certain one was lost from a camel-litter;
The father wandered about, in the night-time, in the
    káfila :

Inquired at every tent; and, hastened in every direction;
Found that light (his son), in the darkness.

When he came to the men of the káraván,
I heard, that he said to the camel-driver :—

" Knowst thou not how I found the path to the friend (my
    son) ?
" Whosoever came before me, I said :—it is he ! "

The pious ones are at the heels of every one, on that
    account,
That they may, perchance, one day, reach a sage, holy man :

410 Bear burdens, for the sake of the pious ;
Endure the thorn (of affliction) for the sake of a single rose.

From the crown of one king-born, in a camel-stable,
A ruby fell, one night, in a stony place.

The father, to his son, said :—" In this night, of dark
    colour,
" How knowst thou,—which is the jewel or stone ?

" Oh son ! take care of all the stones,
" That the ruby may not be out of their midst."

The pure ones of distraught visage, among the rogues,
Are, indeed—the ruby and (precious) stone, in a dark place.

---

408   Whoever seeks runs ; whoever runs finds.
411   In the 'Ikd-i-manzúm, couplets 411 to 426 are omitted.

15 Endure, with pleasure the burden (of violence) of every
       ignorant one,
That, in the end of time, a pious one may fall (to thee).

The person, who is merry of head (enamoured) with a
       friend,—
Seest thou not how he is the enemy's (rival's) load-carrier?

He rends not his garment, rose-like, on account of the
       power of the thorn,
Who, pomegranate-like, laughs, blood gathered in the heart.

Endure the grief of a crowd, for the love of one,
Pay observance to a hundred, for the sake of one.

If those of foot-dust, distraught of head,
Are, in thy sight, contemptible and miserable,

420 Ever look not at them, with the eye of approval;
For, they are approved of God, and that is enough.

The one, who, in thy opinion, is bad,
How knowst thou but that he himself is the possessor of
       saintship?

The door of the knowledge of God is open to those,
In whose face, the doors of men are shut.

---

416   For the good, he endures the violence of the bad.

417   "Khún dar dil uftádan" signifies—ghuṣṣa dar dil dáshtan, wa dar
'ishḳ-i-mahbúbe giriftár búdan. When the pomegranate is red and
ripe, it rends its skin. The rending of the skin they call laughing or
being of happy state. Notwithstanding that, through grief, blood had
fallen (gathered) to his heart, he was content.

    In some copies, the second line runs:—

    (a) Which thorn (rival) may have, snake-like, fallen in thy path.

    (b) In whose heart, blood, pomegranate-like, may have gathered.

420   If the fallen and abject, who are of pure breath, but outwardly dishevelled and wretched, appear to thee contemptible, look not at them;
for, being approved of God, they have no need of thy approbation.

Many of better life, and bitterness-tasting,
May be, in the quarter (Judgment Day), skirt-displaying (in
    majesty).

If thou hast reason and deliberation, thou wilt kiss
The hand of the king-born one (the Man of God) in the
    prison (of this world).

425 For, the day he comes from prison,
He may, when he becomes lofty, give to thee loftiness.

Cause not the rose-tree to burn, in the autumn;
For, it appears to thee excellent, in the fresh spring.

———

A certain one possessed not the power of spending;
Gold, he had; the power of enjoying, he had not.

He used not to eat, that his heart might rest;
Used not to give (in alms), that it might be of use to him
    to-morrow (Judgment Day).

Night and day,—in the entanglement of gold and silver:
—The fetter of the mean one, (is) in gold and silver.—

430 One day, the son, in ambush, knew
Where the miser had placed the gold, in the earth.

He brought it forth from the dust, and gave it to the wind;
I heard, that he deposited a stone in that spot.

For the young man, the gold remained not;
It came to one hand; he enjoyed it with the other.

———

423   "Talkh 'aishán" signifies—persons to whom life, from exceeding
hardship and poverty, is bitter.
    "Dáman-kashán" signifies—kharámán ba náz vavanda.

426   In the autumn of this world, the holy man appears bad; but, in the
fresh spring of the next world, the marks of his goodness will appear.

For this reason that he was one of unclean face (conduct)
    and a low thrower of dice ;
His hat in the bázár; and, trousers pawned.

The father,—clutch placed (in grief) on his own neck ;
The son,—a harp and flute (in enjoyment) brought to the
    front.

435 The father, weeping and lamenting, slept not all night ;
The son, in the morning, laughed ; and said :—

" Oh father ! gold is for the sake of enjoying ;
" For depositing, whether stone or gold,—what matter ? "

They bring forth gold from the hard stone ;
That they may enjoy it with friends and beloved ones.

Gold, in the palm of the man's hand, world-worshipping,
Oh brother ! is yet within the stone.

When, thou art, in life, bad to thy family,
Complain not of them, if they wish thy death.

440 Thy family enjoy thy (wealth) to satiety, at that time,
When thou fallst from the roof of fifty yards to the bottom.

The miser, rich with dínars and silver,
Is a tilism dwelling over the treasure.

His gold remained years, for the reason,
That such a tilism trembles at its head !

With the stone of Fate (death), they suddenly shatter it ;
They make, at ease, division of the treasure.

---

441   " Tilism " signifies—a creature which guards gold. It neither enjoys
the gold, nor permits anyone else to enjoy it. From this word, comes
talisman.

After carrying and collecting, like the ant,
Enjoy,—before that the grave-worm devours thee.

445 The words of Sa'dí are precept and counsel ;
If thou becomest work-performing, they are of use to thee.

It is folly to turn away the face from this ;
Since one can, in this way, obtain empire.

———

A young man had exercised liberality to the extent of a
    dáng ;
He had accomplished an old man's desire.

The sky suddenly caught him, in a crime ;
The Sultán sent him to the slaughtering-place :

The hurrying of soldiers, and uproar of the people ;
Sightseers about the door, and street, and roof.

450 When, within the tumult, the old darvesh beheld
The young man, a captive in the people's hands.

His heart was wounded, on account of the wretched youth,
Who had, once, taken his heart.

He raised a cry, saying :—" The Sultán is dead !
" The world remained ; but, he took away his good dispo-
    sition."

He kept rubbing together the hands of sorrow ;
The soldiers, swords drawn (for slaying) heard.

At the cry, a shout issued from them,—
Palm-striking on head, and face, and shoulder !

———

453   " Turk " signifies—a man of Turkistan, the people of which were
notorious for blood-shedding and fearlessness.

55 On foot, up to the door of the court, with haste,
They ran ; they saw the king on the throne.

The youth went forth from the midst ; they took the old
　　man,
By the neck, a captive, to the Sultán's throne.

He, with awe-inspiring manner inquired ; and, displayed
　　majesty,
Saying :—" To thee,—wherefore was the desiring of my
　　death ?

" Since my disposition and rectitude are good,
" Why, in the end, desirest thou ill (by my death) to
　　men ? "

The resolute old man brought forth a tongue,
Saying :—" Oh (king) ! the world is a ring in the ear (a
　　slave) of thy order !

460 " By a false word—' the king is dead ! '
" Thou didst not die ; and, a helpless one carried off his
　　life."

The king wondered at this tale to such a degree,
That he gave him something, and said nothing.

And, on this side, the youth, falling and rising,
Kept proceeding, running in every direction, helplessly.

One said to him :—" From the four directions of retribution,
" What didst thou, that liberation came to thy soul ? "

458　　See couplet 452.
463　　" Char-sú " signifies—the " square " in which punishments are inflicted and orders issued.

He whispered to his ear—"Oh wise man!
" I escaped from bonds, through a brave soul and a dáng."

465   He places a seed in the dust for the reason,
That it may, in the day of distress, give fruit.

A barley-grain keeps back a great calamity;
Thou hast heard of the staff, that killed 'Új (King of
        Bashan)?

The true account came from the Chosen One (Muhammad),
That—the giving of arms is the repelling of calamity.

Thou seest not an enemy's foot, in this habitation;
For, Abú Bakr, son of Sa'd, is master of the kingdom.

A world joyful by thy face,—Oh (Abú Bakr)! seize
The world, that joy may be on thy face.

470   In thy time, no one endures distress from another;
The rose in the parterre suffers not the violence of the
        thorn.

Thou art the shadow of the grace of God on the earth;
Prophet-like—the mercy of both worlds!

---

466   The mother of 'Új, who lived to the age of three thousand five hundred years, was a daughter of Ádam (on him be peace!); his father was
'Anak. At the time of Noah's deluge, notwithstanding that the water
stood forty yards above the highest mountains of the earth, it reached
only to his waist.

Moses made an attempt against him, upon which 'Új took up a mountain, two farsangs in extent, on his head, with the intention of casting
it on the army of Moses, so that it might be destroyed. God sent the
bird, Hoopoo, which pierced the mountain, so that it became a collar
about his neck.

Moses then struck him on the ankle, so that he fell and died.

467   In the 'Iḳd-i-manzúm, couplets 467 to 472 are omitted.

469   The world having become gladsome through Abú Bakr, the author
invites Abú Bakr to be joyous through the world.

If a person knows not thy worth,—what matter?
They also know not the—" Shab-i-kadr."

In a dream, a person beheld the plain of the place of
    assembling :
The earth's surface, from sun,—molten copper.

From men, complaint kept ascending to heaven;
The brain, through heat, came to boiling.

475 (Beheld) a certain one of this multitude,—in the shade;
An ornament of Paradise, about his neck.

He inquired, saying :—" Oh man, assembly-adorning!
" Who was thy helper, in this assembly ?"

He said :—" I had a vine at my house-door;
" A holy man slept in its shade.

" At this time of despair, that true man
" Asked pardon for my sins from the Ruler of rulers,

" Saying :—' Oh Lord ! forgive this slave;
" ' For once I experienced, through him, ease.' "

480 What said I, when I unloosed this mystery (of the title) ?
—" May glad tidings be to the Lord of Shíráz (Abú-
    Bakr) ! "

For, the grandees, in the shadow of his spirit,
Are resident ; and, at the table of his bounty.

---

472   The " Shab-i-kadr " is the most blessed of nights, on which prayers
are accepted; it is the 27th of the month Ramazán.

480   The author's reply is given in the second line.
    In the 'Ikd-i-manzúm, couplets 480 to 484 are omitted.
    The king,—in whose shade a world is living and at ease at his table
of bounty,—to what dignity will he (in heaven) ascend !

The man of liberality is a tree, fruit-possessing;
When thou passest beyond it,—fuel of the mountain.

If they strike the axe, at the foot of the tree, fit for fuel,—
When strike they at the fruitful tree?

Oh tree of skill (Abú-Bakr)!   Long keep thy foot!
For, thou art fruit-possessing; and, also shady.

485 As to beneficence, I said much;
But, it is not proper for every one.

Enjoy the blood and wealth of the one, man-injuring;
For, of the bad bird,—the feather and wing plucked out is
        best.

One, who is in strife with thy master,
Why givest thou to his hand, the stick and stone?

Cast away the root, that bears the thorn;
Cherish the tree, that produces fruit.

Give the dignity of the great, to that one,
Who to inferiors holds himself, not proudly.

490 Wherever, there is a tyrant,—pardon him not;
For, mercy to him is tyranny to the world.

The lamp of the world-consumer (tyrant) extinguished—is
        best;
One in the fire is better than a people with the stain (of
        tyranny).

Whosoever shows mercy to a thief,
Attacks the káraván, with his own arm.

---

482   "Guzáshtan" signifies—"to abandon" as well as "to pass."
489   "Sar girán dáshtan bar kase" signifies—ghulzat wa ṣaḳl namúdan
ba kase.

Give to the wind (of destruction) the heads of those
    tyranny-practising :
Oppression, on one oppression-practising, is justice and
    equity.

I have heard that a man experienced house-vexation ;
For, a wasp made a nest in his roof.

495 His wife said :—" What thou desirest in respect to them,
    do not ;
" Lest that they should become scattered from their native
    country."

The wise man went to his own work ;
The wasps began, one day, to sting his wife.

About the door, and roof, and street,—the foolish wife
Kept making lamentation.   But, the husband said :—

" Oh woman ! make not thy face bitter towards men ;
" Thou didst say :—' Slay not the poor wasps ! ' "

How may one do good to the bad !
Forbearance to ill-doers increases ill.

500 When thou beholdst a people's injury in a chief,
Cut his throat, with a sharp sword.

What dog, in short, is there—for whom they place a victual-
    tray ?
Order, that they give him a bone.

How well has the old man of the village (Firdausí) ex-
    pressed this proverb :—
" The baggage-animal, leg-striking (kicking), is best under
    a heavy load."

If the watchman shows mercy,
No one is able to sleep at night, for thieves.

In the circle of contest, the spear-reed
Is more precious than a hundred thousand sugar-reeds
    (canes).

505 Not every one is worthy of property ;
This one requires property ; that one, rebuke.

When thou cherishst the cat, it takes away the pigeon ;
When thou makest the wolf fat, it rends Joseph.

The edifice, that has not firm foundations,—
Make it not lofty ; and, if thou dost, tremble for it.

How well said Bahrám, desert-dwelling,
When his thorough-bred, restive, steed threw him to the
    earth,

" It is proper to take from the herd another horse,
" Which it is possible to restrain, if he becomes restive."

510 Oh son ! bind the Euphrates, at low-water ;
For, when the torrent is risen, it is of no use.

When the filthy wolf comes to thy snare,
Slay ; if not, pluck up thy heart from (love for) the sheep.

From Iblís, adoration never comes ;
Nor from the bad jewel,—goodness into existence.

Give neither place nor opportunity to the malignant one ;
The enemy in the pit, and the demon in the glass bottle—
    is best.

---

506   The brothers cast Joseph into a pit, sold him, and represented to their
father that a wolf had devoured him.

508   Bahrám was called Bahrám Gor, "Sahra-nishín," because he loved
the hunting of asses in the desert.
    In the 'Ikd-i-manzúm, couplets 508 to 518 are omitted.

Say not :—" It is proper, to kill this snake with a stick " ;
Strike, when he has his head beneath thy stone.

515 The pen striker (pen-man), who did ill to his inferiors,
To make, with the sword, his hand a pen (to sever it)—is
    best.

The deliberator, who introduces bad regulations,
Takes thee, that he may give thee to hell-fire.

Say not :—" For the country, this deliberator is enough " ;
Call him not deliberator, who is unfortunate.

The fortunate one acts upon Sa'dí's speech,
Because, it is the (cause of) increase of country, and deli-
    beration, and judgment.

CHAPTER III.

On Love.

1 Oh happy the time of those distraught in love of Him,
   Whether they experience the wound (of separation); or,
      the plaster (of propinquity to Him)!

Beggars from royalty fleeing;
In the hope of union with Him, in beggary, long-suffering.

---

1   This chapter is on Ṣúfí-ism (taṣawwuf), or mysticism; the language used is mystical (mutaṣawwif). The one who practises Ṣúfí-ism is called—Ṣúfí; ahl-i-ḥál; 'áshiḳ-i-sádiḳ; ahl-i-ṭaríḳat; ahl-i-dil; ṣáḥib-dil; sálik; ṣáḥib-i-ma'rifat; 'árif.

    The student should on this subject see—
    (a) A summary of the tenets of Ṣúfí-ism, by Sir William Jones.
    (b) De Bode's Bakhárá.
    (c) Sind, by Richard Burton, World-traveller, chap. viii.
    (d) Hughes' Notes on Muhammadanism, p. 227.

    For a general view of the tenets of the Muslim religion, see Lane's Modern Egyptians, vol. i. chap. iii.

    The season of those distraught in love for God Most High is, in every state, very happy. Whether they experience the wound of separation, through the thorn of pain of love for Him, or become wounded by the axe of separation, life-penetrating, and the arrow of affliction of separation, heart-stitching; or, by obtaining propinquity to the presence of God, and the fortune of union with Him, receive the healing plaster for the heart-wound, and drink the draught, pleasant-tasting, of beholding Him.

2   In "pádsháhí" the word "pád" signifies—pás; "sháh" signifies—khudáwind.

Time to time, they drink the wine of pain (of love for Him);
And, if they consider it bitter, they draw breath (are
    patient).

In the pleasure of wine, there is the evil of head-sickness;
The thorn is the armour-bearer of the rose-branch.

5 Patience, which is in remembrance of Him, is not bitter;
For bitterness from a friend's hand is sugar.

His captive descries not release from bonds;
His prey seeks not freedom from the snare.

Sultáns of retirement, beggars of Hai!
Stages of God recognisers, foot-trace lost.

Intoxicated with (the love of) the friend (God), reproach-
    enduring;
The camel, intoxicated, more easily bears the load.

How, may people find the path to their state?
For, like the water of life, they are in darkness.

----

4   For the wine-drinkers of the carpet of love, head-sickness of pain
and affliction is inevitable; and, for rose-pluckers of the gardens of the
knowledge of God,—the skirt, full of thorns.

    Then, head-sickness from wine-drinking and the thorn of the rose-
branch are as guards, so that the father of lust may not, without
bitterness, obtain the taste of pleasure, nor easily bring to his hand the
rose (of the beloved).

7   The true lovers of God apparently wander about villages, and appear,
in the sight of superficial observers, beggars, foodless and wretched.
But, in retirement, they are kings of the time, and road-recognisers,
that is, they have reached the stage and are as those trace-lost, so that
no one finds information regarding their track, or becomes acquainted
with the work which they do.

    " 'Uzlat " here signifies—khilwat wa tanhá,í, or the mystery belonging
to God, into which a stranger has no entrance.

    " Gum karda pai " signifies—be nishán búdan, one who so does his
work that another cannot find the clue to his purpose.

    " Manázil-shinásán " signifies —murshidán wa 'árifán, holy men.

9   In the first line, " sar " is redundant.

    " Waḳt " here signifies—waḳt-i-ḥuẓúr, the time of being present before
God.

10 Like the holy house (Jerusalem), within—full of towers
    (pomp);
Without,—the wall left desolate.

Moth-like, they set fire to themselves;
Silk-worm-like, they spin not on themselves (a protection).

Mistress in embrace,—mistress-seeking;
On the stream-bank, lip dry with thirst.

I say not that, as to water, they are powerless;
But they are, on the Nile, dropsical.

———

The love of one, like thyself—of water and clay,
Ravishes patience and heart-ease.

15 In wakefulness,—enamoured of her cheek and mole;
In sleep,—foot-bound, in thought of her.

In truth, thou placest thy head (life) at her feet, in such a
    way,
That, thou considerst the world, in comparison with her
    existence, non-existent.

When thy gold comes not to the eye (of approval) of thy
    mistress,
Gold and dust appear to thee the same.

———

As regards the water of life, see the Sikandar Náma, Discourses 69
and 70. English translation by Clarke.

10   Their interior is prosperous; exterior, wretched.

12   Their love of God is insatiable. A dropsical patient is never wearied
of drinking water.

14   There are two kinds of love, one *superficial*—the love of man for man;
the other, *real*—the love of the creature for the Creator.

To thee,—desire for another appears not ;
For, with her,—place for another remains not.

Thou sayst :—" Her lodging is within my eye " ;
And, if thou closest together the eye—" It is in my heart."

20 Neither, thought of any one, lest thou shouldst become
        disgraced,
Nor, power that thou shouldst, for a moment, become
        patient.

If she desires thy life, thou placest it on the palm of her
        hand ;
And, if she puts the sharp sword on thy head, thou placest
        thy head (in submission).

When love, whose foundation is on desire,
Is, to such a degree, tumult-exciting and command-issuing,

Hast thou wonder at the travellers of the path of God,
That they should be immersed in the sea of truth ?

In passion for the Beloved, with soul engaged ;
In remembrance of the Friend (God), careless of the world.

25 In memory of God, they have fled from the world ;
So intoxicated with (the splendour of) the Cup-bearer
        (God) that they have spilled the wine !

---

24   " Mushtaghil," in the first line, signifies—fárigh ; mashghúl shavanda ;
and kár kunanda.
      " Mushtaghil," in the second line, signifies—gháfil ; ná-parwá ; rúo
gardánída.
      " Janán" signifies—ma'shúk, a mistress.
25   In Súfí-ism, " sákí " signifies—murshid-i-kámil, a holy spiritual guide ;
and hence God, who, cup-bearer-like, gives the wine of love to His
lovers, and makes them non-existent in His beauty.
      The second line means—With the splendour of the Cup-bearer (God)
they are to such a degree intoxicated, and become non-existent, that
they have spilled the wine of love, and have no need of wine for causing
intoxication (masti), and selflessness (be-khudí).

It is impossible to effect their cure with medicine;
For, none is acquainted with their pain (of love).

From eternity without beginning, to their ear comes:—
    " Am I not your God ? "
With clamour, in a shout, they utter:—" Yes ! "

A crowd,—office-holding, corner-sitting ;
Feet, clayey; breath fiery,—

Pluck up, with a shout, a mountain from its place ;
Heap together, with a cry, a city :

30 Are, wind-like, invisible, and swift-moving ;
Are, stone-like, silent, but praise-uttering.

In the morning, they weep to such a degree that the water
Washes down from their eyes the collyrium of sleep.

Steed (of the body) slain, with the great (austerity), with
        which they have urged the night ;
In the morning, shouting, saying :—" They are wearied ! "

---

27   Before the creation of A'dam, God Most High made all the souls,
and said, " Am I not your God ? "
    They gave evidence to the truth, and said, " Yes ! "
    When they came into the world, many, by reason of worldly affections,
forgot that covenant ; but, as to the true lovers, the sound of those
words is yet in the ear of their hearts ; and they are in shout till now,
in exclaiming, " Yes ! "

28   This crowd of men possessed of majesty, though they are apparently
dismissed from office and are sitting in retirement, are, by reason of the
heart, possessed of office. Outwardly, they appear contemptible ; yet,
from the effects of the fire of love, they bring forth hot sighs, sparks-
raining.

32   " Shab rándan " signifies—shab ravání kardan ; shab bedár búdan.
They have slain lust ; exercised night-watching ; opened the door of the
knowledge of God to their own faces ; and with these qualities, are in
shout, saying :— * * * *
    After passing through the stage " ilạ Alláh " (to God), they proceed
to " fí Alláh " (in God), to which there is no limit.

Night and day, in the sea of phrenzy and burning;
From perturbation, they know not night from day.

So enamoured of the splendour of the figure-painter (God),
That they have no occupation with the beauty of the out-
    ward form.

35 The pious ones gave not their hearts to the covering (ex-
    ternal beauty);
And, if a fool gave,—he is brainless, and fleshless.

That one drank the pure wine of the Unity (of God),
Who forgot this world and the next.

———

I have heard that, once upon a time, one, beggar-born,
Had affection for one, king-born.

He went, and cherished a vain desire;
Imagination plunged its teeth in desire.

Mile-stone like, he used not to be free (absent) from his (the
    prince's) plain;
Bishop-like, at all times, at the side of his horse.

40 His heart became blood, and the secret remained in his
    heart;
But, his feet, through weeping, remained in the mire (of
    desire).

The guards obtained intelligence of his grief;
They said to him :—" Wander not again here !"

---

37   In the 'Ikd-i-manzúm, couplets 37–66 are omitted.
      " Nazar dáshtan " signifies—'ishk dáshtan.
      " Dandán ba kám faro burdan " signifies—kám-yáb wa mastaulí
shudan.
39   At chess, the Bishop is next the Knight (horse).

A moment, he went; recollection of the friend's face
    came to him;
Again, he pitched his tent, at the head of his friend's
    street.

A slave broke his head, and hand, and foot,
Saying :—" Said we not once to thee,—come not here ? "

Again, to him,—patience and rest remained not;
On account of his friend's face, patience remained not.

45 Like flies from off the sugar, with violence, him,
They used to drive away; but, with speed, he used to
    return.

One said to him :—" Oh impudent one of insane appear-
    ance !
" Thou hast wonderful patience as to (blows of) stick and
    stone."

He said :—" This violence, against me, is through his
    tyranny ;
" It is not proper to complain of a friend's hand.

" Behold, I express the breath of friendship ;
" If he holds me friend ; or, if enemy.

" Expect not, without him, patience from me ;
" Nay—even with him, repose has no possibility.

50 " Neither the power of patience, nor room for anger ;
" Neither the possibility of being (stopping), nor the foot
    of flight.

" Say not,—turn aside the head from this door of the
    Court ;
" Though he place my head, like a tent-peg in the tent-
    rope.

" Nay,—the moth, life given at its friend's foot,
" Is better than alive in its dark corner."

He said :—" If thou shouldst suffer the wound of his club?"
He replied :—" I will fall, at his feet, ball-like."

He said :—" If, with the sword, he cuts off thy head?"
He replied :—" This much even, I grudge not.

55 " To me,—indeed, there is not so much knowledge,—
" Whether, the crown, or the axe, be at my head.

" Display not reproof with me impatient ;
" For, patience appears not, in love.

" If my eye becomes white (diseased) like Yakúb,
" I abandon not hope of seeing Yusúf.

" One who is happy (in love) with another,
" Is not vexed with him, for every little thing."

On day, the youth kissed his (the prince's) stirrup ;
He became angry ; and turned the rein from him.

60 He laughed, and said :—" Turn not the rein ;
" For, the Sultán turns not away the rein (face) from any.

" To me—by thy existence, existence remains not ;
" To me,—in memory of thee, self-worshipping remains
        not.

" If thou observst a crime, reproach me not :
" Thou art head brought forth (produced) from my collar
        (of existence).

---

57   Yakúb, from much weeping for Yusúf, became blind ; he still kept
the hope of seeing him. The meeting eventually took place.

58   See couplet 168.

62   Whenever the degree of love reaches the perfection of exaltation,
there is in the lover's heart no room for another. To such a degree
does this occur, that the lover forgets his own existence, and considers
himself indeed the beloved one. Thus Majnúm, in fancy of Laila,
regarded his own body as Laila, and said, " I am Laila ! " The beggar,
even so, regarded his own body to be that of his beloved, and recognised
not himself.

" I fixed my hand in thy stirrup with that boldness ;
" For, I brought not myself in the account.

" I drew the pen on (effaced) my own name ;
" Placed my foot on the head of my own desire.

65 " The arrow of that intoxicated eye slays me indeed ;
" What need that thou shouldst bring thy hand to the
        sword.

" Set fire to the reed, and pass ;
" So that in the forest neither dry, nor green, thing may
        remain."

I have heard, that at the chanting of a singer,
One of Parí face began to dance.

From the fire of the distracted hearts around her,
A candle-flame caught in her skirt.

She became troubled in heart and vexed ;
One of her lovers said :—" What fear ?

70 " Oh love ! as to thee,—the fire burned the skirt ;
" As to me,—it burned, all at once, the harvest (of
        existence)."

If thou art a lover, express not a breath about thy self ;
For, it is infidelity (to speak of) lover and one's self.

I recollect hearing from a knowing old man, in this way,
That one, distraught with love, turned his head to the
        desert.

----

66   The work which is accomplished with ease, make not difficult ; and
useless labour endure not.
    Again :— Cast the fire of love into my heart and go, so that all my
body may burn.
71   Notwithstanding the existence of thy beloved, to consider thy own
existence is disloyalty and infidelity.

The father, through separation from him, neither ate nor
    slept ;
They reproached the son ; he said :—

" From that time, when the Friend called me one of his
    own,
" Further love for any one remained not to me.

75 " By God ! when He showed me His beauty,
" Whatever else I beheld appeared to me fancy."

He, who turned away from the people became not lost ;
For he found again his own lost one (God).

There are, beneath the sky, shunners of men,
Whom one can call, at once, wild beast and also angel.

Like the angel, they rest not from remembering the King
    (God) ;
Like the wild beast, they, night and day, shun men.

Strong of arm (by spirituality) ; but short of hand (by
    materiality) ;
Wise,—(outwardly) mad ; sensible—(outwardly) intoxi-
    cated.

80 Sometimes, tranquil in a corner, religious habit-stitching ;
Sometimes, perplexed in society, religious habit-burning.

Neither passion as to themselves ; nor, solicitude for any
    one ;
Nor place for any one, in the cell of their unitarianism.

Perturbed of reason, confused of sense ;
Ear-stuffed to the word of the adviser.

---

79   Strong, by spirituality ; weak, by materiality ; wise as to the next
world ; mad as to this world ; sensible, not having drunk of the cup of
lust ; intoxicated, with the cup of truth.

82   The adviser is one, who tries to lead them to the world.

The duck will not become drowned in the river (of lust) ;
The samundar ! what knows he of the torment of burning ?

Empty of hand, men of full stomach (proud) ;
Desert wanderers, without a Káfila :

85 They have no expectation of the people's approbation;
For, they are approved of God ;—and that is enough.

Dear ones (of God) concealed from the people's eye ;
Not those waist-cord-possessing, clothed in the habit of the
      darwesh.

They are full of fruit, and shady, vine-like ;
Are not like us,—of black deeds, and blue garment-dyers.

Head plunged in themselves (in reflection), oyster-like ;
Not, foam (on mouth) gathered, river-like.

If wisdom be thy friend, be afraid of them, (those foam-
      gathered) ;
For, they are demons in the garb of men.

90 They are not men indeed of bone and skin ;
A true soul is not in every form.

The Sultán (God) is not the purchaser of every slave ;
Not, beneath every religious garment is there a living man.

If every drop of hail had become a pearl,
The bázár would have become full of them like small shells.

---

83   The samundar is an animal, lizard-like, which dwells in the fire ;
when it comes forth from the fire, it dies. Sultáns make caps of its
skin.

87   In former times, Súfís wore blue-coloured woollen garments.

89   Regard not their outward weakness ; be not careless of their spiritual
powerfulness.

They fasten not the (wooden) clog to themselves, juggler-
    like ;
For, the wooden clog moves hardly from its place.

Companions of the house of retirement—"Am I your
    God ?"
They are, with a draught, intoxicated until the blast of
    the trumpet (of Saráfíl).

95 For the sword, they take not off their grasp from desire
    (of God) ;
For abstinence and love are as the mirror and the stone.

A certain one had a mistress in Samarkand ;
Thou wouldst say :—" She possessed sugar, in place of
    speech."

A beauty,—pledge taken from the sun !
Piety's foundation became ruined by her coquetry.

God Most High !—of beauty, to such a degree,
That thou wouldst think it a sign of the mercy (of God) !

She used to walk ;—and, eyes were behind her ;
Lover's hearts, life placed in exchange for her.

100 That lover used, covertly, to glance at her ;
She once, with severity, looked ; and, said :—

---

93   Not like jugglers do they display devotion, by way of deceit ; for
devotion on the foot is like the wooden clog, which goes with difficulty
from place to place.

94   " Khilwat-sará,e " refers to—the covenant "Am I your God ? " It
means God's abode at that time.

95   As the stone shatters the mirror, so does love abstinence.

96   In the 'Ikd-i-manzúm, couplets 96–113 are omitted.

97   The Sun pledged its goods for her beauty.

99   Men used to glance after her.

" Oh perverse one ! so much, thou runst after me ;
" Knowst thou not, that I am not the bird of thy net ?

" If, again, I see thee (at my heels), with the sword,
" Like an enemy, pitiless, I will cut off thy head."

One said to him :—" Now take thy resolve ;
" Choose a more easy object than this one.

" I think not thou mayst acquire this desire ;
" God forbid ! that thou shouldst place thy life in the
        heart's desire."

105 When he,—mad with love, heart-lost,—heard this reproach,
He drew forth with sorrow a cry from his heart,

Saying :—" Allow,—that the wound of the sword of de-
        struction
" May cause my corpse to roll in blood and sweat.

" Perhaps, before friend and enemy, they will speak,
" Saying :—' This is one slain by her hand and sword ! '

" I see not the (way of) flight, from the dust of street ;
" Say :—in tyranny, spill not my honour !

" Oh self-worshipper ! For me,—thou dictatest repen-
        tance ;
" For thee,—repentance of this speech is better.

110 " Pardon me ; for, whatever she does,
" She does well—even if there be desire for my blood.

" Every night, her fire (of love) causes me to burn ;
" In the morning, I become alive by her pleasant perfume.

" If, to-day, I die, in the street of my beloved,
" In the Resurrection, I will pitch my tent by my beloved."

Yield not, so long as thou canst, in this battle (of love) ;
For Sa'dí is alive, whom love slew.

A certain one thirsty was saying, while he surrendered his
    soul :—
" Happy is that fortunate one, who in water died ! "

115 One of deficient understanding said to him,—" Oh wonder !
" When thou art dead,—whether moist or dry of lip, what
    matter ? "

He said:—" In the end, do I not make my mouth moist,
" Until, I lay down even my precious life ? "

The thirsty one falls into the deep basin ;
For, he knows that the one drowned dies water-satiated.

If thou art a lover, seize her skirt ;
And, if she says :—" Surrender thy life ! " say :—" Take
    it."

Thou mayst enjoy ease of life, at that time,
When thou passest over the hill of non-existence.

120 The heart of seed-sowers may be afflicted ;
(But), when the harvest is accomplished, they sleep plea-
    santly.

In this assembly (of love to God), those arrive at their
    desire,
Who, in the last circulation, attain the cup (of love).

---

113   Lovers of God do not die. Sa'dí was a Súfí.
118   Some say that " O " refers to God. The line will run :—seize the
skirt of God.
121   " Daur-i-ákhir " signifies—piyála,e ákhirín-i-hazm-i-sharáb, the last
circulation of the cup.
    " Jám " signifies—jám-i-ma'rifat wa rísálat.

I have a tale of this sort—of the men of the way of God,
Rich mendicants; king beggars;

—That an old man went, in the morning, for the purpose
    of begging;
He beheld the door of a masjid; and, gave the mendicant's
    cry.

One said to him :—" This is not the people's house;
" Where they give thee anything; stand not here, in im-
    pudence."

125 He said to him :—" Then, whose is this house,
" In which, there is no bestowing (of alms) to any one ? "

He said :—" Be silent; what faulty word is this ?
" The lord of this house is our Lord God ! "

The old man glanced within; he beheld candle and
    prayer-arch,
He drew forth, with burning, a lament from his liver.

Saying :—" It is a pity, to go farther hence;
" It is a pity, to go disappointed from this door.

" In disappointment, I went not forth from any street;
" Why should I go, yellow-of-face, from God's door ?

130 " Even here, I may make the hand of entreaty long;
" For, I know that I may not return empty of hand."

I have heard that, for a year, he sate, a sojourner,
Like those redress-seeking, hand-uplifted.

One night, the foot of his life descended into the clay (of
    death).
Through weakness, his heart began to palpitate.

---

122   Outwardly mendicants, inwardly rich.
            Outwardly beggars, inwardly kings.
129   An Eastern becomes yellow, not pale, with fear or distress.

In the morning, a person brought a lamp near to his head ;
He beheld a spark of life in him, like the morning-lamp.

From gladness, clamour-making, he kept saying :—
" Whosoever beats (knocks at) the door of the Merciful
　　One, that door becomes opened.

5 The seeker of God must be patient and submissive ;
I have not heard that the alchymist is (ever) dejected.

How much gold do they put in the obscure dust,
That they may, possibly, one day, make a piece of copper
　　gold !

Gold, for the sake of purchasing a thing, is good ;
What wilt thou buy better than friend and lover ?

If through one, heart-ravishing,—thy heart is straitened,
Another consoler may come to thy grasp.

For one of bitter face, endure not life-bitterness ;
With the water (of beauty) of another, draw out the fire
　　(of love) for her.

10 But if she have, in beauty, no equal ;
Abandon her not, for a little heart-annoyance.

It is possible to disengage the heart from that one,
Without whom, thou knowst it is possible to be content.

———

I heard that an old man kept awake the night ;
In the morning, he raised the hand of need to God.

A voice from heaven cast into the old man's ear :—
—" Thou art profitless ; go ; take thy own way."

143　　" Sar-i-khwesh giriftan " signifies—dar-kār-i-khud búdan.
　　　See couplet 103.

" At this door (of God), thy prayer is unacceptable ;
" Go, in contempt ; or stand, in lamentation."

145 The next night, from recitation of the name of God and
        devotion, he slept not ;
A disciple obtained news of his state, and said :—

" When thou sawst that the door on that side was closed,
" Endure not uselessly such a struggle."

On his cheek, tears of ruby-colour
Rained, in regret ; and, he said :—" Oh youth !

" I would, in hopelessness, have turned away,
" From this door, at the time when I could have found
        another way.

" Think not, if the friend broke the reins,
" That I would take off the hand from his saddle-strap.

150 " When the asker becomes disappointed at a door,
" What grief, if he recognises another door ?

" I have heard that my way is not in this street ;
" But, there is not the semblance of another path."

He was in this talk,—head on the ground of devotion,
When, in the ear of his soul, they uttered this sound :—

" The prayer is accepted, though to him is no goodness ;
" For save us, to him is no other shelter."

––––––––

A new young bride complains,
To an old man (her father), of her unkind husband,

––––––––––––––––––––

150   But for me there is no other door.
154   In the 'Ikd-i-manzúm, couplets 154–163 are omitted.

155 Saying :—" Approve not so much that, by this son (my
    husband),
" My time should pass in bitterness.

" Those (man and wife) who are with us in this lodging
" —I see not that they are, like me, disturbed in heart.

" The woman and man are together such friends,
" That thou mayst say—they are two kernels, and one
    husk.

" During this time, on my husband's part, I have not seen,
" That, he once smiled in my face."

The old man of happy omen heard this speech;
The man of ancient years was speech-knowing.

160 He gave to her an answer, sweet and pleasant,
Saying :—" Endure the burden of his violence, if he be
    beautiful of face."

It is a pity to turn away from one,
Like whom, it is not possible to find another.

Why art thou arrogant with one who, if he be arrogant,
Draws the pen on the letter of (effaces) thy existence?

Acquiesce, slave-like, to the order of God;
For, thou seest not a master like Him.

One day, my heart burned (in pity) on account of a slave;
Who, while his master was selling him, was saying :—

165 " To thee,—many a slave, better than I, may chance;
" To me,—a master, like thee, no one may be.

In Marv, there was a physician of Parí cheek,
Whose stature, in the garden of the heart, was a cypress.

To him,—no knowledge of the grief of torn hearts ;
To him,—no knowledge of his own sick eye.

A sorrowful wanderer relates a tale,
Saying :—" Some time, I had love for the physician.

" I desired not my own health ;
" Lest that the physician should not, again, come to me."

170 There is much strong, brave, wisdom,
Which the passion of love subdues.

When the passion of love rubs wisdom's ear,
Sense is unable, again, to raise its head.

————

A certain one established (by training) an iron grasp,
Who wished to grapple with the lion.

When the lion drew him within his own grasp,
He found not, again, any force in his own grasp.

————

166   In the 'Ikd-i-manzúm, couplets 166–171 are omitted.
167   "Chashm-bímár " signifies—chashm-i-ním-khwáb, the eye, half-asleep,
of lovers ; red and intoxicated.
      With the intoxication of the wine of beauty and loveliness, he was so
intoxicated and senseless that, apart from (kata'-i-nazar) the remedy for
the heart-pain of lovers, he had not even knowledge of his own sick eye,
so that he might prepare a remedy for it.
168   " Bá kase saram khúsh búd " signifies—
              Bar kase 'áshik shudam.
              Bá kase ta'ashshuk wa mail-i-dil dashtam.
See couplets 58 and 268.

One, at length, said to him :—" Why sleepst thou, woman-
    like ?
" Strike him (the lion) with the iron fist."

175 I heard that the wretch, beneath that (lion), said :—
" It is not possible with this grasp to battle with the lion."

When love becomes audacious, as to the wisdom of the
    sage,
This, indeed, is an iron grasp and a lion.

Thou art a woman, in the grasp of lion-men,
What advantage may the iron grasp render thee ?

When love comes, speak not again of reason ;
For the ball (of reason) is captive in the power of the
    Chaugán (of love).

———

Between two uncle-born ones, marriage occurred :
Two of sun-face, of high descent.

180 To one (the wife)—it (the marriage) had chanced very
    agreeably ;
The other had become shunning and avoiding.

One possessed courtesy and Parí-like grace ;
The other kept his face towards the wall.

---

175   The first line may otherwise be rendered :—
        I heard the wretch in that (state) beneath (the lip) say :—
177   To obtain release, by the power of resolution and strong resolve,
from the grasp of imperious lust, and to arrive at the stage of thy
desire (like the pure lovers of desire, those life-playing in the valley of
the knowledge of God), is a work and labour indeed.
179   In the 'Ikd-i-manzúm, couplets 179–187 are omitted.
180   " Zan rá az mard khúsh uftáda búd " signifies—
        (a) Ta'alluk wa mihr-i-tamám ba shauhar dásht.
        (b) Zan ba shauhar rághib wa masrúr búd.
    The student should note the use of " uftádan " in these two lines.

One used to adorn her own body ;
The other used to ask for his own death from God.

The old men of the village caused the husband to sit (before
    them),
Saying :—" To thee, is no love for **her** ; to her, give the
    dowry."

He laughed and said :—" With a hundred sheep,
" Deliverance from bonds is not loss ! "

185 The one of Parí-face, with her own nail, flayed her skin,
Saying :—" With this number of sheep, how can I ever be
    patient, as to my friend ?

" Not a hundred sheep, but six hundred thousand,
" Are unnecessary,—without seeing the face of my lover ! "

Whatever keeps thee engaged with a friend,
—If thou desirest truth,—it is thy heart-ease (mistress).

A certain one to one of distraught state, wrote,
Saying :—" Desirest thou hell, or heaven ? "

He said :—" Ask not of me, this matter ;
" I approve what He approves for me."

190 A certain one spoke to Majnún, saying :—" Oh one of
    auspicious foot !
" What happened to thee, that thou comest not again to
    Hayy ?

" Perhaps, the passion for Laila, in thy brain, remains not ;
" Thy fancy turns ; and desire remains not ? "

When the helpless one heard, he wept bitterly,
Saying :—" Oh sir !   Keep thy hand from my skirt.

---

185   "Taghábun" signifies—ziyán-kárí áwardan.

" I have, indeed, a heart,—sorrowful and torn ;
" Pour not thy salt on my wound.

" Separation is not a proof of patience ;
" For, separation is often a necessity."

195 He said :—" Oh one fidelity-possessing, of happy disposi-
        tion !
" Utter the message, which thou hast for Laila."

He replied :—" Take not my name before the beloved ;
" For (to mention) my name, where she is, is violence."

———

A certain one took up reproach against Mahmúd of Ghaznín,
Saying :—" Áyáz has no (great) beauty.   Oh wonder !

" The rose, which has neither colour nor perfume,—
" The nightingale's passion for it is wonderful."

One uttered this matter to Mahmúd ;
He writhed much on himself, in reflection,

200 Saying :—" Oh sir ! my love is for his disposition,
" Not, for his stature, and good height."

I heard that, in a defile, a camel
Fell ; and, a chest of pearls broke.

The king expanded his sleeve for plunder ;
And, thence urged his horse with speed.

The horsemen (of the retinue) went after the pearls and
        coral ;
They became, in search of plunder, separated from the king.

Of the attendants, neck-exalting, there remained
None, behind the king, save Áyáz.

205 He glanced, saying :—" Oh one heart-enchanting, fold in
        fold !
    " What hast thou brought from the plunder ? "   He
        replied :—" Nothing.

    " I galloped in rear of thee ;
    " I quitted not service for wealth."

If thou hast propinquity, in the Court (of God),
Be not careless of the King, for wealth.

It is contrary to religion, that the friends of God ;
Should ask for anything, save God, from God.

If, as to a friend, thy eye is intent upon his beneficence,
Thou art in the desire of thyself, not in the desire of thy
        friend.

210

So long as thy mouth is open, through avarice ;
The secret (of God) from the hidden comes not to the ear
        of the heart.

Truths are a decorated house ;
Lust and concupiscence are dust up-raised.

Seest thou not, that wherever the dust has risen,
The sight beholds not, though man be possessed of vision.

———

By chance I and an old man from Faryáb
Arrived at a water (of a river) in the soil of the West.

---

205   " Dilbur pech pech " signifies—
                (a) Maḥbúb-i-muẓá'af wa mustaḥkam.
                (b) Dil-rabáyanda dar kham-i-zulf-i-tábdár.
        Oh heart-ravisher, in the curl of the curling-curl !
208   The Persians often use the Arabic plural in a singular sense, as :—
                Sing. ḥúr   Plur. ḥúrí.
                „ ḥamám   „ ḥamámat.
211   Truths are a decorated house, around which lust and concupiscence
    are as dust up-raised. Therefore the eye of those possessed of avarice
    reaches not to it (the decorated house), and admittance to them is denied.
213   Faryáb is a town in Turkistán.
        In the 'Iḳd-i-manẓúm, couplets 213–236 are omitted.

I had one diram; they took
Me, in a boat; and, left the darvesh.

215 The Ethiopians (boatmen) urged the vessel, like smoke;
For the commander of that vessel was one, God-not
    fearing.

From thought of my companion, to me weeping came;
He laughed a horse-laugh, at my weeping, and said :—

" Oh one full of wisdom! suffer not grief for my sake;
" That One, who takes the boat, brings me."

He spread the prayer-carpet on the surface of the water;
—I thought, is it fancy; or (do I behold it) in a dream?—

From amazement, my eye, that night, slept not;
In the morning, the old man glanced at me, and said :—

220 " Oh friend of happy judgment! remainst thou astonied ?
" A boat brought thee ! and, God me ! "

Why do not the people of prayer believe to this extent,
That certain pious men may go in water and fire ?

The child, who has no knowledge of fire,
The loving mother protects.

Then those, who are immersed in religious fervour,
Are, night and day, in the eye of the protection of God.

---

215   "Ná-khudá" is contracted from—náv-khudá. Had the commander
of the vessel feared God he would have taken the darvesh.

221   " Abdál" (*sing.* badíl) are those by reason of whom God continues the
world in existence; they go fearlessly into fire and water, and pass un-
harmed; they are seventy in number, of whom forty are in Syria and
the remainder elsewhere.

    "Ahl-i-da'wa" signifies—ahl-i-dunyá, people attentive to the exterior,
but who know not God from the heart (the Pharisee).

God preserves (Ibráhím) the friend of God from the heat
    of the fire;
As the wooden-cradle of Musa (the speaker of God) from
    the whirl-pool of the Nile.

225 When a boy is in the hand of a swimmer,
    He fears not, though the Euphrates be broad.

How mayst thou walk on the surface of the sea,
Like men (of God), when, on dry land, thou art wet of
    skirt (sin-stained)?

———

Wisdom's path is not, save turning on turning;
Before holy men there is nothing, save God.

One can say this to the one truths-knowing;
But, the people of argument cavil,

Saying:—"Then the sky and earth—what are they?
"The son of Ádam, and rapacious and non-rapacious
    beasts what are they?"

230 Oh wise man! thou didst ask an approved matter;
If the answer be agreeable to thee, I will speak,

Saying:—"The plain, and sea, and mountain, and sky,
" Parí and Ádam-born, and demon, and angel—

" All, whatever they are,—are less than He;
" For, they took the name of existence by His existence.

---

225   In the first line "bar" is redundant.

228   "Haká-ik-shinás" signifies—'urfá (*sing.* 'árif), those who make a
certainty of attaining their objects by purification and bringing themselves to perfection.
    "Ahl-i-kiyás" signifies—sages who make proof of religious points by
sight and argument.

232   The author utters not a negation as to their existence, for all things
are of God; without Him there is nothing, as is the belief of some sects
of Súfís.

" Before thee, the sea, in wave-motion, is mighty ;
" The shining sun, in the zenith, is lofty.

" But, how do people of external form find the trace,
" To the country, where the lords of truth are ?

235　" Saying :—' If it be a sun, it is not even an atom ;
" And, if it be seven rivers, it is not even a drop of water.' "

When the Sultán of Honour (God) draws forth His
　　　standard (appears),
The world draws its head into the collar of non-existence.

———

The Ra,is of a village, with his son, on a certain road,
Passed by the centre of a monarch's army.

The son beheld the heralds, and sword, and battle-axe ;
Coats of satin, waist-belts of gold.

Warriors, bow-possessing, and prey-striking ;
Slaves, quiver-bearing, and arrow-casting.

According to the author, the possible existence (of a creation) in connection with the necessary existence (God the Creator) is in the stage
of nonentity ; and, though possibilities (of creation) are great, they are
small in comparison with the greatness of God.

With the Ṣúfís the display of argument on the part of sages is impossible, for they say that reason, in the understanding of this, is dismissed, even as in the understanding of probabilities the senses are out
of office.

They call the Ṣúfís " ṭá,ifa,e wujúdiya." The word Ṣúfí comes from
the Arabic word " ṣúf " signifying wool. In former days the Ṣúfís wore
a blue woollen garment of harsh texture ; for good clothing could not
then be made of wool. In Persia, the educated people are in favour of
Ṣúfí-ism. The belief, set forth in couplet 232, is attributed to Revelation and Apocalypse.

234　" Ahl-i-ṣúrat " signifies—aṣḥáb-i-ẓáhir, which is opposed to ahl-i-
ma'ní.

235　To those regarding God's grandeur, the sun, world-illuminating, is
less than an atom.

240 This one,—a garment of painted silk on his body ;
That one,—a royal cap on his head.

The son, when he beheld all that pomp and splendour,
Saw the exceeding meanness of his father,

Whose state changed, and whose colour went ;
From fear, he fled to a cave.

The son said, at length, to him :—" Thou art the Ra,is of
        a village ;
" Thou art, in chieftainship, of the great ones.

" What chanced to thee, that thou didst sever the hope of
        life ;
" Didst tremble, willow-like, with the blast of terror ? "

245 He replied :—" Yes ; I am chief, and order-giver ;
" But, my honour is (only) so long as I am in the village."

The great ones (holy men) are terror-struck, on that
        account,
That they have been in the Court of the King (God).

Oh simpleton ! thou art, in the village, inasmuch
As thou attributest such importance to thy own person.

The eloquent uttered no word,
On which, Sa'dí utters not a parable.

———

Perhaps, thou mayst have seen, in the garden or meadow,
        how
The fire-fly gleams at night, lamp-like ?

---

243   In the second line the second " sar " is redundant.
249   " Kirmake " comes from " kirm."   The " ak " is added to render the
    word diminutive ; the final " e " is " yá,e waḥdat."

250 One said to it:—" Oh fire-fly, night-illuminating !
　　" What is the matter with thee, that thou comest not forth
　　　　by day ? "

Behold—the fiery fire-fly, earth-born,
What answer it gave from its head of luminosity.

" Day and night, save in the desert, I am not ;
" But, in the sun's presence, I am not manifest."

————

In a city of Syria, tumult occurred ;
They seized an old man of happy nature.

Within my ear, still is that speech,
—When they placed fetters on his feet and hands,—

255 Which he uttered :—" If the Sultán (God) makes not the
　　　　signal,
　　" To whom, is there the boldness to plunder ? "

It is proper to hold such an enemy (the plunderer), a friend ;
For, I know the Friend (God) appointed him over me.

If there be respect and rank ; or, if contempt and bonds,—
I know that they come from God, not from 'Umar and Zayd.

Oh wise man ! have no fear of disease ;
For, the Physician (God) sends bitter medicine.

Enjoy whatever comes from the hand of the friend ;
The sick one is not wiser than the physician.

————

260 A certain one uttered praise as to Sa'd (son) of Zangí ;
Saying :—" May there be much mercy on his tomb ! "

————

257　　" 'Umar va Zayd " stand for—A. and B.
260　　For the examination for " High-Proficiency," couplets 260–267 are
　　omitted.

He gave money, and a dress of honour; and cherished him;
Prepared for him, a dignity conformable to his skill.

When he saw—" Alláh va bas,"—on a picture of gold,
He was agitated; and plucked off the robe from his body.

From perturbation, such a flame caught his soul,
That he arose, and took the path to the desert.

One of those desert-sitting said to him :—
" What sawst thou, that thy state became changed?

265   " Thou didst, first, kiss the ground in three places ;
      " Thou shouldst not, in the end, strike the back of the
            foot (on the gold)."

He laughed, saying :—" First, from fear and hope,
" A trembling, willow-like, fell on my limbs.

" Finally, from the majesty of—' Alláh va bas "
" Neither thing, nor person, appeared (worthy) in my
      eye."

———

Of a certain one like me, the heart to the power of a
      person
Was pledged; and, he endured much contempt.

After (regarding him for) learning and wisdom,
They proclaimed him by (beat of) drum for madness.

---

262   " Alláh va bas " signifies—Alláh káfí; the word " va " is redundant.
On seeing the illumination of " Alláh va bas," which, in gold, was embroidered on that robe, he severed his heart from the world; and
drawing it off from his shoulder, in perturbation, rent it.

265   " Zadan pusht-i-pá,e " signifies—lakad zadan ; tark zadan.

268   " Dil ba dast-i-kase girán búdan " signifies—bar kase 'áshik shudan.
See couplet 168.
      In the 'Ikd-i-manzúm, couplets 268 to 283 are omitted.

270 For the friend, he used to bear the violence of the enemy;
For the poison (even) of a friend is a great antidote.

He used to suffer pushing on the back of the head, from
    the hands of his friends ; .
Forehead brought forward (to the blows) nail-like.

Fancy made tumult as to his head, in such a way,
That, it made the roof of his brain kick-suffering.

Of his friends' reproaching, to him was no knowledge,
As one drowning has no knowledge of rain.

He, whose heart's foot has come against the stone (of love)
Reflects not regarding the gloss of name and fame.

275 One night the demon (Shaitán) made himself like one of
    Parí-face ;
He hastened into that young man's embrace.

In the morning, to him, was no power of prayer ;
Of his friends none was acquainted with his secret.

He plunged into a piece of water, near the roof (building),—
A marble-door, on it ice fixed.

An adviser began to reproach,
Saying :—" Thou wilt kill thyself, in this cold water."

From the just youth, a cry issued,
Exclaiming :—" Oh friend ! be silent as to so much
    reproach.

270   Everything from a friend's hand is good.
271   Kafá khurdan " signifies—gardaní khurdan, to suffer pushing, by
nape of the neck seizing.
275   " Bar wai " should be—burná.   See couplet 268.
277   The cold had fixed a door of ice upon the surface of the water.

280   " Five days, this boy fascinated my heart ;
  " For love of him, I am in such a state that I cannot be
   patient.

  " He asked not once, with sweet throat, (as to my condition),
  " Behold,—how long I endure, with soul, the burden of
   his tyranny.

  " Then as to Him,—who created my body from the dust ;
  " Created within it, by His power, the pure soul,—

  " Hast thou wonder, if I bear the burden of His order,
  " When I am perpetually immersed in His beneficence and
   grace ? "

If thou art a man of love, lose thyself ;
And, if not,—take the path of ease.

285   Fear not that God may, through love, make thee clay ;
For thou remainst, if God destroys thee.

From true grains, vegetation springs not,
Unless, first, dust gathers about them.

That gives thee acquaintance with God,
Which gives thee deliverance from thy own hand.

---

280   See couplets 268, 275.
284   " Gum <u>kh</u>wesh gír " signifies—
   (a) I<u>kh</u>tiyár-i-nístí kun.
   (b) Tark-i-<u>kh</u>udí kun, va dar yád-i-ma'shúk <u>kh</u>ud vá farámosh
    kun.
  In the 'Ikd-i-manzám, couplets 284–304 are omitted.
285   Fear not that God may through love make thee clay, or destroy thee ;
for thou wilt obtain everlasting life from this non-existence.
286   Change of state is the cause of fruition.
287   So long as thou art a captive to thyself thou canst not have knowledge of God.

For, so long as thou art self-possessing, the path to thyself
　　　is not;
And, with this subtlety, the self-less one only is acquainted.

Not the musician,—but the sound of the animal's hoof,
Is song (samá'), if thou hast love (to God) and passion
　　　(for Him).

290 The fly beats not its wings, before the one heart-dis-
　　　traught,
Who strikes not, fly-like, his hands on his head.

The one distraught in affairs (the lover of God) knows
　　　neither the bass nor the treble note;
The fakír weeps at the voice of the fowl.

The Singer (God) Himself becomes not silent;
But, not every time, is the ear open.

When those distraught practise wine-adoration,
They express intoxication, at the sound of the water-wheel.

Like a water-wheel, they begin gyrating;
Like a water-wheel, they weep bitterly on themselves.

288　So long as thou art not self-less (bekhud), thou knowst not thyself
　　—who thou art or whence thou camest, as they have said :—
　　　　" Whosoever regards himself self-less, he is informed."

290　If a fly beat its wings before the lover of God, he becomes enraptured
　　at the sound; strikes, fly-like, his hands on his head, and exhibits
　　ecstacy and " samá'."
　　　　" Samá' " signifies—hearing, song, the circular dance of the darvesh.

291　" Bum " signifies—áwáz-i-girán, a great noise.
　　　　" Zer " signifies—áwáz-i-sabuk wa barík wa narm, a quick, gentle, and
　　soft note.

292　The hidden Singer and Player (God) is never silent and never reposes ;
　　but the hearer's ear is not always open.

293　When those distraught with the wine of the love of God, and with
　　the draught of the worshippers of the wine-tavern of love, come into
　　tumult by reason of the intoxication of the wine of love, and into
　　clamour by the intoxication of the wine of affection, they display rapture
　　and ecstacy at the sound of the water-wheel.

295 With resignation, they carry their head into the collar (of
    reflection);
When power (of patience) remains not, they rend the
    collar (in perturbation).

Reproach not the darvesh, bewildered and intoxicated
    (with love),
Who is immersed in the sea of God; for that reason, he
    strikes hand and foot.

Oh brother! I say not samá', what it is (lawful, or not);
Perhaps, I know not the hearer, who he is (a lover of
    God, or not)?

---

295   "Sar dar giríban burdan" signifies—
        (*a*) Gardan nihádan.
        (*b*) Murákibat kardan.
        (*c*) Fikr wa andesha kardan.

In resignation to God, they sit, head on the knee of reflection; and
whenever, in the stage of witnessing the splendour of God, power of
restraining the effulgence of the rays of glory remains not, they rend
the collar in perturbation.

296   In the phraseology of Súfí-ism the hearing of a pleasant sound is
"samá'." By a certain quality this sound brings the hearer into
motion, as they have said:—

    "The hearing of a pleasant modulated sound is the inciter of the
        heart."

When the hearer comes, by reason of this sound, into motion, I
observe that the motion is either modulated, or not modulated. If it
be modulated, they call it *dancing* (rakṣ), and, if not modulated, *agitation* (iẓṭiráb), or "samá'."

When the "samá'" is the cause of motion, they call the motion itself
"samá'," after the fashion of naming the thing caused (rakṣ) by the
name of the cause (samá').

When a person hears this pleasant sound, a certain state, called
ecstasy (wajd) is created within him. When, involuntarily, not through
sport or in the way of the sinner, such a state (wajd) is produced within
him, "samá'" is lawful, otherwise unlawful. The impropriety (ḥurmat)
of sport and mirth, on hearing a pleasant sound, is not because the
"samá'" is modulated, or that it is a pleasant sound. The listening to
modulated metrical utterances of God's word, and the traditions of His
Prophet, and the words of pious men, and to nightingales and men of
fine voice, would then have been unlawful; but no one has said so.

If from the tower of truth (of God), his bird (soul) flies,
The angel remains below his journeying.

If he be a man of sport and pastime and mirth,
The demon (of lust) becomes stronger within his brain.

300 How is the lust-worshipper a man of samá' ?
At the pleasant sound, the one sleeping rises, not the one
    intoxicated.

By the moving wind, the rose becomes disturbed ;
Not, the fire-wood, which one can split only with an axe.

The world is full of samá', and intoxication, and distraction,
But, what does the blind man behold in the mirror ?

---

299   The difference between song (sarod) and melody (naghma) depends
upon the degree of ability and rank of the hearer.

    If the bird of fancy is the hearer from the tower of the knowledge of
God (that is, the nest of truth, " ma'ní," is in his fancy), his flight will
reach to a place where the angel is impotent as to his flight.

    But, if he be a lust-worshipper, his imperious lust will become
stronger, and will incline him to his sins.

300   " Mard-i-samá' " signifies—ḳábil-i-samá'.

    The lust-worshipper is incapable of hearing " samá' " and song (sarod),
for he is in the sleeping stage [careless of intoxication (masti) and the
relish of the love of God], not intoxicated and senseless with wine of the
love of God.   He, sleeping, becomes awake at the pleasant sound.

    The lovers of God are all, with wine of love, intoxicated and senseless.

    Again :—He who is a lust-worshipper is not of the people of " samá'."
When the lovers of God hear the sound of the song of praise to God,
the hearing of such sound is lawful.   Hence, they have said :—

    " ' Samá' ' is lawful to that one to whom the sound of the harp
and of the shutting of a door are the same as regards enjoyment and
pleasure."

301   The one, rose-like (tender), is affected by everything.

302   Those of blind heart find not God.   They say that 'Alí (may God be
satisfied with him !) heard the sound of a conch.   One who was with
him asked, " Understandest thou what this conch says ? "

    Another of the assembly replied, " God and His Prophet, and the
Cousin of His Prophet ('Alí) know."

    Then 'Alí said, " This conch exclaims ' Oh God ! Oh God ! Oh God !
Oh truth ! Oh truth ! Oh truth ! ' "

Seest thou not—the camel at the rousing of the Arab's
    (recitation),
How joy brings him to dancing ?

What ! the camel has, in his head, tumult and joy ;
If a man has not—he is an ass.

---

305 A young man of sugar-lip used to blow the flute ;
In such a way, that he used to burn hearts in the fire,
    reed-like.

The father, oftentimes, hurled shouts at him,
With severity ; and, used to set fire to the flute.

One night, he listened to his son's performance ;
The hearing of it made him confused and senseless.

The father spoke—sweat cast up on his face,
Saying :—" This time, the reed (flute) set fire to me."

Knowst thou not—the intoxicated phrenzied ones
Why they spread forth the hands in dancing ?

310 Through events, a door opens on his heart,
He scatters his hand as to (abandons) the universe.

In memory of his Friend (God), dancing was lawful to him,
In whose every sleeve is a soul.

---

303   On their journeys the Arabs recite poetry. The camels become joyful
and display celerity.

305   Observe the rare meaning of " ámokhtan." Here it means " na-
wákhtan."
    In the 'Iḳd-i-manzúm, couplets 305–314 are omitted.

310   " Wáridát " (sing. wárid) signifies — ḥázir shavanda. In the
phraseology of Súfí-ism, wárid means that which descends into the
heart without the labour of acquisition.

311   Whosoever has these qualities, that thou mayst say " A soul of truth
is in his sleeve," dancing and hand-scattering (abandoning) are to him
lawful, in order that he may scatter the ready money of life on the
head of his friend, and the jewel of faith (in Islám) on his feet.

I allow—that thou art vigorous in swimming;
Naked,—thou canst better strike the hand and foot.

Pluck off the ragged garments of name and reputation,
    and hypocrisy;
For a man, powerless by his garment, may be drowned.

Worldly connection is a veil, and profitless;
When thou breakst the ligature, thou art one joined (to
    God).

———

315 A person said to a moth :—" Oh contemptible one !
  " Go; take a friend suitable to thyself,

  " Go on such a path, that thou mayst see the way of hope;
  " Thou, and the love of the candle is from where to where ?

  " Thou art not the samundar; circle not around the fire;
  " For, manliness is (first) necessary (for man), then con-
    flict.

  " The blind mouse (bat) goes hidden from the sun;
  " For, force is foolish against an iron grasp.

———

312   " Giriftan " signifies—farẓ kardan.

In the sea of love, calamity-exciting, and in the sea of the knowledge
of God, blood-shedding, thou canst not swim with the garments of fame
and reputation, nor with the raiment of fraud and hypocrisy.

Then pluck off the garment of existence from thy back; cast off the
ragged robe of worldly affections from thy breast.

314   " Ta'alluḳ " signifies—ta'alluḳ-i-ḥirṣ va hawá,e nafsání va amr-i-dun-
yaviy.

" Wáṣil," in Ṣúfí-ism, signifies—one who has escaped from himself;
joined God Most High ; dived into the sea of non-existence; and carried
his foot to the shore of existence, so that his trace is not visible, just as
a drop in the ocean becomes untraceable.

" Ḥijáb " signifies—a veil, or hinderer of union, between thee and
God.

316   The candle is a burner, and thou (the moth) hast a capacity for
burning. The love of the candle, which is the enemy of thy life, befits
thee not.

" The person, whom thou knowst to be thy enemy ;
" To take for a friend is not (the part) of wisdom."

320 No one says to thee :—" Thou dost do good
" When thou placest thy life in the desire of his love.

" The beggar who, of a king, asked (in marriage) for his
        daughter,
" Suffered pushing on the back of his head, and nurtured
    a vain passion.

" How may she bring into reckoning a lover like thee,
" For, the faces of kings and sultáns are towards her ?

" Think not that, in such an assembly, she
" Will exercise courtesy to a poor one like thee.

" Or if she practise gentleness towards the whole creation,
" —Thou art a helpless one ;—she will exercise severity
    to thee."

325 Behold ! the ardent moth
What it said :—" Oh wonder displayer ! if I burn, what
    fear ?

" Like Ibráhím, a fire (of love) is in my heart,
" That, thou mayst consider this (candle-) flame is to me
    a rose.

---

319   " Ján dar sar-kár-i-kase kardan " signifies—
        Fidá sákhtan-i-ján dar sar o kár-i-kase, wa 'umr-i-khud ¿irf
            namúdan.
320   " Sar o kár " signifies—
                (a) Awwal kár wa kár-i-ákhir.
                (b) Saudá,e 'ishk.
322   This may be rendered :—
            Into reckoning, a lover like thee, how may that one bring,
            Towards whom the faces of kings and sultáns are (turned) ?
325   " 'Ajab " signifies—ta'ajjub kunanda.
326   Nimrúd threw Ibráhím into the fire. God made the fire a rose-garden
        for Ibráhím's sake.

" My heart draws not the skirt of the ravishing one (the
    candle) ;
" But its love draws the collar of my soul.

" Voluntarily, I take not myself to the fire ;
" But, the chain of love is about my neck.

" Even so, I was far, when it burned me ;
" Not this moment, when the fire of love kindled in me.

330 " A beloved one, in regard to loveliness, does not do that,
" That one can speak to her of continence.

" Who reproaches me for love of the friend,
" When, slain at the friend's foot, I am content ?

" Knowst thou, why I have a lust for destruction,
" When it (the candle) is, if I am not,—it is proper.

" I will burn because it is the approved beloved,
" In whom, the burning of the friend (the moth) makes
    circulation.

" How long speakst thou to me, saying :—' Suitable to
    thyself
" ' Get a companion, compassionate to thyself ? '

335 " Admonition to that one of distraught state is as if
" Thou shouldst say to one scorpion-bitten—lament not !

" Oh astonished one ! utter not advice to that person,
" In whom, thou knowst that it will take no effect.

" To the helpless one, rein-gone from the hand,
" They say not :—' Oh boy ! urge slowly.' "

---

327   I am not the allurer of my beloved ; but, love is my allurer.
336   " Shiguft " signifies—muta'ajjib.
337   In the 'Iḳd-i-manzám, couplets 336–347 are omitted.

How pleasantly occurred this witticism in the book—Sind-
    bád :—
—" Oh son ! love is fire ; advice, wind."

The fierce fire, by the wind, becomes more lofty ;
The panther, by striking, becomes more angry.

340 When I saw, thoroughly, thou doest evil,
That thou placest my face opposite to one like thyself.

Seek one better than thyself, and reckon it gain ;
For, with one like thyself, thou losest time.

The self-worshippers go in pursuit of such as themselves ;
Those intoxicated of God go in a dangerous street (of love).

When I first possessed desire for this work,
I took up, at once, my heart from desire (of life).

One head-casting is true as a lover ;
For, one of white-liver is the lover of himself.

345 Death, in ambush, suddenly, slays me ;
It is better, indeed, that the delicate one should slay me.

When, doubtless, destruction is written on my head,
Destruction (is) most pleasant, by the hand of the beloved.

Dost thou not, one day, in helplessness, yield the soul ?
Then, it is best thou surrender it, at the feet of the beloved.

———

One night, I recollect that my eyes slept not ;
I heard that a moth spoke to a candle,

Saying :—" I am a lover; if I burn, it is lawful,
" Wherefore is thy weeping and burning ?"

50 It replied :—" Oh my poor lover !
" Honey (wax), my sweet friend, has departed from me.

" When sweetness (wax) goes away from me,
" Like (the statuary) Farhad, fire goes to my head."

The candle kept speaking,—and, every moment, a torrent
    of grief
Ran down, on its yellow cheeks,—

Saying :—" Oh claimant ! love is not thy business ;
" For, thou hast neither patience, nor the power of
    standing.

" Thou dost fly from before a naked flame ;
" I am standing, until I completely burn.

55 " If the fire of love burns thy feathers,
" Behold me, whom it burns from head to foot.

" Observe not my splendour, assembly-illuminating ;
" Consider the heat and torrent of my heart-burning.

" Like Sa'dí, whose outward form is illuminated ;
" But, if thou lookst,—his vitals are burned."

A portion of the night, even so, had not passed,
When one of Parí-face, suddenly, extinguished it.

While its smoke rose to its head, it kept saying :—
" Oh son ! this is indeed the end of love ! "

---

57   Sa'dí was "ahl-i-ḥál."   See couplet 1.
58   A little of the night yet remained.
59   The end of love is to surrender one's life.

360 This is the way (of God), if thou wilt learn ;
 By being slain, thou wilt obtain ease from the burning (of
  love).

Make not lamentation over the grave of one slain by the
  friend ;
Say :—" Praise be to God ! that he is accepted by Him."

If thou art a lover, wash not the hand of sickness (of love).
Wash the hand, like Sa'dí, of (worldly) design.

The one who sacrifices his life keeps not his hand from his
  object,
Though they rain arrow and stone on his head.

I said to thee " Beware ; go not to the ocean ;
" But, if thou goest, entrust thy body to the storm."

---

360 By dying, thou wilt obtain everlasting life.
  Observe that " kushtan " is used to express in couplet—
    358, the extinguishing of a candle.
    360, the slaying of a man.
362 The first line means—be always sick (with love).
363 " Fidá,i " is one who casts himself into dangerous places, regardless
of life, for the sake of his beloved.

CHAPTER IV.

THE pure Lord created thee from dust,
Then, oh slave, practise humility like dust.

Be not avaricious, and world-consuming, and head-strong;
Of dust, He created thee; be not like fire.

When the horrent fire exalted its neck,
The dust cast down its body in abjectness.

When that (the fire) showed head-exaltation; this, abase-
    ment;
They made—of that, a demon; of this, a man.

———

A rain-drop dropped from a cloud;
It became ashamed, when it beheld the amplitude of the
    ocean.

Some say that the phrase " world-consuming " qualifies " ḥarís."
Couplets 4 and 5 form a " ḳaṭ'a-band."
In the 'Iḳd-i-manzúm, couplets 5 to 21 are omitted.
The Ḳurán says :—" Verily, we have created man from black clay,
kneaded; and, before his creation, jinn, from red fire, flame-possessing
and burning.
" Tan ba becháragí andákhtan " signifies —
        Tawáẓu' farotaní kháksárí kardan.

Saying :—" Where the ocean is, what am I ?
" If it be ; by God ! then, I am not."

When it regarded itself with the eye of contempt,
A shell cherished it with fervour in its bosom.

The sky caused its work to reach to the place (of honour),
Where, it became the famous royal pearl.

It obtained loftiness, in that it became low ;
It beat the door of non-existence, until it became existent.

----

10 A wise youth of pure disposition
Came forth from the sea, at the barrier of Rúm.

They observed in him,—excellence, and austerity, and dis-
    cretion ;
They placed his chattels in a precious place (a masjid).

One day, the chief of the 'Ábids (the shaikh) spoke to the
    man,
Saying :—" Sweep up the chips and dust of the masjid."

As soon as the man, road-travelling (to God) heard this
    speech,
He went forth ; and, none saw again a trace of him.

The religious brethren (the Súfís), and the shaikh con-
    jectured,
Saying :—" The fakír has no solicitude for service."

15 The next day, a servant (of the monastery) seized him on
    the road,
Saying :—" Through faulty judgment, thou didst not well.

----

12   " Sar-i-ṣálihán " signifies—imám ; shaikh ; peshwá,e neko kárán.
13   " Ráh-rau " signifies—sálik ; ravanda,e sharí'yat va taríḳat va haḳíḳat.

" Oh boy, self-approving ! knowst thou not,
" That by service, men attain to rank ?

From the power of truth and ardour, he began to weep,
Saying :—" Oh friend, life-cherishing, heart-illuminating !

" In that abode (the masjid), I beheld neither dust, nor
　　　refuse ;
" In that pure place, I (only) was polluted.

" I consequently took the retreating step,
" Saying :—' The masjid pure of dust and chips (myself)
　　　is well.' "

20 For the darvesh, there is only this path ;
That he hold his own body subjected.

Is exaltation necessary to thee ?　Choose humility ;
For there is only this ladder to that roof (of exaltation).

I have heard that, once upon a time, on the morning of
　　　an 'íd,
Báyizid came out of the hot bath.

22　　They call him Báyizid the Bustání ; but his name was Ṭaifúr bin 'Ísa
bin A'dam Surshán.　His death occurred in A.H. 281 or 304.

　　Abú Músa, his disciple, says that Báyazid relates :—

　　In a dream I beheld God Most High.　I said, " How is the path to
Thee ? "　He replied, " When thou passest out of thyself, thou
arrivest."

　　In a dream they beheld Báyizid, after death, and asked, " What is
thy state ? "　He replied, " The angels said to me, ' Oh, old man, what
hast thou brought ? '　I said, ' When a darvesh goes to a king's country,
they say not to him, " What broughtst thou ? "　but " What wishst
thou ? " ' "

　　Báyizid, at the time of death, said :—

　　　　" Neither did I worship Thee, save with negligence ;
　　　　　Nor did I serve Thee, save with carelessness."

A certain one, unknowingly, a basin of ashes,
Cast down, from a house, on his head.

He spoke,—turban and hair polluted,
Rubbing the palm of his hand thankfully on his face,—

25 Saying :—" Oh lust of mine ! I am worthy of the fire (of
        hell) ;
" Why draw I together my face for a single ash ? "

The great showed not regard to themselves ;
Desire not God-beholding from one self-beholding.

Greatness is not in reputation and speech ;
Exaltation is not in pretension and conceit.

Humility exalts the head of thy sublimity ;
Arrogance casts thee to the dust.

One, head-extending, of fierce temper falls to the neck (in
        a pit) ;
Is exaltation necessary to thee ?—seek not exaltation.

30 Seek not for the way of Islám from one world-proud ;
Seek not God-beholding from one self-beholding.

If rank be necessary to thee,—like the mean,
Look not at persons, with the eye of contempt.

How may the sensible man entertain the idea,
That high worth is in head-mightiness ?

---

30   In the 'Ikd-i-manzúm, couplets 30 to 41 are omitted.
    " Maghrúr-i-dunyá " signifies—one in love with the pomp of the
world.

Seek not rank more renowned than this,
That the people should call thee :—" One of approved dis-
    position."

No ;—when one like thyself uses haughtiness to thee,
Thou, with wisdom's eye, considerst him not great.

35 If thou displayst arrogance,—thou also, even so,
Appearst, as those haughtiness-displaying appear to thee.

When thou art standing on the lofty house,
—If thou art wise—laugh not at the fallen.

There came down off his feet, many a standing one,
Whose place, the fallen took.

I allow that thou art thyself free from defect ;
Exercise not reproaching on the faulty.

This one has, in his hand, the door-ring of the Ka'ba ;
That one is fallen, intoxicated, in the tavern.

40 If God calls this one,—who may not permit him ?
And, if He drives away that one,—who may bring him
    back ?

Neither is that one strength-finder by his own (good)
    deeds !
Nor for this one is the door of repentance shut in the face.

A compiler of the traditions, thus related, in talk,—
That, in the time of 'Ísa (on Him be peace !)

A certain one had squandered his life ;
Had passed it in ignorance and error.

---

42   This tale occurs in the Bible, Luke xviii. 10-13.

One bold, of black deeds, of hard heart ;
Through his uncleanness, Iblís was ashamed of him.

45 His time, uselessly accomplished ;
Through him, not a single soul rested, so long as he lived.

His head void of wisdom, but full of grandeur ;
His belly fat with forbidden morsels.

With non-uprightness, one, garment-stained,
With shamelessness, one, house-plastered.

Neither one of foot straight-travelling, like those seeing ;
Nor one of ear, like the man, advice-hearing.

The people fleeing from him, like the bad year ;
Pointing him out, together from afar, like the new moon.

50 His harvest (of life) lust and concupiscence burned ;
A grain of good repute ungathered.

He of black deeds urged his pleasure in such a way,
That, in the Book, no place for writing (his deeds) re-
        mained.

A sinner, and one self-opiniated, and lust-worshipper,
Night and day, in carelessness, drunk and intoxicated.

I heard that 'Ísa entered from the desert ;
He passed by the cell of a certain 'Ábid.

The recluse came down from a window ;
He fell, head on the earth, at His feet.

---

49   As people dislike the bad (drought) year and avoid it, so they fled
from him, and pointed him out, with the finger, from afar.
    In some copies, "sále búd" occurs instead of "chú sál-i-bad"; the
first line will then run :—
        Like the year, the people were fugitives from him.
    The word " sále" (a year) is introduced, in this case, to mark exces-
sive avoidance and abhorrence ; for, a year is a long period of time.

55 From afar, the ill-starred sinner,
Moth-like, astonied at them, by (their) splendour.

Reflecting, with regret, ashamed ;
Darvesh-like before one wealth-possessing.

Ashamed, beneath his lip excuse-asking, with heart-
      burning,
On account of whole nights passed in carelessness.

Tears of grief raining, cloud-like, from his eye,
Saying :—" Alas ! my life in carelessness passed.

" I threw away the ready money of dear life ;
" A particle of goodness unacquired.

60 " Let there never be one, like me, living ;
" For, his death (is) much better than his living.

" That one escaped, who died in childhood !
" For, he bore not the aged head of shame (to the grave).

" Oh World-Creator ! pardon my sin ;
" For, if it come with me (to the Resurrection) it will be
      a bad companion."

In this corner, the old sinner weeping,
Saying :—" Oh hand-seizer ! come to the complaint of my
      state."

His head, in shame lowered,
The water of remorse, with lamentation and desire running.

65 And, on that side,—the 'Ábid, head full of pride,
His eye-brows gathered together, on the sinner from afar.

Saying :—" Why is this wretch behind us ?
" The ignorant unfortunate one ! what ! is he of the same
      sort as we ?

" One steeped to the neck in fire;
" One life-given to the wind of lust.

" What good came from his soul, wet of skirt,
" That he is society for Masíh (the Messiah) and me ?

" Well would it have been, if he had taken the trouble (of
      his person) from before me ;
" (If) he had gone to hell, after his own deeds.

70 " I am constantly vexed by his unpleasant countenance ;
" Lest that the fire of his sins should fall on me.

" At the place of assembling, when the assembly becomes
      present,
" Oh God! make not Thou my assembling with him."

In this, he was; and, from the One of glorious qualities, a
      revelation
Came to 'Ísa,—on Him be blessing !—

Saying :—" If this one be learned, and that one ignorant,
" The prayers of both have come to My acceptance.

" The one of wasted time, and inverted days,
" Bewailed before Me, with weeping and heart-burning.

75 " Whosoever comes to Me, in helplessness,
" Him, I cast not down from the threshold of mercy.

" I pass over his ugly (sinful) deeds;
" I bring him, by My own grace, into Paradise.

" But, if the devotion-zealot has shame,
" That he should be fellow-sitting with him in Paradise,

" Say—Have no shame of him, on the Resurrection Day;
" For, they will carry that one (the sinner) to heaven;
      and, this one to hell.

" If the liver of that became blood, through heart-burning
　　and sorrow;
" And, if this one relied on his own devotion,

80 " Knew he not that in the Court of the Independent One
　　(God),
" Helplessness is better than pride and presumption?

" Whose garment is pure, but walk of life impure,—
" For him, no key to hell's door is necessary.

" At this threshold of God, thy weakness and wretchedness
" Are better than thy devotion, and self-beholding."

When thou reckonedst thyself among the good, thou art
　　bad;
Self-sufficiency is not contained in godship.

If thou art a man, speak not of thy own manliness,
Not every jockey carries off the ball (of victory).

85 He is an onion, all husk,—that one skill-less,
Who thought there was, within him, a brain pistachio-nut-
　　like.

Devotion of this sort is of no use;
Go; bring excuse for the fault of thy devotion.

That ignorant one enjoys not the fruit of devotion,
Who to himself is good; and, to the people bad.

Whether a vagabond of confused distracted fortune;
Or, a devotee, who, on his body, practises severity—what
　　difference?

81　　The key to hell's door lies in
　　　　　　　　Fisk va fajúr va 'asiyán.
　　See chap. v. complet 168.

Strive with abstinence and fear of God, and truth, and
  purity ;
But add not to the merit of the Chosen One (Muhammad).

90 Desire not whiteness (purity) beyond limit,
Saying :—It is disgusting ; what room for blackness ?

Of wise men speech remains a token ;
Of Sa'dí, remember this one word :—

" The sinner, God-fearing
" Is better than the saint, devotion-displaying."

—————

A certain lawyer of tattered garment, of straitened hand,
Sate down in the foremost ranks, in the hall of the Kází.

The Kází very sharply glanced at him ;
The officer of the court seized his sleeve, saying :—" Rise !

95 " Knowst thou not, that thy place is not the highest !
" Sit lower, or go, or stand.

" Not every one is worthy of the chief-place ;
" Munificence is in grace ; and rank, in worth.

—————————————

89   In Ṣúfí-ism, " zuhd " signifies—berún ámadan az dunyá. Make not
pride thy occupation ; consider not excess lawful ; preserve limit (mode-
ration) in every matter.
 The Prophet—with all his devotion and purity, and power of pro-
phesying, and message-bringing, and sublime rank—chose humility ;
put not his foot beyond limit, in any matter ; and confessed to the
defect of his devotion.
90   Whenever, beyond limit, whiteness increases, it is disgusting, and
resembles disease.
 In every matter, to pass beyond limit and not to preserve bounds, is
indecorous ; nay, it brings loss upon the face of the work.
 When some of the " Companions " exercised asceticism, Muḥammad
forbade their going deeply in devotion.

" What need to thee of anyone's advice ?
" This very shame is to thee sufficient torture.

" Every one, who sate, with honour, lower down,
" Falls not with contempt from above to below.

" Exercise not boldness, in the place of the great ;
" Display not lionishness, when thou hast not the power of
        grasp."

When that wise one of darvesh complexion saw
That his fortune sate down and rose up to battle,

A sigh, like fire, came forth from the helpless one ;
Than the place where he was, he sate lower down.

The lawyers prepared the path of strife ;
They hurled—the " not," and " I do not agree."

They opened together the door of contest ;
Neck made long with—" not ; and—" yes."

Thou wouldst have said—the courageous cocks are in
        battle ;
Entangled, they fell on each other with beak and claw.

This one, from anger beside himself, like one intoxicated ;
That one, beating both his hands on the ground.

They fell into a difficulty, exceedingly intricate ;
In the solution of which, they could find no path.

The one of tattered garment, in the lowest ranks,
Entered the contest, with force, like a roaring lion.

He said :—" Oh chiefs of the law of the Prophet !
" With the traditions, and revelations (of the Kurán), and
        law, and the principles of Islám,

" Proofs, strong and real, are necessary ;
" Not, the veins of the neck (swelling) in hot altercation.

110 " To me, also are the chaugán (bat) of sport and ball."
They said :—" If thou knowst well, speak."

Then he, who sate at the knee of respect,
Opened his tongue, and closed their mouths.

With the reed of eloquence of description, which he possessed,
He pourtrayed on their hearts, like the picture of a ring-
  stone :

Drew his head from the street of simile to reality ;
Drew the pen upon the head of the letter of (effaced) the
  claim.

On every side, they shouted ;—" Afrín ! Afrín ! "
Saying :—" On thy wisdom and genius, a thousand
  praises ! "

115 The dun horse of speech, he urged so far,
That the Kází, ass-like, remained behind in the mire.

He came forth from his robe and turban ;
He sent them, with reverence and courtesy, to the one,
  garment-tattered.

Saying :—" Alas ! I recognised not thy worth ;
" I was not engaged in thanks for thy auspicious arrival.

" With so great a capital of eloquence, I grieve,
" That I behold thee, in such a rank (the lowest)."

The officer of the court came, with cordiality, to him,
That he might place the turban of the Kází, on his head.

120 " With hand and tongue, he forbade him saying :—" Be it
  far from me !
" Place not, on my head, the foot-link of pride.

" For, to-morrow, towards those wearing old garments
　　(the poor),
" Heavy will my head become with the turban of fifty
　　yards.

" When they call me Maula and chief magistrate,
" Men will appear contemptible in my eyes.

" Is drinking-water ever different,
" If its vessel be golden, or earthen ?

" Wisdom and brain, within man's head, are necessary ;
" For me, like thee, a beautiful turban is unnecessary.

" A person is not of worth, through head-greatness ;
" The gourd of great head is even without a kernel.

" Exalt not the neck with turban and beard :
" For, the turban is cotton ; and, the moustache, dry
　　herbage.

" Those who, in form (only) are man-like,
" Best indeed it is, that they be silent, picture-like.

" To the extent of one's skill, it is proper to seek dignity :
" Make not, Saturn-like, loftiness and misfortune.

" Great is the greatness of the mat-reed,
" In which, indeed, is the intrinsic quality of the sugar-
　　reed.

" With this (deficient) wisdom, and spirit,—I call thee no
　　one,
" Even if a hundred slaves go behind thee.

In future my head will be for the poor full of awe ; and they will
appear to me contemptible.
　The student should note the idiom of the original in the first line.
　Even so are the Lords of Eloquence, in every garment and condition ;
difference, in their perfection and greatness, occurs not.

" How well said the small shell in the clay,
" When an ignorant one, full of avarice, took it up,—

" No one will purchase me for any thing;
" Wind me not, in foolishness, in silk (like a jewel).

" A beetle has that very worth which is its,
" Even if it sate amidst tulips.

" The rich man is not, by property, better than a person;
" If the ass puts on satin-housings,—he is an ass."

135 In this way, the sensible man (the lawyer), speech-uttering,
Washed malice, with the water of speech, from the heart.

The speech of one heart-troubled is hard;
When thy enemy falls, display not sluggishness.

When power reaches thee, pluck out the enemy's brain;
For, the opportunity washes down the dust (of grief) from
    the heart.

The Kází remained captive to his own violence, in such a
    way
That he said :—" This is indeed a disastrous day ! "

Through astonishment, he bit his hands, with his teeth;
His eyes, like the two stars near the pole, remained fixed
    on him.

140 And thence, the young man turned the face of resolution;
He went out, and no one again found his trace.

Clamour arose from the chiefs of the assembly,
" Say, whence is one of such a bold eye ? "

---

133   It is said that when a beetle perceives the perfume of the rose,—it dies.
    " Ja'l " signifies—sargín, ghalatang.
135   The first line may otherwise be rendered :—
        In this way, the man, speech-uttering, quickly.

A herald went from the front, and ran in every direction,
Saying :—" Who saw a man of this description and ap-
    pearance ? "

One said ;—" Of this kind of sweet speech,
" We know, in this city, Sa'dí ; and him only.

" On him be a hundred thousand blessings that he thus
    spoke ;
" The bitter truth—behold ! how sweetly he uttered it."

———

15 There was in the town of Ganja,—one king-born,
Who was unclean and tyrannical—may it be far from
    thee !—

Singing and intoxicated, he entered a masjid,
Wine in his head, and bumper-glass in hand.

In a cell, a devotee was dwelling,
One, tongue-entangling (in truth); and, heart-pure (as to
    malice).

Some persons for his talking, assembled.
—When thou art not learned, be not less than the
    hearer.—

When that refractory steed (the prince) exercised disre-
    spectfulness,
Those dear ones (the assembly) became desolate of heart.

50 When the foot of the prince is wicked,
Who is able to express a breath concerning the well-known
    order ?

———

44   In the 'Iḳd-i-manzúm, couplets 145–201 are omitted.
50   When the Prince places his foot on forbidden things.

Garlic overpowers the rose-perfume ;
The sound of the harp becomes weak, through the drum.

If the prohibiting of forbidden things comes from thy
    hand,
It is not proper to sit like one, handless and footless.

And if thou hast not the hand of power, speak ;
For, the disposition becomes pure by admonition.

When as to both hand and tongue, power is not,
Men show manliness by prayer.

155 One (of the hearers) before the sage, sitting in solitude,
Lamented and wept, head on the earth,

Saying :—" On this intoxicated rascal (the prince) once,
" Pray ; for we are tongueless and handless.

" A single ardent breath (sigh) from a thoughtful heart,
" Is stronger than seventy swords and axes."

The one, world-experienced, stretched forth his hand ;
What said he ?   " Oh Lord of high and low !

" Through fortune, this youth,—his time is happy ;
" Oh God ! keep all his time happy."

160 A person said to him :—" Oh exemplar of rectitude !
" Why desirest thou for goodness for this wretch ?

" When thou desirest good for the faithless,
" What ill desirest thou on the citizens ? "

---

151   Even so, legal orders become not current over one who is entangled in
forbidden things—fisk wa fajúr.
155   See couplet 147.

The one beholding with quick intelligence thus spoke :—
" When thou findst not the secret of my speech, agitate
　　not :

" We adorned not the assembly with raving nonsense ;
" We desired his repentance from the justice of the Creator.

" For every one, who returns from bad ways,
" Reaches eternal ease in Paradise.

" This pleasure of wine is indeed for five days ;
" In abandoning it,—perpetual pleasures."

This matter, which the man, speech-making (the recluse),
　　uttered,
One out of that assembly unfolded to the prince.

From rapture, water, cloud-like, came to his eyes ;
A torrent of sorrow rained on his face.

His heart burned with the fires of desire ;
Shame sewed his eyes to the back of his feet.

To the one of good appearance (the recluse) he sent a person,
Knocking at the door of repentance, saying :—" Oh griev-
　　ance-redresser !

" Be pleased to come, that I may lay down my head (at
　　thy feet) ;
" That I may put aside ignorance and non-rectitude."

The adviser (the recluse) came to the prince's court ;
He glanced into the hall of the court.

He saw sugar, and jujube, and candle, and wine ;
The assembly prosperous with wealth ; but, the men in-
　　toxicated.

Sugar and jujube here stand for—the lip of a mistress.
Candle here signifies—joking.

This one unconscious of himself; that one half-drunk;
Another poetry-spouting, wine-flagon in hand.

On one side, the minstrel's cry raised ;
On the other, the cup-bearer's voice saying :—" Drink ! "

175 The companions, with wine of red colour intoxicated,
Through sleep, the head of the harper on his bosom, harp-
  like.

Of the boon-companions, neck-exalting, there was not
An eye of any open there, save the narcissus.

The drum and harp consonant with each other ;
The flute, from the midst, brought forth a lament.

He (the recluse) ordered : they shattered (the drum and
  harp) into small pieces ;
That pure pleasure became changed to dregs.

They broke the harp and snapped the string ;
The speaker put singing out of his head.

180 They struck a stone on the wine-vessel, in the wine-house,
They placed the wine-vessel (before them), and struck off
  its neck.

The wine of red colour from the flagon, head-lowered,
Ran as blood from a slain duck.

The jar was pregnant nine months with wine :
In that calamity (of birth), it quickly cast out the daughter
  (of grapes).

They rent the belly of the leathern (wine) bag to its navel,
The blood eyes of the cup, over it, full of tears.

---

183 In some copies—the eyes of the cup, over it, bloody with tears.

He ordered :—the stone of the court-yard of the building,
They plucked up, and put anew in its place.

For, the rosy colour of the wine of ruby hue
Departed not, by washing, from the marble surface.

It is not wonderful if the sink become intoxicated,
When, it drank, on that day, so much wine.

Whosoever used again to take the harp in his hand,
Used to endure pushing (beating) of his head, drum-like,
　　at men's hands.

And, if a worthless fellow had taken a harp on his neck,
He would have rubbed his ear, guitar-like.

The young man (the prince), head-intoxicated with pride
　　and conceit,
Sate, like old men, in the corner of devotion.

The father had, many times, spoken vehemently to him,
Saying :—" Be of decent gait, and of pure speech."

He endured his father's violence, and prison, and restraint,
It was not so useful to him, as counsel.

If the gentle-speaker (the recluse) had spoken severely to
　　him,
Saying :—" Put youthfulness, and ignorance out of thy
　　head."

Imagination and pride would have prevailed over him,
That he would not have left the darvesh (the speaker) alive.

The roaring lion, through fighting, casts not away the
　　shield (surrenders not) ;
The panther thinks not of the cutting sword.

One can, with gentleness, flay the enemy's skin ;
When thou exercisest severity towards a friend, he is an
　　enemy.

No one made a hard face, anvil-like,
Who suffered not the chastising hammer on his head.

Exercise not vehemence, in speaking to an amír ;
Pursue gentleness, when thou seest that he practises
    severity.

Make thyself, by manners, concordant, with whomsoever
    thou mayst see,
Whether he be inferior, or superior.

For this one (the superior) may draw back his neck from
    pride ;
And, that one may, by thy pleasant speech, draw his head
    within thy noose.

200 One can, by sweet speech, carry away the ball (of power) ;
But one of bad disposition, constantly, endures bitterness.

Take thou, from Sa'dí, the pleasant speech ;
To the one of bitter visage, say :—" Die of bitterness ! "

———

One of sugar-laughter sold honey,
From whose sweetness, hearts become consumed.

A sweet one, waist-girt, sugar-cane like,
The purchasers about her more (numerous) than the flies.

If, for instance, she should have taken up poison,
They would have devoured it like honey from her hand.

205 One of hard life glanced at her work ;
He bore envy, in respect to her market-day.

He went, the next day, running around the world ;
Honey in his hand ; vinegar (ill-temper) on his eye-brow.

Wandered much, before and behind, clamour-making,
But, not a fly sate on his honey.

At night-time, when money came not to his hand,
He sate, with straitened heart, face to the corner.

Like a sinner, face embittered with (God's) threatening ;
Like the eyebrows of prisoners on a day of festival.

210 A woman sportively said to her husband :—
" The honey of one of bitter visage is bitter."

A bad temper takes a man to hell ;
Those of good temper only see Paradise,

Go ; drink warm water from the brink of the rivulet ;
Drink not the cool draught of one of bitter face.

It was forbidden thee to taste the bread of that one,
Who drew together his eye-brows table-cloth-like.

Sir ! put not on thyself difficult work ;
For the one of bad temper is of reversed fortune.

215 I assume—that to thee, there is neither silver, nor gold ;
To thee, the tongue also is not sweet, like Sa'dí's.

I have heard that of a learned man, God-worshipping,—
His collar, a drunken knave seized.

From that one of black heart, the man of pure heart
Suffered head-pushing, but raised not his head from
    tranquillity.

At length, one said to him :—" Art thou not also a man ?
" Endurance, in respect to this indiscreet one, is a pity."

The man of pure disposition heard this speech ;
He said to him :—" Speak not again to me in this way.

220 " The ignorant drunken one rends a man's collar :—
" Who meditates (practises) conflict with a lion-claw ?

" It befits not the learned one, that his hand,
" He should fix in the collar of the drunken, ignorant one.

" The skilful one possesses life in this way :—
" He suffers violence ; and exercises kindness."

———

The foot of one desert-sitting, a certain dog bit
With such anger, that poison dropped from his teeth.

At night, through pain, helpless, sleep took him not ;
There was, in his party, a little daughter.

225 She used violence to her father, and displayed severity,
Saying :—" Hast thou, also, indeed no teeth ?"

After weeping, the man of distressed days
Laughed, saying :—" Oh little mother, heart-illuminating !

" Although, to me—are power and poison,
" I am loth (to use) my jaws and teeth.

" It is impossible, even if I endure a sword blow on my
        head,
" That I should plunge my teeth within the leg of a dog.

" As to dogs, the nature is evil ;
" But, doggishness comes not from man."

———

230 There was a certain great one, skilful in the world ;
His slave was of depraved qualities.

———

220   Couplets 220 and 221 form a " ḳaṭ'a-band."

Through this filthy one, hair dishevelled,
He used to be as one vinegar-rubbed on the face.

Like a large male serpent, his teeth stained with poison ;
From the ugly ones of the city, pledge taken.

Continually on his face, the water of a diseased eye
Used to run, as the smell of onion (issued) from his armpit.

At cooking-time, he used to express a frown on his eye-
　　brow ;
When they had cooked, he used to strike knee (in sitting)
　　with his master.

235 Time to time, for bread-eating, his fellow-sitter ;
But if he (the master) had died, he would not have given
　　water to his hand.

Neither speaking nor the blows of a stick used to exercise
　　effect on him ;
Night and day, the house was in a state of being mined
　　(ruined) by him.

Sometimes, he used to throw thorns and chips on the road ;
Sometimes, he used to fling the hens into the well.

From his aspect, great terror used to arise ;
He used not to go to a work, from which he used to return.

A person said :—" Of this slave of bad qualities,
" What desirest thou,—manners, or skill, or beauty ?

231　　The second line may otherwise be rendered :—
　　　　　　An evil one : one with vinegar rubbed on his face.
232　　The ugly ones had pledged their ugliness to him, so that he possessed
the sum total of ugliness in the city.
　　"Az kase girau burdan" signifies—ba kase sábiķa kardan ; taķad-
dum namúdan ; az kase rihn sitándan.
234　　Observe the phrase—ba kase zánú zadan.
236　　" Kand o kob " signifies—digging and knocking ; tashwísh wa bezárí.

240   " A person, with this unpleasantness, is not worth (so
          much),
      " That thou shouldst approve of his violence, and endure
          his torment.

      " A slave,—good and of correct walk of life, I
      " Will bring to thy hand; take away this to the captive-
          seller.

      " And, if he brings thee the smallest coin, turn not away
          thy head ;
      " He is dear at any price,—if thou wishest the truth."

      The man of good disposition heard this speech ;
      He laughed, saying :—" Oh friend of auspicious family !

      " As to this boy—his nature and disposition are bad; but,
      " By him, my nature becomes good nature.

245   " When I shall have endured much from him,
      " I may be able to endure the violence of everyone."

      Endurance appears, at first, to thee, like poison ;
      But when it grows in the disposition, it becomes honey.

      ————

      No one sought the road to the ancient shaikh Ma'rúf of
          Karkh,
      Who placed not, first, his own renown, out of his head.

      I heard that a certain one came a guest to him ;
      From his sickness to death little remained.

      Head cast as to its hair; and face, as to its purity (of
          complexion) ;
      The soul clinging, by a single hair, to his body.

      ————————

247   Ma'rúf Kirkhí was one of the ancient shaikhs ; he died A.H. 200. His
      grave is at Baghdád, of which Kirkh was a quarter. People go in
      pilgrimage to his tomb to utter prayers.

250 At night, he cast himself down there, and put his pillow ;
Forthwith, he placed his hands—in clamour, and lament.

Nights, one moment, neither used sleep to seize him ;
Nor (was there) sleep to anyone, by reason of his lament.

A disturbed nature, and rough disposition ;
He died not ; but slew a people by his altercation.

From his clamour, and lamenting, and sleeping, and
      rising,—
People took the path of flight from him.

Of the men-inmates of that abode, a person (was not) ;
There remained—the powerless one, and Ma'rúf only.

255 I have heard that, many nights, on account of service,
      Ma'rúf slept not ;
Like men, he bound his waist ; and did whatever he said.

One night, sleep brought an army to his (Ma'rúf's) head ;
—How much power may the non-sleeping man exercise ?—

In a moment, when his eyes began to sleep,
The distressed traveller began to speak,

Saying :—" May there be a curse on this impure race (of
      darveshes),
" Who are (seekers of) name and fame ; but, are fraud
      and wind :

" Filthy believers, purity-wearing ;
" Deceivers, piety-selling.

260 " How knows the glutton, sleep-intoxicated,
" That a helpless one closed not his eyes ? "

----

260   " lat-ambán " signifies—harís va pur khwár va bisiyár khwár va
shikam-parast.

He uttered unlawful words to Ma'rúf,
Saying :—" Why slept he careless of him, one moment ? "

The shaikh, from generosity, endured this matter ;
The concealed ones of the haram (the women) heard.

One spoke secretly to Ma'rúf.
Saying :—" Heardst thou what the lamenting darvesh
    said ?

" Oh shaikh ! go ; after this, say :—take thy own way ;
" Take away reproach ; die in another place.

265 " Goodness and mercy are in their own places ;
    " But, generosity to the bad is evil.

" Place not a round pillow for the head of the mean ;
" The head of the man-injurer (is) best against a stone.

" Oh one of good fortune ! exercise not goodness to the
    bad ;
" For, (only) the fool places the tree in the salt soil.

" I say not—Take no care of a man,
" But waste not generosity on such as are not men.

" Act not, with qualities of softness towards the rough ;
" For, they rub not the dog's back, like the cat.

270 " If thou desirest justice, the dog, right-recognising,
    " Is better, in character, than the man ungrateful.

" Use not mercy, with ice-water, towards the mean ;
" When thou dost,—write the compensation for it on ice.

" I beheld not such a crafty person ;
" Show not mercy to this worthless one."

---

266   The second line means :—It is proper to beat his head on a stone.
270   " Ba yakh nawishtan " signifies—kár-i-taḥáṣil va be ṣabát kardan.

When the lady of the palace (Ma'rúf's wife) uttered this
    reproach,
A cry issued from the good man's heart,

Saying :—" Return, and sleep tranquil of heart ;
" Be not distressed, as to this distressed one, because he
    thus spoke.

275 " If, from indisposition, he shouted at me,
" The unpleasant speech from him came pleasantly to my ear.

" It is proper to listen to the tale of violence of such a
    one,
" Who, from restlessness, cannot slumber."

When thou seest thyself of strong state and happy,
Endure, thankfully, the burden of the feeble.

If thou art, indeed, a mere semblance, tilism-like,
Thou wilt die ; and, thy name, like thy body, will die ;

But if thou causest thyself to cherish the tree of liberality,
Thou mayst, assuredly, enjoy the fruit of good name.

280 Seest thou not that, in Karkh, the tombs are many ?
The tomb of Ma'rúf only is known.

The man pomp-worshipping displays pride ;
He knows not that grandeur is in gentleness.

An impudent one preferred his desire (in beggary) to a
    pious one,
There was not, at that time, a single acquired thing
    (money) in his girdle.

His girdle and hands were void and clean (empty) ;
Otherwise, he would have scattered gold on his face, dust-
    like.

The beggar, malignant of face, hastened out ;
In the street, he began to reproach him,

285 Saying :—" Beware of these silent scorpions ;
" Panther-renders, wool-clad.

" For, they place the knee against the heart, cat-like ;
" But, if a prey chances, they leap up, dog-like.

" The shop of fraud to the masjid brought,
" For, one can seldom find game in a house.

" Lion-men attack the káraván ;
" But, these (Súfís) pluck off the garment of men.

" White and black pieces (of cloth) stitched together ;
" Capital put together ; gold gathered.

290 " Oh excellent ! barley-sellers, wheat-exhibiting ;
" World-wanderers, night-mendicants, harvest-beggars.

" Look not at their devotion, saying :—" They are old and
     lazy ;
" For, in dancing (rapture) and ecstacy, they are young
     and vigorous.

" Why is it necessary to make prayers from a state of
     posture,
" When they can leap up to dance ?

" They are the staff of Músa, much-devouring ;
" Outwardly—so yellow of face, and emaciated.

---

291   See chap. iii.

293   When his holiness Músa went to Far'ún, and invited him to join his
faith, he displayed apparent miracles. Far'ún said, " This is all sorcery
and magic; I also can summon my own sorcerers; let us contend
together ; whichever is superior, truth is on his side." Músa consented.
When the magicians were assembled, they displayed their magic. Músa
feared. But, a revelation from the Glorious One came to him: " Oh,
Músa ! fear not, but cast thy staff on the ground." When the staff left
his hand, lo ! it became snake-like, and immediately swallowed their
sorceries.

    Músa's rod, by swallowing, became not fat ; the same is the case with
these men.

" They are neither abstinent, nor learned ;
" This, indeed, is enough—that they purchase the world
    with religion.

295 " On their body, they put a coarse cloak like that of
    Bilál ;
" With the produce of Abyssinia, they make garments
    for women.

" Of the precepts of Muhammad, thou seest in them no
    sign,
" Save the former sleep (in the afternoon), and the morn-
    ing bread.

" The belly up to the head, they have filled tight with
    morsels ;
" Like the palm-leaf basket of beggary of seventy colours.

" Beyond this, I will not speak on this matter ;
" For, it is a sin to speak of one's own walk of life."

The impudent speaker spoke of this habit (of the Súfís) ;
The eye, fault-finding, sees not skill.

300 One who has made many dishonoured,
What care has he of anyone's reputation ?

A disciple related this speech to the shaikh ;
—If thou wishst the truth, he did not wisely.

An evil one behind me spoke of my defect, and slept ;
Worse than he,—the friend, who brought (the tale) and
    uttered it.

---

295   Bilál, an Abyssinian of black colour, was the crier who announced to
the people when Muhammad prayed.

296   " Nán-i-sihr " signifies—something which Muslims eat at the close of
the night, during the Ramzán.

301   From the second line of 301 to couplet 304 is uttered by the author.

A certain one cast an arrow, and it fell on the road ;
It injured not my existence, and gave me no wound.

Thou didst take it up and come to me ;
Didst strike it violently into my loins.—

305 The pious one of good disposition laughed,
Saying :—" This is easy, say—utter a more difficult matter
        than this.

" Yet what he said ill of me is little ;
" It is one, out of a hundred of those bad deeds I know.

" These that he, through suspicion, attributed to me ;
" I, on my part, truly know that they are so.

" He joined his society with us this year ;
" What knows he of the defects of my seventy years ?

" In the world, better than I, a person, my own defect,
" Knows not,—save the Knower of my secret (God).

310 " I have not seen one of such good intention,
" Who considered my defect was this, and no more.

" At the place of assembling, if he be the evidence of my
        sin,
" I fear not hell ; for, my work is good.

" If my enemy speaks ill of me,
" Come and say :—' Take away the draft (of my defect)
        from before me.' "

Those have been men of the path of God,
Who have been the butt of the arrow of calamity.

They threw off (from the head) the hat of pride ;
They exalted the head with the crown of eminence.

---

307   " Bar man bastan " signifies—ba man isnád kardan.

315 Be submissive, while they rend thy skin ;
For the pious endure the burden of the impudent.

If, of the dust of men, they make a pitcher ;
Those reproach-making will break it with a stone.

———

King Sálih of the kings of Syria
Used to come out early in the morning with his slave.

He used to wander in the quarters of the bázár and streets,
After the manner of an Arab,—a veil bound about his face.

For, he was possessed of discernment, and was the poor
man's friend ;
Whosoever has these two qualities,—he is King Sálih.

320 He discovered two darveshes sleeping in a masjid ;
He found them distressed of heart, and heart disturbed.

In the night, through cold, sleep had not taken their eyes ;
Thinking of the sun, lizard-like.

One of those two was speaking to the other,
Saying :—" Even, on the day of the place of assembling,
there is justice.

" If these kings, neck-exalting,
" Who are in sport and pastime, and possessed of desire
and consequential airs,

" Enter Paradise with those distressed,
" I will not raise my head from the brick of the grave.

325 " Lofty Paradise is our country and abode ;
" For, to-day, the fetter of grief is about our feet.

———

322　　Only, in this world, there is no justice.

" During thy whole life-time, what pleasure didst thou
    experience from them,
" That thou shouldst, in the next world, also endure their
    trouble ?

" If Sálih there, by the garden-wall,
" Enters, I will rend his brain with my shoe."

When the man uttered this speech, and Sálih heard it,
He considered it not wisdom to be (standing) longer there.

A moment passed, when the fountain of the sun,
Washed down sleep from the eyes of the people.

330 Running, he sent for the two men, and called them;
In pomp, he sate; and, in dignity, caused them to sit.

He rained on them the rain of liberality;
He washed down, from their bodies, the dust of contempt.

After distress through cold, and rain, and torrent,
They sate with those renowned of the tribe :

Two beggars, night made day, garmentless,
Perfuming their garments over the aloe-burner.

One of them spoke privately to the king,
Saying :—" Oh king ! the world a ring in the ear (a slave)
    to thy order,

335 Those approved of God attain greatness ;
In us two slaves, what appeared pleasing to thee ?

The monarch expanded from joy, rose-like ;
He laughed, in the face of the darvesh, and said :—

" I am not such a one that, from pride of retinue,
" I contract my face, at those helpless.

---

330   " Duwán yá rawán " signifies—zúd, quickly.
          See couplet 250.

" Put thou also as to me the malignant disposition, out of
        thy head :
" Lest thou shouldst, in Paradise, display discordance.

" I opened, to-day, the door of peace ;
" Shut not, to-morrow, the door on my face.

" If thou art an accepter of the true path, choose a path
        like this ;
" When power reaches thee, take the hand of the darvesh.

" That one took not away the fruit (of pardon) of the
        Túba tree,
" Who sowed not, to-day, the seed of desire (of good
        deeds).

" Thou hast not desire,—seek not happiness ;
" With the chaugán of service, one can carry off the ball
        (of empire)."

To thee, how is there effulgence (of love) lamp-like,
Since, thou art full of thyself, as a lamp with water.

That existence gives light to the assembly,
Whose burning in the bosom is candle-like.

––––––––

A certain one had a little skill in astronomy ;
But, he possessed a head, intoxicated with pride.

From the far road, he came to Koshyár,
—A heart full of desire ; a head, full of pride.—

The sage used to sew up (close) his eyes from him,
He used not to teach him a single letter.

––––––––

In the East, men fill a glass with water and put in it oil and a wick.
This sort of lamp gives but little light.
    Koshyár was the name of a sage of Gílán.

When portionless, he resolved to return,
The sage, neck-exalting, said to him :—

" Thou hast imagined thyself full of wisdom ;
" A vase that is full—how may it take more.

350 " Thou art full of pretension ; on that account, thou goest
        empty from me :
" Come empty ; so that thou mayst become full of truth."

Sa'dí-like, in the world,—of self-consciousness,
Become void, and return full of the knowledge of God.

———

In anger, a slave turned his head from a king (fled) ;
He ordered a person to seek ; no one found him.

When he (the slave) returned, in anger and rancour,
He said to the swordsman :—" Spill his blood ! "

Thirsty for blood, the unkind executioner
Drew forth a sword like a thirsty tongue.

355 I heard that, from his straitened heart, he said :—
" Oh God ! I pardon him my blood,

" Because, always in favour, and pleasure, and fame,
" I have, in his fortune, been a friend.

" God forbid ! that, to-morrow (the Judgment Day), for
        my blood,
" They should seize him, and his enemy become joyful (by
        his punishment)."

When his speech came to the king's ear,
The cauldron of his wrath boiled no further.

———

352   " Dar " is superfluous.
        In the 'Iḳd-i-manzúm, couplets 352 to 363 are omitted.
356   " Iḳbál " signifies—pesh ámadan ; rue áwardan bar chíze ; chíze pesh-i-
kase dáshtan.

He gave (him) many kisses on his head and eyes;
He became lord of the standard, and tambourine, and drum.

360 From such a frightful place, by softness,
He caused his fortune to attain that dignity.

The design of this tale is—that soft speech
Is like water on the fire of a fiery man.

Oh friend! exercise humility to a stern enemy;
For, gentleness makes blunt the cutting sword.

Seest thou not that, in the place of meeting of sword and
  arrow,
They put on the garment of silk, a hundred-fold?

From the desolate place of a holy man, ragged garment-
  clad,
The baying of a dog came to a certain one's ear.

365 To his heart, he said:—" How is the baying of a dog
  here?"
He entered, saying:—" Where is the holy darvesh?"

From before and behind, he saw not the trace of a dog;
Save the pious man, he saw none other there.

Ashamed, he began to return;
For, shame came to him to argue about the mystery.

From within, the holy man heard the foot-sound;
He said:—" Ho! why standst thou at the door? Enter.

" Oh my resplendent eye! thoughtst thou not,
" That, from here, a dog gave tongue? I am the dog.

----

360   " Rifk" signifies—mulátifat, mulá, imat.

370 " When I saw that He purchases helplessness,
    " I put out of my head—pride, and judgment, and wisdom.

    " I made much noise, dog-like, at His door ;
    " For, I beheld not many meaner than a dog."

    When thou desirest that thou mayst attain sublime rank,
    Thou wilt attain to loftiness from the low place of
        humility.

    Those took the chief seat in this presence,
    Who placed their own worth low.

    When the torrent came with fear and haste,
    It fell headlong, from height to depth.

375 When the dew fell—humble and feeble,
    The sky carried it, with love, to the (lofty) red star
        (Pleiades-following).

    A number of the eloquent are of opinion,
    That Hátim was deaf ; believe it not.

    In the morning, there issued the buzzing of a fly,
    Which fell into a spider's net.

    All the spider's weakness and silence was deceit ;
    The fly thought it sugar ; .it was imprisonment.

    From the desire of counsel, the shaikh glanced at the fly,
    Saying :—" Oh foot-bound in avarice ! be still.

380 " Sugar and honey, and candy everywhere, are not ;
    " But nets and fetters, in the corners, are open."

---

376   Hátim, son of 'Amwánu-e-aṣamm, entitled 'Abdu-r-raḥman, belonged
    to the ancient Shaikhs' of Khurásán of Balkh. He died in Baváshjard,
    in Balkh, in A.H. 237.
        In the 'Iḳd-i-manẓúm, couplets 376 to 424 are omitted.

One of that clique of people of judgment said :—
" Oh man of the way of God ! I hold it wonderful,

" How thou didst perceive the fly's noise,
" When it came, to our ears, with difficulty !

" Since thou art acquainted with the fly's sound,
" It is not proper, after this, to call thee deaf."

Hátim, smiling, said to him :—" Oh one of quick under-
      standing !
" To be deaf is better than to be listening to foolish talk.

385 " Those, who are with me in privacy,
" Are defect-concealers and praise-scatterers.

" When I hold concealed mean qualities,
" Existence makes me weak ; (and) lust, vile.

" I show myself as though I heard not,
" Perhaps I may be free from the trouble (of bad qualities).

" When fellow-sitters consider me deaf,
" They utter whatever is good and bad of me.

" If to hear evil is unpleasant to me,
" I withdraw my skirt from bad conduct."

390 Be not at the well (of egotism), with the cord of
      praise ;
Be deaf, like Hátim, and hear thy own defects.

He sought not happiness, and found not safety,
Who turned aside the neck from Sa'di's sayings.

Is a better adviser than this Sa'dí necessary to thee ?
I know not what may chance to thee after him.

There was, in the limits of Tabríz, one dear to God,
Who was always wakeful and night-rising (in devotion).

One night, he saw a place where a thief, a noose,
Twisted and cast upon the side of a roof.

395 He informed the people, and raised a cry;
Men, from every side, arose with sticks.

When the unmanly thief heard the voice of men,
He saw no place of existing, in the midst of the danger.

Through that tumult, fear came upon him;
Flight, in season, became his choice.

From pity, the devotee's heart became wax;
For, the helpless night-thief was disappointed.

In the darkness, he, from behind came to his front;
By another road, he returned in front of him,

400 Saying :—" Oh friend ! go not; for I am a friend of thine ;
" I am, in manliness, the dust of thy foot.

" I have seen no one, like thee, in manliness ;
" Since battle-action lies in two ways only.

" One way is to come manfully before the enemy ;
" The second to carry one's life out of the contest (by
  flight).

" By these two qualities of thine, I am thy slave ;
" How art thou named; for I am the slave of thy name ?

" If, by way of liberality, it be thy opinion ;
" I may guide thee to a place which I know.

405 " It is a house, small; and the door fast shut ;
" I think not the lord of the chattels is there.

" We may place two clods, one on the other ;
" We may put one foot on the shoulder of the other (to
  reach the roof).

" Be satisfied with as much as falls to thy hand;
" It is better, than that thou shouldst return empty of
　　hand."

With cordiality, and flattery, and art,
He drew him (the thief) towards his own house.

The young night-traveller (the thief) held lowered his
　　back;
The lord of sense (the devotee) entered (the house), by his
　　shoulder.

410　Horse-housings, and turbans, and chattels which he had;
He put, from above, into his (the thief's) skirt.

And, thence he raised a shout, saying :—" Thief!
" Oh young men! (there are) recompense, and aid, and
　　hire."

The deceitful thief leaped out from the tumult,
Running, the garment of the devotee under his arm.

The man of good faith became comforted,
Saying :—" The desire of the one head distracted became
　　accomplished."

The filthy one, who pitied no one,—
The heart of a good man forgave.

415　From the mode of life of the intelligent, it is not won-
　　derful,
That they should, from magnanimity, do good to the bad.

411　　The second line means :—
　　　　　　Assist me, for recompense and reward.

In the prosperity of the good, the bad live;
Although, the bad are not people of goodness.

––––––

There was a pure heart, Sa'dí-like, to a certain one,
Who had fallen in love with one of smooth face.

He used to endure violence from the enemy, harsh-speaking,
Used to leap, ball-like, from the chaugán of hardship.

Used not to cast a frown, at any, on his eyebrows,
Used not to relinquish gentleness for harshness.

420 One, at length, said to him :—" To thee is there no shame ?
" Of all this slap-giving and stone-throwing,—is there no
      knowledge ?

" The mean make their own body fat ;
" The feeble make endurance of the enemy.

" It is not proper to pass over the fault of an enemy,
" Lest they say :—' He possessed neither power, nor man-
      liness.' "

The distraught one, distracted of head, gave to him
An answer, which it is fit to write in gold :—

" My heart is the house of the love of my friend only ;
" For that reason, malice to no one is contained in it."

425 How well said Bahlúl of happy temperament,
When he passed by a holy man, battle-seeking,—

––––––––––––––––––––

417   " Ba kase dar uftádan " signifies—bá kase 'áshik gashtan.
419   " Chín bar ábrú andákhtan " signifies—'abúsu-l-wajh gashtan.
425   Bahlúl was a saint, who feigned madness.

" If this claimant had recognised the Friend (God),
" He would not have engaged, in contest with the enemy."

If he had possessed knowledge of the existence of God,
He would have considered all people non-existent.

———

I have heard that Lukmán was of black colour;
Was neither tender, as to body; nor, delicate, as to limb.

A certain one considered him his own slave;
He was vile; he kept him (engaged) on clay-work.

430 He experienced violence, and endured his tyranny and
　　　anger;
He prepared, in one year, a house for his sake.

When the runaway slave came back to him,
Of Lukmán, a great fear came over him.

He fell at his feet, and made apology;
Lukmán laughed, saying:—" What is the use of apology?

" In a year, by thy violence, I make my liver blood;
" In a moment, how may I put grief out of my heart?

" But indeed I forgive thee, oh good man!
" For, thy gain (by my service) made not my loss.

435 " Thou didst make thy sleeping-chamber prosperous;
" For me,—skill and knowledge of God became greater.

———

426　　Whoever is a holy man, God-recognising, and Friend (God) knowing,
regards no one as an enemy.
　　The claimant here means one claiming to be of the circle of holy
men.
428　　Lukmán was a celebrated Greek philosopher. In the Kurán, God
says:—" And, verily, I have given (power of) prophecy to Lukmán."
434　　" Márá," in place of " mará," is for respect.

" Oh one of good fortune! there is, among my followers, a
　　slave,
" Whom I oftentimes order difficult work.

" Again I will not sorely vex his heart;
" When recollection comes to me of the severity of the
　　clay-work."

Whosoever endured not the violence of the great,
His heart burned not for the poor weak folk.

If the word of rulers be hard to thee,
Exercise not harshness towards thy inferiors.

———

440 I have heard that, in the desert of San'á, Juníd
Saw a dog (by old age) the hunting-teeth dug out.

From the power of the grasp, lion-seizing,
He had become weak, like an old fox.

After seizing, on foot, mountain-sheep and antelope,
He used to suffer kicks from the sheep of the tribe of
　　Hayy.

When he beheld it weak, powerless and wounded,
He gave to it a half of his own provisions.

I heard that he said, while he wept blood :—
" Who knows, which of us two is the better ?

445 " To-day, in outward appearance, I am better than this
　　dog;
" In the future, what (decree) may Fate urge against me ?

440　San'á is a town in the district of Yaman, in Arabia Felix.
　　Juníd was a well-known saint of Baghdád; they say that originally
he was of Nihávand; his title was Abú-l-Kásim, and his nickname
Kávarírí of Zajjaj, or Khazzár.　He died in A.H. 287 or 289.
　　All Imáms are directly descended from him; hence they call him
Sayyidu-l-tá,ifa, "chief of the band."

" If the foot of my faith slips not from its place,
" I may place the crown of God's pardon on my head.

" But if, on my body, the garment of holiness
" Remain not, I am less by much than this dog.

" For when the dog, with all its ill-repute, dies
" They will not carry it to hell."

Oh Sa'dí! this is the way—that men of the path of God
Looked not on themselves with honour.

450 They possessed honour above the angels, on that account,
That they regarded not themselves better than a dog.

A certain drunken one had a harp under his arm;
He broke it, at night, on a devotee's head.

When day came, that good gentle man
Carried a handful of silver to that one of stone-heart.

Saying:—" Last night, thou wast proud and intoxicated;
" For thee and me, harp and head are broken.

" As to me, that wound has become well, and fear has
　　risen (and departed);
" As to thee, save by silver, the harp will not be sound."

455 The friends of God are over heads (in power), on that
　　account,
That they endure much on their heads.

I heard that, in the dust of Wakhsh, of the great,
There was one hidden, in the corner of retirement.

456　　Wakhsh was a town in Badakhshán.
　　In the 'Ikd-i-manzúm, couplets 456–501 are omitted.

Naked in truth; not, by the religious garment, a holy one,
Who puts out the hand of need (in beggary) to the
        people.

As to happiness,—the door opened towards him;
The doors of others shut in his face.

An eloquent one, void of wisdom, endeavoured,
Through impudence, to speak ill of that good man,

460 Saying :—" Beware of this deceit, and artifice, and fraud;
" Of sitting, demon-like, in the place of Sulaimán.

" From time to time, they (the Súfís) wash the face, cat-
        like,
" Lusting for the prey of the mice of the street.

" Austerity-enduring, for the sake of name and pride;
" For, far goes the sound of the empty drum."

He kept talking, and the crowd about him a multitude,
Man and woman, making fun of them (the devotee and the
        orator).

I heard that the sage of Wakhsh wept,
Saying :—" Oh Lord! forgive this Thy slave.

465 " Oh pure Lord! if he spoke truth,
" Give to me repentance, that I may not be destroyed.

---

457   He was not a hypocrite, who, by the religious dress, gained his liveli-
hood.

460   The jinn Ṣaḥra having assumed the likeness of Sulaimán, and taken
the finger-ring from a female slave, sate on Sulaimán's throne. In the
end Áṣaf bin Burkhya, Sulaimán's vazír, having discovered this, recited
(for the purpose of revealing the secret) in his presence the book Zabúr.
That accursed one, not having the power to hear the word of God, withdrew himself from the throne, and cast the ring into the sea, whence,
in the belly of a fish, it returned to Sulaimán's hand. Ever after, bands
of jinns and men, and beasts and birds were present, as of yore, in his
court.

" My fault-seeker was agreeable to me ;
" For, he made known to me my bad disposition."

If thou art that which an enemy says, grieve not ;
And, if thou art not, say :—" Go, wind-weigher ! "

If a fool called the musk fetid,
Be thou tranquil ; for, he uttered nonsense.

And, if this speech, as to the onion passes,
Say it is so ; display not a fetid (proud) brain.

170 The wise one of enlightened mind takes not
The mouth-stopper of the enemy (defect-revealing) from
　　　the juggler.

It is not wisdom, and judgment, and understanding,
That a wise man should purchase deceit from a juggler.

Then the wise man sate behind his own work,
He shut against himself the enemy's tongue.

Be thou of good conduct, that the malevolent one
May not obtain the power of speaking to thy injury.

When from the enemy's speech, it comes hard to thee.
See ! what defect he takes up, that do not.

169　　" Ganda maghz " signifies—takabbur kardan ; hirza bar zabán rándan ; durushtí wa kaj khulk namúdan.

170　　Since the hearing of faults from the enemy is the cause of amend-
ment of the disposition, the sage takes no charm from the juggler for
the stopping of men's mouths ; nay, he desires that the enemy should
utter his faults.

　　Hangáma-gir is one who, in public places, utters tales so that men
purchase his amulets.

　　" Zabán-band " signifies—a charm, with which they close an enemy's
mouth, so that he is unable to slander.

　　" Mush 'abid " signifies—hukka-báz ; hangáma-gír.

475 That person only knows good of me,
Who reveals to me my faults.

A certain one brought a difficult matter before 'Alí;—
Peradventure, he may make apparent to him the difficulty.

The chief, enemy-binding, territory-conquering,
Gave to him an answer from the fountain of knowledge
    and judgment.

I heard that, in this assembly, a person
Said:—" Oh Bú-l-Hasan ! it is not so."

Haydar, name-seeking, on account of him, grieved not;
He said:—" If thou knowst better than this, speak."

480 Whatever he knew, he spoke; and suitably spoke;
It is improper to conceal the sun's fountain with clay.

The king of men approved of his answer,
Saying :—" I was in error; and he, in truth.

" He spoke better than I; the Wise One is one only
    (God);
" For, knowledge is not higher than His knowledge."

If, to-day, there had been a lord of rank,
He would not, through his pride, have looked at him.

The chamberlain would have placed him out of court;
They would, without reason, have beaten him.

485 Saying :—" Hereafter, make not one void of reputation;
" Speech is improper before the great."

----

476   'Alí was the fourth Khalífa; he was called Bú-l-Hasan; Haydar i
Sháh-i-Mardán.

One, in whose head, is conceit,—
Think not, that he will ever listen to truth.

From his knowledge, comes sorrow; from admonition, dis-
    grace;
The red tulips grow from rain, not from stone.

If thou hast the pearl of the river of excellence, rise;
Scatter, in admonition, (pearls) at the feet of the darvesh.

Seest thou not that,—in the dust, fallen, wretched,—
The rose grows, and the fresh spring blossoms?

490 In the eye of (wise) people, no one is of account,
Who shows, in himself, much haughtiness.

Oh sage! scatter not sleeves of pearls (of eloquence),
When thou beholdst a rich man, full of himself.

Speak not,—so that a thousand persons may utter thy
    praises;
When thou speakst of thyself, expect not (praise) from
    any.

I heard that, in a narrow street, as regards a beggar,
'Umar placed his own foot on the back of his foot.

The helpless poor man knew not who he was;
For one aggrieved knows not enemy from friend.

495 He was enraged at him, saying:—"Perhaps, thou art
    blind?"
'Umar, the just chief, said to him:—

---

493   'Umar was the second Khalífa.

" I am not blind; the deed passed by mistake;
" I observed not; pass over my fault."

How just have been the great ones of religion.
Who have, with inferiors, been even so.

One sense-choosing is humble;
The branch full of fruit places its head on the earth.

Those humility-practising will, to-morrow, boast;
The head of those neck-exalting will, in shame, be lowered.

500 If thou fearst the day of reckoning,
Forgive the fault of that one, who fears thee.

Exercise not malignant tyranny towards thy inferiors ;
For, there is a power even above thy power.

———

Of good conduct and good disposition, there was a certain
        one,
Who was well-speaking of the bad.

When he passed (in death), a person beheld him in a dream
        (and asked),
Saying :—" Tell me of past events."

He opened a mouth, rose-like, with laughter,
He gave utterance, nightingale-like, with a sweet sound,

505 Saying :—" They used not much severity towards me ;
" For I practised oppression against no one."

———

I have recollection of this sort, that the water-carrier of
        the Nile
Prepared not, one year, water for Egypt.

———

496   " Khatá raft kár" signifies—íu 'amal khatá wáki' shud.

A crowd went towards the mountains;
Became, with supplication, suppliants for rain.

They wept; but, from their weeping, a running rivulet
Came not, save the water of the eyes of women.

One from among them carried news to the Saint Zú-n-Nún,
Saying:—"On the people there is much grief and suffering.

510 " Pray for those distressed;
" For the word of those God-accepted is not rejected."

I heard that Zú-n-Nún fled to Madín;
Much time passed not before rain fell.

After the lapse of twenty days, the news went to Madín,
That the cloud of black heart had wept over them.

The old man made an immediate resolution of returning;
For, by the spring-torrents, the water-pools became full.

A holy man secretly inquired of him,
" What philosophy was there in this thy going away?"
  He replied:—

515 " I heard that for fowl, and ant, and rapacious beast,
" There was scarcity of food, on account of the deeds of
  the wicked.

---

507 In a drought-year, men, by reason of excessive wretchedness, used to
assemble in the mountains and deserts, and to beseech, with lamentation, rain from God.

509 Zú-n-Nún was a saint; his name Subán Ibráhím; title, Abú-l-faẓl;
and nickname, Zú-n-Nún.

 His father was Naubí of the wise ones of Kuresh; his spiritual guide,
Isráfíl; his teacher, Malik-i-Uns. He died in A.H. 245.

511 Madín is the name of a city, on a river of the west, of the tribe of
·Shu'aib (Jethro).

" In this country, I reflected much ;
" I considered no one worse than myself.

" I went, lest that, through my wickedness,
" God should fasten the door of liberality on the people
    (of Egypt)."

Is greatness necessary to thee ? exercise courtesy; for those
    great ones
Beheld not men worse than themselves, in the world.

Thou becomest precious before men, at that time,
When thou reckonst thyself for nothing.

520 The great one, who reckoned himself among the small folk,
Carried away greatness in this and in the future world.

From this dust-holder (the world), that slave went pure,
Who, at the feet of the meanest person, became dust.

Ho ! thou who passest over our dust,
By the dust of dear ones ! (let it be) that thou rememberst
    (me).

For if Sa'dí (after death) became dust—to him what
    sorrow ?
Since he was, in life also, dust (humble).

In humbleness, he gave his body to the dust ;
Although he went, wind-like, around the world.

525 Much time passes not before that the dust (of the grave)
    consumes him,
The wind carries him, again, through the world.

----

522   " Illá ai ki " is a common form of address.
       The second line may mean :—
            That thou rememberst me in auspicious prayer.
       Or, That thou rememberst this speech, in couplet 523.
524   The second line refers to the fact that Sa'dí was a great traveller.

Behold! since the rose-garden of truth blossomed,
No nightingale spoke in it, sweetly, like Sa'dí.

If a nightingale should die in such a way, wonderful,—
That a rose should not grow on its bones!

CHAPTER V.

ON RESIGNATION.

1 ONE night, I kept burning the olive-oil of reflection ;
I lighted up the lamp of eloquence.

A foolish talker heard my speech,
Save to say—To thee be praise !—he saw no way.

From villainy of nature, he also folded within it (the
     following),
—For, from pain of envy a cry involuntarily arises,—

Saying :—" His thought is sublime, and his judgment
     lofty,
" In this matter of the habit of abstinence, and regula-
     tions, and counsel :

5 " Not, in regard to lance and mace and heavy club ;
" For, the conclusion of this matter is for others."

Knows he not that to us there is no desire for battle ;
Otherwise the power of speech is not scanty ?

I am able to draw forth the sword of the tongue ;
To draw forth his existence, in a moment.

Come; so that, in this matter, we may wage war;
(And) may make a stone-pillow for the enemy's head.

Happiness is in the gift of the Ruler (God);
It is not in the grasp and arm of the strong.

10 When the lofty sky gives not wealth,
It comes not, by manliness, into the snare.

Neither, through weakness, did distress come to the ant;
Nor, by grasp of strength, did lions eat.

Since one cannot draw forth the hand against the sky,
It is necessary to be content with its revolution.

If God has written for thee long life,
Neither the snake, nor the sword, nor the arrow may
        injure thee.

And, if, as to thy life, a portion remains not,
The electuary kills thee just as poison.

15 No; when Rustam experienced the end of his days,
Shughdad brought forth the dust (of destruction) from
        his body.

In Sipahán, I had a certain friend,
Who was warlike and fearless and shrewd.

---

13   " Gazáyad " comes from—gazáyídan, *not* from gazídan.
15   Shughád, Rustám's brother, threw Rustam, with his horse Rakhsh,
into a well; he himself was slain by an arrow, which Rustam fired from
the well. The Persians trace his descent from Mamún, son of Benjamin,
son of Jacob.

Continually, his hand and dagger coloured with blood;
The enemy's heart was, through him, like roast meat on
    the fire.

I beheld not the day, on which, he bound not (to his waist)
    the quiver;
And fire leaped not from his steel arrow.

Courageous; strong, with the gripe of an ox,—
Through fear of him, confusion fell upon lions.

20 He used to cast his arrow, with such precision,
That he used to cast down an enemy with every arrow.

The thorn in the rose,—I saw not that it passed in such a
    way,
As his arrow passed not into the shields.

He struck not the helmet of the one contest-seeking,
Whose helmet and head, he shattered not completely.

In battle (enraged) like a sparrow on the locust day,
In slaying,—whether a sparrow, or a man, to him what
    difference?

If it were to him, to attack Firídún,
He would not have given him respite for sword-drawing.

25 Panthers, by the force of his gripe, beneath him;
His fingers plunged in the brain of the lion.

He used to seize the girdle of one strength-tried,
And if he had been a mountain, he would have plucked
    him from his place.

When he used to strike his battle-axe on the one mail-
    clad,
It used to pass through the man, and strike his saddle.

---

19   "Gáv-zor" may signify—rude, violent, brutal.
20   "Da'wa" signifies—claim; but here it means precision.
23   On the swarming of locusts, the sparrow becomes demented; and,
rushing in every direction, seizes every locust it can.

Neither as to manliness, nor as to magnanimity,—to him,
A second, no one saw a man in this world.

He used not to allow me to go a moment from his hand
　　(side) ;
For, he used to have an inclination for those of true dis-
　　position.

30 Suddenly, a journey snatched me from that soil ;
For, in that abode, there was no food for me.

Fate transported me from Media to Syria ;
In that pure dust, my abode was happy.

In short, some time, I became resident ;
In sorrow and in ease ; in hope, and in fear.

Of Syria, my cup again became full ;
The desire of my house drew me.

By chance it so fell,
That my path again fell by Media.

35 One night, my head became lowered in thought ;
That skilled one (of Ispahán) passed to my heart.

The salt (of desire) made fresh my ancient wound ;
For, I was one who had eaten salt from the man's hand.

For seeing him, I went towards Sipáhán ;
In love of him, I became a seeker and inquirer.

I beheld the young man old from time's revolution ;
His poplar arrow (of stature) a bow ; his deep red colour
　　(complexion) yellow.

31　"'Irák-i-'Ajam" signifies—Media ; "'Irák-i-'Arab" signifies—
Chaldea ; "Shám-i-'Arab" signifies—Syria.

34　The student should note the use of "uftádan," in this couplet.

36　"Namak" here signifies—ishtiyák.

38　Arghaván is a tree of deep red colour.
　　Zarír is a yellow grass with which they dye garments.

His head, from snow-hair, like a white mountain;
Water, from the snow of old age, running on his face.

40 Heaven obtained the hand of power over him;
It twisted the tip of his manly hand.

The world put pride out of his head;
The head of powerlessness on his knees.

I said to him:—" Oh chief, lion-seizing !
" What made thee withered like an old fox ? "

He laughed, saying:—" From the day of battle with the
     Tátárs,
" I put out of my head that battle-seeking.

" I beheld the ground, with spears, like a cane-brake,
" The (coloured) standards, fir-like, set in it.

45 " I raised the dust of battle, like smoke ;
" When there is not the power,—of what use is ardour ?

" I am that one who when I used to attack,
" Used to carry off, with a spear, a ring from the hand.

" But, when my star displayed not assistance ;
" They gat themselves about me like a ring.

" I reckoned the way of flight gain ;
" For (only) the fool makes a sharp tussle with Fate.

" How may helmet and cuirass render me aid,
" When my bright star displayed not assistance ?

50 " When victory's key is not in the hand,
" One cannot break victory's door, by the arm.

---

48   " Panja tez kardan " signifies—muḵábila kardan ; koftan-i-panja ba
tezí va shitáb zadagí.

" A crowd, panther-overthrowing, and of elephant-strength,
" Man's head (the rider) and horse's hoof (the ridden)—
      in iron.

" That very moment, when we saw the dust of the army,
" We put on the mail-garment, and the helmet head-
      piece :

" Urged our Arab steeds, cloud-like ;
" Showered down our gleaming arrows, rain-like.

" From ambush, the two armies dashed together ;
" Thou wouldst have said :—On the earth, they dashed
      the sky.

" From the raining of arrows, hail-like,
" Death's storm arose on every side.

" For the chase of lions, conflict-making,
" The dragon-noose, mouth opened.

" With blue dust, the earth became the sky;
" The flash of sword and helmet in it star-like.

" When we overtook the enemy's horsemen,
" On foot, we wove shield within shield.

" Baham bar zadan " signifies—bar ham dígar rekhtan.

Through the display of bravery and assault, they rendered all things topsy-turvy.

" Dar yáftan " signifies—dar rasídan.

" Sipar dar sipar yáftem " signifies—darmíyán-i-má va eshán parda sákhtem.

In the second line, " báftem "—signifying "muttaṣil va paiwand kardem "—sometimes occurs.

When the enemy's horsemen approached and the work of arrow and musket was ended—of necessity, alighting from our horses, and placing the shield in front, we were opposed to the enemy, who did even so.

On both sides, the armies commingled to such a degree that shield to shield became conjoined.

" With arrow and spear, we split the hair ;
" When power was not,—we turned away.

60 " What force does the grasp of man's exertion bring,
" When the arm of God's grace assists not ?

" The sword of those malice-bearing was not blunt ;
" But there was malice, on the part of the angry star.

" A person of our army, forth from the conflict,
" Came not—save with a khaftán bedabbled with blood.

" Within the silken vest, went not the arrow of those
" Of whom, I said :—They may sew (pierce) the anvil
        with an arrow.

" Like a hundred grains, clustered in an ear of corn,
" We fell,—each grain in a corner.

65 " With unmanliness, we became dispersed ;
" Like the fish, which, cuirass-clad, falls to the fish-hook.

" When Fortune, from towards us, was face on the turn ;
" The shield before the arrow of destiny was—nothing."

———

In Ardabíl, a certain one of iron grasp
Caused, continually, the double-headed arrow to pass
        through a spade.

One felt-clad came before him in battle,
A young man, world-consuming, battle-making,

———

65   " Az ham dast dádan " signifies—azyak dígar gashtan ; hazímat
khurdan ; pareshán shudan.
        " Shist " signifies—kulláb, a fish-hook.
67   Ardabíl is a city in Ázar bíján, in Persia ; it is said to have been
founded by Fírúz, Naushíraván's grandfather.

Contest-seeking, like Bahram-Gor,
On his shoulder, a noose of the raw hide of the wild ass.

70　When he of Ardabíl saw the one felt-wearing,
He brought the string to the bow, and the string to the
　　　ear.

He struck him with fifty poplar arrows;
But; not a single arrow passed beyond the felt.

The warrior came like the hero Dastán,
He brought him (of Ardabíl) within the curl (of his noose),
　　　and took him away.

In the camp, at the tent-door, his hand,
He bound to his neck—like bloody thieves.

In the night, from anger and shame, he slept not;
In the morning, a slave-girl, from the tent said :—

75　" Since thou piercest iron with the arrow and dart,
" How didst thou fall a captive to one felt-wearing ? "

I heard that he said, while he wept blood :—
" Knowst thou not that no one lives on the day of death ?

" I am that one, who,—in the act of spear-piercing and
　　　sword-striking,
" Teach Rustam the manner of battle.

" When the arm of my fortune was of strong state,
" The thickness of the spade appeared to me as felt.

" Now, that fortune is not in my grasp,
" The felt is not less than the spade, before my arrow.

69　　Bahrám Gor was a king of Persia, who was fond of hunting wild
asses. He was Naushíraván's grandson.

80 " On the day of death, the spear rends the cuirass ;
    " It passes not beyond the shirt of one deathless.

    " He, in whose rear is the sword of the wrath of death,
    " Is naked,—if his cuirass be manifold.

    " But, if Fortune be his friend ; and, Time supporter—
    " It is impossible to slay him naked—(even) with a large
        knife.

    " Neither did the sage, carry away (save) his life, by
        effort ;
    " Nor, did the fool die, by improper eating."

———

One night, a hero slept not on account of a side-pain ;
There was a physician, in that quarter ; he said :—

8   " Since, he eats the vine-leaf in this fashion,
    " I have wonder if he will finish the night (alive).

    " For, the blade of the Tátár arrow in the chest,
    " Is better than wine-sweetmeats of improper food.

    " If by a single morsel, griping occurs in the bowels,
    " All the life of the ignorant one comes to naught."

By chance, the physician died that night ;
Forty years have passed since this time ; but the hero is
        alive.

———

As to a certain villager,—his ass fell (and died) ;
On a vine-tendril, he placed its head flag-fashion.

---

89   " 'Alam kardan " signifies—dar áwekhtan, to suspend.
    For driving away the evil eye, they used to suspend the head of an
ox, or an ass.

90 **An old** man, world-experienced, passed by it ;
To the vineyard-keeper, laughing, he thus spoke :—

" **Oh soul of father !** think not that this **ass**
" Repels **the evil eye,** from the sown field.

" For, from its own head and buttocks,—this ass, the re-
    pelling (of blows)
" Effected not, so that, feeble and wounded, it died."

What **knows the physician of trouble-removing** from a
    person,
When helpless, **he himself will die of trouble** !

————

I **have** heard that, **from an** indigent person, a **dínár**
Fell ; and that the wretched one sought for **it much.**

95 At length, he turned away **the head of despair ;**
Another, without searching, **found it.**

For bad and good fortune, the pen,
The Fates urge ;—we, yet, in the womb.

By strength **of grasp, they enjoy not their daily food ;**
For those **of strong grip** are more straitened in circum-
    stance.

An old man **struck his son with a stick ;**
He said :—" Oh father ! I am guiltless ; **strike not.**

" For men's violence against **thee,** it is possible **to weep ;**
" **But, when** thou displayst violence, to me what remedy **is**
    there ? "

———

99 It is right to complain *to* God, but not *of* God.

100 Oh lord of sense! cry to the Ruler (God),
Raise not a cry, on account of the Ruler.

———

One of lofty star,—his name Bakht-yár,—
Was of great power, and possessed of capital.

In that place, to him were both gold and property;
Others poor of reversed fortune.

His house was in the street of the beggars;
His gold was like wheat in the measure.

When the darvesh beholds the rich one in affluence,
His heart burns the more by the stain of indigence.

105 A woman joined battle with her husband,
When, in the night-time, he went to her empty-handed,

Saying:—" There is no one, unfortunate, poor, like thee;
" Thou hast only this sting, like the red wasp.

" Learn manliness from the neighbours;
" For I am not, in short, a harlot picked up on the road.

" Persons have gold, and silver, and territory, and household goods,
" Why art thou not of good fortune, like them?"

The one of pure heart, wool-clad, raised
A shout from the heart, drum-like,

110 Saying:—" I possess not the hand of power, as to anything;
" Writhe not in the grasp of the hand of Fate.

———

101   After "tawángar" read "rá."
106   The red wasp has a sting but no honey; so thou hast the power of
doing injury, not of good.

" In my hand they placed not power,
" That I might make myself fortunate."

In the dust of Kísh, a certain poor man,—
How well he said to his ugly partner (wife) ;—

" When the hand of Fate created thee ugly of face,
" Plaster not the rose-colour (rouge) on thy ugly face."

Who acquires good fortune, by force ?
Who makes the blind man's eye seeing, by antimony ?

115 A good deed comes not from those of bad stock ;
Needle-work is impossible to dogs.

All the philosophers of Greece and Rúm
Know not how to make honey from the thorny tree.

It happens not that, from a wild beast, a man becomes ;
Education, (even) with exertion, is lost on it.

One can make clean the mirror from blight ;
But, the mirror comes not from a stone.

The flower grows not from the willow-bough, by effort ;
The Ethiopian becomes not white, by the hot bath.

120 When the poplar-arrow of destiny is not repelled,
For the slave,—there is no shield, save resignation.

A vulture to a kite thus spoke,
Saying :—" There is no one more far-seeing than myself."

---

112   Kísh is the name of a city in an island in the sea of Hurmuz.
115   The disposition of dogs is to rend, not to put together, as in sewing.
121   " Zaghan " signifies—gosht-rabá ; ghalíváj.
       " Kargis " signifies—nasr.

The kite replied :—" It is not proper to pass by this
    matter ;
" Come ; so that thou mayst look at the quarters of the
    desert."

I heard that, to the extent of one day's march,
The vulture viewed from height to depth.

Thus, he spoke :—" I saw, if belief be to thee,
" Where a grain of wheat is on the plain."

125 From astonishment, patience remained not to the kite,
From sublimity, they turned to profundity.

When the vulture came close to the grain,
A long foot-tether became knotted on him.

From his devouring that grain, the vulture knew not
That adverse fortune would cast a snare about his neck.

Not every oyster is pregnant with the pearl ;
Not every time does the expert archer hit the butt.

The kite said :—" From seeing this grain, what profit,
" When to thee, there was not the beholding of the
    enemy's snare ? "

130 I heard that, he, neck in the noose, said :—
" Caution, as to destiny, is unprofitable."

When death brought forth the hand for his blood,
Fate bound his eyes, finely-discerning.

In that water (of eternity), whose shore is unknown,
The swimmer's pride is of no avail.

———

How well said the apprentice of the embroidery-weaver,
When he pourtrayed 'Anká, and elephant, and giraffe :—

---

122   " Dar " belongs to " guzashtan."

" From my hand, there came not a form,
" The plan of which, the Teacher from above pourtrayed
    not."

135 If the form of thy state be bad, or good,
The hand of Fate is its painter.

There is a kind of concealed hypocrisy in this,
Namely—" Zaid injured me, or 'Umar wounded me."

If the Lord of Command gives thee the eye,
Thou seest not again the form of Zaid and 'Umar.

I think not—if a slave rests (from seeking food),
That God draws his pen on (stops) his daily food.

May the World-Creator give thee the means of opening
    (the door) !
For, if He shuts, none can open.

————

140 A young camel, to its mother, said :—
" After travelling, at last, sleep awhile."

She said :—" If the rein had been in my hand
" No one would have seen me a load-carrier in the camel-
    string."

There, where it wishes, Fate takes the vessel,
Although, the captain rends the garment on his body.

Oh Sa'dí ! place not thy eye (of expectation) on anyone's
    power ;
For Omnipotence only is the Giver.

———————————

136 Man's vision should be such that he should see the signs of God, not
those of an abject creature.

If thou worshipst God, of (people's) doors, sufficient for
    thee ;
But if He drives thee away, no one desires thee.

145 If God makes thee a crown-possessor,—raise thy head ;
But, if not, scratch the head of despair.

Worship, with sincerity of intention, is good ;
Otherwise, what comes from the husk, without kernel ?

What,—the idolater's cord on thy waist ? what, the re-
    ligious garment ?
If thou putst them on for the opinion of the people.

I said to thee :—Display not thy own manliness ;
When thou displayst manliness, be not an hermaphrodite.

It is proper to display (religious qualities) to the extent of
    thy capacity ;
Shame overpowered not him, who had not displayed.

150 For, when they draw the borrowed garment from off thy
    head,
The old robe will remain on thy body.

If thou art small, fasten not on wooden feet,
That thou mayst, in children's eyes, appear tall.

And, if copper be silver-plated,
One can expend it on the ignorant.

Oh my life ! place not the gold-water on the valueless coin ;
For the wise banker takes it as nothing.

They take the things gold-washed to the fire ;
Then, it appears which are copper, and which gold.

----

144   The first line means—that people, to whose doors thou goest in
beggary, will give thee alms.
148   See chapter iv. couplet 84.

155 Knowst thou not what the old man of the mountain said,
To the man, who, for reputation, slept not at night?

" Oh soul of father! go; strive for sincerity;
" For, from the people, thou canst not establish any
     (proof)."

Those persons, who have approved of thy acts,
Have yet only seen thy outward form.

What price, does the Khurdís slave fetch,
Who has leprous limbs beneath the over-coat?

It is impossible to enter Paradise, with imposture,
For, the shroud goes back (on the Judgment Day) from
     thy ugly face.

———

160 I have heard that a certain one of immature age kept a
     fast,
With a hundred difficulties, he accomplished one day up to
     the mid-day meal.

The tutor took him not that day to school;
Devotion, on the part of a little boy, appeared to him
     great.

The father kissed his eyes; and, the mother his head;
They scattered almonds and gold on his head.

When a half of the day passed over him,
From his stomach's fire, the burning (of hunger) fell upon
     him.

---

156   " Az khalk bar bastan " signifies—az khalk naf' giriftan.
160   " Sá,ik " comes from " suk," signifying—ádab-ámoz ; atálik.
      " Sábik " signifies—sabak dihanda ; khalífa,e maktab.

To his heart, he said :—" If I eat a few morsels,
" How may my father and mother know of the secret
        (deed) ? "

165 When the boy's face was towards his father and family,
He secretly ate ; but openly carried on the fast.

Who knows, whether thou art in the bonds of God ;
If thou standst unwashed, in prayer ?

Then, this old man is more ignorant than that child,
Who, for the sake of men, is in devotion.

The key of hell's door is that prayer,
Which thou, in men's eyes, makest long.

If, except to God, thy way goes,—
They spread thy prayer-carpet in hell.

———

170 One of black deeds fell from a ladder ;
I heard that, even in a breath, he gave his soul (to God).

For some days, the son took to weeping ;
Took, again, to sitting with his companions :

Beheld, in a dream, his father ; and inquired after his
        state,
Saying :—" How escapedst thou from the assembling, and
        reviving, and questioning ? "

He said :—" Oh son ! desire not news concerning me ;
" From the ladder, I fell into hell."

———

166   " Wuẓú' " signifies—in law, the washing of the face, hands, feet, and
anointing of the head.
168   See chapter iv. couplet 81.
169   If thou performst devotion to be seen of men.

One of good walk of life, outwardly unceremonious,
(Is) better than one of good fame, inwardly evil.

175 In my opinion, the night-going highway-man
Is better than the adulterer of chaste skirt.

One trouble-enduring at the people's door,—
What reward will God give him on the Resurrection Day?

Oh son! expect not reward from 'Umar,
When thou art, at work, in the house of Zaid.

I say not :—he can reach his Friend (God),
In this path ; save that one, whose face is turned towards
    Him.

Go the right way, that thou mayst reach the stage,
(Oh hypocrite !) thou art not on the path ; for this reason,
    thou art lagging.

180 Like the ox, whose eyes the oil-presser binds up,
Though running till the night,—at night, even there where
    it is.

The person, who turns away his face from the altar,
The people of eloquence give evidence as to his infidelity.

Thou also art, in prayer, back to the Kibla,
If thy face of supplication be not towards God.

That tree, whose root is firm,
Cherish—that one day it may give thee the fruit of fruit.

If the root of sincerity be not in thy soil,
No one is disappointed like thee, at this door (of God).

---

179   The one, who is a hypocrite, does much, but makes no progress. How,
then, can he reach the stage?

180   The ox is always circling.

185 Whosoever casts seed on the rock-surface,
At the time of in-come, not a grain comes to his grasp.

Put not honour upon the reputation of (acquired by)
    hypocrisy;
For, this (hypocrisy) has mire beneath the (lustrous) water.

When thou art, in secret, bad and dust-like,
What profit,—the water of hypocrisy on the surface of the
    work?

On the surface of hypocrisy, it is easy to stitch the reli-
    gious garment,
If thou canst sell it to God.

How may men know who is in the religious habit?
The writer knows what is in the register (of deeds).

190 What weight may the leathern bag, full of wind, show in
    the place
Where there is the scale of justice, and the book of equity?

The hypocrite, who showed so much austerity,
They see there is nothing in his leathern bag.

They make the outside of the coat cleaner than the lining;
For, this is behind a veil, and that before the sight.

The great possessed indifference as to men's eyes,
For that reason, they possessed a painted silk lining.

If thou wishst renown spread abroad in the country,
Place the cloak outside; say:—Fill the interior with cotton.

---

187   "Námús" here signifies—riyá, hypocrisy.
190   A hypocrite's work is compared to a bag full of wind.
193   They are clothed with good deeds; because they desire not renown.
194   " Hulla" signifies—azár; radá.
       The second line means:—
              Cause thy exterior to be decked with hypocrisy.

195 Báyizíd uttered not, in sport, this speech :—
" I am safer from the disbeliever, than from the disciple."

Those, who are sultáns and monarchs,
Are altogether beggars at this Court (of God).

The man of truth fixes not his desire (of help) upon the
　　beggar ;
It is improper to take the hand of the fallen.

This indeed is best,—if thou be pregnant with a jewel,
That thou shouldst take thy head within thyself,—oyster-
　　like.

When the face of thy adoring is towards God,
If Jibrá,il see thee not,—it is proper.

200 Oh son ! Sa'dí's counsel is enough for thee,
If thou hearst it, like a father's counsel.

If, to-day, thou hearst not my word,
God forbid ! that, to-morrow, thou shouldst be abashed.

Than this (Sa'dí) is a better adviser necessary to thee ?
I know not what may chance to thee, after me.

195　The disbeliever tells me of my ill-doing ; but the disciple, of my
well-doing.
197　The beggar is described in couplet 196.
202　See chapter iv. couplet 392.

CHAPTER VI.

ON CONTENTMENT.

1 HE knew not God and worshipped not,
Who displayed not contentment with his fortune and daily
    food.

Contentment makes a man rich;
—Inform the greedy one, world-travelling.—

Oh one without permanence! bring tranquillity to thy
    hand.
For, vegetation grows not on the rolling stone.

If thou art a man of judgment and sense, cherish not thy
    body;
For, when thou cherishst it,—thou slayst it.

5 Wise men are skill-cherishers;
But body-cherishers are feeble in skill.

Eating and sleeping is the way of beasts alone;
To be in this way is the habit of the unwise.

That one attended to a manly life,
Who silenced first the dog of lust.

Happy that fortunate one, who, in a corner,
Gathers to his hand road-provisions of the knowledge of
    God.

Those, to whom God's mystery became revealed,
Preferred not the false to it.

10 But, when he knows not darkness from light,
Whether the sight of a demon, or the cheek of a húrí—to
    him what difference?

Thou didst cast thyself into a well, on that account,
That thou didst not recognise the well from the road.

How may the young hawk fly to the zenith of the sky,
When, in its long feathers, the stone of desire is bound?

If from lust's claw, thy skirt free,
Thou shouldst make, thou wouldst go to the lotus-tree
    (in Paradise).

By eating less food than one's custom,
One can make the body of angelic temperament.

15 How may the brutal lion reach the angel state?
It cannot fly from earth to sky.

Practise first the human temperament;
Think after that of the angelic temperament.

Thou art on the flanks of a refractory colt;
Take care that it twist not its head from thy order.

For, if it should tear the halter from thy hand,—
It would slay thy body, and spill thy blood.

If thou art a man, eat food within limit;
Such a fully belly!—art thou a man, or a jar?

---

10   The demon (of falsehood) and the "húrí" (of truth) are alike to
him.

20 Within the body, is a place for food, and reflection on God,
    and breath ;
Thou thinkst it is for bread only.

In the wallet of lust, where is remembrance of God con-
    tained ?
With difficulty, he breathes,—leg extended.

The body-cherishers have no knowledge,
That—the full stomach is void of wisdom.

The two eyes and stomach became not filled with any-
    thing ;
These bowels, coil on coil, are best empty.

Like hell which they fill with fuel,
Again, there is a shout, saying :—" Is there any more ? "

25 Thy 'Ísa (the soul) continually dies of weakness ;
Thou art in that desire, that thou mayst cherish thy ass
    (the body).

Oh one of little worth ! buy not the world, in exchange
    for religion ;
Purchase not thou the ass with the gospel of 'Ísa.

Perhaps, thou seest not that as to rapacious and non-
    rapacious animals,
Only the greed of eating casts into the snare.

The panther, which stretches its neck (in pride) among
    the beasts.
Falls, mouse-like, into the snare, through the greed of
    eating.

Mouse-like, whose bread and cheese thou eatst,
Into his snare, thou fallst and sufferst his arrow.

---

24   This occurs in the Súra of Káf in the Kurán.

30   *   *   *   *   *   *

If food be delicious, or if it be simple,
When delay occurs to thy hand, thou eatst pleasantly.

35 The sage places his head on the pillow at that time when,
Sleep takes him, with violence, into its net.

So long as thou obtainst not the power of speech,—speak
    not;
When thou seest not the plain (of power), beware of the
    ball (of speech).

Speak not; and, so long as thou canst, plant not thy foot
Outside of limit, or inside of limit.

––––––

Go; acquire a pure heart;
The belly will not become full, save with the dust of the
    grave.

A Hájí gave me an ivory comb,
Saying:—" May the mercy of God be on the good quali-
    ties of pilgrims !"

40 I heard that once upon a time he had called me a dog,
For his heart was, in some way, dejected about me.

I threw away the comb, saying :—" This bone,
" Is unnecessary for me ; another time, call me not a dog.

" Think not, if I swallow my own vinegar,
" That I will endure the violence of the lord of sweet-
    meats."

Oh soul ! be content with a little
That thou mayst consider the sultán and darvesh as one.

––––––––––––––––––––

30   In the 'Ikd-i-manzúm, couplets 30 to 37 are omitted.
    For obvious reasons, couplets 30 to 33 are here omitted.

Why goest thou before the king, with entreaty ?
When thou placest avarice aside, thou art a king.

45 And, if thou art a self-worshipper, make the belly a
        drum ;
Make the door of this and that (man)—a Kibla.

And, if every moment, thy lust says :—give,
It causes thee to wander, village to village, in beggary.

Oh man of sense ; contentment exalts the head ;
The head full of avarice comes not forth from the shoulder.

———

A certain one, possessed of avarice, before King Khwárazm,
—I heard—went early in the morning.

When he saw Khwárazm, he became doubled and straight ;
He rubbed his face, moreover, on the earth ; and arose.

50 His son said :—" Oh little father, name-seeking !
" I ask of thee a difficulty ; explain it.

" Didst thou not say, that the dust of Hijáz was thy
        Kibla ?
" Why didst thou, to-day, pray in this direction (towards
        the king) ? "

Display not devotion to the lust of the lust-worshipper ;
Since, it has, every hour, another Kibla.

Avarice spilled the reputation of honour ;
It poured out a skirt (full) of pearls for two barley-grains.

When thou wishst to become satiated with the rivulet-
        water,
Why spillst thou face-water (honour) for the sake of ice ?

———

47   For, every moment, he is bowing in humility (ruḳú') ; and, in submission (khuzú').

55 Perhaps, thou art a patient one as to happiness ;
But if not, thou art, of necessity, (begging) at doors.

Sir ! go ; make short the hand of avarice ;
What need to thee of the long sleeve (of beggary) ?

Of him, who folded up the casket of avarice,
It is unnecessary to write—" Slave or servant to any one."

Expectation will drive thee from every assembly,
Drive it from thyself, so that no one may drive thee.

To one of the holy men, a fever came,
A person said :—" Ask for sugar from such a one."

60 He said :—" Oh son ! the bitterness of my dying
" Is better than my bearing the oppression of one of
　　　bitter face."

The wise man ate not sugar from the hand of that one,
Who, through arrogance, made his face vinegar (bitter)
　　　towards him.

Go not, in pursuit of whatever thy heart desires
For the strengthening of the body diminishes the soul's
　　　light.

Imperious lust makes a man contemptible ;
If thou art wise, hold it not dear.

If thou enjoyst whatever may be thy wish,
Thou wilt endure much disappointment from the revolu-
　　　tion of time.

55　Oh, covetous one ! exercise patience as to affluence : and moderate
thy desire.

65 To heat constantly the oven of the belly
   May, in the day of want, be a misfortune.

In straitened circumstances, thy face causes not its com-
    plexion to be shed
If, in the time of plenteousness, thou makst the belly
    tight.

The man, full-devourer, endures the belly-load ;
And, if he obtain not food, he endures the grief-load.

Thou mayst often see the belly-slave greatly ashamed,
In my opinion, the belly straitened is better than the heart
    (straitened).

Alas ! thou art one man-born, full of dignity,
Who is like the beasts—" Nay ; they are lost ! "

70 Show not pity to the ox of great weight ;
   For, it is a great sleeper, and great devourer.

If fatness, ox-like, be necessary to thee,
Submit thy body, ass-like, to the tyranny of persons.

————

Knowst thou what wonderful thing I brought from Basra?
—A tale, which is sweeter than the green date.

We—a few individuals in the religious garb of the true
    (Súfís)—
Passed by the side of a date-garden.

One amongst us was a stomach-barn (a glutton) ;
He was, through this narrow-eyedness, a belly-enjoyer.

—————————————

68   The belly straitened, by want of food, is better than the heart
straitened by not obtaining its desire.
69   The second line comes from the Súra A'ráf of the Ḳurán.
    In the 'Iḳd-i-manẓúm, couplets 69 to 71 are omitted.
72   Baṣra is a town near the Persian gulf ; it is sometimes called Balsora.
See Lane's Arabian Nights Entertainments.

75 The **wretched one bound his loins, and** ascended the (date)
    tree;
And, **thence fell heavily headlong.**

The **Ra,is of the village came, saying :—" Who slew this
    man ? "**
I said :—" **Express not against us a harsh word.**

" The belly **drew his skirt down from the branch."**
—The **one of narrow heart is of capacious bowels.—**

Not every **time, can one eat the date and carry it away ;**
The stomach-barn (the glutton) suffered a **bad end, and**
    died.

The **belly is the hand-fetter, and foot-chain ;**
A belly-slave rarely worships God.

80 The **locust is assuredly altogether belly;**
The **ant of small belly drags the locust by the foot.**

A certain one had **sugar-cane, on a small plate,—**
A wanderer, left and right, for a purchaser.

In a corner of the **village, to a pious man, he spoke,**
Saying :—" Take ; **and pay, when thou hast the means."**

That wise **man of** adorned disposition uttered
An answer, that should be written on the eye.

" Perhaps, to thee, patience (as to payment) may not be
    (exercised) towards **me ;**
" **But, to me, (patience) is, as to the sugar-cane."**

---

77   " Rúdgán " is a word of the same character as—rozgárán ; bahárán.
78   " Lat-ambán " signifies—lat-nabáz ; lat nabar.
80   The belly extends from the locust's neck to its hinder extremity.

85 Sugar, in its reed, has no sweetness,
When, behind it, is the bitter demand (for its price).

———

To one of the men of illumined mind,
The Amír of Khután gave a piece of silk cloth.

He expanded, through gladness, like the laughing rose-
    leaf;
Kissed his hands; clothed himself; and said :—

" How good is the garment of honour of the King of
    Khután !
" But, my own religious garment is more beautiful than it."

If thou art noble, sleep on the earth; for, it is enough :
Perform no one's ground-kiss (in obeisance) for a costly
    carpet.

———

90 A certain one had no bread-food, save an onion ;
He had no resources and means, like others.

One said to him :—"Oh one of foolish time !
" Go ; bring something cooked from the tray of plunder
    (the king's table).

" Oh sir ! ask, and have fear of none ;
" For the one ashamed is cut as to his victuals."

He bound about him his over-coat, and quickly folded his
    hand (sleeve);
They rent his coat, and broke his hand.

———

86   Khután is a country in Turkistán, near Khatá, or Tartary.
90   "Nán-khurish" signifies—the condiments eaten with bread.   See
couplet 95.

I have heard that he said, while he wept blood :—
" What is the remedy for the deed done by one's self !

95　" The captive of avarice is one calamity-seeking,
" After this—I and my house; bread and onion (are
enough)."

The barley-loaf, which I eat by the power of my arm,
Is better than flour (twice sifted) on the tray of people of
liberality.

Last night, how heart-straitened slept that worthless one,
Who kept the ear (of expectation) upon the Kibla of
others !

———

In an old woman's house, there was a certain cat,
Which was of reversed fortune, and of bad state.

It went running to the amír's guest-house,
The slaves of the sultán struck it with arrows.

100　It ran, blood dropping from its bones (wounds),
While from fear of life it ran, it kept saying :—

" If I escape from the hand of this arrow-caster,
" I and the mouse, and the old woman's desolate abode
(are enough)."

Oh my soul ! honey is not worth the sting's wound ;
Contentment with one's own syrup of dates is best.

The Lord God is not satisfied with that slave,
Who is not content with his Lord's portion.

———

A certain child had cut its teeth,
The father was head-lowered in reflection,

———

95　See couplet 101.

5 Saying :—" Whence may I bring bread food for him?
" It is not manliness to abandon him."

When helpless, he uttered this speech to his partner (his
    wife),
Behold how like a man she spoke to him!

" Suffer not fear of Iblís, until he surrenders life (to God).
" That same Person, who gives teeth, gives bread."

The Lord of Days (God) is, in short, able
To cause daily food to arrive; vex not thyself so much.

He is the Pourtrayer of the boy within the womb;
He is also the Writer (Computer) of its age, and daily
    food.

110 That lord, who bought a slave,
Maintains him. How much more God, who created the
    slave!

To thee, there is not that reliance on the Omnipotent,—
As to the slave, on his lord.

I heard that, in ancient times,
A stone used, in the hands of the pious, to become silver.

Thou thinkst not this speech is unreasonable?—
When thou becomest content, silver and stone are alike to
    thee.

---

107   In the Ḳurán :—
        "Through fear of want, kill not thy children; we give thee and
            them daily food."
109   " Navísauda" here signifies—andáza kunanda.
112   " Abdál" (sing. badíl) signifies—religious men, for whose sake God
    preserves the world; they are, in number, seventy. Of these, forty are
    in Syria, and the remainder elsewhere.

When the child has a heart free from avarice,
In its mind, whether a handful of gold, or dust, what
　difference ?

115 Give news to the darvesh, sultán-worshipping,
Saying :—" The sultán is more wretched than the **darvesh.**"

A diram of **silver makes the beggar satiated** ;
Firídún, with the kingdom **of Persia,**—half satiated.

The guardianship of the country and of the empire is a
　calamity ;
The beggar is king, but his name is beggar.

The beggar, on whose heart is no desire,
Is better than a king, who is unhappy (through dis-
　content).

The villager and his partner (wife) sleep pleasantly,
With a pleasure, with which the sultán, in the palace,
　sleeps not.

120 If he be king ; or, if garment-stitcher,—
When they sleep, the night of both becomes day.

And, if the torrent of death comes and takes both,
Whether the sultán on the throne ; or the wanderer in the
　desert—what difference ?

When thou seest the rich man, head intoxicated with pride,
Oh one of straitened hand ! go ; give thanks to God.

Praise be to God ! thou hast not those resources,
That, by thy power, any one's injury may arise.

———

I have heard that a pious one, a good man,
Made a house conformable to his stature.

120　　In each case the night terminates and day begins

125 One said :—" I know thy means (are such),
  " That thou mayst construct a better house than this."
      He replied :—" Enough.

  " Why should I desire to raise a house above my head ?
  " This indeed is enough, for the sake of leaving, (after
      death)."

Oh slave ! make not a house in the path of the torrent (of
    this world);
Because, for none did this edifice become complete.

Through knowledge of God, and wisdom, and judgment,—
    it is not
That one of a káraván constructs a house on the road (of
    this world).

As to a certain one, empire-ruling, possessed of pomp, —
His sun (life) desired to descend to the mountain (in
    death).

130 He left his territory to the shaikh of that place ;
For he had, in his house, no successor.

When the recluse heard the drum of empire,
He experienced not again pleasure in the corner of retire-
    ment ;

He began to lead his army, left and right ;
Began to strengthen the heart of those hearty :

Became so strong of arm, and sharp of grip,
That he sought contest with those battle-seeking.

He killed a number of a scattered tribe ;
The rest assembled together, confederates and allies.

135 They drew him within a fence so tightly,
That he became distressed with the arrow and stone-
    raining.

He sent a person to a good man,
Saying :—"I am much distressed; come to my call for
    help.

" Assist by blessing; for, the sword and arrow
" Are not a help in every battle."

When the 'ábid heard, he laughed and said :—
" Why ate he not half a loaf, and slept ? "

Kárún, wealth-worshipping, knew not,
That the treasure of safety was in retirement.

---

140 The perfection (of existence) is the breath (spirit) of a
    gentle man,
If he have not gold,—what loss or fear ?

Think not,—if a mean one becomes rich,
That his base disposition becomes changed.

But if the one liberality practising gets not bread,
His nature may still be rich (generous).

Generosity is the soil; capital, the sown-field;
Give,—that the root may not be destitute of a branch.

That God, who makes man from dust,—
I have wonder if He makes lost humanity,

145 Seek not greatness, by gathering wealth;
For, stagnant water makes an unpleasant smell.

Strive for liberality; for, the running water,
Aid from heaven reaches with the flood.

---

144   It is inconceivable that God should ruin humanity, or that He should
cause the source of liberality to disappear.

If a mean one fall from rank and fortune (or, be dismissed),
He rarely again becomes erect (reinstated).

But, if thou art a precious jewel, have no care ;
For, time causes thee not to be destroyed.

A clod—although it be fallen on the road,—
Thou seest not that any one looks at it.

150 But, if a fragment of gold from the teeth (blade) of the
 scissors,
Falls,—they will search again (and again) for it, with a
 candle.

They extract glass-ware from stone ;
Where remains the mirror, beneath the blight ?

Skill, and religion, and excellence, and perfection,—are
 necessary ;
For rank and wealth sometimes come ; sometimes depart.

From men of sweet discourse, I have heard,
That, there was within the city (of Shíráz) a certain ancient
 old man ;

Much experienced as to kings, and the period of command ;
A lifetime brought to an end from the era of 'Umar.

155 The ancient tree had fresh fruit (a son),
Who kept, by his goodness (of beauty), the city full of
 noise.

----

151 They make the mirror clean and free from blight.
153 In the 'Ikd-i-manzúm, couplets 153 to 174 are omitted.

Wonder,—as to the (apple-like) chin of that one, heart-
    fascinating;
For, there was never an apple on the cypress (of stature).

On account of his sauciness and lacerating of men,
The old man found pleasure in shaving his head.

With an old razor, the age of small hope (the old man)
Made his (the son's) head white, like the hand of Moses.

That one of iron heart (the old man), from the impetuosity
    which he had,
Opened (his own) tongue, as to the defect of the one of
    Parí-cheek.

160 As to the razor, which made diminution of his beauty,
Men placed, at once, its head in its belly.

The head of the one of beautiful countenance, from shame,
    harp-like,
Lowered; and, his hair fallen, in front, (on the ground).

As to a certain one,—in whom the heart had gone,—
He was infatuated like his (the boy's) eyes, heart-binding.

A person said:—" Thou didst experience violence and
    pain;
" Wander not again in regard to a vain fancy.

" Turn away, moth-like, from love for the boy;
" For the scissors have extinguished the candle of his
    beauty."

---

156   One has never seen an apple on the cypress. But, his stature was as
a cypress; and his chin, the apple on it.
158   " Músa, in the first line, signifies a razor; in the second, Moses.
160   After shaving, men put the razor-blade into the razor-handle (its
belly).
    A commentator says that the second line may be rendered:—
    " Men placed, at once, the loss of the beauty of his head, in secret,
        within their own belly."

165 A cry arose from that true lover :—
" The covenant of those of wet skirt (sin-stained) is
    sluggish.

" A son of pleasant temperament and handsome face—is
    necessary ;
" To his father, say :—In ignorance, cast away his hair.

" My soul has mingled with his love ;
" My heart is not attached to his hair."

When thou hast a handsome countenance, suffer not grief;
For, if the hair falls, it will again grow.

The vine gives not always a green cluster ;
It sometimes sheds its leaves ; sometimes gives fruit.

170 Sun-like, the great fall under a veil (of eclipse) ;
Spark-like, the envious fall into the water.

The sun comes forth from beneath the cloud,
Gradually ; but, the spark perishes in the water.

Oh approved friend ! fear not the darkness,
In which it is possible there is the water of life.

Did not the world find rest, after motion ?
Did not Sa'dí travel, until he found his desire ?

Consume not thy heart, from failure of desire ;
Oh brother ! the night is pregnant with the day.

---

165   I am not of those. Nay, I am a lover, violence-enduring. I love the
    nature of the beloved one, not his forelock (kákul).
172   The Water of Life is to be found in a very dark place. See translation
    of the Sikandar-Náma, by Clarke.

CHAPTER VII.

ON EDUCATION.

1 THE language (of this chapter) is on integrity, and delibe-
    ration, and disposition;
Not on the steed, and the battle-field, and the ball-game.

Thou art fellow-lodger with the enemy,—lust;
Why art thou a stranger in the art of conflict?

Those turning back the rein of lust, from forbidden things,
Surpassed Rustam and Sám in manliness.

Chastise thyself, with a stick, boy-like;
Beat not men's brains with the heavy mace.

5 No one has concern for an enemy like thee,
Who prevailst not against thy own body.

1

This couplet means:—Our language is on the correcting of the
passions, and deliberating on the future world, and perfecting the disposition; not on reining the steed, and galloping in the battle-field.
2   Thou shouldst slay so near an enemy; but wonderful to say—thou
art careless of him, and a stranger as to contest with him.

Thy body is a city full of good and bad ;
Thou art sultán ; and wisdom (is) the prime-minister.

Know for sure, that the mean, neck-exalting,
In this city are—pride, and passion, and avarice.

Resignation and the fear of God are the free of good report ;
Lust and concupiscence are highway-men and cut-purses.

When the sultán displays favour to the bad,
How may ease remain for the wise ?

10 Lust, and avarice, and pride, and envy
Are like blood in thy veins ; and, like the soul in thy body.

If these enemies should obtain nurture,
They would turn aside their heads from thy order and
    judgment.

On the part of lust and concupiscence, opposition remains
    not,
When they experience the grasp of sharp wisdom.

The Ra,is, who punished not the enemy,
Ruled not also,—by reason of the enemy's power.

What need to say much in this chapter,
When a word is enough, if a person acts upon it ?

15 If thou bringst thy feet, mountain-like, (firmly) beneath
    thy skirt,
Thy head will pass beyond the sky in grandeur.

Oh man, much-knowing ! draw within the tongue ;
For, at the Resurrection, there is no register, as to the
    tongueless.

---

16   At the Resurrection, there will be no reckoning of deeds done by
tongueless animals. It is possible that the expression "tongueless"
here means—little-speaking. For, in truth, nothing casts men headlong into hell-fire, save the requital of words spoken by the tongue.

Those scattering the jewel of secrets, oyster-like,
Opened not their mouths, save for pearls (of lustrous
    words).

The one great in speech (loquacious) is stuffed as to his
    ears (deaf);
He takes not advice, save in silence.

When thou wishst to speak incessantly,
Thou findst not pleasure from the speech of any.

20 It is improper to utter unprepared speech;
It is unfit, to cut (to stop a person's speech) not cast out
    (delivered).

Those reflecting on falsehood and truth,
Are better than triflers, ready of answer.

In man's soul, speech is perfection;
Make not thyself of less account, by speech.

Thou seest not the little talker ashamed;
A grain of musk is better than a heap of clay.

Exercise caution as to the fool having the speech of ten
    men;
Utter, like a wise man, one prepared speech.

25 Thou didst cast a hundred arrows, and each of the hun-
    dred is a miss;
If thou art wise, cast one straight.

Why does a man utter in secret that thing,
When, if it becomes known, his face becomes yellow?

---

21   " Zhazh " signifies—a grass excessively hard, which the camel eats.
    "Zhazh-khá" is opposed to " shakr-khá "; it is synonymous with
"behúda-go"; " sakht-go."
24   Nizámí says :—
    "If thou knowst, say little;
      Utter not one thing a hundred times; say a hundred things once."

Detract not, in front of a wall,
Behind which, it often happens some one has his ear.

The interior of thy heart is the rampart of a secret,
Take care that it may not see the city-door open.

The wise man has sewn up his mouth, for that reason,
That he sees the candle is consumed by its tongue (wick).

------

30 Takash uttered a secret to his slaves,
Saying :—" It is improper to unfold this secret to any
    one."

In one year, it came from the heart to his lip ;
In one day, it became published in the world.

He ordered the merciless executioner,
Saying :—" Take off the heads of these, with the sword."

One, from amongst the slaves, while he asked for pro-
    tection, said :—
" Slay not the slaves ; for, this crime arose from thee.

" At first, when it was a mere fountain, thou didst not
    bind it ;
" When it became a torrent, of what use is binding ? "

35 Reveal thou not the heart's secret to any one,
Who will, indeed, utter it to every one.

Entrust the jewel to the treasury-guards ;
But, keep guard over the secret thyself.

So long as thou utterst not speech, to thee, there is power
    over it ;
When it becomes uttered, it obtains mastery over thee.

Thou knowst that when the demon has departed from
　　bonds,
He returns not again at the—Lá haul—of any one.

Speech is a confined demon in the heart's well;
Let it not go to the height of palate and tongue.

40 One can give way to the ugly demon;
But, one cannot seize him again by fraud.

A child may take off the tether from (the steed) Rakhsh;
It comes not within the noose, with a hundred Rustams.

Utter not that which, if it falls on an assembly (becomes
　　revealed),
A person, on its account, falls into calamity.

How well said the woman to the ignorant villager,—
" Utter speech, with wisdom; or, express not a breath."

Utter not what thou hast not the power to hear;
For, having sown barley, thou wilt not reap wheat.

45 How well, (the Indian sage) Barhaman expressed this
　　proverb :—
" Every one's dignity is of himself."

It is unnecessary that thou shouldst play much,
In order that thou mayst shatter thy own value.

A certain one was of good disposition, but ragged garment
　　clad,
Who was silent for some time, in Egypt.

38　" Lá haul walá ḳúwata illá bi-lláh "—there is no power, nor strength,
but in God !
41　Rakhsh was the name of Rustam's steed.

The wise men, from near and far,
Around him, moth-like, light-seeking.

One night, within his own heart, he reflected,
Saying :—" A man is hidden under his own tongue.

50 " Even so, if I lower my head to myself ;
" How many men know whether I am wise ? "

He spoke ; and enemy and friend knew
That he was indeed, in Egypt, more ignorant than himself.

Those who used to be in his presence became dispersed ;
    and his work ruined ;
He made a journey ; and, on the arch of a masjid, wrote :—

" If I had, in a mirror, beheld myself,
" I would not, in foolishness, have rent the curtain.

" So ugly,—I lifted the screen from it ;
" For, I thought myself of good visage."

55 For the one little speaking, there is great fame ;
When thou spakest, and splendour remained not to thee,—
    fly.

Oh lord of sense ! for thee, silence
Is dignity ; and, for the worthless one, a curtain.

If thou art a sage, take not away fear of thyself (as to
    uttering speech) ;
And, if thou art a fool, rend not thy own screen.

Display not quickly the idea of thy own mind ;
For, whenever thou wishst, thou canst reveal it.

---

49   'Alí, cousin and son-in-law of Muḥammad, spoke as given in the
second line.
50   The first line signifies—" If I keep silent."

But, when a man's **secret** is discovered,
One cannot, by endeavour, make it again secret.

60 How well the pen concealed the sultán's secret,
   At the head of which, so long as the knife was not, it
       spoke not.

The wild beasts are silent,—mankind speakers ;
The foolish speaker is worse than the wild beast.

It is proper **to utter speech with sense, like a man** ;
Or, otherwise, to be silent like a wild-beast.

By articulation and sense, **one man-born is known** ;
Be not loquacious and foolish, parrot-like.

A certain foolish **one spoke at the time of quarrelling** ;
With the **hand, they rent his collar.**

65 He suffered blows on the back of his head ; and sate naked
       and weeping ;
   One, world-experienced, said to him :—"Oh self-wor-
       shipper !

" If thou hadst, rose-bud-like, been mouth-closed,
" Thou wouldst not have seen thy shirt rent, rose-like."

The confounded **one utters speech full of folly** ;
Like a brainless (hollow) drum, much-boasting.

Seest thou not, that the tongue is only **a fire** ?
One **can** extinguish it, in a moment, with water.

If a **man be possessed of skill,**
Skill itself will speak, **not the possessor of skill.**

70 If thou **hast pure musk, speak not** ;
   For, if it be (existent),—it becomes known by its **smell.**

To say, with an oath,—"the gold is of the **West**,"
What need? the touch-stone, indeed, will say what it is.

A thousand calumniators will speak, for this reason,
Saying:—"Sa'dí is neither skilful nor sociable."

It is allowable if they rend my **fur-coat** (slander me);
For, I have not the power (of endurance) that they should
     take my brain (by much talking).

The son of King 'Azúd was very ill;
Patience was far from his father's nature.

75 A certain pious one spoke to 'Azúd, by way of advice,
Saying:—"Let go the wild fowls from confinement."

He broke the cages of the birds, morning-singing;
—Who remains in confinement, when the prison is
     broken?

The king kept on the arch of the garden-house,
One famous nightingale, a sweet singer.

The son, in the early morn, hastened towards the garden;
He found only that bird, on the arch of the hall.

He laughed, saying:—"Oh nightingale of pleasant voice!
" Thou art left in a cage, on account of thy sweet speech."

80 No one has business with thee, speechless;
But, when thou spakest, bring its proof.

Like Sa'dí, who, for some time, closed his tongue;
(And) escaped from the calumny of calumniators.

----

81   This couplet may be rendered:—
              Like Sa'dí, who, while he was tongue-bound,
              Was free from the calumny of calumniators.

That one takes ease of heart into his bosom,
Who, from people's society, takes the edge (of the road).

Oh wise man ! make not evident the people's defect ;
Be occupied with thy own defect, not with that of the
    people.

When they speak falsely, apply not the ear (listen not) ;
When thou seest one uncovered, cover thy eyes.

---

85 I have heard that, at a banquet of intoxicated slaves,
A disciple broke the minstrel's tambourine and harp.

They drew him, at once, by the hair, harp-like,
The slaves struck him on the face, drum-like.

At night, from pain of stick and slap, he slept not ;
The next day, an old man said to him, by way of admoni-
    tion :—

" Thou wishst not to be face-wounded drum-like ;
" Oh brother ! cast down thy head, in front, harp-like."

Two persons beheld dust, and tumult, and conflict ;
Shoes scattered ; stones flying.

90 This one saw the commotion ; he turned away from its
    direction ;
The other went into the midst, and broke his head.

No one is happier than one lord of himself ;
For, he has no concern with the good and bad.

---

83   Note the difference between " ba chíze mashghúl búdan " and " az
chíze mashghúl búdan."

They placed thy eye and ear in the head ;
The mouth, the place of speech ; and, the heart the place
    of sense.

Perhaps, thou mayst again know descent from ascent ;
Thou mayst not say :—" This is short, that long."

———

Thus spoke an old man of approved sense,
—The words of old men are pleasing to the ear.—

95 Saying :—In India, I went down to a corner ;
What saw I ?   A black man, long, like the longest winter-
    night.

In his embrace, a girl, moon-like,
His teeth lowered to her lips.

In his embrace, so tightly gathered,
That thou wouldst say :—the night covers the day.

The well known command of God seized my skirt ;
Presumption became a fire and seized me.

From before and behind, I sought for a stick or stone,
Saying :—" Oh one fearing not God ! nameless and shame-
    less."

100 With reproach, and abuse, and outcry, and force,
I separated the white (girl) from the black (man) as the
    dawn.

From above the garden, that horrible cloud departed ;
From beneath the crow, that egg appeared.

———

93   Thou mayst be cautious in thy gait.
94   In the 'Iḳd-i-manẓúm, couplets 94 to 116 are omitted.
98   It is proper to dissuade a person from violating an order of God.

From the reciting of—Lá haul—that demon-form leaped
  forth ;
The hand of the one of Parí-form clung to me.

Saying :—" Oh thou of the prayer-carpet of hypocrisy,
  blue-clad ;
" Of black deeds, world-purchaser, religion-seller !

" A long time, my heart had gone from the hand
" To this person ; and, my soul was desirous of him.

105 " Now became cooked my raw morsel,
" Which hot thou didst put out of my mouth."

She brought an accusation of tyranny, and uttered complaint,
Saying :—" Compassion fell down, and mercy remained
  not.

" None of the young men remained a helper,
" Who might take justice from me, from this old man,

" To whom shame of his old age comes not,
" To fix his hand in the veil of a woman, unlawful to him."

My skirt in her grasp, she kept complaining ;
From shame, my head remained in the collar.

110 Like garlic, I immediately went out of my garment ;
For, I feared the rebuke of young and old.

Naked, I went running from before the woman ;
For, my garment in her hand was better than myself.

After a time, she passed by me,
Saying :—" Knowst thou me ? "   I replied :—" Beware !

" On account of thy hand, I have repented,
" Saying,—I wander not again about a matter of inter-
  ference."

Such a matter comes not before that one,
Who wisely sits behind his own work.

115 Through this disgrace, I took up this counsel,
I regarded, in future, the thing seen, un-seen.

If thou hast sense and wisdom, draw within the tongue;
Like Sa'dí, utter speech; if not, be silent.

A certain one sate before Dá'ud of the tribe of Tai,
Saying:—" I saw a certain Súfí fallen drunk.

" His turban and shirt, vomit-stained;
" A crowd of dogs, a ring around him."

When the one of happy disposition heard this tale,
He gathered together his eyebrows at the speaker.

120 For a time, he was amazed, and said :—" Oh companion !
" A kind friend is of use to-day.

" Go; bring him from that shameful place;
" For it is forbidden in the law; and, a disgrace as to the
        religious garb.

" Bring him on thy back, like men, for the intoxicated one
" Has not the rein of safety in his hand."

Through this speech, the hearer became straitened in
        heart;
He descended into thought, like an ass in the mire.

Neither the boldness, that he might refuse the order;
Nor the power, that he might bring the drunken one on
        his shoulder.

---

117   Abú Sulaimán Dá,ud bin Naṣr belonged to the great Shaikhs, and to
the Lords of Ṣúfí-ism. He was the pupil of Abú Ḥanífa the Kúfíte.

125 He contorted himself, for a while ; but, saw no remedy ;
He saw no way of drawing his head out of the order.

He bound his loins, and without choice, on his back,
Brought him ; and, a city about him, in ferment.

One reviled him, saying :—" Behold the darvesh (Súfí) !
" Oh wonderful devotees of pure religion !

" See thou these Súfís, who have drunk wine ;
" (Who) have pawned the patched garment for aromatic
        wine."

Pointing with the hand to this one and the other,
Saying :—" This one is altogether drunk ; and, that one,
        half drunk."

130 The sword of the enemy's violence on the neck
Is better than the disgrace of a city, and the clamour of
        the people.

He suffered calamity ; and, with trouble, passed one day ;
He carried him, without desire, to a place that he had.

During the night, from shame and thought, he slept not ;
The next day Tai laughed, and said :—

" Spill not a brother's reputation in the street,
" That adverse fortune may not spill thy reputation, in a
        city."

In respect to the man, good or bad,—ill
Utter not. Oh young man endowed with understanding !

135 For, thou makest the bad man thy enemy ;
And, if he be a good man, thou doest ill.

---

130   " Josh-i-'awamm " signifies—hujúm-i-anám.

Whosoever says to thee, a certain one is bad ;
Know this much, that he is censuring himself.

For, the proof of (the bad) act of a person is necessary ;
And, his (the calumniator's) bad act appears clear.

In ill-speaking, when thou expressest breath,
If thou speakst the truth even, thou art bad.

A person made long his tongue, in slander ;
A sagacious one, head-exalting spoke to him,

140 Saying :—" Render not bad the memory of persons, before
          me ;
    " Make me not evilly suspicious, as to thyself.

    " I admit—there may be diminution of his dignity ;
    " There will be no increase to thy rank."

    A person said—I thought it was a jest—
    " Thieving is more upright than slandering."

    I said to him :—" Oh friend of distracted sense !
    " That tale came strangely to my ear.

    " What goodness, seest thou in dishonesty,
    " That thou preferst it to slander ? "

145 He replied ,—" Yes ; thieves display ardour ;
    " By the manly arm, they fill the belly.

---

136   " Dar postín-i-khud búdan " signifies—mazimmat-i-khud kardan.   See
couplet 162.

" From slander, what does that simpleton desire,
" Who blackened his record-book (with God) and enjoyed
  not anything ? "

In the Nizámiya, I had a pension ;
Night and day, there was instruction and repetition.

I said to my teacher :—" Oh one full of wisdom !
" A certain friend bears me envy.

" When I give the gift of signification, as to the traditions,
" His polluted heart becomes disturbed."

50 When the leader of morals heard this **speech,**
He was greatly enraged, and said :—" How wonderful !

" Thy friend's enviousness is disagreeable to thee ;
" Who informed thee that detraction is good ?

" If he, through baseness, took hell's path,
" Thou, by this other path, reachst it."

A certain one said :—" Hujjáj is a blood-devourer,
" His heart is like a piece of black stone.

" He fears neither the sigh, nor the complaint of the
      people ;
" Oh God ! Take from him the justice due to the people."

55 One, world-experienced, an old man of ancient birth,
Gave to a young man, a piece of counsel, worthy of an old
      man,

---

47   The Nizámiya was a college at Baghdád. It was founded by Nizámu-
l-Mulk Túsí, the vazír of Sultán Sanjár of Persia.
53   Hujjáj, son of Yusuf, ruled 'Irák-i-'Arab, in 685 A.D. He was notorious for cruelty.

Saying :—" The justice, of (due to) his wretched oppressed
    ones,
" They will demand (on the Judgment Day); and, from
    the others (his slanderers) revenge.

" Restrain thy hand (of criticism) from his and his time ;
" For, time itself makes him powerless.

" Neither does injustice on his part appear to me happy ;
" Nor, slander even, on thy part, appear to me pleasant."

Sin carries to hell the ill-fated one,
Who made full his measure ; and black (with entries) his
    record-book.

160 The other person, by slander, runs behind him,
Lest that he should go alone to hell.

I have heard that one of the pious
Laughed, jestingly, at a boy.

The other devotees, sitting in retirement,
Fell, in slander, on his fur-garment.

At length, this story remained not concealed ;
They unfolded it to that one of clear sight.   He said :—

" Rend not the curtain over the friend of perturbed state ;
" Neither is pleasantry unlawful; nor, slander lawful."

---

165 In my childhood, the desire of fast-keeping arose ;
I used not to know, which was left, and which right.

---

162   See couplet 136.
164   " Parda darídan " signifies—'aib kardan ; nám-i-kase ba badí yád kardan ; mazimmat-i-kase kardan.

A certain 'ábid of the pious of the street
Used constantly to teach me the washing of hand and foot,

Saying :—" First, according to tradition, say :—In the
    name of God !
" Secondly, summon resolution; thirdly, wash the palms
    of the hands.

" Wash, after that, the mouth and nose three times,
" Scratch the nostrils, with the little finger.

" Rub the front teeth, with the fore-finger;
" For, after the declining (of the sun the tooth-brush) is
    forbidden during a fast.

" And throw, after that, three handfuls of water on the
    face;
" From the growing-place of the hair, down to the chin.

" Wash again the hands up to the elbow;
" Utter whatever thou knowst of praise and recitation of
    the names of God.

" Again, stroking of the head; after that, washing of the
    feet;
" This is indeed (ablution); and its conclusion,—' in the
    name of God.'

" As to this custom (of ablution), no one knows better
    than I,
" Seest thou not that the old man of the village has become
    doting ? "

---

67   Among the Sunnís there are four sects (mazhab). The titles are
derived from the names of the chief of the sect, thus :—Mazhab-i-
hanífa; Mazhab-i-shafi'í; Mazhab-i-hambl; Mazhab-i-málik.
    At the beginning of ablution, to say—" Bimi-lláhu-r-rahmanu-r-
rahím,"—was Muhammad's command.
69   The tooth-brush (miswák) consists of a piece of soft wood, the end of
which is rubbed against the teeth. These tooth-brushes are sold in
small bundles in the bázárs.

The ancient village-holder heard this speech;
He was confounded, and said :—" Oh execrable filthy one !

175 " Saidst thou not that, the tooth-brush during a fast is a
    crime ?
" To eat the dead sons of Ádam is lawful.

" Say—first, the mouth from things unfit to be uttered,
" Wash—to that one who has washed as to things fit to be
    eaten."

The person, whose name is mentioned in public,
Recite his name and praises, in the sweetest way.

When always thou sayst that men are asses
Entertain not the idea, that they, like men, will mention
    thy name.

Speak of my mode of life, within the street, even as
Thou canst speak of it to my face.

180 And, if thou hast shame of the one present
  Oh sightless one ! is not the Secret-Knower (God)
    present ?

Shame comes not to thee of thyself
That thou hast freedom as to Him, and shame as to me ?

———

Those path-recognising of firm foot
Sate, some time, together in privacy.

One from amongst them began to slander,
He opened the door of remembrance of a helpless one.

A person said to him :—" Oh friend of perturbed com-
    plexion !
" Hast thou ever made war against the infidels in Europe ? "

85 The slanderer said :—" From behind my four walls,
" I have not, during my whole life, placed my foot in front
(of them)."

The darvesh of pure breath thus spoke :—
" I have not beheld a person, to such a degree greatly distraught,

" That the infidel sits secure from contest with him ;
" (But) a Muslim escapes not from the violence of his
tongue."

How well a distraught one of Marghàz uttered
A saying, from the subtlety of which thou mayst bite the
lip with the teeth :—

" If I defame the name of men,
" I only utter the slander of my mother.

90 " For the wise educated ones know,
" That that devotion is indeed best which the mother
takes."

Oh one of good name ! a friend, who is absent,—
As to him, two things are unlawful.

One is that they should wrongfully enjoy his property ;
The second that they should defame him.

Whosoever defames men,
Expect not thou thy own thanks from him.

---

90   'Abdu-llàh says :—" If I slander anyone, I ought to slander my father
and mother ; for they are worthy of my good deeds. When a person
slanders another, the angels give the slanderer's good deeds to the
slandered."

In the traditions, it is stated :—" If a person oppresses, the boldness
of the oppressed goes to the oppressor ; and the goodness of the oppressor
to the oppressed.

For, he utters that very thing in thy absence,
Which he utters before thee, behind men.

195 In my opinion, that person is world-wise,
Who is engaged about himself, and careless of the world.

As to three persons, I have heard that slander is lawful;
When thou exceedst this, the fourth is a sin.

First, the king, reproach-approving,—
From whom, thou mayst observe injury as to the people's
     heart,—

It is lawful to carry information regarding him;
Perhaps, the people may be cautious of him.

Secondly,—draw not the screen on the shameless one;
For, he himself rends the screen of his own body.

200 Oh brother! guard not, from the (shallow) pool, him,
Who falls, up to the neck, in a well.

Thirdly—the one of crooked balance, of dishonest disposi-
     tion,
Utter whatsoever thou knowst of his bad deeds.

I have heard that a thief entered from the desert,
He passed by the gate of Sístán.

The green-grocer robbed him of half a dáng,
The thief of black deeds raised a cry :—

------

201   This couplet describes the fraudulent trader.
202   Rustam used to live in Sístán.

" Oh God ! burn not Thou in the fire the night-traveller
    (robber) ;
" For, an inhabitant of Sístán road travels (robs) by day."

---

205 A certain one said to a Súfí, possessed of purity ;—
" Knowst thou not what a certain person said behind thy
    back ? "

He replied :—" Oh brother ! be silent ; go to sleep :
" What the enemy said,—best unknown."

Those persons, who bear the enemy's message,
Are, assuredly, more an enemy than the enemy.

Bears the enemy's word to a friend, no one,
Save that one, who is, in enmity, the enemy's friend.

The enemy is unable to express violence to me,
To such a degree that my body should tremble at hearing
    (his words).

210 Thou art the greater enemy, who bringst to the mouth
    (openly),
What the enemy said, in secret.

The word-plucker makes fresh the ancient feud ;
He brings the good, meek, man to anger.

So long as thou canst, fly from that fellow-sitter,
Who said to the dormant trouble—" Arise ! "

(To be) a man of black condition (in distress),—in it, foot-
    bound,
Is better than to carry strife from place to place.

Contest, between two persons, is like fire ;
The unfortunate tale-bearer is the fire-wood cutter.

---

215 Fírídún had an approved vazír,
Who possessed an illumined heart, and far-seeing eye.

First, he used to preserve resignation to God;
Next, he used to keep observance of the king's command.

The mean functionary places trouble upon the people,
Saying :—" It is the administration of the country and the
      augmentation of the treasury."

If thou keepst not God's side,
God causes injury to reach thee from the king.

A certain one went, in the morning, to the king,
Saying :—" May ease and desire every day be thine !

220 " Consider it not design ; accept counsel from me ;
" This vazír is, in secret, thy enemy.

" Of the high and low of the army—none have remained,
" Who have not loans of silver and gold from him.

" On the condition that,—when the king, neck-exalting,
" Dies,—they give back that gold and silver.

" That self-worshipper wishes not thee, alive ;
" Lest that he should not regain his money."

Often, towards the vazír, the asylum of the kingdom,
The king, with the eye of punishment, used to glance,

225 Saying :—" In the semblance of friends, before me,
" Why art thou, in heart, my enemy ? "

The vazír kissed the ground before his throne and said :
" Since thou askst, it is now improper to conceal.

" Oh renowned king ! I this wish,
" That the world, like me, may be thy well-wisher.

" When thy death is the stated period for (the return of)
    my silver,
" They will, from fear of me, wish thee greater perma-
    nency.

" Desirest thou not that men, with sincerity and supplica-
    tion,
" Should wish thy head green, and thy life long.

230 " Men reckon prayer—a gain;
" For, it is the cuirass against the arrow of calamity."

The monarch approved of what he said:
The rose of his face, from freshness, expanded.

Of the rank and station, which the prime-minister
    possessed,
He increased its dignity, and exalted its rank.

Than a calumniator, I have seen no one more afflicted;
Of more reversed fortune, and overturned state.

Through the ignorance and obscurity of judgment, which
    is his,
He casts altercation between two friends.

235 Another time, this and that (the two friends) make glad
    their hearts;
He, between them, unfortunate and ashamed,

To kindle a fire between two persons;
To consume oneself in the midst—is not wisdom.

Like Sa'dí, that one tasted the delight of retirement,
Who, from both worlds, withdrew his tongue.

Whatever thou knowst of profitable speech—utter;
Though it be acceptable to no one.

For, to-morrow (the Judgment Day), he penitent may raise
    a cry,
Saying :—" Alas ! why did I not listen to the truth ? "

———

240 A good, order-bearing, chaste wife
Makes a poor man, a king.

Go ; strike five times (in joy) at thy door,
That a concordant mistress is in thy bosom.

If, all day, thou endurest grief,—have no care,
When, at night, the dear companion is in thy embrace.

Whose house is prosperous, and bed-fellow, a companion—
God's glance is, in mercy, towards him.

When the wife of beautiful face is chaste,
The husband, by beholding her, is in Paradise.

245 That person took up, from the world, his heart's desire,
Whose mistress was concordant with him.

If she be chaste, and pleasant of speech,
Look not at her beauty, or deformity.

From the one of Parí-face, of bad disposition,—takes
    away (the ball of empire),
The woman of demon-face of pleasant disposition.

From her husband's hand, she takes vinegar, like sugar ;
Face vinegar plastered, she eats not sweetmeats.

250 The woman, well-wishing is the heart's-ease ;
But, from the bad woman,—oh God ! protect me.

As a parrot, for whom a crow was companion,
Considers freedom from the cage,—gain,—

Place thy head in wandering, in the world ;
Place, otherwise, thy heart on helplessness.

To go bare-foot,—better than the tight shoe ;
The toil of travel,—better than contention in the house.

A captive in the kází's dungeon,—better
Than, in the house, to see contraction on the eyebrow (of
    the wife).

255 Travel is a festival to that house-master,
In whose house is a wife of bad disposition.

Shut the door of joyfulness on that house,
From which, the wife's clamour issues loudly.

When the wife takes the path to the bázár, strike ;
Otherwise, sit, in the house, wife-like.

If the wife has no ear for her husband,
Clothe the man in her black garment.

The wife, who is ignorant and dishonourable,
Thou didst ask for a calamity on thy head,—not a woman.

260 When, in the barley-measure, she breaks faith,
Wash thy hand of the wheat-store.

God has desired good to that slave,
For whom, the heart and hand of the wife are true.

When the wife laughs in the stranger's face,
To the husband, say :—" Boast not further of manliness."

May the woman's eyes be blind, as to strangers !
When she goes out of the house, may it be to her grave !

When the wanton wife places her hand in the fried meat,
Say :—" Go ; put thy hand in a man's face."

---

260   The wife who abandons rectitude,—as to her being a harlot, have no
doubt.

265 When thou seest that the woman's foot is not in one place.
Silence is not the part of wisdom and judgment.

Fly from her hand, into the crocodile's mouth ;
For dying is better than life, in distress.

Cause her face to be covered from the strange man ;
And, if she hear not,—then whether wife, or husband,—
    what difference ?

The beautiful wife of pleasant disposition is fortune and
    companion ;
Release (divorce) the wife, ugly, discordant.

How well came this single speech from those two persons,
Who were bewildered by a woman's hand.

270 This one said :—" Let there not be a bad wife for any
    one ! "
The other said :—" Let there not be a woman, in the world
    itself !"

Oh friend ! every fresh spring, take a new wife ;
For, last year's almanac is of no use.

Whomsoever, thou seest captive to a woman ;
Do not—oh Sa'dí ! reproach him not.

Thou also mayst suffer violence, and endure her burden,—
If, one night, thou drawst her into thy embrace.

A young man, from want of concordance with his wife,
Bewailed to an old man, and said :—

---

271   The first line may be rendered :—
           Take a virgin woman.

75 " A heavy load, from the hand of this bold enemy,
" I endure, even as the nether mill-stone."

He said to him :—" Oh sir ! place thy heart on distress ;
" No one, by patience exercising, becomes ashamed.

" Oh one house-burning ! at night, thou art the upper
      mill-stone ;
" In the day, why art thou the nether stone ? "

When thou mayst have experienced pleasure from a rose-
      bush,
If thou endurest the burden of its thorn, it is proper.

The tree, whose fruit thou constantly enjoyst,
At that time,—when thou sufferst its thorn,—be patient.

------

80 When a boy has passed ten years of age,
   Say :—" Sit apart from those not unlawful (to him in
      marriage)."

It is not right to kindle a fire on cotton ;
For, while thou winkst the eye, the house is burned.

When thou wishst that thy name may remain in place
      (of honour),
Teach the son wisdom, and judgment.

When his skill and judgment are insufficient,
Thou wilt die ; and, none of thy family will remain.

He endures severity for much time,
The son,—whom the father tenderly cherishes.

------

276   " Ba sakhtí dil nihádan " signifies—to be content with hardship.
277   " Kháua-soz " is a word of the same class as " jahán-soz." It signifies
—one complaining of others ; time-stricken ; shameless ; unjust.

285 Keep him wise and abstinent;
If thou lovest him, keep him not by endearing expressions.

Rebuke and instruct him, in childhood;
Exercise promise and fear, as to his good and bad deeds.

For the young student,—commendation, and praise, and reward
(Are) better than the master's reprimand, and threatening.

Teach the one matured, hand-toil;
Even if, Kárún-like, thou hast command as to wealth.

How knowst thou—the revolution of time
May cause him to wander, in exile, in the country?

290 Rely not on that resource which is;
For, it may be, that wealth may not remain in thy hand.

When, for him—there are the resources of trade,
How may he bear the hand of beggary before any one?

The purse of silver and gold reaches its limit;
The purse of the trader becomes not empty.

Knowst thou not how Sa'dí obtained his object?
He neither traversed the desert, nor ploughed the sea.

In childhood, he suffered slaps from the great;
In matureness, God gave him purity.

295 Whosoever places his neck (in submission) to order,
Not much time passes, but he gives orders.

Every child, who the violence of the teacher,
Experiences not,—will suffer the violence of time.

Keep the son good and cause ease to reach him,
That his eyes (of expectation) may not remain on the hands of others.

Whosoever endured not grief for his son,
Another suffered grief and abused him.

Preserve him from the bad teacher;
For, the unfortunate and road-lost one makes him, like
    himself.

300 Desire not one of more black deeds than that herma-
    phrodite,
Whose face becomes black (with sin) before the sprouting
    of the beard.

From that one, void of honour, it is proper to fly;
For, his unmanliness spilled the water (of honour) of men.

The boy who sate among Kalandars,
To his father, say :—" Wash thy hands of his welfare."

Suffer not regret as to his destruction and ruin,
For, the degenerate son, dead before his father, (is) best.

———

One night, in my street, there was a convivial meeting;—
Men of every class, in that assembly.

---

302   The Kalandar, or Kalandar, or Kanda,e nátarashída, has, in perfection,
the disposition of going alone to Makka; of leading a solitary life; and
of strenuously exerting himself in the demolishing of customs and forms
of worship. He has no religious teacher; at the same time, he does not
refuse to take muríds or disciples. The Súfís blame the order.

   The Malámatí is one who keeps secret the worship of God from
others, who displays neither goodness nor beauty, and who conceals
neither wickedness nor evil.

   The Sáfí is one whose heart is not engaged with the people.

   The Sáfí is higher than the other two, because they are obedient to
saints and prophets.

   They apply the word Kalandar to wicked men, on account of their outward similarity to Kalandars, and to wine-drinkers. Of these three
sects, the Kalandar alone shaves his head.

305 When the musician's voice entered from the street,
The há,e hú,e of lovers went to the firmament.

One of fairy face was my beloved;
I said to him :—" Oh my beautiful toy !

" Why comest thou not, with thy companions, to the
    assembly,
" That thou mayst illumine our assembly, candle-like ? "

I heard that he went, and by himself,
Kept saying to me :—" Oh my lover !

" When thou hast not a beard, like men ;
" It is not manliness to sit before men."

———

310 The beardless boy, house-mining, ruins thee ;
Go ; make the house prosperous with a pleasant woman.

It is improper to play at love, with a rose,
Which has, every morning, a fresh nightingale.

Since, in every assembly, he made himself a candle,
Wander not again, about him, moth-like.

A woman, good, and of pleasant disposition and adorned,—
How does she resemble the ignorant youth ?

Blow a breath of fidelity upon her, rose-bud-like,
Who follows thee, with laughing, rose-like.

---

310   " Khána kan" signifies—ná-khalaf, one who does wicked deeds.
313   That woman, good and pleasant, is like a rose-bud.
    Then, as the rose-bud, with the breath of the morning wind, laughs—
do thou breathe the breath of fidelity, and see that, rose-like, with
much laughter, she will fall in rear and display cordiality.

315 Not like a beloved boy, impudent,
Whom one cannot break with a stone.

Consider him (the boy) not charming, like the húrí of
    Paradise,
For whom, the face of another is ugly, demon-like.

If thou dost kiss his feet, he has no thanks (to give);
And, if thou art the dust (in humility), he has no fear.

Make void thy head of brain, and hand of money,
When thou givest thy heart to the son of man.

Exercise not the evil glance, towards the son of man;
Lest evil should arise to thy own son.

————

320 Once upon a time, it reached my ear in this city (of
    Shíráz),
That a certain merchant purchased a slave.

*   *   *   *   *   *

The one of fairy-face, whatever fell to his hand,
Broke, in malice, the head and brain of the foolish mer-
    chant.

*   *   *   *   *   *

He summoned God and His Prophet to himself, as witness,
Saying :—" I will not again wander about folly."

325 In this week, journeying chanced to him,
Heart-wounded, and head-bound, and face-torn.

———

315   " Pech bar pech " here signifies—mahbúb.
321   For obvious reasons, couplets 321 and 323 are omitted.

When he went one or two miles out of Kazrún
A dangerous, stony place appeared before him.

He inquired, saying :—" What is the name of this
castle?"
Saying :—" Whosoever lives sees many wonderful things."

An intimate companion of the káraván thus spoke to
him :—
" Thou knowst not, perhaps, the place called—tang-i-
turkán ?"

The merchant grieved when he heard the name—tang-i-
turkán ;
Thou wouldst have said, that he had beheld the sight of
an enemy.

330 He raised a great shout at the black,
Saying :—" Why urgest thou farther ? Throw away the
goods.

" To me, there is not a barley-grain of wisdom, nor know-
ledge,
" If I again go to the—tang-i-turkán."

Shut the door of lust of the ungrateful soul ;
Or, if thou art a lover,—suffer the kick, and bind the
head.

When thou cherishst a slave,
Bring him up in awe, so that thou mayst enjoy advantage
from him.

And, if the lord bite with the teeth (kisses) his slave's lip,
He (the slave) matures the fancy of lordship.

---

326   Kazrún is at a distance of two karoh (twenty miles) from Shíráz.
One míl = four thousand camel-paces = one-third of a farsang.
327   The merchant thought the lofty rocks a castle.
328   " Turk " signifies—mahbúb.

335 The slave should be water-drawer, and brick-maker ;
    The cherished slave is a fist-striker.

A crowd sate with a pleasant youth,
Saying :—" We are honourable lovers, and possessed of
        discernment."

Ask (their state) of me, time-wearied ;
For the fast-keeper suffers regret at the table-cloth.

The sheep eats the date-seed, for that reason,
That there is a lock and fastening on the dates.

The head of the oil-presser's ox is towards the grass, for
        that reason,
That, its tether is short of the rape-seed.

---

340 A certain (chaste) one saw a form possessed of beauty ;
    Through phrensy of love and ecstacy for her, he changed.

Helpless, he cast forth perspiration, to the same degree,
As the dew on the leaf of the April-tree.

The sage Bukrát, riding, passed by him ;
He inquired, saying :—" What matter befell this one ? "

A person said to him :—" This is a chaste 'ábid,
" From whose hand sin never sprang.

---

335   In some copies, in the second line, "khisht," in place of "musht,"
occurs.
       Then " khisht-zan," in the first line means—brick-maker ; in the
second, brick-caster.
337   This couplet is uttered by Sa'dí, in reproach of the statement made in
couplet 336.
342   " Bukrát " signifies—Hippocrates.

" Day and night, he goes into the plain and mountain ;
" From society, fleeing ; and, with men, disgusted.

345 " One, heart-ravishing, has snatched his heart ;
" The foot of his vision has descended into the clay (of
        love).

" When the reproach of the people comes to his ear,
" He says :—Of so much reproach, be silent.

" Say not, if I complain, that he is not excusable ;
" For, my complaint is not far from cause.

" This picture snatches not the heart from my hand ;
" He (God) takes the heart, who pourtrayed this picture."

The man, work-tried, heard this speech ;
Old in years, one cherished, of ripe judgment.

350 He said :—" Although, the soul of goodness goes forth (in
        these words),
" With whatever thou mayst utter, every one goes not.

" Of the Painter (God) indeed is this picture ;
" Which snatched, in rapine, the heart of the distraught.

" Why does not the child of one day (in age) ravish his sense,
" For, in beholding the creating of God, whether of ripe
        age, or tender,—what difference ? "

The asserter of God's truth looks at the camel, in the
        same way,
As, at the beauties of Chín and Chigál.

---

352   The poet saith :—
        " From sky to earth, if thou lookst with wisdom,
        There is not an atom in which there is not a strange mystery."
353   In Chigal and Turkistán the people are very handsome.

Every line of mine of this book (the Bustán) is a woman's
    veil
Lowered on the cheek of the one, heart-alluring.

355 There are meanings (clear) beneath the black letters,
    Like the beloved one behind the curtain; or the moon
        behind the cloud.

In the times of Sa'dí sorrow is not comprehended;
For, there is so much beauty of thought behind the screen
        (of black letters).

For me,—there are words, assembly adorning,
In them, fire-like, illumination (for the seeker) and burning
        (for the envious).

I grieve not of enemies, if (through envy) they tremble;
For, through this Persian fire, they are in burning.

            ———

If he has escaped in the world, from the (people of the)
    world,
It is he, who has closed the door on himself, against the
    people.

360 No one escaped from the violence of tongues,
    Whether he be self-displaying, or truth-worshipping.

If, angel-like, thou dost fly from the sky,
Ill-thought will cling to thy skirt.

One can, with effort, bind the Tigris;
One cannot bind the enemy's tongue.

---

354   The author compares the book Bustán to a woman's veil; and its
meaning to a lovely one.

357   As in fire there are illumination and heat, so in Sa'dí's language
splendour and heart-burning.

Those wet of skirt (sin-stained) sit together,
Saying :—"This is dry devotion; and that a trap for
    gaining bread."

Turn not thy face from worshipping God,
Abandon ;—so that people may reckon thee as nothing.

365 When the pure God becomes satisfied with the slave,
If these (people) be not contented,—what matter ?

The enemy of the people is not acquainted with God ;
Through the tumult of the people, there is no way for him
    to God.

They have not found the path to the place (of their desire)
    for that reason,
That, they have missed their foot, at the first step.

Two persons apply their ears (listen) to a tradition :
From this one, to that—as far as from Ahrimán (Satan) to
    Surosh (Gabriel).

One accepts advice; the other, odious,
Through word-seizing (slandering), is not occupied with
    the advice.

370 Dejected, in the dark corner of a place,
What may he find from the cup, world-displaying ?

If thou art a lion, or a fox, think not
That thou mayst escape from these (slanderers) by man-
    liness, or stratagem.

If a person chooses the corner of retirement ;
Because he has not much solicitude for society,—

They make him contemptible, saying :—" (This one's work)
    is fraud and deceit ;
" He flies from man, as from the demon."

If he be of laughing face and sociable,
They consider him not chaste and abstinent.

5 With slander, they rend the rich man's skin,
Saying :—" If, in the world, there be a Far'ún, it is he."

If one, foodless, weeps, with heart-burning,
They call him :—" Unfortunate and unhappy."

If a poor man be in distress,
They will say it is—from calamity and misfortune.

And, if a prosperous one comes down from his footing,
They regard it (his fall) as gain, and God's grace.

Saying :—" How long this dignity and arrogance ?
" In the rear of happiness, is unhappiness."

10 If as to a straitened one of narrow means,—
Fortune makes his rank high,

In malice towards him, they gnash their teeth with poison,
Saying :—" This base time is the cherisher of the mean."

When they behold a work perfect in thy hand,
They reckon thee covetous, and world-worshipping.

And if thou holdst the hand of resolution from the work
      (of the world),
They consider thee of the beggar-trade, and cooked food-
      devourer.

And, if thou art an orator,—thou art a drum full of
      nonsense ;
If thou art silent,—thou art a picture (lifeless) of the
      bath-room.

---

7   " Idbár " signifies—pusht dádan.
13   " Pukhta-khwár " signifies—one who gives no toil to his body, but
devours the earnings of others. It means, also, one who eats the cooked
food of others, and who is present at their time of eating.

385 They call not those, patience-exercising, men,
    Saying :—" The helpless one, through fear, raised not his
       head."

And, if in his head (nature) there be awe and manliness,
They fly from him, saying :—" What madness is this ? "

If he be a little eater, they slander him,
Saying :—" His property is perhaps the fortune of another."

And, if his food be excellent and pure,
They call him :—" Belly-slave, and body-cherisher."

And, if the wealth-possessor lives without pomp,
    Saying :—" Decoration is a reproach to people of discern-
       ment."

390 They apply the tongue (of reproach) to his torture, sword-
       like,
    Saying :—" The unfortunate one withholds gold from his
       own body ! "

If he constructs a palace and painted hall ;
Makes a splendid dress for his own body.

He is ready to die, from the power of cavillers,
Saying :—" He adorned himself woman-like."

If a devotee travelled not,
Those, who have made journies call him not a man,

    Saying :—" For him, not advanced beyond his wife's
       embrace,
" What is his skill, or judgment, or knowledge ? "

395 They even rend the skin of one, world-experienced,
    Saying :—" He is one, head-revolving, of overturned
       fortune.

" If of fortune, there were for him, a portion and share,
" Time would not drive him from city to city."

The one viewing critically contemns the bachelor,
Saying :—" The earth is vexed with his sleeping and
    rising."

And, if he marries, he says :—" From the power of the
    heart,
" He has fallen headlong, in the mire, ass-like."

The one of ugly face escapes not from man's oppression ;
Nor the lovely one, from the unmanly one of ugly speech.

10 If, one day, anger plucks (a man) from his place,
They call him :—" Insane, and of obscure judgment."

And, if he exercises patience with any,
They will say :—" He has not sufficient spirit."

They say, by way of counsel, to the generous one,—
    " Enough !
" For, to-morrow, both thy hands may be (in beggary)
    before a person."

And if he becomes contented and self-possessing,
He becomes captive to the reproaching of a crowd,

Saying :—" This mean man wishes to die like his father.
" Who gave up wealth, and took away regret."

15 Who is able to sit in the corner of safety,
When the Prophet escaped not from the villainy of the
    enemy ?

Of God,—who resemblance, and partner and co-equal,
Has not,—heardst thou what the Christian said !

---

10   In the 'Ikd-i-manzúm, couplets 400 to 407 are omitted.
15   The infidels say :—" How is he (Muhammad) a prophet, who eats
like us, and wanders in the streets and bázár ? "

No one escapes from a person's hand,
The remedy for the captive is patience only.

————

There was a young man, skilful and learned,
Who was, as regards admonishing, vigilant and manly.

Of good repute, and pious, and God-worshipping,
The beard of his face more beautiful than his hand-
 writing.

410 Strong in eloquence, and clever in grammar;
But, he used not to utter truly the letters of the Abjad.

Perhaps, he had stammering in the tongue,
For, he used not to explain the truth of the Mu'jam.

I spoke to one of the pious,
Saying :—" A certain one has no front teeth."

At my folly, he became red of face,
Saying :—" Speak not again, in this foolish way.

" Thou didst see in him that very defect, which is existent;
" From how much skill, thy wisdom's eye was shut !

415 " Listen truly to me; for, in the day of certainty (Resurrection),
" The man, good-seeing, will not experience evil.

" One, who has grace, and science, and judgment,
" —If the foot of his integrity slips from its place.—

" Approve not violence against him, for one small matter.
" What have the sages said :—Take what is clean."

Oh wise man ! the thorn and the rose are together :
Why art thou in the fetter of the thorn ? fasten thou the
 rose-bouquet.

————

415 Couplets 415 and 416 form a " kat'a-band."

He—in whose nature, is the ugly disposition,
Sees not the peacock,—only his ugly foot.

120 Oh one of malevolent face! acquire purity (of heart);
For, the dark mirror displays not the face.

Seek a path by which, thou mayst escape from punishment
　　　　(of hell);
Not a word (of man), on which thou mayst lay the finger
　　　　(of criticism).

Oh wise one! place not in front (expose not) the people's
　　　　defects;
For it sews up thy eyes from thy own defects.

Why do I inflict punishment on the one of stained skirt,
When I know, within myself, that I am of wet (stained)
　　　　skirt?

It is improper that thou shouldst exercise violence against
　　　　a person,
When thou dost aid thyself by artifice of speech.

125 When evil is unpleasant to thee, do not do it thyself;
Say, after that, to thy neighbour:—" Do not evil."

If I am God-worshipping; or if self-displaying;
I preserve my exterior for thee, my interior for God.

When I adorned my exterior with chastity,
Interfere not with my crookedness, or uprightness.

If my way of life be good; or if bad,
God is more acquainted than thou, with my secret.

Punish for bad conduct that person,
Who hopes from thee the reward of goodness.

130 If I am good or bad, be thou silent;
For, I am myself the porter of profit and loss.

For a good deed by a man of good judgment,—
For one, God writes ten.

Oh son ! of whomsoever, thou also a single talent
Mayst observe,—pass by his ten defects.

Count not upon the finger one defect of his ;
Bring forth a world of excellence for nothing.

Like the enemy, who, on the poetry of Sa'dí,
Glances with scorn, heart ruined.

435 He has no ear for the hundred beautiful subtleties ;
When he beholds a defect, he raises a shout.

That one, bad-approving,—to whom, there is only this
    reason,—
Envy plucked out his eyes, good-discerning.

Did not God's creating create the people ?
Black, and white, and beautiful, and ugly—came.

Not every eye nor eyebrow, that thou seest, is good ;
Eat the kernel of the pistachio nut ; cast away its husk.

---

431   Thus it is written in the Ḳurán.

CHAPTER VIII.

On Thanks.

1 I CANNOT express a breath for thanks to my Friend (God);
For, I know not a word of praise that is worthy of Him.

Every hair on my body is a gift from Him;
How may I perform thanks for every hair?

Praise to the Lord-Giver,
Who, from nonentity, made the slave existing.

To whom, is there the power of description of His beneficence?
For, His praises are immersed in His dignity.

5 That inventor, who creates a person from clay,
Gives soul, and wisdom, and sense, and heart.

From the father's back-bone to the limit of old age,
Behold to what extent, He, from the unseen, gave thee
honour!

---

4   If one utters thanks to God,
How may he utter thanks for the grace of thanks to God?

When God created thee pure, be sensible and pure;
For, it is a shame to go unclean to the dust (of the grave).

Shake off continually the dust (of mean qualities) from the
    mirror (of the heart);
For, it takes not polish, when the blight eats it.

In the beginning, wast thou not water of man's seed?
If thou art a man, put presumption out of thy head.

10 When, thou bringst, with effort, victuals to thyself,
Rely not on the strength of thy own arm.

Oh self-worshipper! why dost thou not see God
Who brings into revolution the arm of the hand?

When by thy striving, a thing happens,
. Know by God's grace (it is); not, by thy own effort.

By violence no one has carried off the ball;
Utter praise to the Lord of Grace.

Of thyself, thou art not erect one step;
From the hidden, aid arrives momently.

15 Wast thou not a child, tongue-bound as to boast (of
    speech)?
Food, from the navel, kept coming within thee.

When they severed the umbilical cord, thy daily food was
    broken off;
Thy hand clung to thy mother's breast.

A traveller, before whom adverse time brings sickness,
They give to him water from his own city, as medicine.

Then he obtained nourishment in the belly;
He obtained food from the store of the bowels.

---

17   When a person drinks the water of his native place, he obtains
(they say) convalescence.

The two breasts,—that, to-day, are heart-pleasing to him,—
Are also two fountains of his nurturing-place.

The bosom and breast of the mother, heart-pleasing,
Are paradise; and, the breast is for him, a stream of milk.

Her stature, life-nourishing, is a tree;
The offspring, on her bosom,—a delicate fruit.

Are not the veins of the breast, within the heart?
Then, if thou wilt consider, milk is the heart's blood.

Teeth, sting-like, plunged in her blood;
Love for her own blood-devourer created within her.

When God made the arm strong; and, the teeth, dense—
The nurse anoints her breast with aloes.

The aloe makes it (the offspring) silent (forgetful) of milk, so
That it forgets the breast and its milk.

Oh sir! thou also art, as to repentance, a child of the path
    of God;
By bitterness, sin becomes forgotten by thee.

A young man turned his head from his mother's judgment,
Her sorrowful heart burned like fire.

When she became helpless, she brought a cradle before
    him,
Saying :—" Oh one languid of love and forgetful of the
    time (of infancy)!

" Wast thou not weeping, and tired and small,
" When nights, from thy power, sleep overpowered me
    not?

30 " No; to thee, in the cradle there was not the strength of
          thy (present) state;
   " To thee, there was not the power to drive away a fly
          from thyself.

   " Thou art that one, who used to be vexed with a single
          fly,
   " Who, to day, art chief and powerful."

   Thou mayst again be in that state, at the bottom of the
          grave,
   When thou canst not repel an ant from thy body.

   Again how may the eye light up its lamp,
   When the worm of the grave devours the fat of the brain?

   Like one clothed as to the eye (blind), seest thou not that
          the road
   He knows not, at the time of going, from the well?

35 Thou who art possessed of vision, if thou didst perform
          thanks (knowst the path from the well);
   If not, thou also art one clothed as to the eye (blind).

   The instructor taught thee not understanding and judg-
          ment;
   God created these qualities in thy existence.

   If He had refused thee a heart, truth-hearing,
   Truth would have appeared to thy eye the essence of false-
          hood.

———

   Behold one finger, with how many joints,
   God, by creating, cast together.

   Then, it is madness and foolishness,
   That thou shouldst place thy finger (of cavilling) on the
          word of His creating.

For the sake of man's motion, consider
Him, who fixed the sinews and placed the articulations of
    so many bones.

For, without the revolution of the ancle, and the knee, and
    the foot,
It is impossible to raise the foot from its place.

Prostration (on the ground) is not difficult for a man, on
    that account,
That, the joint in his back-bone is not of one piece.

God has arranged two hundred joints within one another,
Who has finished like thee (oh God!) a clay-joint?

Oh one of agreeable disposition! the veins in thy body
Are a land,—in it, are three hundred and sixty streams.

In the head,—vision, and thought, and judgment, and dis-
    cretion;
The limb of the body for the dear heart; (and) the heart
    for dear wisdom.

The wild beasts, with the countenance downcast, are con-
    temptible;
Thou, Alif-like, art a rider on thy feet.

They, head-lowered, for the sake of eating;
Thou, with dignity, bringst thy food to the head.

It beseems thee not, with so much chieftainship,
That thou shouldst lower thy head, save in devotion (to
    God).

By His own beauty, God gave thee knowledge; behold!
He made thee not, like the animals, head in the grass.

"Pai zadan" signifies—ba a'záb band kardan.
The letter Alif is straight and upright.

50 But, with this form, heart-enchanting,
Be not fascinated ; take a good walk of life.

A straight path is necessary, not erect stature ;
For, the infidel is also like us, in outward form.

He, who gave thee eye and mouth, and ear ;
If thou art wise,—strive not in opposition to Him.

I grant, that thou mayst beat the enemy with a stone,
Wage not war, at least from ignorance, with the Friend
      (God).

Those of wise disposition, obligation-recognising,
Sew up the favour (of God), with the nail of thanks.

———

55 One king-born fell from a black horse ;
A joint in his neck became dislocated.

The neck, elephant-like, descended to his body ;
His head used not to turn, so long as his body moved not.

The physicians were astonied at this ;
But, a philosopher, from the Greek-land,

Twisted back his head, and the vein became right,
And, if he had not been present, he would have become
      paralytic.

Again, he came near to the king ;
That mean one looked not at him.

60 The sage's head became plunged in shame ;
I heard that he went, and gently said :—

" If, yesterday, I had not twisted his neck,
" He would not, to-day, have turned his face from me."

He sent a seed, by the hand of a slave,
Saying :—" It is proper that thou shouldst place it on the
　　censer, aloe-burning."

To the one, king-born, through the smoke, sneezing came,
His head and neck became even as they were.

With apology, they hastened after the philosopher;
They sought much, but found little.

65 Turn not thy head from thanks to a benefactor,
Lest that thou shouldst, in after days, raise thy head for
　　nothing.

———

A certain one severely rubbed a boy's ears (chastised him),
Saying :—" Oh father of wonderful judgment, of overturned
　　fortune !

" I gave thee an axe, saying :—Split fire-wood;
" I said not :—Undermine the masjid-wall."

The tongue came (from God) for thanks and praise;
The grateful one moves it not in slander.

The ear is the thoroughfare for the Kurán and counsel;
Strive not to listen to calumny and falsehood.

70 Two eyes, for the sake of (beholding) the creating of God,
　　are good;
Lower the eyes from the defect of brother and friend.

———

For the sake of thy ease, the night and day are;
The resplendent moon and the sun, world-illuminating.

For thy sake, the west wind, chamberlain-like,
Causes constantly to be spread the carpet of spring.

If wind, and snow, and rain, and hail are,
And if the Chaugán expresses thunder, and the sword
    lightning,—

All are work-performers, and order-bearers (of God)
Who cherish thy seed in the dust.

75 And, if thou remainst thirsty, rage not through affliction;
For, the Water-carrier brings thee a cloud of water on His
    back.

From the dust, He brings colour, and perfume, and food;
Amusement for the eye, and brain, and palate.

He gave thee honey from the bees; and manna, from the
    sky;
He gave thee the green date, from the date-tree; and the
    date-tree from the seed-stone.

All the gardeners gnaw the hand
In astonishment, saying:—"No one planted such a date-
    tree!"

The sun and moon and Pleiades all are for thee;
They are the candles of the roof of thy house.

80 He brings thee a rose from the thorn; musk, from the
    (animal's) navel:
Gold, from the mine; and the green leaf, from the dry
    wood.

---

77 "Manna" is an Arabic word. The substance so called is produced
in Europe from the ash.

    In Persia, from a willow growing in moist ground.

    In Arabia, from a tamarisk, in the district of Mount Sinai. This
"manna" is called "ṭúfra."

    In India and Syria, from the camel-thorn. This "manna" is called
"al ḥaj."

    "Manna" is of red colour, very sweet; it melts in water. In India,
it is used as medicine.

He pourtrayed thy eye and eye-brow, with His own hand;
For, one cannot leave the intimate friend to strangers.

The powerful One, who cherishes the delicate,
Cherishes thee, with various favours.

Breath by breath, with soul, it is proper to utter (praise);
For, thanks to Him is not a work of the tongue only.

Oh God! my heart became blood, and eye wounded,
When I see thy reward is greater than my speech (of
　　thanksgiving).

85 I speak not of the rapacious and non-rapacious beast, and
　　ant, and fish,
But, of the army of angels above heaven's summit.

Yet, they have uttered a little Thy praise;
They have uttered one out of so many thousands (which
　　they should have uttered).

Oh Sa'dí! go; wash thy hand, and the book;
Hasten not on the path, that has no end.

———

A person knows not the value of a day of pleasure,
Save on that day when he falls to hardship-enduring.

The winter-season of the darvesh, in the narrow year,—
How easy is it to the lord of wealth?

90 One healthy,—who, once complaining, slept not,—
Uttered not thanks to God for sound health.

When thou art a manly mover, and swift of foot,
Stand, with thanks (to God) by those slow of foot.

———

81　　By strangers are meant angels. Thou, an intimate friend of God's,
art not left to the angels.

The young man bestows to the ancient old man,
The powerful one displays pity for the powerless.

What do the people of the Jíhún know of the value of
    water?
Ask those wearied utterly in the sun.

To the Arab, who is sitting by the Tigris
What care is there as to the thirsty ones of the (desert of)
    Zarúd?

95 That one recognised the value of healthiness,
Who, once, helpless sweltered in fever.

How may the dark night appear long to thee,
Who rollst, from side to side, in comfort?

Think of one falling and rising in fever;
For, the sick one knows the lengthiness of the night.

At the sound of the drum, the rich man becomes awake;
What knows he, how the watchman passed the night?

———

I have heard that Tughril, one night, in the autumn,
Passed a Hindú watchman,

100 From the pouring of snow, and rain, and torrent,
Fallen to trembling, like the star Canopus.

His heart, from pity for him, suffered agitation;
He said :—" Behold ! put on my fur garment.

" Wait a moment, by the terrace-side ;
" For, I will send it out by the hand of a slave."

He was in this (speech) ; and, the morning-breeze blew.
The monarch entered the royal hall.

He had, in his retinue, a slave of Parí-form,
For whom, his disposition had a little inclination.

The sight of the beloved chanced so agreeably to him,
That the wretched Hindú passed from his memory.

The (word) fur-coat passed to his (the watchman's) ear,
It came not, through misfortune, to his shoulders.

Perhaps the torment of toil was not enough for him,
Since, the sky's revolution added to it expectation.

When the sultán slept in carelessness, behold,
What the watchman said to him, in the morning!

" Perhaps (the watchman) " Nek-Bakht " was forgotten
      by thee,
" When thy hand went to the bosom of (the slave-girl)
      " Aghosh."

" For thee, the night passes in ease and joy;
" As to us, what knowst thou how the night passes?"

One of a káraván, head-lowered to the caldron,—
To him, what care of those sunk in sand?

Oh Lord of the Zaurak! keep on the water;
For the water has passed over the head of those helpless.

Oh vigorous young men! stay;
For, in the káraván, are sluggish old men.

Thou hast slept well in the haudaj of the káraván,—
The camel-rein, in the camel-driver's hand.

Whether plain or mountain; whether stone or sand,—to
      thee what matter?
Ask the state (of the road) from those lagging behind.

The camel of burden, mountain-form, carries thee;
What knowst thou of the foot-man, who devours the blood
      (of grief)?

23

Those sleeping, in comfort of heart, in the house,
What know they of the state of the hungry belly.

The night-guard had bound a certain one's hand;
He was, all night, afflicted, and heart-broken.

In the night of dark colour, there came to his ear,—
A person kept complaining of his straitened hand
(poverty).

120 The thief had, neck-fastened, heard this speech, and
said :—
" How long lamentst thou of helplessness?   Sleep.

" Oh one of straitened hand (poor)! go; give thanks to
God,
That the night-guard bound not straitly thy hand."

Make not much lamentation, as to foodlessness,
When thou seest one more foodless than thyself.

One of naked body made loan of one diram;
He made for his body a garment of raw hide.

He complained, saying :—" Oh perverse fortune!
" I am cooked with heat, within this raw hide."

125 When the uncooked (foolish) one, with fierceness, began to
boil,—
One from the prison-pit said to him :—" Silence!

" Oh raw one ! offer thanks to God,
" That thou art not like me—raw-hide (bound) on hand
and foot."

A certain one passed by a holy man,
He came to his sight, in the form of a Jew.

He struck him a blow, on his neck;
The darvesh gave him his shirt.

He became ashamed saying :—" What passed from me was
    a fault.
" Pardon me; what room (need) is there for giving (a
    shirt) ? "

He said :—On this (shirt-giving), I am firm, in thanks (to
    God),
" That that one whom thou didst think me, I am not."

———

One left behind on the road was weeping,
Saying :—" Than I in this desert, who is more wretched ? "

An ass, load-carrier, said to him :—" Oh one without dis-
    cretion !
" How long bewailst thou also of the tyranny of the
    heavens ?

" Go; thank God although thou art not on an ass,
" That thou art, in short, a son of Adam, not an ass."

A lawyer passed by one fallen drunk ;
He became proud of his own abstinence.

Through haughtiness, he looked not at him,
The young man raised his head, saying :—" Oh old man !

" Go; thank God, when thou art in prosperity,
" For disappointment comes from pride.

" Laugh not at one, whom thou seest in bonds ;
" Lest that, suddenly, thou shouldst fall into confinement.

" In short, is it not, in the possibility of fate,
" That thou mayst be to-morrow fallen drunk like me ? "

Heaven wrote for thee the inscription on the Masjid (of
    Islám),
Express not reproach on others in the fire-temple.

140 Oh Musalmán ! join the hands, in thanks,
That He bound not the idolater's cord about thy waist.

Whosoever is a seeker of Him, goes not by himself ;
The favour of the friend (God) drawing takes him by force.

Behold, whence destiny travelled !
For it is blindness to place reliance on another (God).

God has created the power of convalescence in honey,
Not to such an extent that it exercises power over death.

Honey makes pleasant (benefits) the constitution of those
    alive ;
But, the pain of dying has no remedy.

145 For the one, in whom a spark of life remained,—when life
    from his body
Issues, what use (is) honey in the mouth ?

A certain one suffered (a blow of) a steel mace on his head
One said :—" Rub sandal wood on his wound."

Fly, so long as thou canst, from danger ;
But strive not sharply with destiny.

So long as the interior is capable of drinking and eating,
The body is fresh of face, and pure of form.

This house (of the body) becomes altogether bad, at that
    time,
When the constitution and food agree not.

Thy temperament is moist and dry; and hot, and cold;
Man's constitution is compounded of these.

When one of these obtains the mastery over the others,
It breaks the balance of the equilibrium of thy temper-
　　　ament.

If the wind of a cold sigh passes,
The stomach's heat brings the soul into agitation.

And if the caldron of the stomach agitates the food,
The work of the delicate body becomes immature.

The one possessed of knowledge binds not his heart to
　　　these (four elements),
Which will not always agree with each other.

Consider not powerfulness of body, from food;
But, God's grace gives thee sustenance.

By God! if, on sword and knife,—the eye,
Thou placest, thou wilt not perform thanks to Him.

When thou placest thy face on the ground, in service,
Utter praise to God; and regard not thyself.

Praising God, and repeating the name of God, and having
　　　the heart towards Him—are acts of beggary;
For the beggar, it is improper that he should be proud.

I admit, that thou thyself hast done a service to God;
Hast thou not constantly enjoyed His portion on feudal
　　　tenure?

First, He placed in thy heart desire of worship,
Then His slave placed his head (in devotion) at His thres-
　　　hold.

If the grace of a good act arrives not from God,
How may a good act arrive to a stranger from a slave?

Why observest thou the tongue which gave confession ?
Behold Him, who gave speech to the tongue.

The door of the knowledge of God is man's eye,
Which He has opened on sky and earth.

To thee, how could there have been understanding of
    ascent and descent,
If He had not opened this door (of the eye) on thy face ?

165 He brought the head and hand from nonentity to existence,
He placed in this, liberality ; in that, adoration.

And, if not, how would liberality have come from thy
    hand ?
It is impossible that adoration would have come from thy
    head.

He gave thee a tongue endowed with wisdom ; and, created
    the ear,—
Which are the keys of the heart's chest.

If the tongue had not possessed (the power of) narration,
When would a person have possessed knowledge of the
    heart's secret ?

And, if there were not effort on the part of the news-
    gatherer of the ear,
When would news have reached the sultán of sense (the
    mind) ?

170 He gave to me the sweet word of the narrator ;
He gave to thee the ear and perception of the understander.

These two are perpetually, like chamberlains, at the door ;
They carry news from sultán to sultán.

Why reflectst thou of thyself, saying :—" My action is
    good ! "
Glance at that door ; because, it is His grace.

The gardener carries to the king's hall,
As first-fruit, even the rose from the king's garden.

———

I beheld an idol of ivory in the (idol-temple) Somnáth,
Gemmed like the (idol) Manát, in (the days of) ignorance.

75 The painter had so pourtrayed its form,
That one more beautiful than it may not be imagined.

From all countries, káraváns going,
For the seeing of that soul-less form.

The chiefs of Chín and Chigal greedily desired
Fidelity, like Sa'dí, from that idol of stone-heart.

The eloquent ones, set out from every abode,
Supplication-making before that tongueless form.

I was exhausted as to the revealing of this matter,
Saying :—" Why does the living one worship a mineral ? "

80 Of an idolater, who was partner with me,
One speaking well of me, and of the same cell, and friend,

I inquired, with gentleness,—" Oh Barhaman !
" I have wonder at the proceedings of this house.

———

174　Somnáth was an idol-temple in Gújerat ; it was destroyed by Mahmúd of Ghazní in A.D. 1024. For its maintenance, the revenues of two thousand villages had, by various princes, been granted. There officiated at the ceremonies (which at the time of eclipses were attended by two hundred thousand votaries) two thousand priests, five hundred dancing women, and three hundred musicians. The gold chain, supporting a bell, struck at the time of prayer, weighed sixteen thousand pounds. The idol was washed daily with water brought from the Ganges, one thousand miles distant ; it was of hollow stone, five yards in height, of which two were concealed in the earth. Mahmúd, striking the idol with a mace, exposed the interior, which was filled with jewels far exceeding in value the sum offered by the priests for its preservation.

181　" Barhaman " is a term applied to the learned of the idolaters, and Hindús, and fire-worshippers.

" For, they are distracted about this powerless form ;
" They are imprisoned in the pit of error.

" In it, neither power of hand, nor motion of foot ;
" And, if thou cast it down, it rises not from its place.

" Seest thou not, that its eyes are of amber !
" To seek fidelity from stone-eyes (lovely ones) is a mis-
    take."

185 At this speech, that friend became angry ;
He became, with anger, fire-like, and caught me.

He informed the idolaters and the old men of the temple ;
I saw not, in that assembly, a face of goodness.

The idolaters, Zand-reading, fell
Dog-like upon me, for the sake of that bone (the idol).

When that crooked way was, in their opinion, straight,
The straight road appeared, in their eyes, crooked.

For, although a man be wise and pious,
He is, in the opinion of the ignorant, foolish.

190 Like a drowning person, I was destitute of remedy ;
Beyond courtesy, I saw no path (of escape).

When thou seest the ignorant ones bent on malice,
Safety is in surrender ; and, in being gentle.

I loudly praised the chief of the Barhamans,
Saying :—" Oh explaining old man, and Zand-teacher !

" To me, also, the painting of this idol is agreeable ;
" For, it is a beautiful form, and a heart-alluring shape.

---

187   Ten little books (ṣaḥf) were revealed to Ibráhím ; the name of the
tenth is Pázand, which comprehends counsel, philosophy, and the mystery
(of God).

" In my sight, its form appears rare ;
" But, I have no information as to its meaning.

195　" Because, lately, I am the traveller of this place ;
" The foreigner seldom recognises bad from good.

" Thou knowst ; because thou art the learned man (queen)
　　　of this chess-board ;
" Thou art the adviser of the king of this abode.

" What is the meaning in the form of this idol ;
" For, I am the first (chief) among its worshippers ?

" Worship, in imitation, is seduction ;
" He who is acquainted is pleasing to the wayfarer."

The Barhaman's face kindled with joy ;
He approved and said :—" Oh one of approved counte-
　　　nance !

200　" Thy question is right, and thy deed excellent ;
" Whoever desires proof arrives at the stage (of his
　　　desire).

" Much, like thee, I wandered in travel ;
" I beheld idols, void of knowledge of themselves.

" Except this idol, which, in the morning from this place
　　　where it is,
" Raises its hand to God, the Ruler !

" And if thou wishst, stay even here to-night ;
" So that, to-morrow, this idol's mystery may be revealed
　　　to thee."

By the old man's order, I remained there the night,
Like Bezhan, a captive, in the pit of calamity.

204　Bezhan, the son of Rustam's sister, was known as " dukhtar-záda."
He became enamoured of Munizha, daughter of Afrásiyáb, King of
Persia. Afrásiyáb finding him one day in Munizha's house, seized and
confined him in a pit, whence he was delivered by Rustam.

205 That night, long like the Judgment Day;
The idolaters, unwashed, in prayer around me.

The priests, ever water untroubled,
Their arm-pits,—like a corpse in the sun.

Perhaps, I had committed a great sin;
For, I endured much torment, during that night.

All night afflicted in this bondage of grief;
One hand on my breast; the other, in prayer.

When, suddenly the drum-striker beat the drum;
The Barhaman, cock-like, suddenly called out.

210 Night,—preacher, black-clad—without opposition,
Drew forth the sword of day from the scabbard.

The fire of the morning fell upon tinder;
A world became, in a moment, illumined.

Thou wouldst have said that, in the country of Zangbár,
A Tátár had suddenly issued from a corner.

The idolaters, of ruined judgment, of unwashed face,
Appeared from door, and plain and street.

Of man or woman, none remained in the city;
For a needle, there remained no room in that idol-temple.

215 I—through anguish, afflicted; and through sleep, intoxicated;
When, suddenly, the image raised its hand!

---

211 "Sokhta" signifies — harráḳa; lutta va ámata,e parcha,e ním-
sokhta.
212 The people in Zangbár are black; in Turkistán, fair.

A shout immediately issued from them;
Thou wouldst have said, that a sea had come into agita-
    tion.

When the idol-temple became void of the assembly,
The Barhaman, laughing, glanced at me,

Saying :—" I know, a difficulty remains not to thee ;
" Truth became evident; and falsehood remained not."

When I saw that ignorance was strong within him ;
(And that) an absurd fancy was concealed within him.

220 I again prepared not any speech of truth ;
For, it is proper to conceal the truth from the false.

When thou seest the superior powerful of arm,
It is unmanliness to break one's fist.

In hypocrisy, I wept for a while,
Saying :—" I am become penitent, as to what I said."

By weeping, the hearts of the infidels inclined towards
    me ;
By a torrent, if a stone rolls,—it is not wonderful.

Those service-performing ran towards me ;
They seized, with respect, my arm.

225 Excuse-uttering, I went to the person of ivory (the idol),
On a chair of beaten gold, on a throne of ebony,

I gave a kiss on the hand of that worthless idol,
Saying :—" May a curse be on it; and, on the idol-wor-
    shipper!"

Hypocritically, I became an infidel for a few days ;
I became, in the sayings of Zand, a Barhaman.

When I saw that I was safe in the temple,
Through joy, I contained not myself in the earth.

One night, I firmly fastened the temple-door ;
Ran, left and right, scorpion-like :

230 Looked beneath and above the throne ;
Saw a screen, gold-bordered :

Behind the screen, an arch-priest, a fire-worshipper,
Sitting, the end of a cord in his hand.

Immediately, the state as to that (idol) became known to
        me,
Like David, when the iron became (soft as) wax to him.

That when he pulls the cord, of necessity,
The idol raises its hand, redress-seeking.

The Barhaman from before my face went ashamed ;
For, the quilting, on the face of the work was a disgrace.

235 He ran, and I hastened after him ;
I threw him headlong into a well.

For I knew if that Barhaman, alive,
Remained, he would strive for my blood :

Would desire, that he might bring forth my destruction,
Lest I should make display of his secret.

When thou obtainst information of the work of a perni-
        cious one,
Bring him forth from his power, when thou findst him.

For, if thou leavest him alive, that unskilful one
Will not wish thee further life.

240 And if he places his head in service at thy door,
If he prevail, he will cut off thy head.

---

232   Iron, in David's hand, became wax ; of which he made a coat of
mail.
234   "Bakhiya bar rúc kár uftádan" signifies—ifshá,e ráz kardan.

Plant not thy foot on the deceiver's foot ;
When thou goest and seest him, give him not respite.

I slew him, that impure one, outright with a stone ;
For, from a corpse, the tale issues not.

When I saw that I excited tumult,
I escaped from that land and fled.

When thou setst fire to the cane-brake,
If thou art wise, shun the tigers.

245 Slay not the young of the snake, man-biting ;
If thou slayst, stand no longer in that dwelling.

When thou disturbst the house of the wasp,
Fly quickly, from that quarter,—lest thou fall.

Cast not thy arrow at one more expert than thyself;
When it falls, seize thy skirt with the teeth (and fly).

In the leaves of Sa'dí, there is only this advice :—
" When thou minest the foundation of a wall,—stand not
        there."

After that resurrection day, I came to Hind ;
And, thence, by way of Yaman, to Hijáz.

250 From that amount of bitterness, which passed over me,
To-day only, my mouth became sweet.

In the fortune, and strengthening of Abú Bakr (son) of
        Sa'd ;
Like whom, neither before nor after, a mother produces.

I came, justice-seeking, from heaven's violence ;
I came to this shelter of the shelter-spreader (Abú Bakr).

I am, slave-like, a prayer-utterer for this kingdom ;
Oh God ! keep perpetually, this shadow,

Which placed not on me a plaster, worthy of the wound;
But, worthy of his own favours and honours.

255 How may I perform thanks for this favour,
Though my head become foot in his service?

After those bonds (of trouble) I obtained joy;
Yet, of those counsels, at my ear, is

One that, at that time, when the hand of supplication,
I raise to the Court of the Knower of Secrets (God),

That Chinese puppet comes to my hand,
It puts dust in the eye of my self-conceit.

I know that the hand, I raised,
I exalted not through my own power.

260 The pious draw not up (of themselves) their hands;
For, they draw the end of the cord through the One unseen
  (God).

The door of goodness and devotion is open; but,
Every one is not powerful as to good deeds.

This, indeed, is the hinderer that—into the Court,
Save by the King's order, it is improper to go.

The key of destiny is in no one's hand;
God is absolutely powerful, and that is enough.

Then, oh man running on the straight path!
Thanks are not for thee; they are for God.

265 When He, in the hidden, created thy disposition good,
Bad conduct issues not from thy disposition.

This sweetness from the bee, made appear,
That very Person, who created poison in the snake.

When He wishes to lay waste a country,
He first makes a people afflicted by thee.

And if His bounty be over thee,
He causes ease to reach the people from thee.

Display not pride on the path of truth;
For, they (angels) seized thy hand, and thou didst rise.

270 Speech is profitable, if thou wilt listen;
Thou mayst attain to the (stage of the) men of God, if
　　thou travel the path of religion,

If they guide thee, thou wilt obtain an abode,
Where, they place thy table-cloth (victual-spread), on the
　　tray of respect.

But, it is improper that thou shouldst eat alone;
Thou shouldst remember the distressed darvesh (Sa'dí).

Thou didst, perhaps, send mercy upon me;
For, I am not confiding to my own work.

CHAPTER IX.

ON REPENTANCE.

1 OH, thou whose age has passed to seventy years! Come;
Thou wast, perhaps, asleep that thy life went to the wind.

Thou didst prepare every requisite of being (in this
world);
Didst not engage thyself in the thought of going (to the
next world).

On the Resurrection Day, when they lay out the market of
heaven,
They give dignities for good deeds.

Stock in trade, as much as thou bringst, thou takest
away;
And, if thou art poor, thou takest away shame.

5 For, the more full the market, just so much,
The more distressed (is) the heart of the one of empty hand.

If out of fifty dirams, five become wanting,
Thy heart, with the grasp of grief, becomes torn.

When fifty years have gone forth from thy hand,
Consider it gain that there is a space of five days.

If the wretched corpse had possessed a tongue,
He would have raised a shout, in lament and cry,

Saying:—"Oh living one! when there is the power of
    speech,
" Let not the lip sleep (cease), corpse-like, from uttering
    the name of God.

10 " Since our time, in carelessness passed,
" Do thou, at least, reckon a few moments,—opportunity."

One night, in youth and the pleasure of affluence (of
    youth),
We, young men, sate sometime together.

Nightingale-like, singing; rose-like, fresh of face;
From hilarity, clamour cast into the street.

An old man, world-experienced, apart from us,
The blackness of his hair white, through the violence of
    Time,

Was tongue-bound, as to speech, nut-like;
Was unlike us, lip from laughter, pistachio-nut-like.

15 A youth went before him, saying:—" Oh old man!
" Why sittest thou, with sorrow, in the corner of regret?

" Raise once thy head from the collar of grief;
" Move jauntily, with ease of heart, with the young men."

---

10   " Shumár" is the root of " shumárídan"; and " shumar" of " shu-
murdan."   Both verbs have the same meaning.

He year-stricken raised his head from concealment,
Behold his answer! how like an old man, he spoke :—

" When the morning breeze blows over the garden,
" It befits the young tree to move to and fro.

" The green corn, so long as it is young and the head
        green,—waves ; .
" When it reaches mellowness, it becomes broken.

20 " In the spring-time, when the wind brings (the fragrance
        of) the musk-willow,
" The ancient tree sheds its dry leaves.

" It does not beseem me to move jauntily with young men,
" When the morning of old age has blossomed on my
        cheek.

" The male falcon (of my soul), which was within my
        bonds,
" Wishes, from time to time, to snatch the end of the
        thread (of life).

" Yours is the time to sit at this tray (of enjoyment) ;
" For, we have washed our hands of luxurious enjoyment.

" When the dust of venerability sits on the head,
" Look not again for the pleasure of youth.

25 " Snow rained on my raven feathers (hair),
" The spectacle of the garden, nightingale-like, is not suit-
        able to me.

" The peacock, possessed of beauty, makes display ;
" What desirest thou of the hawk, feather-stripped ?

" For me, the reaping of the corn is near ;
" For you, now the fresh verdure (of the beard) grows.

" The freshness of our rose-garden has passed ;
" Who binds the rose-bouquet, when it has become
        withered ?

" Oh soul of father ! my reliance is on a staff ;
" Further reliance on life is a mistake.

30 " For the young man, it is reserved to leap on his feet ;
" For old men prefer a request for aid to the hands (of
        others).

" Behold the red rose of my face,—pure yellow ;
" When the sun becomes yellow, it descends.

" To entertain lust, on the part of an immature youth.
" Is not so odious, as on the part of an old man.

" It is proper for me to weep, like children,
" For shame of my sins ; not to live, child-like (in sport)."

Lukmân spoke well saying :—" Not to live
" Is better, than to live years in sin."

35 Even, to shut the shop-door in the morning
Is better than to give from the hand (to squander) the
        profit and capital of life.

While the young man causes the blackness (of hair) to
        attain to light (whiteness),
The wretched old man takes his whiteness to the grave.

———

One of ancient years came to a physician,
From his weeping, near to dying,

Saying :—" Oh one of good judgment ! place thy hand on
        my vein ;
" For my foot rises not from its place.

" This my bent stature resembles that,
" That thou mayst say,—I have descended into the clay (of
    the grave)."

40 He said to him :—" Part asunder from the world,
" That thy foot may, in the Resurrection, issue from the
    clay."

Seek not the joy of youth from old men ;
For the running stream returns not to the rivulet.

If, in the time of youth, thou didst exercise hand and foot
    (in lust) ;
In the season of old age, be sensible and reasonable.

When the revolution of age exceeds forty (years),
Exercise not hand and foot in lust; for the water (of life)
    has passed over thy head.

Joy began to be afraid of me, at that time,
When my evening (black hair) began to blossom as the
    down (white hair).

45 It is necessary to put lust out of the head,
When the season of lustfulness comes to an end.

How may my heart with freshness become green,
When verdure will spring from my clay ?

Sporting in lust and concupiscence,
We passed over the dust of many.

Those who are yet invisible (unborn)
Will come, and pass over our dust.

Alas ! that the season of youth has departed ;
Life, in sport and pastime, has departed.

50 Alas ! time, soul-cherishing, in such a way,
Passed over us as the lightning of Yaman.

From the passion for this I wear, and that I eat,
I became not free, that I might suffer care for religion.

Alas! we became engaged in falsehood;
We remained far from God, and became careless.

How well spoke the teacher to the boy,
Saying :—" We did not a single work; but, time passed."

———

Oh young man; to-day (in youth), take the path of salva-
    tion ;
For, to-morrow, youth comes not from old age.

55 Thou hast leisure of mind, and strength of body;
When the plain is spacious, strike the ball (of life).

I understood not the value of that day (of youth);
Now I know it, when I have played it away.

Fate snatched for me such a time,
Every day of which was a night of power.

What effort may the old ass (of the body) beneath the
    load (of devotion) make ?
Do thou go; who art a rider on a wind-footed steed.

If they cleverly piece together the broken goblet,
It will not fetch the price of the perfect one.

———

57   " Shab-i-ḳadr " signifies—lailatu-l-ḳadr. There is much explanation
of this, in the glorious Ḳurán, that angels descend on that night of
all nights most honoured. It is the 27th night of the Ramazan, on
which night the Ḳurán descended from heaven.
59   The old man (who is like the broken cup), though he mightily strives,
the work of youth comes not truly from him.
    Devotion in old age cannot attain to austerity in youth; but such
devotion is at least better than that thou shouldst go empty-handed, and
have no bank-draft in thy hand.

60 Since the cup fell, in negligence, from thy hand,—now,
There is no way save to fasten anew.

Who said to thee :—" Throw thy body into the Jihún ?
" When thou hast fallen, strike (in swimming) hand and
foot."

Thou didst, in carelessness, give pure water (honour) from
thy hand,
What remedy now, except purifying with dust ?

When, from those expert in running,—the wager,
Thou didst not carry off, go (on the path of religion) even
falling and rising (as a cripple).

If those wind-footed steeds (pious men) went quickly,
Do thou, footless and handless, arise from sitting.

———

65 One night, in the desert of Faid, sleep
Bound down my foot of running with fetters.

A camel-driver came, with fear-inspiring and rancour,
He struck the camel-rein on my head, saying :—" Arise !

" Perhaps, thou hast fixed thy heart on dying in rear (of the
káfila),
" Since thou risest not, at the sound of the bell (of de-
parture) ?

" To me as to thee, sweet sleep is in the head ;
" But, the desert is in front.

" When, from sweet sleep, at the sound of—Al rahíl ! Al
rahíl ! thou
" Risest not, when wilt thou again reach the track (of the
káfila) ? "

70 The camel-driver (death) beat the camel-drum (of de-
        parture),
The first of the káraván reached the stage.

Happy, those sensible of auspicious fortune,
Who, before the drummer, bound up their chattels.

When those sleeping on the road raise their heads,
They see not a trace of those who have travelled the road.

That wayfarer excelled, who arose quickly ;
To be awake, after translation (to the next world),—what
        profit ?

A certain one scatters barley, in the spring ;
How may he take wheat, at reaping-time ?

75 Oh sleeping one ! how it is necessary to be awake ;
When death fetches thee from sleep,—what advantage ?

When on the face of youth, white hair comes forth,
The night (black hair) becomes day (white hair),—pluck up
        the eye from sleep (of carelessness).

That day, I plucked up hope of life,
When, within my blackness (black hair), white occurred.

Alas ! precious life has passed ;
These few moments will also pass.

Whatever passed ; in non-rectitude, passed ;
And, if thou takest not advantage of this, it will also pass.

80 If thou art solicitous, now is the seed-time ;
If thou hast hope, that thou mayst take the harvest.

Go not empty of hand to the city of Resurrection ;
For, there is no reason to sit in regret.

If to thee be an eye to wisdom, and deliberation as to the
    grave,—
Act now, when the ant (of the grave) has not devoured
    thine eye.

Oh son! one can make profit, with capital;
What profit comes to that one, who enjoyed his capital?

Strive now, when the water possesses (only) thy waist;
Not, when the torrent passes over thy head.

85 Now, when thou hast an eye,—rain a tear;
The tongue is in thy mouth,—bring forth excuse (for sin).

The soul is not always in the body;
The tongue turns not always in the mouth.

Now, it is necessary to utter excuse for sin;
Not when the spirit of articulation sleeps (rests) from
    speaking.

To-day, from the learned, hear the word (of Nakír and
    Munkir);
For, to-morrow, Nakír may question thee with terror.

Reckon this precious soul,—gain;
For the cage, birdless, has no value.

90 Waste not thy life, in regret and sorrow;
For opportunity is precious; and, time, a sword.

———

Fate cut the vein of Life of one living;
Another, through grief, rent his collar.

A beholder, with sharp sense, thus spoke,
When complaint and lament reached his ear:—

"With your hand, the corpse, on its own body,
"Would have rent the shroud,—if there had been to it a
    hand,

" Saying :—' Writhe not so much, through care and sorrow
    for me,
" ' That I prepared (for the next world), a day or two,
    before thee.

95 " ' Thou didst, perhaps, forget regarding thy own death,
" ' Since my death has made thee powerless and wounded ? ' "

When the teacher of truth lets fall clay on the corpse,
His heart will burn, not for it,—but for himself.

In separation from that child, who went into the dust (of
    the grave),
Why lamentst thou ? for he came pure, and departed pure.

Thou camest pure (into this world) ; be firm as to caution
    and purity ;
For, it is a shame to go unclean to the dust (of the grave).

Now, it is necessary to bind the foot of this bird (of the
    soul) ;
Not, at the time when it takes the end of the string from
    thy hand.

100 Thou didst sit much in another's place ;
Another one will sit in thy place.

If thou art a warrior ; or, if a swordsman,
Thou wilt only carry the shroud (out of the world).

If the wild ass causes the noose to snap,
He becomes foot-bound, when he sticks in the sand.

Thou also hast such arm-power,
For, thy foot has not gone into the sand of the grave.

Place not thy heart on this year-stricken house (of the
    world) ;
For, a walnut rests not a dome.

105 When yesterday passed; and, to-morrow comes not to the
        hand,
Make reckoning of this one moment that is.

A certain delicate one (a son) of (King) Jamshíd descended
        (to the grave),
A shroud of silk, he made him, like the silk-worm.

After a few days, he came to the tomb,
That he might, with lament and heart-burning, weep over
        him.

When he beheld the silken shroud, rotten,
He thus, in thought, spoke to himself :—

" I had plucked it (the silk), with force, from the silk-
        worm ;
" The grave-worms plucked it again from him."

110 One day, two couplets made my liver (as it were) roast meat ;
When the minstrel, with the stringed instrument, kept
        saying :—

" Alas ! without us, many a time,
" The rose will grow ; and, the fresh spring blossom.

" Many a fourth, tenth and second month
" Will appear,—when we are dust and brick."

———

As to one of devotee-disposition, God-worshipping,—
A golden brick fell to his hand.

His wise head became as stupid
As his illumined heart became obscure through phrensy.

———

112   The sun is in—the Crab in the fourth month; Capricorn, in the tenth
month ; the Bull, in the second month.

115 All night, in thought, saying:—"This treasure and pro-
    perty,
" To it, so long as I live, the way of decline will come not.

" Again, for begging, my weak stature
" It is unnecessary to make bent and straight (in bowing)
    to any.

" I may make a house,—its foundation, marble;
" The timber of its roof,—all native aloe.

" A special room for friends;
" The chamber-door in the garden-mansion.

" I am wearied of stitching rag on rag;
" The effulgence of others has burned (with envy) my eyes
    and brain.

120 " In future, inferiors may cook my food;
" In ease, I may give sustenance to my soul.

" This woollen bed has slain me with its hardness;
" I go after this, and spread a gorgeous bed."

Imagination made him a dotard and crazy-like,—
A crab's claw plunged in his brain.

For him,—leisure for prayers and secrets (with God) re-
    mained not;
For him,—eating and sleeping, and reciting the name of
    God, and prayers remained not.

Head intoxicated with consequential airs he came to a
    desert,
For, he had no place for sitting at ease.

125 A certain one, at the head of a grave, kneaded clay,
That he might get bricks from that clay of the grave.

The old man descended, for a while, in thought,
Saying :—" Oh soul of little vision ! take advice (from the
    brick-maker's action).

" Why attachest thou thy heart to this golden brick,
" When one day he will make a brick out of thy clay ?

" Of avarice, the mouth is not open to such a degree,
" That avarice causes it to sit (tranquil) with one morsel.

" Oh mean one ! restrain thy hand from this (gold) brick ;
" For, it is impossible to dam the Jíhún (of avarice) with a
    single brick."

130 Thou art careless as to thought of profit and wealth,
While the capital of life becomes trodden under foot.

The morning breeze will pass over this dust, in such a way,
As will carry every atom of us to some place, or other.

The dust of lust stitched up wisdom's eye;
The simúm (hot wind) of desire consumed the sown field
    of thy life.

Make clean from the eye, the antimony of carelessness;
For, to-morrow, thou wilt become collyrium, in the eye of
    the dust.

———

Between two persons, there was enmity and strife,
Through pride, head above the other, panther-like.

135 Flying from the sight of each other, to such a degree,
That the sky used to appear narrow for both.

Death brought his army to the head of this one;
Days of ease arrived at an end for him.

The heart of his enemy became joyful ;
He passed, after a while, by his grave.

He saw the bed-chamber of his grave, clay-plastered ;
But, he once saw (in life) his house gold-plastered.

He came, proudly-walking opposite to his pillow ;
Kept saying to himself, lip open with laughter ;—

140 " Oh happy is the tranquil time of that one, who is
" After an enemy's death, in the friend's embrace.

" It is unnecessary to weep for the death of that one,
" Who lived a single day, after his enemy's death."

By way of enmity, with a powerful arm,
He plucked up a plank, from the surface of his grave.

He beheld—his crowned head, in the pit ;
His two eyes, world-seeing, dust-stuffed ;

His existence, a captive in the prison of the grave ;
His body, the food of worms, and the plunder of ants ;

145 His bones tightly stuffed with dust, just as
The collyrium-casket of ivory, full of collyrium :

From the sky's revolution, the full moon of his face,—the
　　　new moon ;
From Time's violence, his cypress stature,—a tooth-pick :

The palm of the hand of powerful grasp ;
Time-separated, joint from joint.

From his heart, pity for him came to him, in such a way,
That he made clay, with weeping on his dust.

He became penitent, as to his deeds and bad disposition ;
He ordered them to write on his tomb-stone ;—

150 " Rejoice not at any one's death ;
" For, after him, thy time remains not long."

A holy wise man heard this speech.
He bewailed, saying :—" Oh powerful Omnipotence !

" Wonderful !—if thou awardst not mercy to him,
" Over whom, the enemy, with lamentation, wept.

" May our body also, one day, become so
" That the heart of enemies may grieve over it.

" Perhaps, in the heart of my Friend (God) pity may come,
" When He sees that my enemy forgave me.

155 " The head, slowly or quickly, reaches that state,
" In which—thou mayst say—there never was an eye."

One day, I struck a mattock on a dust-heap;
A sorrowful lament came to my ear,

Saying :—" If thou art a man, take care (to strike) more
    gently ;
" For the eye, and lobe of the ear, and face, and head—are
    here."

———

One night, I had slept with the intention of making a
    journey ;
In the morning, I followed a káraván.

A frightful wind and dust arose,
Which made the world dark to the eyes of men.

160 The guide had a house-daughter
With the mi'jar, she wiped the dust from her father.

The father said to her :—" Oh dear face of mine !
" Who hast the love of my distracted heart,

" In this eye (after death) dust sits, not to such a degree,
" That one can, again, make it clean with the mi'jar."

Thy beautiful spirit, like an impetuous animal,
Takes thee running to the marge of the bottom of the
    grave.

Death will suddenly cause thy stirrup to break ;
One cannot hold back the rein from the profundity (of the
    grave).

---

165 Oh bone-cage ! knowst thou
That thy soul is a bird ; and its name, spirit ?

When the bird departs from the cage (of the body), and
    snaps its chain ;
It becomes not, by effort, again, thy prey.

Take care of opportunity ; for, the world is for a moment ;
In the opinion of the wise, a moment (of life) is better than
    a world.

Sikandar, who held sway over a world,
Abandoned the world, at that time when he died.

To him, it was unattainable that—a world from him,
They might take ; and give him, in return, a moment's
    respite.

170 They departed, and every one reaped what he sowed ;
There only remains—good and bad name.

Why place we the heart on this káraván-place,
From which, friends have departed ; and, we are on the
    road ?

After us,—the garden gives this very rose ;
Friends sit with one another.

---

167   Because, a moment of life is attainable by none, even though the
world be given for it.

Fix not the heart on this mistress of the world ;
For she sate with no one, whose heart she ravished not.

When a man sleeps in the dust-place of the grave,
The Resurrection Day will scatter the dust from his face.

175 Bring forth, now, the head from the pocket of carelessness
That, to-morrow (the Resurrection Day) it may not remain
　　　lowered in regret.

No ; when thou desirest to enter Shíráz,
Thou wilt wash the head and body from the dust of travel.

Oh one dusty with sin ! then, presently,
Thou wilt make a journey to a foreign city (in the next
　　　world).

Urge a stream from the two fountains of the eye ;
And, if thou hast impurity,—wash it from thyself.

———

I remember, in my father's time,
—The rain of mercy, every moment on him !—

180 That he purchased, in my childhood, a tablet and book ;
He bought, for my sake, also, a gold ring.

Suddenly, a purchaser took off
The ring, from my hand, for a single date.

When the little boy understands not (the value of) a ring,
They can take it away from him, for a sweetmeat.

Thou, also, didst not recognise life's value,
When thou didst throw it away for sweet ease.

On the Resurrection Day, when the good attain to the
　　　highest (dignity),
They rise from the bottom of the grave-ashes to the
　　　Pleiades.

85 Thy head will, from shame, remain (lowered) before thee,
When thy (bad) deeds arise around thee.

Brother! have shame of the work of the bad;
For, thou wilt become ashamed in the presence of the good.

On that day, when they ask of thy deeds and words,
The body of the lords of resolution (the prophets) will
　　　tremble from fear.

In the place, where the prophets suffer fear,
—Come—what excuse for sin, hast thou?

Those women, who, with pleasure, perform devotions
Surpass (in rank) the non-devout men.

190 Does not shame come to thee of thy own manliness,
That there should be greater favour (in God's Court) for
　　　women, than for thee?

By the established excuse, that exists for women,
They sometimes withhold the hand from devotion.

Thou, excuseless, sittest apart, woman-like (excuse-pos-
　　　sessing);
Oh less than woman! go; boast not of manliness.

I may not indeed have eloquence;
The poet 'Ansar, king of speech, thus spoke :—

" When thou passest out of straightness, it is crookedness;
" What kind of man is he, who is less than a woman?"

187　Ulú-l-'azm are the prophets, masters of the new law. They are :—
Núh, Ibráhím, Músa, 'Ísa, Muhammad.

191　" 'Uzr-i-mu'aiyin " refers to—haiz and nafás, during which times
women are excused from praying.

195 Suppose—lust cherished, with kindness and joy;
Accept—in the passing of time, a strong-made enemy.

A certain one cherished a wolf's whelp;
When it became fully matured, it rent its master.

When he slept on the brink of life—surrendering,
An eloquent one went to his head, and said :—

" When thou tenderly cherishst such an enemy,
" Knowst thou not that thou wilt, inevitably, suffer its
wound ?"

No; Iblís expressed reproach as to us,
Saying :—" Only evil comes from these."

200 Lament as to the evils that are in us;
For, I fear the opinion of Iblís is true.

The accursed one—when our punishment became agreeable
to him,
God drove him, for our sake, from the door.

How may we bring forth the head from this reproach and
shame,
When we are at peace with him; and, at war, with God?

Thy friend rarely glances at thee,
When thy face is towards the enemy's face.

If to thee be necessary, a friend, from whom thou mayst
enjoy profit,
It is improper that thou shouldst take the enemy's order.

205 He holds estrangement right from that friend,
Who chooses the enemy for a companion.

Knowst thou not that the friend seldom plants his foot
(within the house)
When he sees that an enemy is within.

Behold, what wilt thou buy with black silver (base deeds),
Who will sever thy heart for love for Joseph (God)?

If thou art wise, turn not from a friend,
That the enemy may be unable to glance at thee (to thy
 injury).

A certain one used contention with a king;
He consigned him to his enemy, saying:—" Spill his
 blood."

210 A captive, in the power of that one, revenge-seeking,
He kept saying to himself, with lamentation and heart-
 burning :—

" If I had not vexed my friend the king against myself,
" How should I have suffered violence from the enemy's
 hand?"

With his nails, his enemy's skin, he tore,
That friend, who vexed not a friend against himself.

With a friend, be thou of one heart, and of one speech;
For the friend brings forth the enemy's root from the
 foundation.

I consider not this infamy good :—
For an enemy's pleasure, a friend's injury.

----

215 A certain one, by fraud, enjoyed a man's property.
When it arose (and departed), he cursed Iblís.

Iblís, on the path, thus spoke to him,
Saying:—" I have never seen a fool, like thee.

----

210 " Kína-toz" signifies—kína-kosh; kína-kash.

" To thee with me (there was) concord.   Oh certain one !
" Why didst thou rise to battle with me ? "

It is a pity that the deed ordered by the ugly demon
    (Shaitán),
The hand of an angel (who is pure) should write against
    thee.

From thy ignorance and fearlessness, thou holdst it lawful,
That the pure ones (angels) should write unclean things
    of thee.

220 Find a better path, and seek the peace (of God) ;
Raise an intercessor ; and utter thy acknowledgment (of
    sin).

For, safety, for a moment, appears not
When, by time's revolution the measure (of life) is full.

And, if thou hast not the hand of power, for a (good)
    work,
Bring forth, like the helpless, the hand of lamentation.

And, if thy evil doing passed beyond limit,
When thou saidst :—" Evil went (from me)," thou wast
    good.

Rise ; and come forward, when thou seest the door of
    peace open ;
For the door of repentance becomes suddenly shut.

225 Oh son ! go not beneath the load of sin.
For the burden-carrier becomes wearied on a journey.

---

218   The author says :—" Oh one subject to Satan (curses be on him !),
pity comes to me that thou performst Satan's command and doest evil
deeds; because, the hand of an angel (who is pure) will write in the
Book of Deeds thy bad deeds, which are instigated by Satan."

223   In the traditions :—Whosoever repented one day before death, God
turned on him with pardon.

It is proper to hasten after good men;
For, whosoever sought for this happiness—found it.

But, thou art in rear of the base demon (Shaitán),
I know not, when thou mayst arrive among the holy.

The Prophet (Muhammad) is an intercessor for that one,
Who is on the highway of the law of the Prophet.

———

One clay-stained took the path to a masjid;
From fortune of reversed fortune, in astonishment.

230 One forbade him, saying:—" May both thy hands be
　　　destroyed!
" Go not, skirt-stained, into a pure place."

As to this matter, a tenderness entered my heart;
Because, lofty Paradise is pure and joyful.

In that place (Paradise) of the hopeful pure ones,
For one clay-stained with sin,—what business?

That one takes Paradise, who bears devotion,
To whom, ready money is necessary,—let him take his
　　　trade-stock.

Do not;—wash the skirt from the dust of vileness;
For, from above, they suddenly close the stream (of puri-
　　　fication).

235 Say not:—" The bird of wealth has leaped from my
　　　bonds";
Thou hast, yet, the end of the cord in thy hand.

———

226　　In the traditions:—Death is ease for believers.
227　　The signs of happiness are:—Truth in the heart; fear of God in
religion; abstinence in the world; modesty in the eye; fear in the
body.
235　　" Murgh-i-daulat " signifies—kudrat-i-tauba; zamán-i-jawání.

And, if there was delay (in repenting), be impetuous and
    active;
A perfect work has no concern as to late coming.

Death has not yet bound thy hand of entreaty (to God);
Raise thy hand to the Court of the Omnipotent.

Oh one sin-committed, sleeping! sleep not; arise;
Pour out eye-water (tears), in acknowledgment of sin.

Since it is an order of necessity that, their reputation,
They (sinners) should spill; on this dust of the street (of
    the world, let them spill it).

240 And, if water (of repentance) remains not to thee,—bring
    an intercessor,
Whose reputation (before God) is greater than thine.

If God drives me, in anger from His door;
I may bring the souls of the great, as intercessors.

———

Recollection keeps coming to me of the time of childhood,
When, on an 'Íd, I came out with my father.

I became engaged in the pastime of the men;
I became lost as to my father, through the tumult of the
    people.

Through restlessness, I raised a shout;
My father suddenly rubbed my ear,

245 Saying:—" Oh saucy one! at least, several times, to thee,
" Said I not:—Keep not thy hand from off my skirt."

The little child knows not how to go alone;
For one can, with difficulty, travel the unseen road.

Oh fakír! thou also art a child of the road; with effort,
Go; seize the skirt of those road-knowing (spiritual-
    guides).

Sit not with mean men ;
When thou dost, wash thy hand of respect.

Affix thy grasp to the saddle-strap of the pure ;
For the holy one has no shame of beggary.

250 The disciples are, in strength, less than children ;
The shaikhs are like a strong wall.

Learn motion from that little child ;
How he prefers a request for aid to the wall !

He escaped from the chain of the impure,
Who sate in the circle of the devout.

If thou hast any need,—take this society (of the devout) ;
For, the sultán (even) has no flight from this door.

Go ; be an ear-of-corn gatherer, like Sa'dí,
That thou mayst gather the harvest of the knowledge of
     God.

255 Ho ! oh revellers in the prayer-niche of affection,
When, to-morrow, you sit at the holy table,

Turn not away the face from the beggars of the tribe ;
For, the lords of generosity turn not away the humble
     companion.

Now, it is proper to become a partner with wisdom ;
For, to-morrow, the path of returning remains not.

A certain one heaped up the corn of the autumn month
     Mardad ;
He set his heart at ease, as to the care of the spring month
     Dai.

---

254   Be a corn-gatherer of those of the path of God.
255   In the 'Ikd-i-manzúm, couplets 255 to 257 are omitted.
258   In the fifth month, Mardad (July), the sun is in Leo.

One night, he became drunk ; he kindled a fire ;
The foolish one of reversed fortune burned his harvest.

260 The next day, he sate gleaning ears of corn,
For, a single grain of his harvest remained not to him.

When they saw the poor man afflicted,
One said to his own cherished one,

Thou wishst not, that thou shouldst be of such dark days ?
Burn not thy harvest, in madness.

If thy life passed from thy hand, in evilness,
Thou art he, who set fire to his own harvest.

It is a disgrace to gather ears of corn (to beg),
After burning thy own harvest.

265 Oh my soul! do not; sow the seed of religion and
        justice ;
Give not the harvest of good fame to the wind.

When one of reversed fortune falls into bonds,
Those of happy fortune take warning from him.

Before punishment, beat thou the door of pardon ;
For, lament, beneath the rod, has no profit.

Bring forth thy head from the collar of carelessness ;
That shame may not remain, to-morrow, in thy breast.

———

A certain one was consenting to a forbidden deed ;
One of good qualities passed by him.

270 He sate, perspiring as to his face, through shame,
Saying :—" Have I become ashamed of the shaikh of the
        street ? "

The shaikh of illumined soul heard this speech,
He was confounded at him, and said :—" Oh youth !

" Does not shame come to thee of thyself,
" That God is present ; and thou hast shame of me ?

" Have such shame of the lord of self,
" As shame is to thee of strangers and relations.

" Thou restst not at any one's side ;
" Go ; look towards God only."

When Zulaikhá became intoxicated with the wine of love,
She fixed her hand on the skirt of Yúsuf.

The demon of lust had given consent, to such a degree,
As when the wolf had fallen upon Yúsuf.

The lady of Egypt (Zulaikhá) had an idol of marble,
She was, morning and evening, assiduous in its devotion.

At that time, she covered its face and head,
Lest that her act might, in its sight, be disagreeable.

Yúsuf, grief-stricken, sate in a corner,
Hand over the head, through the lust of the tyrant (Zulai-
     khá).

Zulaikhá kissed both his hands and feet,
Saying :—" Oh one of sluggish covenant, perverse !

" Contract not thy face, with anvil heart ;
" Waste not the sweet time, in harshness."

From his eye, a stream went running on his face,
Saying :—" Return ; and, seek not this uncleanness from
     me.

" Thou didst become ashamed, in the face of thy stone
     idol ;
" Does not shame come to me of Omnipotence ? "

What profit,—if repentance comes to hand,
When thou hast squandered the capital of life.

285 They drink wine, for the sake of a ruddy face;
But, they bear, in the end, through it, a yellow face.

Make entreaty, to-day, with supplication for pardon for
    sin;
For, to-morrow, (the Resurrection Day), the power of
    speech remains not.

The cat makes pollution, in a pure place;
When it appears filthy, he covers it with dust.

Thou art free (from fear) of filthy deeds,
Thou fearst not, that the eyes (of men) may fall on them.

Reflect on that sinful slave,
Who is, sometimes, disobedient to his master.

290 If he returns, in truth and supplication,
They bring him not back to chains and fetters.

Thou art, in malice, in strife with that Person (God),
From whom, there is for thee remedy (for ills), or flight.

It is necessary to make reckoning of thy deeds, now,
Not, at the time when the Book (of Deeds) becomes spread
    open.

Although, a person did evil,—he did not evil,
When, before the Judgment Day, he suffered grief for
    himself.

Although the mirror becomes obscured by a sigh;
The heart's mirror becomes bright by a sigh.

295 Be afraid of thy sins, this moment,
That thou mayst fear no one, in the Judgment Day.

I came a traveller into a city of Abyssinia;
Heart, from care, free; head, through ease, happy.

On the road, I beheld a lofty prison;
In it, some wretched ones foot-bound.

I immediately prepared for journeying;
I took to the desert, like a bird from the cage.

One spoke, saying :—" These fettered **ones are night-
　　prowlers ;
" They **take not advice ; and hear not truth."

When **oppression comes to no one from thy hand;**
If the watchman seize the world,—to thee what care?

No **one takes captive the one of good name;**
Fear God ; but, fear not **the amír.**

The agent, **treachery unused in business,**
Cares **not for the deciding of court-officials.**

But, if there **be deceit beneath** his (apparent) integrity,
The tongue of **his account-giving becomes** not bold.

When thou performst approved service,
Thou thinkst not of the malignant enemy.

If the slave **exerts himself, slave-like,**
The lord holds him **dear.**

But if he be, in service, dull of judgment,
He falls from soul-guarding to áss-slaving.

Plant **the** foot (of devotion) forward, that thou mayst
　　surpass the angels ;
For, **if thou** remainst **behind, thou art less** than a rapa-
　　cious animal.

———

The King of Damighán, with a chaugán, a certain one,
Struck, so that his cry, drum-like, came forth.

At night, from restlessness, he could not sleep;
A devotee passed by him, and said :—

310 " If, at night, he had borne his heart-burning (for crime) to
          the watchman,
    " In the day, the crime would not have taken his repu-
          tation."

On the day of the place of assembling (Judgment Day)
          that one becomes not ashamed,
Who, nights, preferred his heart-burning to the Court (of
          God).

Still, if thou hast desire for peace (with God), what fear ?
The Merciful One (God) fastens not the door against those
          pardon-seeking.

If thou art wise,—of the ruler (God), desire
Forgiveness for the sin of the day, on the night of re-
          pentance.

That Merciful One (God), who brought to thee existence,
          from non-existence,
Will seize thy hand, if thou shouldst fall.   Oh wonderful !

315 If thou art a slave,—bring forth the hand of need, (at
          God's Court);
And, if ashamed,—rain the water of repentance (weep).

There came to this door, pardon-asking, no one,
Whose sin the water of penitence washed not away.

---

313   There are certain nights on which prayers are answered.

God spills the honour of none,
Whose sin pours forth much eye-water (tears).

In Sin'á, a child of mine passed away (in death) ;
Of that which passed over my head,—what may I say ?

Fate drew not a picture of beauty, Yúsuf-like,
Which the fish of the grave devoured not, Yúnas-like.

This garden (of the world), that cypress became not lofty,
Whose root, the wind of death plucked not from its foun-
    dation.

It is not wonderful, if the rose blossoms on his dust ;
For, many a rose-limb sleeps in the dust.

To my heart, I said :—" Oh shame of men ! die ;
" For, the boy goes pure (to God) ; and, the old man,
    stained."

Through madness and perturbation regarding his stature
    (of body),
I uplifted a stone from his tomb.

In that place, dark and narrow,—through fear,
My state became confounded, and complexion changed.

From that changed state, when I returned to sense ;
From the son, heart-binding, there came to my ear :—

" If fear comes to thee, of the dark place (of the grave),
" Be wise ; and, enter endowed with light.

" Thou wishst the night of the grave, illumined day-
    like?
" Here (in this world), kindle the lamp of (good) deeds."

Sin'á is the name of a town.

The body of the work-performer trembles with fever (of
    anxiety),
Least that his date-tree should not bring forth dates.

A multitude of excessive avarice entertain the idea,
That they may, wheat unscattered, take up the harvest.

330 Oh Sa'dí! that one enjoyed the fruit, who planted the
    root;
That one took the harvest, who scattered the seed.

CHAPTER X.

Come; let us raise a hand from the heart;
For, to-morrow, (after death), one cannot raise the hand
    from the clay (of the grave).

In the autumn season, seest thou not the tree,
Which, from severe cold, remains leafless!

It uplifts the empty hands of supplication.
It returns not, through God's mercy, empty-handed (leaf-
    less).

Fate gives to it a renowned dress of honour;
Destiny places fruit, within its bosom.

At that door, which God never closed,—think not,
That he, hands raised (in supplication), becomes hopeless.

All bring devotion; and the wretched, supplication;
Come, so that at the Court of the Cherisher of the
    Wretched (God),

We may raise the hand, like the naked (leafless) branch;
For, one cannot sit longer than this, without means (leaf-
    less).

Oh Lord! look with bounty,
When sin comes into existence (issues) from Thy slaves.

Sin issues from the dust-like slave,
In hope of the pardon of the Lord.

10 Oh Merciful One! we are cherished by Thy bounty;
We are accustomed to Thy favour and grace.

When a beggar experiences liberality, and grace, and
    tenderness,
He turns not back from the rear of the giver.

Since Thou didst make us precious in the world,
We have expectation of this same (dearness), in the future
    world.

Thou alone givest preciousness and despicability;
One, dear to Thee, experiences contempt from none.

Oh God! by Thy honour, make me not contemptible (in
    the future world);
By the baseness of sin, make me not ashamed.

15 Make not, a person like unto myself, ruler over me;
If I bear punishment, it is best from Thy hand.

There is no evil, in the world, worse than this,—
To suffer oppression from the hand of one like unto my-
    self.

Shame of Thee is for me enough;
Make me not further ashamed before any.

If a shadow from Thee falls on my head,
For me,—the sky is of the lowest rank.

If Thou grantst a crown, it exalts my head;
Raise Thou me, so that none may cast me down.

———

My body trembles, when I bring to recollection,
The prayers of one distraught, in the sacred enclosure at
    Makka,

Who, with much lamentation, was saying to God:—
" Cast me not away; for no one takes my hand.

" Call me, with kindness, to Thy door; or, drive me from
    Thy door;
" —My head is only at Thy threshold.

" If Thou knowst that we are wretched, and helpless;
" We are wearied of imperious lust.

" This headstrong lust hastens to such a degree,
" That reason cannot seize its rein.

" Who, by force, prevails over lust and Shaitán?
" The battle-ranks of panthers come not from the ant.

" Give me a path, by the holy men of Thy path,
" Give me protection, from these enemies (lusts).

" Oh God! by the nature of Thy Lordship,
" By Thy qualities, matchless and unequalled,

" By—I await Thy command—of the pilgrim of the holy
    house (the Ka'ba),
" By the buried Muhammad,—peace be on him!

" By the extolling of Thee of men, sword-exercising,
" Who reckon the man of war, a woman.

" By the worship of old men adorned (with devotion),
" By the truth of young men, newly risen,—

" (I pray) saying :—In that whirlpool of a breath (death-
    throes),
" Help us from the shame of saying, two (Gods).

" There is hope from those who perform devotions ;
" For, they make intercession for those devotionless.

" Keep me far from pollution, by the pure ;
" And hold me excused, if any sin passes from me.

" By the old men, back bent with devotion ;
" Eye from shame of sin (stitched) to the back of the foot.

35 " (I pray) saying :—Close not my eye from the face of
    happiness ;
 " Bind not my tongue, at the time of witnessing.

" Hold the lamp of truth opposite my path ;
" Keep my hand short of doing evil.

" Cause my eyes to turn from that unfit to be seen ;
" Give me no power, as to disgraceful deeds.

" I am that atom, standing in Thy air,
" My existence, or non-existence, through despicability, is
    one.

" A single ray of the sun of Thy grace is sufficient ;
" For no one sees me, save in Thy effulgence.

40 " Glance at the evil one, that he may be better ;
" A glance from the king is enough for the beggar.

" If Thou, in justice and equity, seizest me,
" I will complain, saying :—Thy pardon gavest not to me
    this condition.

---

38   A mote, from the sun's effulgence and moon's luminosity, becomes
visible ; in obscurity, its existence and non-existence are one.

" Oh God ! drive me not, in contempt, from Thy door ;
" For no other door appears to me.

" And if I become, through ignorance, absent a few days,
" Shut not the door, in my face, when I return.

" What excuse may I bring for the shame of wet-skirted-
    ness,
" Unless I offer submission, saying :—Oh independent One !

45 " I am a poor man ; take me not in crime, and sin ;
" The rich man has pity for the poor.

" Why is it necessary to weep for the weakness of my state ?
" If I am weak, my shelter is Thou.

" Oh God ! in carelessness, we broke the covenant ;
" What force may the hand of struggle bring against
    destiny ?

" What issues from the hand of our deliberation ?
" This reliance is, indeed, enough,—confession of our sin.

" Whatever I did, Thou didst strike it all together (upset
    it) ;
" What power may one's self exert against God ?

50 " I take not my head beyond Thy order ;
" But Thy command thus passes over my head."

―――――

A certain one called one of blackish colour, ugly ;
He gave to him an answer of such a sort that he remained
    astonied.

" I have not created my own form,
" Which thou considerest my fault, saying :—I have done
    ill.

" If I am ugly of face, what business (oh sneerer!) hast
    thou with me?
" I am not, in short, the pourtrayer of the ugly and
    beautiful."

Beyond that which Thou didst write on my forehead,
Oh Slave-cherisher! I did neither less nor more.

55 Thou art, in short, the Knower that I am not powerful;
Thou art absolutely powerful;—who am I?

If Thou art my Guide, I arrive at safety;
But, if Thou shouldst lose me, I remain behind in journey-
    ing.

If the World-Creator affords not assistance,
How may the slave exercise abstinence?

———

How well said the darvesh of short hand,
Who, in the night, vowed; and, in the morning, broke his
    vow :—

" If He gives repentance, it will remain steadfast;
" For, our covenant is unstable and languid."

60 By Thy truth! stitch up my eyes from falsehood;
By Thy light! consume me not, to-morrow, in hell.

My face, through poverty, went into the dust;
My sin's dust ascended to Heaven.

Oh Cloud of Mercy! rain Thou once;
For dust, in the presence of rain, remains not.

———

54   Couplets 54–57 are uttered by the poet.

Through sin, to me, in this kingdom (of the world) is no
    rank;
But, to the next world, there is no path.

Thou knowst the intention of those tongue-bound;
Thou placest the plaster, on those heart-wounded.

----

65 An idolater was door shut as to his face against the world;
He was loin-girt in an idol's service.

After some years, as to that one of despised religion
—Fate brought before him, a difficult matter.

At the idol's foot, in the hope of good,
He helplessly rolled, in the dust of the temple,

Saying:—" Oh idol! I am distressed; help me;
" I am ready to die; pity my body."

Many times, in its service, he groaned;
But, any deeds for his arrangement issued not.

70 How may an idol accomplish a person's important affairs,
Which cannot drive a fly from its face?

He was confounded, saying:—" Oh one foot-bound in
    error!
" I worshipped thee several years, in folly:

" Accomplish the important matter, which I have before
    me;
" Otherwise, I will ask it from the Omnipotent."

His face, still stained with dust from (prostration before)
    the idol,
When the pure God accomplished his wish.

One truths-recognising became astonished at this;
—For, his pure time became to him obscured,—

75 Saying :—" A mean, false, perturbed worshipper,
   "—His head still, with the wine of the wine-tavern, in-
        toxicated,—

" Washed not his heart from infidelity; nor his religion
        from treachery,
"—God fulfilled that desire, which he sought ! "

His heart descended into this difficulty,
When a message (from God) came to the ear of his heart,

Saying :—" The old man of deficient wisdom, before the
        idol,
" Uttered much; but, his prayer was unacceptable.

" If he be also repulsed from Our Court,
" Then, from the idol to the Lord God,—what difference ?"

80 Oh friend ! it is necessary to bind the heart on the Lord
        God ;
Than the idol whatever (or whosoever) it be—who are
        more helpless ?

If thou placest thy head (in devotion) at this door, it is
        impossible,
That the hand of need should return to thee empty.

Oh God ! we came deficient in work ;
We came empty of hand, but hopeful.

———

I have heard that one intoxicated with the heat of the
        date-wine,
Ran to the most sacred place of a masjid.

He bewailed at the threshold of mercy,
Saying :—" Oh Lord ! take me to the loftiest Paradise ?"

85 The Mu,azzin seized his collar, saying:—" Make haste,
" Oh one careless of wisdom and religion!—a dog and a
　　masjid.

" What worthy deed didst thou, that thou seekst Para-
　　dise?
" Grace beseems thee not with an ugly face."

The old man uttered this speech, while intoxicated one
　　wept,
Saying:—"Oh sir! I am drunk; keep thy hand from me.

" Hast thou wonder at the grace of the Omnipotent,
" When a sinner is hopeful?

" I say not to thee (oh Mu,azzin!)—accept my excuse;
" The door of repentance is open, and God is helper."

90 I have constantly shame of the grace of the Merciful One;
For, I call my sin great, in comparison with his pardon.

When old age brings down a person from his feet,—
When thou seizest not his hand, he rises not from his place.

I am that old man, fallen from his feet;
Oh God! help me, by Thy own grace.

I say not:—Give me greatness and rank;
Pardon me the cause of my wretchedness (sin), and my
　　crime.

If a friend knows a little defect regarding me,
He makes me notorious for foolishness.

95 Thou seeing, and we fearful of each other;
For Thou art the Screen-coverer (of sin), and we the
　　screen-render.

85　" Hín " signifies—zúd básh.
90　The author here begins to speak.

Men from without (the screen) have raised a shout (on
    finding a defect) ;
Thou art always within the screen and screen-coverer.

If slaves, in foolishness, turn their heads (from order),
The lords draw the pen (efface the crime).

If Thou pardonst sin to the extent of Thy liberality,
There remains no captive in existence.

And, if Thou becomest angry to the extent of sin,—
Send to hell ; and, ask not for the balance.

100 If Thou helpst me, I may arrive at the (appointed) place ;
And, if Thou castest me down,—no one assists.

Who uses violence, if Thou givest assistance?
Who seizes, when thou givest deliverance?

In the place of assembling, there will be two parties ;
I know not which path they may assign to me.

If my road be from the right hand,—it is wonderful ;
For, only crookedness arose from my hand.

My heart gives, time to time, hope,
That God has shame of my white hair.

105 I have wonder, if He has shame of me,
For shame comes not to me of myself.

Did not Yúsuf—who experienced such calamity and im-
    prisonment,
When his command became current, and his rank lofty,—

Pardon the crime of the offspring of Ya'kúb ?
For a good appearance has virtue.

---

104   In the traditions, it is stated :—Him, who became old in Islám, God
is ashamed to punish.

He imprisoned them not, for their bad conduct;
He rejected not their small capital.

We also, from Thy grace, have expectation of this very
    (treatment),
Oh dear One ! forgive the sin of this one, without capital.

110 No one has seen one of blacker deeds than me
Of whom no deed is approved.

Besides this that to me there is hope of Thy assistance ;
To me, there is hope of Thy forgiveness.

I have brought no capital, save hope ;
Oh God ! make me not hopeless of pardon.

---

109   We have hope that our small capital may not be rejected, for it is a
reason for mercy.   Nay, our prayers, without capital, are a cause of
compassion.
    We lament and supplicate and prefer excuse for sin.   After saying—
Oh Lord !—we depreciate ourselves and our deeds.

SUPPLEMENTARY NOTE.

*In some copies, the following version of the passage,
couplets 685 to 706, in Chapter I., occurs.*

He saw an ass, fleet and load-carrying;
Strong, powerful, and effective.

A certain man,—a bone in his hand,
He so struck it, that he broke its bone.

The king was astonied and said :—" Oh youth !
" Thy cruelty to this tongueless one has passed bounds.

" Since thou art strong, make not this self-display ;
" Exercise not strength against the fallen."

The idle words of the king came not pleasing to him ;
He expressed a shout, in terror, against the king.

Saying :—" I chose not, in folly, this action ;
" Since thou knowst not,—go about thy own business.

" Many an one, who is in thy opinion not excused,
" —If thou wilt look well into the matter,—is not far from
    good counsel."

To the king, his reply seemed severe;
He said :—" Come ; what right hast thou ?

" I think thou art a stranger to reason ;
" Thou art, assuredly, not drunk,—but mad."

The man laughed, saying :—" Oh foolish soldier ! silence ;
" The tale of Khizr has not perhaps come to thy ears ?

695 " No one calls him either mad, or intoxicated ;
" Why broke he the ship of the feeble folk ? "

The king said :—" Oh tyranous one !
" Knowst thou not, why Khizr so acted ?

" In that sea, was a king, a tyrant,
" On whose account, hearts were a sea of terror.

" Creatures, from his deeds, full of lamentation ;
" A world, by his power, like a river in agitation.

" Then, for the sake of the good, he broke (in pieces) that
          ship ;
" That the chief, the tyrant, might not acquire it.

700 " A broken (article of) property, that is in thy hand,
" Is better than that whole (should be) in the enemy's
          power."

The villager of enlightened mind laughed,
Saying :—" O Amír ! the right is in my hand.

" Not, through stupidity, do I break the ass's leg ;
" But, through the oppression of the unjust sultán.

" The ass, in this place, lame and pain-suffering,
" Is better than that (ass) which (is) a load-carrier before
          the king.

" Fie upon such (a tyrant king) who ruled (this) country
          and empire !
" On whom, shame will remain till the Judgment Day.

05 " If the woman, burden-bearing (pregnant) brings forth a
    snake,
" It is better than one man-born of demon-form."

The tyrant exercised tyranny on his own body ;
He exercised it not on the state of the poor darvesh.

For, to-morrow, in that assembly of fame and infamy,
The darvesh will seize, in his grasp, the tyrant's collar and
    beard.

The darvesh places the load of his own sins, on his neck ;
He (the tyrant) is unable to raise his head.

I grant—that the ass now carries his load ;
How will he (the tyrant) bear the load of asses, on that
    Day (of Judgment).

710 If thou askest justice, he is ill-starred,
To whom, another's sorrow is joy.

These very fine days of delight, he has
Whose delight is in the grief of men.

If that dead-heart (ignorant one) rise not (from his sleeping-
    garment), it is better than that
Men should, on his account, sleep heart-distressed.

INDEX.

The tales, or discourses, marked :—

a are not contained in the 'Ikd-i-manzúm ;

b do not properly belong to the 'Ikd-i-manzúm ;

a and *c* need not be read for the High Proficiency Examination in Persian, in India.

As to examinations, see Appendix to Clarke's " Persian Manual."

The following Table shows the Couplets, belonging to the Bustán, which are omitted in the 'Iḳd-i-Manẓúm.

From	To	Total Couplets.	Chapter.
54	67	14	Intro-duction.
72	97	26	
104		1	
107	190	84	
		125	
1	21	21	1
39	41	3	
69	264	195	
297	302	6	
318	319	2	
322	358	37	
370	414	45	
418	421	4	
452	479	28	
512	547	36	
559	560	2	
581	588	8	
618	636	19	
651	655	5	
663	677	15	
714	718	5	
742	747	6	
753	797	45	
822	880	59	
891	971	89	
		630	
1	28	28	2
55	121	67	
229	234	6	
263	265	3	
411	426	16	
467	472	6	
480	484	5	
508	518	11	
		142	
37	66	30	3
96	113	8	
154	163	10	
166	171	6	

From	To	Total Couplets.	Chapter.
179	187	9	
213	236	24	
268	283	16	
284	304	21	
305	314	10	
336	347	12	
		146	
5	21	17	4
30	41	12	
145	201	57	
352	363	12	
376	424	49	
456	501	46	
		193	
		0	5
		0	
30	37	8	6
69	71	3	
153	174	22	
		33	
94	116	23	7
310	358	49	
400	407	8	
		80	
		0	8
		0	
255	257	3	9
275	286	12	
		15	
		0	10
		0	

Total number of couplets in the Bustán · · · 4,099
    ,,   ,,   ,, omitted in the 'Iḳd-i-manẓúm · 1,344

Hence total number of couplets in the 'Iḳd-i-manẓúm · 2,755

London: Printed by W. H. Allen & Co., 13, Waterloo Place.

Works issued from the India Office, and Sold by Wm. H. ALLEN & Co.

Tree and Serpent Worship ;

Or, Illustrations of Mythology and Art in India in the First and Fourth Centuries after Christ, from the Sculptures of the Buddhist Topes at Sanchi and Amravati. Prepared at the India Museum, under the authority of the Secretary of State for India in Council. Second edition, Revised, Corrected, and in great part Re-written. By James Fergusson, Esq., F.R.S., F.R.A.S. Super-royal 4to. 100 plates and 31 engravings, pp. 270. Price £5 5s.

Illustrations of Ancient Buildings in Kashmir.

Prepared at the Indian Museum under the authority of the Secretary of State for India in Council. From Photographs, Plans, and Drawings taken by Order of the Government of India. By Henry Hardy Cole, Lieut. R.E., Superintendent Archæological Survey of India, North-West Provinces. In One vol.; half-bound, Quarto. Fifty-eight plates. £3 10s.

The Illustrations in this work have been produced in Carbon from the original negatives, and are therefore permanent.

Pharmacopœia of India.

Prepared under the Authority of the Secretary of State for India. By Edward John Waring, M.D. Assisted by a Committee appointed for the Purpose. 8vo. 6s.

Archæological Survey of Western India.

Report of the First Season's Operations in the Belgâm and Kaladgi Districts. January to May, 1874. Prepared at the India Museum and Published under the Authority of the Secretary of State for India in Council By James Burgess, Author of the " Rock Temples of Elephanta," &c., &c., and Editor of " The Indian Antiquary." Half-bound. Quarto. 58 Plates and Woodcuts. £2 2s.

Adam W. (late of Calcutta) Theories of History.
8vo. 15s. (See page 27.)

Advice to Officers in India.
By JOHN McCOSH, M.D. Post 8vo. 8s.

Allen's Series.
1.—World We Live In. (See page 30.) 2s.
2.—Earth's History. (See page 6.) 2s.
3.—Geography of India. (See page 8.) 2s.
4.—2000 Examination Questions in Physical Geography. 2s.
5.—Hall's Trigonometry. (See page 9.) 2s.
6.—Wollaston's Elementary Indian Reader. 1s. (See page 30.)
7 —Ansted's Elements of Physiography. 1s. 4d.

Analytical History of India.
From the earliest times to the Abolition of the East India Company in 1858. By ROBERT SEWELL, Madras Civil Service. Post 8vo. 8s.
₄ The object of this work is to supply the want which has been felt by students for a condensed outline of Indian History which would serve at once to recall the memory and guide the eye, while at the same time it has been attempted to render it interesting to the general reader by preserving a medium between a bare analysis and a complete history.

Ancient and Mediæval India.
2 vols. 8vo. 30s. (See page 17.)

Anderson's (P.) English in Western India.
8vo. 14s.

Andrew's (W. P.) India and Her Neighbours,
With Two Maps. 8vo. 15s.

Ansted's (D. T.) Elements of Physiography.
For the use of Science Schools. Fcap. 8vo. 1s. 4d.

Ansted's (D. T.) Physical Geography.
5th Edition. With Maps. Crown 8vo 7s. (See page 23.)

Ansted's (D. T.) World We Live In.
Fcap 2s. 25th Thousand, with Illustrations. (See page 30.)

Ansted's (D. T.) Earth's History.
Fcap. 2s. (See page 6.)

Ansted's (D. T.)
Two Thousand Examination Questions in Physical Geography. pp. 180. Price 2s.

Ansted's (D. T.) Ionian Islands.
8vo. 8s. (See page 14.)

Ansted's (D. T.) and R. G. Latham's Channel Islands.
8vo. 16s. (See page 14.)

Ansted's (D. T.) Water, and Water Supply.
Chiefly with reference to the British Islands. — Surface Waters. 8vo. With Maps. 18s.

Archer's (Capt. J. H. Laurence) Commentaries on the Punjaub Campaign—1848-49. Crown 8vo. 8s. (See page 5.)

Atterbury Memoirs, &c.
The Memoir and Correspondence of Francis Atterbury, Bishop of Rochester, with his distinguished contemporaries. Compiled chiefly from the Atterbury and Stuart Papers. By FOLKESTONE WILLIAMS, Author of "Lives of the English Cardinals," &c., 2 vols. 8vo. 14s.

Authors at Work.
By CHARLES PEBODY. Post 8vo. 10s. 6d.

Bengal Artillery.
A Memoir of the Services of the Bengal Artillery from the formation of the Corps. By the late CAPT. E. BUCKLE, Assist - Adjut. Gen. Ben. Art. Edit. by SIR J. W. KAYE. 8vo. Lond. 1852. 10s.

Bernays, (Dr. A. J.) Students' Chemistry.
Crown 8vo. 5s. 6d. (See page 26.)

Binning's (R. M.) Travels in Persia, &c.
2 vols. 8vo. 16s.

Birth of the War God.
A Poem. By KALIDASA. Translated from the Sanscrit into English Verse. By RALPH T. H. GRIFFITH. 5s.

Blanchard's (S.) Yesterday and To-day in India.
Post 8vo. 6s. (See page 30.)

Blenkinsopp's (Rev. E. L.) Doctrine of Development
In the Bible and in the Church. 2nd edit. 12mo. 6s. (See page 6.)

Boileau (Major-General J. T.)
A New and Complete Set of Traverse Tables, showing the Differences of Latitude and the Departures to every Minute of the Quadrant and to Five Places of Decimals. Together with a Table of the lengths of each Degree of Latitude and corresponding Degree of Longitude from the Equator to the Poles; with other Tables useful to the Surveyor and Engineer. Fourth Edition, thoroughly revised and corrected by the Author. Royal 8vo. 12s. London, 1876.

Boulger (D. C.) The Life of Yakoob Beg, Athalik Ghazi and Badaulet, Ameer of Kashgar. 8vo. With Map and Appendix. 16s.

Boulger (D. C.) England and Russia in Central Asia. With Appendices and Two Maps, one being the latest Russian Official Map of Central Asia. 2 vols. 8vo. 38s.

Bowring's Flowery Scroll.
A Chinese Novel. Translated and Illustrated with Notes by SIR J. BOWRING, late H.B.M. Plenipo. China. Post 8vo. 10s. 6d.

Boyd (R. Nelson). Coal Mine Inspection; Its History and Results. 8vo. 14s.

Bradshaw (John) LL.D. The Poetical Works of John Milton, with Notes, explanatory and philological. 2 vols. post 8vo. 12s. 6d.

Brandis' Forest Flora of North-West and Central India.
Text and plates. £2 1s. (See page 8.)

Briggs' (Gen. J.) India and Europe Compared.
Post 8vo. 7s.

Browne's (J. W.) Hardware; How to Buy it for Foreign Markets. 8vo. 10s. 6d. (See page 9.)

Canal and Culvert Tables, based on the Formula of Kutter, under a Modified Classification. with Explanatory Text and Examples. By LOWIS D'A. JACKSON, A.M.I.C.E., author of "Hydraulic Manual and Statistics," &c. Roy. 8vo. 28s.

Catholic Doctrine of the Atonement.
An Historical Inquiry into its Development in the Church. with an Introduction on the Principle of Theological Development. By H. NUTCOMBE OXENHAM, M.A. 2nd Edit. 8vo. 10s. 6d.
"It is one of the ablest and probably one of the most charmingly written treatises on the subject which exists in our language."—*Times.*

Celebrated Naval and Military Trials.
By PETER BURKE, Serjeant-at-Law. Author of "Celebrated Trials connected with the Aristocracy." Post 8vo. 10s. 6d.

Central Asia (Sketches of).
By A. VAMBERY. 8vo 16s. (See page 28.)

Cochrane, (John) Hindu Law. 20s. (See page 13.)

Commentaries on the Punjaub Campaign 1848-49, including some additions to the History of the Second Sikh War, from original sources. By Capt. J. H. LAWRENCE-ARCHER, Bengal H. P. Crown 8vo. 8s.

Cruise of H.M.S. "Galatea,"
Captain H.R.H. the Duke of Edinburgh, K.G., in 1867—1868. By the Rev. John Milner, B.A., Chaplain; and Oswald W. Brierly. Illustrated by a Photograph of H.R.H. the Duke of Edinburgh; and by Chromo-Lithographs and Graphotypes from Sketches taken on the spot by O. W. Brierly 8vo. 16s.

Cyprus: Historical and Descriptive.
Adapted from the German of Herr Franz Von Löher. With much additional matter. By Mrs. A. Batson Joyner. Crown 8vo. With 2 Maps. 10s. 6d

Danvers (Fred. Chas.) On Coal.
With Reference to Screening, Transport, &c 8vo. 10s. 6d.

Doctrine of Development in the Bible and in the Church.
By Rev. E. L. Blenkinsopp, M.A., Rector of Springthorp. 2nd edition. 12mo. 6s.

Doran (Dr. J.) Annals of the English Stage.
Post 8vo. 6s. (See p. 26.)

Down by the Drawle.
By Major A. F. P. Harcourt, Bengal Staff Corps, author of "Kooloo, Lahoul, and Spiti," "The Shakespeare Argosy," &c. 2 Vols. crown 8vo. 21s.

Drain of Silver to the East,
And the Currency of India. By W. Nassau Lees. Post 8vo. 8s.

Drury.—The Useful Plants of India,
With Notices of their chief value in Commerce, Medicine, and the Arts. By Colonel Heber Drury. Second Edition, with Additions and Corrections. Royal 8vo. 16s.

Earth's History,
Or, First Lessons in Geology. For the use of Schools and Students. By D. T. Ansted. Third Thousand. Fcap. 8vo. 2s.

East India Calculator,
By T. Thornton. 8vo. London, 1823. 10s.

Edinburgh (The Duke of) Cruise of the "Galatea."
With Illustrations 8vo. 16s.

Edwards' (H. S.) Russians at Home.
With Illustrations. Post 8vo. 6s. (See page 25.)

Edwards' (H. S.) History of the Opera.
2 Vols., 8vo. 10s. 6d. (See page 10.)

Elementary Mathematics.
A Course of Elementary Mathematics for the use of candidates for admission into either of the Military Colleges; of applicants for appointments in the Home or Indian Civil Services; and of mathematical students generally. By Professor J. R. YOUNG. In one closely-printed volume 8vo., pp. 648. 12s.

"In the work before us he has digested a complete Elementary Course, by aid of his long experience as a teacher and writer; and he has produced a very useful book. Mr. Young has not allowed his own taste to rule the distribution, but has adjusted his parts with the skill of a veteran."—*Athenæum.*

English Cardinals.
The Lives of the English Cardinals, from Nicholas Breakspeare (Pope Adrien IV.) to Thomas Wolsey, Cardinal Legate. With Historical Notices of the Papal Court. By FOLKESTONE WILLIAMS. In 2 vols. 14s.

English Homes in India.
By MRS. KEATINGE. Part I.—The Three Loves. Part II.—The Wrong Turning. Two vols., Post 8vo. 16s.

Entombed Alive, and other Songs and Ballads. (From the Chinese.) By GEORGE CARTER STENT, M.R.A.S., of the Chinese Imperial Maritime Customs Service, author of "Chinese and English Vocabulary," "Chinese and English Pocket Dictionary," "The Jade Chaplet," &c. Crown 8vo. With four Illustrations. 9s.

Eyre, Major-General (Sir V.), K.C.S.I., C.B. The Kabul Insurrection of 1841–42. Revised and corrected from Lieut. Eyre's Original Manuscript. Edited by Colonel G. B. MALLESON, C.S.I. Crown 8vo., with Map and Illustrations. 9s.

Final French Struggles in India and on the Indian Seas.
Including an Account of the Capture of the Isles of France and Bourbon, and Sketches of the most eminent Foreign Adventurers in India up to the period of that Capture. With an Appendix containing an Account of the Expedition from India to Egypt in 1801. By Colonel G. B. MALLESON, C.S.I. Crown 8vo. 10s. 6d.

First Age of Christianity and the Church (The).
By John Ignatius Döllinger, D.D., Professor of Ecclesiastical History in the University of Munich, &c., &c. Translated from the German bv Henry Nutcombe Oxenham, M.A., late Scholar of Baliol College, Oxford. Third Edition. 2 vols. Crown 8vo. 18s.

Forbes (Dr. Duncan) History of Chess.
8vo. 7s, 6d. (See page 10.)

Forest Flora of North-Western and Central India.
By Dr. Brandis, Inspector General of Forests to the Government of India. Text and Plates. £2 18s.

Franz Schubert.
A Musical Biography, from the German of Dr. Heinrich Kreisle von Hellborn. By Edward Wilberforce, Esq., Author of "Social Life in Munich." Post 8vo. 6s.

Gazetteers of India.
Thornton, 4 vols., 8vo. £2 16s.
 ,, 8vo. 21s.
 ,, (N.W.P., &c.) 2 vols., 8vo. 25s.

Gazetteer of Southern India.
With the Tenasserim Provinces and Singapore. Compiled from original and authentic sources. Accompanied by an Atlas, including plans of all the principal towns and cantonments. Royal 8vo. with 4to. Atlas. £3 3s.

Gazetteer of the Punjaub, Affghanistan, &c.
Gazetteer of the Countries adjacent to India, on the northwest, including Scinde, Affghanistan, Beloochistan, the Punjaub, and the neighbouring States. By Edward Thornton, Esq 2 vols. 8vo. £1 5s.

Geography of India.
Comprising an account of British India, and the various states enclosed and adjoining. Fcap. pp. 250. 2s.

Geological Papers on Western India.
Including Cutch, Scinde, and the south-east coast of Arabia. To which is added a Summary of the Geology of India generally. Edited for the Government by Henry J. Carter, Assistant Surgeon, Bombay Army. Royal 8vo. with folio Atlas of maps and plates; half-bound. £2 2s.

German Life and Manners
As seen in Saxony. With an account of Town Life—Village Life—Fashionable Life—Married Life—School and University Life, &c. Illustrated with Songs and Pictures of the Student Customs at the University of Jena. By Henry Mayhew, 2 vols. 8vo., with numerous illustrations. 18s.

A Popular Edition of the above. With illustrations. Cr. 8vo. 7s.
"Full of original thought and observation, and may be studied with profit by both German and English—especially by the German." *Athenæum.*

Glyn's (A. C.) Civilization in the 5th Century.
2 vols. post 8vo. £1 1s.

Goldstucker (Dr.) The Miscellaneous Essays of.
With a Memoir. 2 vols. 8vo. 21s.

Grady's (S. G.) Mohamedan Law of Inheritance & Contract.
8vo. 14s. (See page 13.)

Grady's (S. G.) Institutes of Menu.
8vo. 12s. (See page 13.)

Griffith's (Ralph T. H.) Birth of the War God.
8vo. 5s. (See page 4.)

Hall's Trigonometry.
The Elements of Plane and Spherical Trigonometry. With an Appendix, containing the solution of the Problems in Nautical Astronomy. For the use of Schools. By the Rev. T. G. HALL, M.A., Professor of Mathematics in King's College. London. 12mo. 2s.

Hamilton's Hedaya.
A new edition, with the obsolete passages omitted, and a copious Index added by S. G. Grady. 8vo. £1 15s.

Handbook of Reference to the Maps of India.
Giving the Lat. and Long. of places of note. 18mo. 3s. 6d.
₊ *This will be found a valuable Companion to Messrs. Allen & Co.'s Maps of India.*

Hardware; How to Buy it for Foreign Markets.
By J. WILSON BROWNE. (See page 5.)
This is the most complete Guide to the Hardware Trade yet brought out; comprising all the principal Gross Lists in general use, with Illustrations and Descriptions. 8vo. 10s. 6d.

Hedaya.
Translated from the Arabic by WALTER HAMILTON. *A New Edition,* with Index by S. G. GRADY. 8vo. £1. 15s.

Henry VIII.
An Historical Sketch as affecting the Reformation in England. By CHARLES HASTINGS COLLETTE. Post 8vo. 6s.

Hindu Law.
By Sir Thomas Strange. 2 vols. Royal 8vo., 1830. 24s. (See page 13.)

Historical Results
Deducible from Recent Discoveries in Affghanistan. By H. T. PRINSEP. 8vo. Lond. 1844. 15s.

Histories of India.
Mill, 9 vols., cr. 8vo. £2 10s. (See page 22.)
Thornton, 6 vols., 8vo. £2 8s. (See page 27.)
Thornton, 1 vol., 8vo. 12s. (See page 27.)
Trotter, 2 vols., 8vo. 32s. (See page 28.)
Sewell (Analytical) Crown 8vo. 8s. (See page 3.)
Owen, India on the Eve of the British Conquest. 8s. (See page 22.)

History of Civilization in the Fifth Century.
Translated by permission from the French of A. Frederic Ozanam, late Professor of Foreign Literature to the Faculty of Letters at Paris. By ASHBY C. GLYN, B.A., of the Inner Temple, Barrister-at-Law. 2 vols., post 8vo. £1 1s.

History of Chess,
From the time of the Early Invention of the Game in India, till the period of its establishment in Western and Central Europe. By DUNCAN FORBES, LL D 8vo 7s. 6d.

History of the Opera,
From Monteverde to Donizetti. By H. SUTHERLAND EDWARDS Second edition. 2 vols., Post 8vo. 10s. 6d.

History of the Punjaub,
And of the Rise, Progress, and Present Condition of the Sikhs. By T. THORNTON. 2 Vols. Post 8vo. 8s.

Horses of the Sahara, and the Manners of the Desert.
By E. DAUMAS, General of the Division Commanding at Bordeaux, Senator, &c , &c. With Commentaries by the Emir Abd-el-Kadir (Authorized Edition). 8vo. 6s.

"We have rarely read a work giving a more picturesque and, at the same time, practical account of the manners and customs of a people, than this book on the Arabs and their horses."—*Edinburgh Courant.*

Hough (Lieut.-Col. W.) Precedents in Military Law.
8vo. cloth. 25s.

Hughes's (Rev. T. P.) Notes on Muhammadanism.
Second Edition, Revised and Enlarged. Fcap. 8vo. 6s.

Hydraulic Manual and Working Tables, Hydraulic and
Indian Meteorological Statistics. Published under the patronage of the Right Honourable the Secretary of State for India. By LOWIS D'A JACKSON. 8vo. 28s.

Illustrated Horse Doctor.

Being an Accurate and Detailed Account, accompanied by more than 400 Pictorial Representations, characteristic of the various Diseases to which the Equine Race are subjected: together with the latest Mode of Treatment, and all the requisite Prescriptions written in Plain English. By EDWARD MAYHEW, M.R.C.V.S. 8vo. 18s. 6d.

CONTENTS.—The Brain and Nervous System.—The Eyes.—The Mouth.—The Nostrils.—The Throat.—The Chest and its contents.—The Stomach, Liver, &c.—The Abdomen.—The Urinary Organs.—The Skin.—Specific Diseases.—Limbs.—The Feet.—Injuries.—Operations.

"The book contains nearly 600 pages of valuable matter, which reflects great credit on its author, and, owing to its practical details, the result of deep scientific research, deserves a place in the library of medical, veterinary, and non-professional readers."—*Field.*

"The book furnishes at once the bane and the antidote, as the drawings show the horse not only suffering from every kind of disease, but in the different stages of it, while the alphabetical summary at the end gives the cause, symptoms and treatment of each."—*Illustrated London News.*

Illustrated Horse Management.

Containing descriptive remarks upon Anatomy, Medicine, Shoeing, Teeth, Food, Vices, Stables; likewise a plain account of the situation, nature, and value of the various points; together with comments on grooms, dealers, breeders, breakers, and trainers; Embellished with more than 400 engravings from original designs made expressly for this work. By E. MAYHEW. A new Edition, revised and improved by J. I. LUPTON. M.R.C.V.S. 8vo. 12s.

CONTENTS.—The body of the horse anatomically considered PHYSIC.—The mode of administering it, and minor operations SHOEING.—Its origin, its uses, and its varieties. THE TEETH.—Their natural growth, and the abuses to which they are liable. FOOD.—The fittest time for feeding, and the kind of food which the horse naturally consumes. The evils which are occasioned by modern stables. The faults inseparable from stables. The so-called "incapacitating vices," which are the results of injury or of disease. Stables as they should be. GROOMS.—Their prejudices, their injuries, and their duties. POINTS.—Their relative importance and where to look for their development. BREEDING.—Its inconsistencies and its disappointments. BREAKING AND TRAINING.—Their errors and their results.

India Directory (The).

For the Guidance of Commanders of Steamers and Sailing Vessels. Founded upon the Work of the late CAPTAIN JAMES HORSBURGH, F.R.S.

PART I.—The East Indies, and Interjacent Ports of Africa and South America. Revised, Extended, and Illustrated with Charts of Winds, Currents, Passages, Variation, and Tides. By COMMANDER ALFRED DUNDAS TAYLOR, F.R.G.S., Superintendent of Marine Surveys to the Government of India. £1 18s.

PART II.—The China Sea, with the Ports of Java, Australia and Japan and the Indian Archipelago Harbours, as well as those of New Zealand. Illustrated with Charts of the Winds, Currents, Passages, &c. By the same. (*In the Press.*)

India and Her Neighbours.

By W. P. ANDREW. 8vo. With 2 Maps. 15s.

Indian Administration.

By H. G. KEENE. Post 8vo. 5s.

The India List, Civil and Military,

Containing Names of all Officers employed by the Indian Government, including those of the Public Works, Educational, Political, Postal, Police, Customs, Forests, Railway and Telegraphs Departments, with Rules for Admission to these Services, Furlough Rules, Retiring Pensions, Staff Corps Regulations and Salaries, &c., with an Index. Issued in January and July of each year, by permission of the Secretary of State for India in Council. 8vo. 10s. 6d.

Indian Code of Civil Procedure.

In the Form of Questions and Answers. With Explanatory and Illustrative Notes. By ANGELO J. LEWIS. 12s. 6d.

Indian Criminal Law and Procedure,

Including the Procedure in the High Courts, as well as that in the Courts not established by Royal Charter; with Forms of Charges and Notes on Evidence, illustrated by a large number of English Cases, and Cases decided in the High Courts of India: and an APPENDIX of selected Acts passed by the Legislative Council relating to Criminal matters. By M. H. STARLING, ESQ., L.L.B. & F. B. CONSTABLE, M.A. Third edition. 8vo. £2 2s.

Indian Penal Code.

In the Form of Questions and Answers. With Explanatory and Illustrative Notes. By ANGELO J. LEWIS. 7s. 6d.

Indian and Military Law.

Mahommedan Law of Inheritance, &c. A Manual of the Mahommedan Law of Inheritance and Contract; comprising the Doctrine of the Soonee and Sheea Schools, and based upon the text of Sir H. W. MACNAGHTEN's Principles and Precedents, together with the Decisions of the Privy Council and High Courts of the Presidencies in India. For the use of Schools and Students. By STANDISH GROVE GRADY, Barrister-at-Law, Reader of Hindoo, Mahommedan, and Indian Law to the Inns of Court. 8vo. 14s.

Hedaya, or Guide, a Commentary on the Mussulman Laws, translated by order of the Governor-General and Council of Bengal. By CHARLES HAMILTON. Second Edition, with Preface and Index by STANDISH GROVE GRADY. 8vo. £1 15s.

Institutes of Menu in English. The Institutes of Hindu Law or the Ordinances of Menu, according to Gloss of Collucca. Comprising the Indian System of Duties, Religious and Civil, verbally translated from the Original, with a Preface by SIR WILLIAM JONES, and collated with the Sanscrit Text by GRAVES CHAMNEY HAUGHTON, M.A., F.R.S., Professor of Hindu Literature in the East India College. New edition, with Preface and Index by STANDISH G. GRADY, Barrister-at-Law, and Reader of Hindu, Mahommedan, and Indian Law to the Inns of Court. 8vo., cloth. 12s.

Indian Code of Criminal Procedure. Being Act X of 1872, Passed by the Governor-General of India in Council on the 25th of April, 1872. 8vo. 12s.

Indian Code of Civil Procedure. In the form of Questions and Answers, with Explanatory and Illustrative Notes. By ANGELO J. LEWIS, Barrister-at-law. 12mo. 12s. 6d.

Indian Penal Code. In the Form of Questions and Answers. With Explanatory and Illustrative Notes. By ANGELO J. LEWIS, Barrister-at-Law. Post 8vo. 7s. 6d.

Hindu Law. Principally with reference to such portions of it as concern the Administration of Justice in the Courts in India. By SIR THOMAS STRANGE, late Chief Justice of Madras. 2 vols. Royal 8vo., 1830. 24s.

Hindu Law. Defence of the Daya Bhaga. Notice of the Case on Prosoono Coomar Tajore's Will. Judgment of the Judicial Committee of the Privy Council. Examination of such Judgment. By JOHN COCHRANE, Barrister-at-Law. Royal 8vo. 20s.

Law and Customs of Hindu Castes, within the Dekhan Provinces subject to the Presidency of Bombay, chiefly affecting Civil Suits. By ARTHUR STEELE. Royal 8vo. £1 1s.

Chart of Hindu Inheritance. With an Explanatory Treatise, By ALMARIC RUMSEY. 8vo. 6s. 6d.

Manual of Military Law. For all ranks of the Army, Militia and Volunteer Services. By Colonel J. K. PIPON, Assist. Adjutant General at Head Quarters, & J. F. COLLIER, Esq., of the Inner Temple, Barrister-at-Law. Third and Revised Edition. Pocket size. 5s.

Precedents in Military Law: including the Practice of Courts-Martial; the Mode of Conducting Trials; the Duties of Officers at Military Courts of Inquests, Courts of Inquiry, Courts of Requests, &c., &c. The following are a portion of the Contents:—
1. Military Law. 2. Martial Law. 3. Courts-Martial. 4. Courts of Inquiry. 5. Courts of Inquest. 6. Courts of Request. 7. Forms of Courts-Martial. 8. Precedents of Military Law. 9. Trials of Arson to Rape (Alphabetically arranged.) 10. Rebellions. 11. Riots. 12. Miscellaneous. By Lieut.-Col. W. HOUGH, late Deputy Judge-Advocate-General, Bengal Army, and Author of several Works on Courts-Martial. One thick 8vo. vol. 25s.

The Practice of Courts Martial. By HOUGH & LONG. Thick 8vo. London, 1825. 26s.

Indian Infanticide.

Its Origin, Progress, and Suppression. By JOHN CAVE-BROWN, M.A. 8vo. 5s.

Indian Wisdom,

Or Examples of the Religious, Philosophical and Ethical Doctrines of the Hindus. With a brief History of the Chief Departments of Sanscrit Literature, and some account of the Past and Present Condition of India, Moral and Intellectual. By MONIER WILLIAMS, M.A., Boden Professor of Sanscrit in in the University of Oxford. Third Edition. 8vo. 15s.

Ionian Islands in 1863.

By PROFESSOR D. T. ANSTED, M.A., F.R.S., &c.] 8vo., with Maps and Cuts. 8s.

Jackson's (Lowis D'A.) Hydraulic Manual and Working Tables, Hydraulic and Indian Meteorological Statistics. 8vo. 28s. (See page 10.)

Jackson (Lowis D'A.) Canal and Culvert Tables. Roy. 8vo. 28s. (See page 5.)

Japan, the Amoor and the Pacific.

With notices of other Places, comprised in a Voyage of Circumnavigation in the Imperial Russian Corvette *Rynda*, in 1858—1860. By HENRY A. TILLEY. Eight Illustrations. 8vo. 16s.

Jersey, Guernsey, Alderney, Sark, &c.

THE CHANNEL ISLANDS. Containing: PART I.—Physical Geography. PART II.—Natural History. PART III.—Civil History. PART IV.—Economics and Trade. By DAVID THOMAS ANSTED, M.A., F.R.S., and ROBERT GORDON LATHAM, M.A., M.D., F.R.S. New and Cheaper Edition in one handsome

8vo. Volume, with 72 Illustrations on Wood by Vizetelly, Loudon. Nicholls, and Hart ; with Map. 16s.

"This is a really valuable work. A book which will long remain the standard authority on the subject. No one who has been to the Channel Islands, or who purposes going there will be insensible of its value."— *Saturday Review.*

"It is the produce of many hands and every hand a good one."

Jerrold's (Blanchard) at Home in Paris.
2 Vols. Post 8vo. 16s.

Kaye (Sir J. W.) The Sepoy War in India. (See page 25.)
Vol. 1. 18s.
Vol. 2. £1.
Vol. 3. £1.

Kaye (Sir J. W.) History of the War in Affghanistan.
New edition. 3 Vols. Crown 8vo. £1. 6s.

Kaye (Sir J. W.) H. St. G. Tucker's Life and Correspondence.
8vo 10s.

Kaye's (Sir J. W.) Memorials of Indian Governments.
By H. St. George Tucker. 8vo. 10s.

Keene's (H. G.) Mogul Empire.
8vo. 10s. 6d. (See page 22.)

Keene's (H. G.) Administration in India.
Post 8vo 9s.

Keene (H. G.). The Turks in India.
Historical Chapters on the Administration of Hindostan by the Chugtai Tartar, Babar, and his Descendants. 12s. 6d.

Kenneth Trelawny.
By Alec Fearon. Author of "Touch not the Nettle." 2 vols. Crown 8vo. 21s.

Lady Morgan's Memoirs.
Autobiography, Diaries and Correspondence. 2 Vols. 8vo, with Portraits. 18s.

Latham's (Dr. R. G.) Nationalities of Europe.
2 Vols. 8vo. 12s. (See page 22.)

Latham's (Dr. R. G.) Russian and Turk,
From a Geographical, Ethnological, and Historical Point of View. 8vo. 18s.

Law and Customs of Hindu Castes,
By Arthur Steele. Royal 8vo. £1. 1s. (See page 13.)

Lee (Rev. F. G., D.C.L.) The Words from the Cross: Seven
Sermons for Lent, Passion-Tide, and Holy Week. Third edition revised. Fcap. 3s. 6d.

Lee's (Dr. W. N.) Drain of Silver to the East.
Post 8vo. 8s.

Lewin's Wild Races of the South Eastern Frontier of India.
Including an Account of the Loshai Country. Post 8vo. 10s. 6d.

Lewis's (A. J.) Indian Penal Code
Post 8vo. 7s. 6d. (See page 12.)

Lewis's Indian Code of Civil Procedure.
Post 8vo. 12s 6d. (See page 12.)

Leyden and Erskine's Baber.
MEMOIRS OF ZEHIR-ED-DIN MUHAMMED BABER, EMPEROR OF
HINDUSTAN, written by himself in the Jaghatai Turki, and
translated partly by the late JOHN LEYDEN, Esq., M.D., and
partly by WILLIAM ERSKINE, Esq., with Notes and a Geographical and Historical Introduction, together with a Map of
the Countries between the Oxus and Jaxartes, and a Memoir
regarding its construction. By CHARLES WADDINGTON, of the
East India Company's Engineers. 4to. Lond. 1826. £1 5s.

Liancourt's and Pincott's Primitive and Universal Laws of
the Formation and development of language ; a Rational and
Inductive System founded on the Natural Basis of Onomatops.
8vo. 12s. 6d.

Lockwood's (Ed.) Natural History, Sport and Travel.
Crown 8vo. With numerous Illustrations. 9s.

McBean's (S.) England, Egypt, Palestine & India by Railway.
Popularly Explained. Crown 8vo., with a coloured Map. 4s.

MacGregor's (Col. C. M.) Narrative of a Journey through
the Province of Khorassan and on the N. W. Frontier of
Afghanistan in 1875. By Colonel C. M. MACGREGOR,
C.S.I., C.I.E., Bengal Staff Corps. 2 vols. 8vo. With
map and numerous illustrations. 30s.

Mahommedan Law of Inheritance and Contract.
By STANDISH GROVE GRADY, Barrister-at-Law. 8vo. 14s.
(See page 13.)

Malleson's (Col. G. B.) Final French Struggles in India.
Crown 8vo. 10s. 6d. (See page 7.)

Malleson's (Col. G. B.) History of the Indian Mutiny,
1857–1858, commencing from the close of the Second
Volume of Sir John Kaye's History of the Sepoy War.
Vol. I. 8vo. With Map. £1.
CONTENTS. BOOK VII.—Calcutta in May and June.—
William Tayler and Vincent Eyre.—How Bihar and Calcutta
were saved. BOOK VIII.—Mr. Colvin and Agra.—Jhansi
and Bandalkhand.—Colonel Durand and Holkar.—Sir George
Lawrence and Rajputana.—Brigadier Polwhele's great battle

and its results.—Bareli, Rohilkhand, and Farakhabad. BOOK
IX.—The relation of the annexation of Oudh to the Mutiny.
—Sir Henry Lawrence and the Mutiny in Oudh.—The siege
of Lakhnao.—The first relief of Lakhnao.

VOL. II.—Including the Storming of Delhi, the Relief
of Lucknow, the Two Battles of Cawnpore, the Campaign
in Rohilkhand, and the movements of the several Columns
in the N.W. Provinces, the Azimgurh District, and on the
Eastern and South-Eastern Frontiers. 8vo. With 4 Plans.
20s.

Malleson's (Col. G. B.) History of Afghanistan, from the
Earliest Period to the Outbreak of the War of 1878. 8vo.
2nd Edition. With Map. 18s.

Manning (Mrs.) Ancient and Mediæval India.
Being the History, Religion, Laws, Caste, Manners and
Customs, Language, Literature, Poetry, Philosophy, Astronomy,
Algebra, Medicine, Architecture, Manufactures, Commerce,
&c., of the Hindus, taken from their writings. Amongst the
works consulted and gleaned from may be named the Rig Veda,
Sama Veda, Vajur Veda, Sathapatha Brahmana, Baghavat
Gita, The Puranas, Code of Menu, Code of Yajna-valkya,
Mitakshara, Daya Bagha, Mahabharata, Atriya, Charaka,
Susruta, Ramayana, Raghu Vansa, Bhattikavia, Sakuntala
Vikramorvasi, Malali and Madhava, Mudra Rakshasa, Retna-
vali, Kumara Sambhava, Prabodah, Chandrodaya, Megha Duta,
Gita Govinda, Panchatantra, Hitopadesa, Katha Sarit, Sagara,
Ketala, Panchavinsati, Dasa Kumara Charita, &c. By Mrs
MANNING, with Illustrations. 2 vols., 8vo. 30s.

Manual of Military Law.
By Colonel J. K. PIPON, and J. F. COLLIER, Esq., of the
Inner Temple, Barrister-at-Law. 5s.

Mayhew's (Edward) Illustrated Horse Doctor.
8vo. 18s. 6d. (See page 11.)

Mayhew's (Edward) Illustrated Horse Management.
New edit. By J. I. LUPTON. 8vo. 12s. (See page 11.)

Mayhew's (Henry) German Life and Manners.
2 vols., 8vo. 18s.
Also a cheaper edition, Post 8vo. 7s. (See page 8.)

Max Muller's Rig-Veda-Sanhita.
The Sacred Hymns of the Brahmins; together with the
Commentary of Sayanacharya. Published under the Patron-
age of the Right Honourable the Secretary of State for India in
Council. 6 vols., 4to. £2 10s. per volume.

Meadow's (T.) Notes on China.
8vo. 9s.

Military Works—chiefly issued by the Government.

Field Exercises and Evolutions of Infantry. Pocket edition, 1s.

Queen's Regulations and Orders for the Army. Corrected to 1874. 8vo. 3s. 6d. Interleaved, 5s. 6d. Pocket Edition, 1s.

Musketry Regulations, as used at Hythe. 1s.

Dress Regulations for the Army. 1875. 1s. 6d.

Infantry Sword Exercise. 1875. 6d.

Infantry Bugle Sounds. 6d.

Handbook of Battalion Drill. By Lieut. H. C. Slack. 2s; or with Company Drill, 2s. 6d.

Handbook of Brigade Drill. By Lieut. H. C. Slack. 3s.

Red Book for Sergeants. By William Bright, Colour-Sergeant, 37th Middlesex R.V. 1s.

Handbook of Company Drill, also of Skirmishing, Battalion, and Shelter Trench Drill. By Lieut. Charles Slack. 1s.

Elementary and Battalion Drill. Condensed and Illustrated, together with duties of Company Officers, Markers, &c., in Battalion. By Captain Malton. 2s. 6d.

Cavalry Regulations. For the Instruction, Formations, and Movements of Cavalry. Royal 8vo. 4s. 6d.

Cavalry Sword, Carbine, Pistol and Lance Exercises, together with Field Gun Drill. Pocket Edition. 1s.

Manual of Artillery Exercises, 1873. 8vo. 5s.

Manual of Field Artillery Exercises. 1877. 3s.

Standing Orders for Royal Artillery. 8vo. 3s.

Principles and Practice of Modern Artillery. By Lt.-Col. C. H. Owen, R.A. 8vo. Illustrated. 15s.

Artillerist's Manual and British Soldiers' Compendium. By Major F. A. Griffiths. 11th Edition. 5s.

Compendium of Artillery Exercises—Smooth Bore, Field, and Garrison Artillery for Reserve Forces. By Captain J. M. McKenzie. 3s. 6d.

Principles of Gunnery. By John T. Hyde, M.A., late Professor of Fortification and Artillery, Royal Indian Military College, Addiscombe. Second edition, revised and enlarged. With many Plates and Cuts, and Photograph of Armstrong Gun. Royal 8vo. 14s.

Notes on Gunnery. By Captain Goodeve. Revised Edition. 1s.

Text Book of the Construction and Manufacture of Rifled Ordnance in the British Service. By STONEY & JONES. Second Edition. Paper, 3s. 6d., Cloth, 4s. 6d.

Handbooks of the 9, 16, and 64-Pounder R. M. L. Converted Guns. 6d. each.

Handbook of the 9 and 10-inch R. M. L. Guns. 6d. each.

Handbook of 40-Pounder B. L. Gun. 6d.

Handbooks of 9-inch Rifle Muzzle Loading Guns of 12 tons, and the 10-inch gun of 18 tons. 6d. each.

Treatise on Fortification and Artillery. By Major HECTOR STRAITH. Revised and re-arranged by THOMAS COOK, R.N., by JOHN T. HYDE, M.A. 7th Edition. Royal 8vo. Illustrated and Four Hundred Plans, Cuts, &c. £2 2s.

Military Surveying and Field Sketching. The Various Methods of Contouring, Levelling, Sketching without Instruments, Scale of Shade, Examples in Military Drawing, &c., &c., &c. As at present taught in the Military Colleges. By Major W. H. RICHARDS, 55th Regiment, Chief Garrison Instructor in India, Late Instructor in Military Surveying, Royal Military College, Sandhurst. Second Edition, Revised and Corrected. 12s.

Treatise on Military Surveying; including Sketching in the Field, Plan-Drawing, Levelling, Military Reconnaissance, &c. By Lieut.-Col. BASIL JACKSON, late of the Royal Staff Corps. The Fifth Edition. 8vo. Illustrated by Plans, &c. 14s.

Instruction in Military Engineering. Vol. 1., Part III. 4s.

Elementary Principles of Fortification. A Text-Book for Military Examinations. By J. T. HYDE, M.A. Royal 8vo. With numerous Plans and Illustrations. 10s. 6d.

Military Train Manual. 1s.

The Sappers' Manual. Compiled for the use of Engineer Volunteer Corps. By Col. W. A. FRANKLAND, R.E. With numerous Illustrations. 2s.

Ammunition. A descriptive treatise on the different Projectiles Charges, Fuzes, Rockets, &c., at present in use for Land and Sea Service, and on other war stores manufactured in the Royal Laboratory. 6s.

Hand-book on the Manufacture and Proof of Gunpowder, as carried on at the Royal Gunpowder Factory, Waltham Abbey. 5s.

Regulations for the Training of Troops for service in the Field and for the conduct of Peace Manœuvres. 2s.

Hand-book Dictionary for the Militia and Volunteer Services, Containing a variety of useful information, Alphabetically arranged. Pocket size, 3s. 6d. ; by post, 3s. 8d.

Gymnastic Exercises. System of Fencing, and Exercises for the Regulation Clubs. In one volume. Crown 8vo. 1877. 2s.

Army Equipment. Prepared at the Topographical and Statistical Department, War Office. By Col. Sir HENRY JAMES, R.E., F.R.S., &c., Director.

PART. 1.—*Cavalry.* Compiled by Lieut. H. M. HOZIER, 2nd Life Guards. Royal 8vo. 4s.

PART 4.—*Military Train.* Compiled by Lieut. H. M. HOZIER, 2nd Life Guards. Royal 8vo. 2s. 6d.

PART 5.—*Infantry.* Compiled by Capt. F. MARTIN PETRIE. Royal 8vo. With Plates. 5s.

PART 6.—*Commissariat.* Compiled by Lieut. H. M. HOZIER, 2nd Life Guards. Royal 8vo. 1s. 6d.

PART 7.—*Hospital Service.* Compiled by Capt. MARTIN PETRIE. Royal 8vo. With Plates. 5s.

Text-Book on the Theory and Motion of Projectiles; the History, Manufacture, and Explosive Force of Gunpowder; the History of Small Arms. For Officers sent to School of Musketry. 1s. 6d.

Notes on Ammunition. 4th Edition. 1877. 2s. 6d.

Regulations and Instructions for Encampments. 6d.

Rules for the Conduct of the War Game. 2s.

Medical Regulations for the Army, Instructions for the Army, Comprising duties of Officers, Attendants, and Nurses, &c. 1s. 6d.

Purveyors' Regulations and Instructions, for Guidance of Officers of Purveyors' Department of the Army. 3s.

Priced Vocabulary of Stores used in Her Majesty's Service. 4s.

Transport of Sick and Wounded Troops. By DR. LONGMORE. 5s.

Precedents in Military Law. By LT-COL. W. HOUGH. 8vo. 25s.

The Practice of Courts-Martial, by HOUGH & LONG. 8vo. 26s.

Manual of Military Law. For all ranks of the Army, Militia, and Volunteer Services. By Colonel J. K. PIPON, and J. F. COLLIER, Esq. Third and Revised Edition. Pocket size. 5s.

Regulations applicable to the European Officer in India. Containing Staff Corps Rules, Staff Salaries, Commands, Furlough and Retirement Regulations, &c. By GEORGE E. COCHRANE, late Assistant Military Secretary, India Office. 1 vol., post 8vo. 7s. 6d.

Reserve Force; Guide to Examinations, for the use of Captains and Subalterns of Infantry, Militia, and Rifle Volunteers, and for Serjeants of Volunteers. By Capt. G. H. GREAVES. 2nd edit. 2s.

The Military Encyclopædia; referring exclusively to the Military Sciences, Memoirs of distinguished Soldiers, and the Narratives of Remarkable Battles. By J. H. STOCQUELER. 8vo. 12s.

The Operations of War Explained and Illustrated. By Col. HAMLEY. New Edition Revised, with Plates. Royal 8vo. 30s.

Lessons of War. As taught by the Great Masters and Others: Selected and Arranged from the various operations in War. By FRANCE JAMES SOADY, Lieut.-Col., R.A. Royal 8vo. 21s.

The Soldiers' Pocket Book for Field Service. By Col. SIR GARNET J. WOLSELEY. 2nd Edition. Revised and Enlarged. 4s. 6d.

The Surgeon's Pocket Book, an Essay on the best Treatment of Wounded in War. By Surgeon Major J. H. PORTER. 7s. 6d.

A Precis of Modern Tactics. By COLONEL HOME. 8vo. 8s. 6d.

Armed Strength of Austria. By Capt. COOKE. 2 pts. £1 2s.

Armed Strength of Denmark. 3s.

Armed Strength of Russia. Translated from the German. 7s.

Armed Strength of Sweden and Norway. 3s. 6d.

Armed Strength of Italy. 5s. 6d.

Armed Strength of Germany. Part I. 8s. 6d.

The Franco-German War of 1870—71. By CAPT. C. H. CLARKE. Vol. I. £1 6s. Sixth Section. 5s. Seventh Section 6s. Eighth Section. 3s. Ninth Section. 4s. 6d. Tenth Section. 6s. Eleventh Section. 5s. 3d. Twelfth Section. 4s. 6d.

The Campaign of 1866 in Germany. Royal 8vo. With Atlas, 21s.

Celebrated Naval and Military Trials By PETER BURKE. Post 8vo., cloth. 10s. 6d.

Military Sketches. By SIR LASCELLES WRAXALL. Post 8vo. 6s.

Military Life of the Duke of Wellington. By JACKSON and SCOTT. 2 Vols. 8vo. Maps, Plans, &c. 12s.

Single Stick Exercise of the Aldershot Gymnasium. 6d.

Treatise on Military Carriages, and other Manufactures of the Royal Carriage Department. 5s.

Steppe Campaign Lectures. 2s.

Manual of Instructions for Army Surgeons. 1s.

Regulations for Army Hospital Corps. 9d.

Manual of Instructions for Non-Commissioned Officers, Army Hospital Corps. 2s.

Handbook or Military Artificers. 3s.

Instructions for the use of Auxiliary Cavalry. 2s. 6d.

Equipment Regulations for the Army. 5s. 6d.

Statute Law relating to the Army. 1s. 3d.

Regulations for Commissariat and Ordnance Department 2s.

Regulations for the Commissariat Department. 1s. 6d.

Regulations for the Ordnance Department. 1s. 6d.

Artillerist's Handbook of Reference for the use of the Royal and Reserve Artillery, by WILL and DALTON. 5s.

An Essay on the Principles and Construction of Military Bridges, by SIR HOWARD DOUGLAS. 1853. 15s.

Mill's History of British India,
With Notes and Continuation. By H. H. WILSON. 9 vols. cr. 8vo. £2 10s.

Milton's Poetical Works, with Notes.
By JOHN BRADSHAW, LL.D., Inspector of Schools, Madras. 2 vols. post 8vo. 10s. 6d.

Mogul Empire.
From the death of Aurungzeb to the overthrow of the Mahratta Power, by HENRY GEORGE KEENE, B.C.S. 8vo. Second edition. With Map. 10s. 6d.

This Work fills up a blank between the ending of Elphinstone's and the commencement of Thornton's Histories.

Mysteries of the Vatican;
Or Crimes of the Papacy. From the German of DR. THEODORE GREISENGER. 2 Vols. post 8vo 21s.

Nationalities of Europe.
By ROBERT GORDON LATHAM, M.D. 2 Vols. 8vo. 12s.

Natural History, Sport and Travel.
By EDWARD LOCKWOOD, Bengal Civil Service, late Magistrate of Monghyr Crown 8vo. 9s.

Nirgis and Bismillah.
NIRGIS; a Tale of the Indian Mutiny, from the Diary of a Slave Girl: and BISMILLAH; or, Happy Days in Cashmere. By HAFIZ ALLARD. Post 8vo. 10s. 6d.

Notes on China.
Desultory Notes on the Government and People of China and on the Chinese Language. By T. T. MEADOWS, 8vo. 9s.

Notes on the North Western Provinces of India.
By a District Officer. 2nd Edition. Post 8vo., cloth. 5s.

CONTENTS.—Area and Population.—Soils.—Crops.—Irrigation.—Rent.—Rates.—Land Tenures.

Owen (Sidney) India on the Eve of the British Conqnest.
A Historical Sketch. By SIDNEY OWEN, M.A. Reader in Indian Law and History in the University of Oxford. Formerly Professor of History in the Elphinstone College, Bombay. Post 8vo. 8s.

Oxenham (Rev. H. N.) Catholic Eschatology and Universalism. An Essay on the Doctrine of Future Retribution. Second Edition, revised and enlarged. Crown 8vo. 7s. 6d.

Oxenham's (Rev. H. N.) Catholic Doctrine of the Atonement. 8vo. 10s. 6d. (See page 5.)

Ozanam's (A. F.) Civilisation in the Fifth Century. From the French. By The Hon. A. C. Glyn. 2 Vols. post 8vo. 21s.

Pathologia Indica,
Based upon Morbid Specimens from all parts of the Indian Empire. By Allan Webb. B.M.S. Second Edit. 8vo. 14s.

Pelly (Sir Lewis). The Miracle Play of Hasan and Husain. Collected from Oral Tradition by Colonel Sir Lewis Pelly, K.C.B., K.C.S.I., formerly serving in Persia as Secretary of Legation, and Political Resident in the Persian Gulf. Revised, with Explanatory Notes, by Arthur N. Wollaston, H.M. Indian (Home) Service, Translator of Anwari-Suhaili, &c. 2 Vols. royal 8vo. 32s.

Pharmacopœia of India.
By Edward John Waring, M.D., &c. 8vo. 6s. (See page 2.)

Physical Geography.
By Professor D. T. Ansted, M.A., F.R.S., &c. Fifth Edition. Post 8vo., with Illustrative Maps. 7s.
Contents:—Part I.—Introduction.—The Earth as a Planet.—Physical Forces.—The Succession of Rocks. Part II.—Earth—Land.—Mountains.—Hills and Valleys.—Plateaux and Low Plains. Part III.—Water.—The Ocean.—Rivers.—Lakes and Waterfalls.—The Phenomena of Ice,—Springs Part IV.—Air.—The Atmosphere. Winds and Storms.—Dew, Clouds, and Rain.—Climate and Weather. Part V.—Fire.—Volcanoes and Volcanic Phenomena—Earthquakes. Part VI. –Life.—The Distribution of Plants in the different Countries of the Earth.—The Distribution of Animals on the Earth.—The Distribution of Plants and Animals in Time.—Effects of Human Agency on Inanimate Nature.
"The Book is both valuable and comprehensive, and deserves a wide circulation."—*Observer.*

Pilgrimage to Mecca (A).
By the Nawab Sikandar Begum of Bhopal. Translated from the Original Urdu. By Mrs. Willoughby Osborne. Followed by a Sketch of the History of Bhopal. By Col. Willoughby Osborne, C.B. With Photographs, and dedicated, by permission, to Her Majesty. Queen Victoria. Post 8vo. £1. 1s.
This is a highly important book, not only for its literary merit, and the information it contains, but also from the fact of its being the first work written by an Indian lady, and that lady a Queen.

Pebody (Charles) Authors at Work.
Francis Jeffrey—Sir Walter Scott—Robert Burns—Charles
Lamb—R. B. Sheridan—Sydney Smith—Macaulay—Byron
Wordsworth—Tom Moore—Sir James Mackintosh. Post 8vo.
10s. 6d.

Pollock (Field Marshal Sir George) Life & Correspondence.
By C. R. Low. 8vo. With portrait. 18s.

Practice of Courts Martial.
By Hough & Long. 8vo. London. 1825. 26s.

Precedents in Military Law;
By Lieut.-Col. W. Hough. One thick 8vo. Vol. 25s.

Prichard's Chronicles of Budgepore, &c.
Or Sketches of Life in Upper India. 2 Vols., Foolscap 8vo. 12s.

Primitive and Universal Laws of the Formation and
Development of Language. 8vo. 12s. 6d. (See page 16.)

Prinsep's (H. T.) Historical Results.
8vo. 15s.

Prinsep's (H. T.) Thibet.
Post 8vo. 5s.

Prinsep's Political and Military Transactions in India.
2 Vols. 8vo. London. 1825. 18s.

Races and Tribes of Hindostan.
The People of India. A series of Photographic Illustrations
of the Races and Tribes of Hindustan. Prepared under the
Authority of the Government of India, by J. Forbes Watson
and John William Kaye. The Work contains about 450
Photographs on mounts, in Eight Volumes, super royal 4to.
£2 5s. per volume.

Red Book for Sergeants.
By W. Bright. Colour-Sergeant. 37th Middlesex R.V. Fcap.
interleaved. 1s.

Regiments of the British Army (The).
Chronologically arranged. Showing their History, Services,
Uniform, &c. By Captain R. Trimen, late 35th Regiment.
8vo. 10s. 6d.

Republic of Fools (The).
Being the History of the People of Abdera in Thrace, from
the German of C. M. Von Wieland. By Rev. Henry Christmas, M.A. 2 Vols crown 8vo. 12s.

Richards (Major W H.) Military Surveying, &c.
12s. (See page 19.)

Russians at Home.
Unpolitical Sketches, showing what Newspapers they read, what Theatres they frequent; and how they eat, drink and enjoy themselves; with other matter relating chiefly to Literature, Music, and Places of Historical and Religious Interest in and about Moscow. By H. Sutherland Edwards. Second Edition, post 8vo., with Illustrations. 6s

Russian and Turk, from a Geographical, Ethnological, and Historical point of View. By R. G. Latham, M.A., M.D., &c. 8vo. 18s.

Sanderson's (G. P.) Thirteen Years among the Wild Beasts of India. Small 4to. 25s. (See page 27.)

Sepoy War in India.
A History of the Sepoy War in India, 1857—1858. By Sir John William Kaye, Author of "The History of the War in Affghanistan." Vol. I, 8vo. 18s. Vol. II. £1. Vol. III. £1.

Contents of Vol. I. :—Book I.—Introductory.—The Conquest of the Punjab and Pegu.—The "Right of Lapse."—The Annexation of Oude.—Progress of Englishism. Book II.—The Sepoy Army: its Rise, Progress, and Decline.—Early History of the Native Army.—Deteriorating Influences.—The Sindh Mutinies.—The Punjaub Mutinies. Discipline of the Bengal Army. Book III.—The Outbreak of the Mutiny.—Lord Canning and his Council.—The Oude Administration and the Persian War.—The Rising of the Storm.—The First Mutiny.—Progress of Mutiny.—Excitement in Upper India —Bursting of the Storm.—Appendix.

Contents of Vol. II.:—Book IV.—The Rising in the North-west. The Delhi History.—The Outbreak at Meerut.—The Seizure of Delhi.—Calcutta in May.—Last Days of General Anson.—The March upon Delhi Book V.—Progress of Rebellion in Upper India —Benares and Allahabad.—Cawnpore.—The March to Cawnpore.—Re-occupation of Cawnpore. Book VI.—The Punjab and Delhi.—First Conflicts in the Punjab.—Peshawur and Rawul Pinder.—Progress of Events in the Punjab.—Delhi —First Weeks of the Siege.—Progress of the Siege.—The Last Succours from the Punjab.

Contents of Vol. III. :—Book VII.—Bengal, Behar, and the North-west Provinces.—At the Seat of Government.—The Insurrection in Behar.—The Siege of Arrah.—Behar and Bengal. Book VIII.—Mutiny and Rebellion in the North-west Provinces.—Agra in May.—Insurrection in the Districts.—Bearing of the Native Chiefs.—Agra in

June, July, August and September. Book IX.—Lucknow and Delhi.—Rebellion in Onde.—Revolt in the Districts.—Lucknow in June and July.—The siege and Capture of Delhi.

Sewell's (Robert) Analytical History of India.
Crown 8vo. 8s. (See page 3.)

Sherer. Who is Mary?
A Cabinet Novel, in one volume. By J. W. Sherer, Esq., C.S.I. 10s. 6d.

Simpson. Archæologia Adelensis; or a History of the Parish of Adel, in the West Riding of Yorkshire. Being an attempt to delineate its Past and Present Associations, Archæological, Topographical, and Scriptural. By Henry Traill Simpson, M.A., late Rector of Adel. With numerous etchings by W. Lloyd Fergussen. Roy. 8vo. 21s.

Sin : Its Causes and Consequences.
An attempt to Investigate the Origin, Nature, Extent and Results of Moral Evil. A Series of Lent Lectures. By the Rev. Henry Christmas, M.A., F.R.S. Post 8vo. 5s.

Social Life in Munich.
By Edward Wilberforce. Second Edition. Post 8vo. 6s.
"A very able volume. Mr. Wilberforce is a very pleasant and agreeable writer whose opinion is worth hearing on the subject of modern art which enters largely into the matter of his discourse."—*Saturday Review.*

Starling (M. H.) Indian Criminal Law and Procedure.
Third edition. 8vo. £2 2s.

Student's Chemistry.
Being the Seventh Edition of Household Chemistry, or the Science of Home Life. By Albert J. Bernays, Ph. Dr. F.C.S., Prof. of Chemistry and Practical Chemistry at St. Thomas' Hospital, Medical, and Surgical College. Post 8vo. 5s. 6d.

Strange's (Sir T.) Hindu Law.
2 Vols. Royal 8vo. 1830. 24s. (See page 13.)

"Their Majesties Servants" :
Annals of the English Stage. Actors, Authors, and Audiences. From Thomas Betterton to Edmund Kean. By Dr. Doran, F.S.A., Author of "Table Traits," "Lives of the Queens of England of the House of Hanover," &c. Post 8vo. 6s.
"Every page of the work is barbed with wit, and will make its way point foremost. . . . . . provides entertainment for the most diverse tastes."—*Daily News.*

Textile Manufactures and Costumes of the People of India,
As originally prepared under the Authority of the Secretary of State for India in Council. By J. FORBES WATSON, M.A., M.D., F R.A.S., Reporter on the Products of India. Folio, half-morocco. With numerous Coloured Photographs. £3. 5s.

This work—by affording a key to the Fashions of the People, and to the Cotton, Silk, and Wool Textiles in actual use in India—is of special interest to Manufacturers, Merchants, and Agents; as also to the Student and lover of ornamental art.

Theories of History.
An Inquiry into the Theories of History,—Chance,—Law,— Will. With Special Reference to the Principle of Positive Philosophy. By WILLIAM ADAM. 8vo. 15s.

Thirteen Years among the Wild Beasts of India; their Haunts and Habits, from Personal Observation; with an account of the Modes of Capturing and Taming Wild Elephants. By G. P. SANDERSON, Officer in Charge of the Government Elephant Keddahs at Mysore. With 21 full page Illustrations and three Maps. Second Edition. Fcp. 4to. £1 5s.

Thomson's Lunar and Horary Tables.
For New and Concise Methods of Performing the Calculations necessary for ascertaining the Longitude by Lunar Observations, or Chronometers; with directions for acquiring a knowledge of the Principal Fixed Stars and finding the Latitude of them. By DAVID THOMSON. Sixty-fifth edit. Royal 8vo 10s.

Thornton's History of India.
The History of the British Empire in India, by Edward Thornton, Esq. Containing a Copious Glossary of Indian Terms, and a Complete Chronological Index of Events, to aid the Aspirant for Public Examinations. Third edition. 1 vol. 8vo. With Map. 12s.

*** *The Library Edition of the above in 6 volumes, 8vo., may be had, price £2. 8s.*

Thornton's Gazetteer of India.
Compiled chiefly from the records at the India Office. By EDWARD THORNTON. 1 vol., 8vo., pp. 1015. With Map. 21s.

*** *The chief objects in view in compiling this Gazetteer are :—*

1st. To fix the relative position of the various cities, towns, and villages with as much precision as possible, and to exhibit with the greatest practicable brevity all that is known respecting them ; and

2ndly. To note the various countries, provinces, or territorial divisions, and to describe the physical characteristics of each, together with their statistical, social, and political circumstances.

To these are added minute descriptions of the principal rivers and chains of mountains ; thus presenting to the reader, within a brief compass, a mass of information which cannot otherwise be obtained, except from a multiplicity of volumes and manuscript records.

The Library Edition.
4 vols., 8vo. Notes, Marginal References, and Map. £2 16s.
Thugs and Dacoits of India.
A Popular Account of the Thugs and Dacoits, the Hereditary Garotters and Gang Robbers of India. By James Hutton. Post 8vo. 5s.
Tibet, Tartary, and Mongolia.
By Henry T. Prinsep, Esq. Second edition. Post 8vo. 5s.
Tilley's (H. A.) Japan, &c.
8vo. 16s. (See page 14.)
Tod's (Col. Jas.) Travels in Western India.
Embracing a visit to the Sacred Mounts of the Jains, and the most Celebrated Shrines of Hindu Faith between Rajpootana and the Indus, with an account of the Ancient City of Nehrwalla. By the late Lieut.-Col. James Tod. Illustrations. Royal 4to. £3 3s.
*** This is a companion volume to Colonel Tod's Rajasthan.*
Trimen's (Capt. R., late 35th Regiment) Regiments of the British Army chronologically arranged. 8vo. 10s. 6d.
Trotter's (L. J.) History of India.
The History of the British Empire in India, from the Appointment of Lord Hardinge to the Death of Lord Canning (1844 to 1862). By Lionel James Trotter, late Bengal Fusiliers. 2 vols. 8vo. 16s. each.
Trotter's (L. J.) Warren Hastings, a Biography.
Crown 8vo. 9s.
Turkish Cookery Book (The).
A Collection of Receipts from the best Turkish Authorities. Done into English by Farabi Efendi. 12mo. Cloth. 3s. 6d.
Vambery's Sketches of Central Asia.
Additional Chapters on My Travels and Adventures, and of the Ethnology of Central Asia. By Armenius Vambery. 8vo. 16s.
" A valuable guide on almost untrodden ground."--*Athenæum.*

View of China,
For Philological Purposes. Containing a Sketch of Chinese Chronology, Geography, Government, Religion, and Customs. Designed for the use of Persons who study the Chinese Language. By Rev. R. Morrison. 4to. Macao, 1817. 6s.
Waring's Pharmacopœia of India.
8vo. 6s. (See page 2.)
Warren Hastings: a Biography. By Captain Lionel James Trotter. Bengal H. P., author of a " History of India," " Studies in Biography," &c. Crown 8vo. 9s.

Water, and Water Supply, chiefly in Reference to the British
Islands.—Surface Waters. By Professor D. T. ANSTED, M.A.,
F.R.S., F.G.S., &c. 8vo. With numerous Maps. 18s.

Watson. Money.
By JULES SANDIEU. Translated from the French by MAR-
GARET WATSON. Crown 8vo. 7s. 6d.

Watson's (Dr. J. Forbes) Textile Manufactures of India.
Folio. £3. 5s. (See page 27.)

Watson's (Dr. J. F.) and J. W. Kaye, The People of India.
A Series of Photographs. Vols. 1 to 8, £18.

Webb's (Dr. A.) Pathologia Indica.
8vo. 14s. (See page 23.)

Wellesley's Despatches.
The Despatches, Minutes, and Correspondence of the Marquis
Wellesley, K.G., during his Administration in India. 5 vols.
8vo. With Portrait, Map, &c. £6. 10s.
This work should be perused by all who proceed to India in the
Civil Services.

Wellington in India.
Military History of the Duke of Wellington in India. 1s.

Wilberforce's (Edward) Social Life in Munich.
Post 8vo. 6s. (See page 26.)

Wilberforce's (E.) Life of Schubert.
Post 8vo. 6s.

Wilk's South of India.
3 vols. 4to. £5. 5s.

Wilkins. Visual Art; or Nature through the Healthy Eye.
With some remarks on Originality and Free Trade, Artistic
Copyright, and Durability. By WM. NOY WILKINS, Author of
" Art Impressions of Dresden," &c. 8vo. 6s.

Williams' (F.) Lives of the English Cardinals.
2 vols., 8vo. 14s. (See page 7.)

Williams' (F.) Life, &c., of Bishop Atterbury.
2 vols., 8vo. 14s. (See page 4.)

Williams' Indian Wisdom.
8vo. 15s. (See page 14.)

Wilson's Glossary of Judicial and Revenue Terms, and of
useful Words occurring in Official Documents relating to the
Administration of the Government of British India. From the
Arabic, Persian, Hindustani, Sanskrit, Hindi, Bengali, Uriya,
Marathi, Guzarathi, Telugu, Karnata, Tamil, Malayalam, and
other Languages. Compiled and published under the authority of the Hon. the Court of Directors of the E. I. Company.
4to., cloth. £1 10s.

Wollaston's (Arthur N.) Anwari Suhaili, or Lights of Canopus
Commonly known as Kalilah and Damnah, being an adaptation
of the Fables of Bidpai.   Translated from the Persian.   Royal
4to., with illuminated borders, designed specially for the work,
cloth, extra gilt.   £3 13s. 6d.

Wollaston's (Arthur N.) Elementary Indian Reader.
Designed for the use of Students in the Anglo-Vernacular
Schools in India.   Fcap.   1s.

Woolrych's (Serjeant W. H.)
Lives of Eminent Serjeants-at-Law of the English Bar.   By
HUMPHRY W. WOOLRYCH, Serjeant-at-Law.   2 vols. 8vo. 30s.

World we Live In.
Or First Lessons in Physical Geography.   For the use of
Schools and Students.   By D. T. ANSTED, M.A., F.R.S., &c.
25th Thousand.   Fcap. 8vo.   2s.

Wraxall's Caroline Matilda.
Queen of Denmark, Sister of George 3rd.   From Family and
State Papers. By Sir Lascelles Wraxall. Bart. 3 vols., 8vo. 18s.

Wraxall's Military Sketches.
By SIR LASCELLES WRAXALL, Bart.   Post 8vo.   6s.
    "The book is clever and entertaining from first to last."—*Athenæum*.

Wraxall's Scraps and Sketches, Gathered Together.
By SIR LASCELLES WRAXALL, Bart. 2 vols., Post 8vo.   12s.

Yakoob Beg (the Life of), Athalik Ghazi and Badaulet.
Ameer of Kashgar.   By DEMETRIUS CHARLES BOULGER.
Member of the Royal Asiatic Society.   8vo.   With Map and
Appendix.   16s.

Yesterday and To-Day in India.
By SIDNEY LAMAN BLANCHARD.   Post 8vo.   6s.
    CONTENTS.—Outward Bound.—The Old Times and the New.—
Domestic Life.—Houses and Bungalows.—Indian Servants —
The Great Shoe Question.—The Garrison Hack —The Long
Bow in India.—Mrs. Dulcimer's Shipwreck.—A Traveller's
Tale, told in a Dark Bungalow.—Punch in India.—Anglo-
Indian Literature.—Christmas in India.—The Seasons in
Calcutta.—Farmers in Muslin.—Homeward Bound.—India
as it Is.

Young's (J. R.) Course of Mathematics.
8vo.   12s.   (See page 7.)

A SELECTION FROM

MESSRS. ALLEN'S CATALOGUE

OF BOOKS IN THE EASTERN LANGUAGES, &c.

HINDUSTANI, HINDI, &c.

[Dr. Forbes's Works are used as Class Books in the Colleges and Schools in India.]

Forbes's Hindustani-English Dictionary in the Persian Character, with the Hindi words in Nagari also; and an English Hindustani Dictionary in the English Character; both in one volume. By DUNCAN FORBES, LL.D. Royal 8vo. 42s.

Forbes's Hindustani Grammar, with Specimens of Writing in the Persian and Nagari Characters, Reading Lessons, and Vocabulary. 8vo. 10s. 6d.

Forbes's Hindustani Manual, containing a Compendious Grammar, Exercises for Translation, Dialogues, and Vocabulary, in the Roman Character. New Edition, entirely revised. By J. T. PLATTS. 18mo. 3s. 6d.

Forbes's Bagh o Bahar, in the Persian Character, with a complete Vocabulary. Royal 8vo. 12s. 6d.

Forbes's Bagh o Bahar in English, with Explanatory Notes, illustrative of Eastern Character. 8vo. 8s.

Eastwick (Edward B.) The Bagh-o-Bahar—literally translated into English, with copious explanatory notes. 8vo. 10s. 6d.

Forbes's Tota Kahani; or, "Tales of a Parrot," in the Persian Character, with a complete Vocabulary. Royal 8vo. 8s.

Small's (Rev. G.) Tota Kahani: or, "Tales of a Parrot." Translated into English. 8vo. 8s.

Forbes's Baital Pachisi; or, "Twenty-five Tales of a Demon," in the Nagari Character, with a complete Vocabulary. Royal 8vo. 9s.

Platts' J. T., Baital Pachisi: translated into English. 8vo. 8s.

Forbes's Ikhwanu s Safa; or, "Brothers of Purity," in the Persian Character. Royal 8vo. 12s. 6d.

[For the higher standard for military officers' examinations.]

Platts' Ikhwanu S Safa; translated into English. 8vo. 10s. 6d.

Platts' Grammar of the Urdu or Hindustani-Language. 8vo. **12s.**

Forbes's Oriental Penmanship; a Guide to Writing Hindustani in the Persian Character. 4to. **8s.**

Forbes's Hindustani-English and English Hindustani Dictionary, in the English Character. Royal 8vo. **36s.**

Forbes's Smaller Dictionary, Hindustani and English, in the English Character. **12s.**

Forbes's Bagh o Bahar, with Vocaby., English Character. **5s.**

Hindustani Selections, with a Vocabulary of the Words. By James R. Ballantyne. Second Edition. 1845. **5s.**

Singhasan Buttisi. Translated into Hindi from the Sanscrit. A New Edition. Revised, Corrected, and Accompanied with Copious Notes. By Syed Abdoolah. Royal 8vo. **12s. 6d.**

Robertson's Hindustani Vocabulary. **3s. 6d.**

Eastwick's Prem Sagur. 4to. **30s.**

Akhlaki Hindi, translated into Urdu, with an Introduction and Notes. By Syed Abdoolah. Royal 8vo. **12s. 6d.**

Sakuntala. Translated into Hindi from the Bengali recension of the Sanskrit. Critically edited, with grammatical, idiomatical, and exegetical notes, by Frederic Pincott. 4to. **12s. 6d.**

SANSCRIT.

Haughton's Sanscrit and Bengali Dictionary, in the Bengali Character, with Index, serving as a reversed dictionary. 4to. **30s.**

Williams's English-Sanscrit Dictionary. 4to., cloth. **£3. 3s.**

Williams's Sanskrit-English Dictionary. 4to. **£4 11s. 6d.**

Wilkin's (Sir Charles) Sanscrit Grammar. 4to. **15s.**

Williams's (Monier) Sanscrit Grammar. 8vo. **15s.**

Williams's (Monier) Sanscrit Manual; to which is added, a Vocabulary, by A. E. Gough. 18mo. **7s. 6d.**

Gough's (A. E.) Key to the Exercises in Williams's Sanscrit Manual. 18mo. **4s.**

Williams's (Monier) Sakuntala, with Literal English Translation of all the Metrical Passages, Schemes of the Metres, and copious Critical and Explanatory Notes. Royal 8vo. **21s.**

Williams's (Monier) Sakuntala. Translated into English Prose and Verse. Fourth Edition. **8s.**

Williams's (Monier) Vikramorvasi. The Text. 8vo. **5s.**

Cowell's (E. B.) Translation of the Vikramorvasi. 8vo. **3s. 6d.**

Thompson's (J. C.) Bhagavat Gita. Sanscrit Text. 5s.

Haughton's Menu, with English Translation. 2 vols. 4to. 24s.

Johnson's Hitopadesa, with Vocabulary. 15s.

Hitopadesa, Sanscrit, with Bengali and English Trans. 10s. 6d.

Johnson's Hitopadesa, English Translation of the. 4to. 5s.

Wilson's Megha Duta, with Translation into English Verse. Notes, Illustrations, and a Vocabulary. Royal 8vo. 6s.

PERSIAN.

Richardson's Persian, Arabic, and English Dictionary. Edition of 1852. By F. Johnson. 4to. £4.

Forbes's Persian Grammar, Reading Lessons, and Vocabulary. Royal 8vo. 12s. 6d.

Ibraheem's Persian Grammar, Dialogues, &c. Royal 8vo. 12s. 6d.

Gulistan. Carefully collated with the original MS., with a full Vocabulary. By John Platts, late Inspector of Schools, Central Provinces, India. Royal 8vo. 12s. 6d.

Gulistan. Translated from a revised Text, with Copious Notes. By John Platts. 8vo. 12s. 6d.

Ouseley's Anwari Soheili. 4to. 42s.

Wollaston's (Arthur N.) Translation of the Anvari Soheili. Royal 8vo. £2 2s.

Keene's (Rev. H. G.) First Book of The Anwari Soheili. Persian Text. 8vo. 5s.

Ouseley's (Col.) Akhlaki Mushini. Persian Text. 8vo. 5s.

Keene's (Rev. H. G.) Akhlaki Mushini. Translated into English. 8vo. 3s. 6d.

Clarke's (Captain H. Wilberforce, R.E.) The Persian Manual. A Pocket Companion.

    PART I.—A concise Grammar of the Language, with Exercises on its more Prominent Peculiarities, together with a Selection of Useful Phrases, Dialogues, and Subjects for Translation into Persian.

    PART II.—A Vocabulary of Useful Words, English and Persian, showing at the same time the difference of idiom between the two Languages. 18mo. 7s. 6d.

A Translation of Robinson Crusoe into the Persian Language. Roman Character. Edited by T. W. H. Tolbort, Bengal Civil Service. Cr. 8vo. 7s.

BENGALI.

Haughton's Bengali, Sanscrit, and English Dictionary, adapted
for Students in either language ; to which is added an Index, serving
as a reversed dictionary. 4to. 30s.

Forbes's Bengali Grammar, with Phrasesand dialogues. Royal
8vo. 12s. 6d.

Forbes's Bengali Reader, with a Translation and Vocabulary
Royal 8vo. 12s. 6d.

Nabo Nari. 12mo. 7s.

ARABIC.

Richardson's Arabic, Persian and English Dictionary. Edition
of 1852. By F. Johnson. 4to., cloth. £4.

Forbes's Arabic Grammar, intended more especially for the use of
young men preparing for the East India Civil Service, and also for the
use of self instructing students in general. Royal 8vo., cloth. 18s.

Palmer's Arabic Grammar. 8vo. 18s.

Forbes's Arabic Reading Lessons, consisting of Easy Extracts
from the best Authors, with Vocabulary. Royal 8vo., cloth. 15s.

Matthew's Translation of the Mishkat-ul-Masabih. 2 vols in 1.
By the Rev. T. P. Hughes, Missionary to the Afghans at Peshawur.
(*In the press.*)

TELOOGOO.

Brown's Dictionary, reversed ; with a Dictionary of the Mixed
Dialects used in Teloogoo. 3 vols. in 2, royal 8vo. £5.

Campbell's Dictionary. Royal 8vo. 30s.

Bromn's Reader. 8vo. 2 vols. 14s.

Brown's Dialogues, Teloogoo and English. 8vo. 5s. 6d.

Pancha Tantra. 8s.

Percival's English-Teloogoo Dictionary. 10s. 6d.

TAMIL.

Rottler's Dictionary, Tamil and English. 4to. 42s.

Babington's Grammar (High Dialect). 4to. 12s.

Percival's Tamil Dictionary. 2 vols. 10s. 6d.

GUZRATTEE.

Mavor's Spelling, Guzrattee and English.   7s, 6d.

Shapuaji Edalji's Dictionary, Guzrattee and English.   21s.

MAHRATTA.

Molesworth's Dictionary, Mahratta and English.   4to.   42s.

Molesworth's Dictionary, English and Mahratta.   4to.   42s.

Stevenson's Grammar.   8vo., cloth.   17s. 6d.

Esop's Fables.   12mo.   2s. 6d.

Fifth Reading Book.   7s.

MALAY.

Marsden's Grammar.   4to.   £1 1s.

CHINESE.

Morrison's Dictionary.   6 vols. 4to. £10.

Marshman's—Clavis Sinica, a Chinese Grammar.   4to.   £2 2s.

Morrison's View of China, for Philological purposes; containing a
Sketch of Chinese Chronology, Geography, Government, Religion and
Customs, designed for those who study the Chinese language. 4to. 6s.

MISCELLANEOUS.

Reeve's English-Carnatica and Carnatica-English Dictionary.
2 vols. (Very slightly damaged).   £8.

Collett's Malayalam Reader.   8vo.   12s. 6d.

Esop's Fables in Carnatica.   8vo. bound.   12s. 6d.

A Turkish Manual, comprising a Condensed Grammar with
Idiomatic Phrases, Exercises and Dialogues, and Vocabulary.   By
Captain C. F. MACKENZIE, late of H.M.'s Consular Service.   6s.

MAPS OF INDIA, etc.

Messrs. Allen & Co.'s Maps of India were revised and much improved during 1876, with especial reference to the existing Administrative Divisions, Railways, &c.

District Map of India; corrected to 1878;
> Divided into Collectorates with the Telegraphs and Railways from Government surveys. On six sheets—size, 5ft. 6in. high; 5ft. 8in. wide, £2; in a case, £2 12s. 6d.; or, rollers, varn., £3 3s.

A General Map of India; corrected to 1876;
> Compiled chiefly from surveys executed by order of the Government of India. On six sheets—size, 5 ft. 3 in. wide; 5 ft. 4 in. high, £2; or, on cloth, in case, £2 12s. 6d.; or, rollers, varn., £3 3s.

Map of India; corrected to 1876;
> From the most recent Authorities. On two sheets—size, 2 ft. 10in. wide; 3 ft. 3 in. high, 16s.; or, on cloth, in a case, £1 1s.

Map of the Routes in India; corrected to 1874;
> With Tables of Distances between the principal Towns and Military Stations. On one sheet—size, 2 ft. 3 in. wide; 2 ft. 9 in. high, 9s.; or, on cloth, in a case, 12s.

Map of the Western Provinces of Hindoostan,
> The Punjab, Cabool, Scinde, Bhawulpore, &c., including all the States between Candahar and Allahabad. On four sheets—size, 4 ft. 4in. wide; 4 ft. 2 in. high, 30s.; or, in case, £2; rollers, varnished, £2 10s.

Map of India and China, Burmah, Siam, the Malay Peninsula, and the Empire of Anam. On two sheets—size, 4 ft. 3 in. wide; 3 ft. 4 in. high, 16s.; or, on cloth, in a case, £1 5s.

Map of the Steam Communication and Overland Routes
> between England, India, China, and Australia. In a case, 14s.; on rollers, and varnished, 18s.

Map of China,
> From the most Authentic Sources of Information. One large sheet—size, 2 ft. 7 in. wide; 2 ft. 2 in. high, 6s.; or, on cloth, in case, 8s.

Map of the World;
> On Mercator's Projection, showing the Tracts of the Early Navigators, the Currents of the Ocean, the Principal Lines of great Circle Sailing, and the most recent discoveries. On four sheets—size, 6ft. 2 in. wide; 4 ft. 3 in. high, £2; on cloth, in a case, £2 10s; or, with rollers, and varnished, £3.

Handbook of Reference to the Maps of India.
> Giving the Latitude and Longitude of places of note. 18mo. 3s. 6d.

Russian Official Map of Central Asia. Compiled in accordance with the Discoveries and Surveys of Russian Staff Officers up to the close of the year 1877. In 2 Sheets. 10s. 6d., or in cloth case, 14s.

THE

ROYAL KALENDAR,

AND

COURT & CITY REGISTER

FOR

𝕰𝖓𝖌𝖑𝖆𝖓𝖉, 𝕴𝖗𝖊𝖑𝖆𝖓𝖉, 𝕾𝖈𝖔𝖙𝖑𝖆𝖓𝖉, 𝖆𝖓𝖉 𝖙𝖍𝖊 𝕮𝖔𝖑𝖔𝖓𝖎𝖊𝖘

FOR THE YEAR

1 8 7 9.

CONTAINING A CORRECT LIST OF THE TWENTY-FIRST IMPERIAL PARLIAMENT, SUMMONED TO MEET FOR THEIR FIRST SESSION—MARCH 5TH, 1874.

House of Peers—House of Commons—Sovereigns and Rulers of States of Europe—Orders of Knighthood—Science and Art Department—Queen's Household—Government Offices—Mint—Customs—Inland Revenue—Post Office—Foreign Ministers and Consuls—Queen's Consuls Abroad—Naval Department—Navy List—Army Department—Army List—Law Courts—Police—Ecclesiastical Department—Clergy List—Foundation Schools—Literary Institutions—City of London—Banks—Railway Companies—Hospital and Institutions—Charities—Miscellaneous Institutions—Scotland, Ireland, India, and the Colonies; and other useful information.

Price with Index, 7s.; without Index, 5s.

O

www.ingramcontent.com/pod-product-compliance
Lightning Source LLC
Chambersburg PA
CBHW052348110726

47901CB00005B/1401